Don't Want You Like a Best Friend

Don't Want You Like a Best Friend

A Novel

EMMA R. ALBAN

An Imprint of HarperCollins*Publishers*

This book is a work of fiction. References to real people, events, establishments, organizations, or locales are intended only to provide a sense of authenticity, and are used fictitiously. All other characters, and all incidents and dialogue, are drawn from the author's imagination and are not to be construed as real.

HarperCollins books may be purchased for educational, business, or sales promotional use. For information, please email the Special Markets Department at SPsales@harpercollins.com.

FIRST EDITION

Designed by Diahann Sturge

Library of Congress Cataloging-in-Publication Data has been applied for.

ISBN 978-0-06-331200-5

24 25 26 27 28 LBC 9 8 7 6 5

For my parents,
thank you, for everything

PROLOGUE

April 1857

Beth

Beth wishes Mother could just leave well enough alone. The alcohol stings against her back and she shudders as Mother blows on the spot at the bottom of her left shoulder. Beth really doesn't think one blemish would be the death of her. They're lucky she didn't break out in hives in front of the queen; one pimple can't make that much difference now.

Beth stares at her reflection in her bedroom mirror as Mother adjusts her shift. Her makeup's been done, dull brown hair coiled and wrapped artfully high on the back of her head, with careful pieces left framing her face. She looks no less a painted peacock than she did this afternoon, only now she's exhausted, and hungry, and they haven't even wrestled her into her hoop yet.

"You look wonderful," Mother says, wrapping her arms about Beth's shoulders and leaning down so their faces are level.

"*You* look wonderful," Beth corrects.

Viscountess Cordelia Demeroven always looks perfect. High, sharp cheekbones, dark piercing brown eyes, bountiful hair swept back in an elegant chignon—she's beautiful, and graceful, and (now that she's out of her mourning colors) cheerful. She's a constant social delight. Beth would rather sink straight into the floor than muster up that energy.

"You'll be the talk of the ball," Mother insists, gingerly nudging Beth's head with her own. "The queen thought you beautiful, and I've already arranged a number of morning calls for us. All you have to do is smile."

Beth glowers at her mother, who simply laughs and reaches around to tickle her. Beth shrieks and jumps away. Mother snickers. Twenty years and she's never managed to curb that reflex, and Mother still revels in it any chance she gets.

"See," Mother says, pointing at Beth's suddenly flushed cheeks and reluctant laugh. "Beautiful. Now, let's finish getting you ready."

Beth sighs, but dutifully lets Mother help her into her corset, adjusting the modest padding. Beth has a naturally trim waist, but even the tightest stays can't give her a bosom. Mother, by contrast, has ample curves beneath the lavender lace across her chest—modest, but coquettish.

She looks stunning in her purple skirts and Beth wishes for the thousandth time that she was more like her mother than her late father. They've divested themselves of everything else of his, but Beth's figure isn't something she can lock away in a trunk, out of sight, out of mind. Her round face, flat chest, and skinny frame are all his side of the family.

Beth steps into the hoop cage and helps Mother gather it to settle on her small waist. Together they adjust the hoops and then gingerly slip a petticoat over the curved steel and taping. Beth marvels at the lightness of her skirt and smiles as Mother winks. It beats the seven petticoats she would have worn last year, had she been presented as planned.

Beth steps to the side to allow Mother to slip around her and pick up the skirt from her bed. Her hoops knock the vanity chair, and it scrapes loudly against the wooden floor. Beth groans and Mother laughs.

"You'll adjust," she promises.

"Right. I'll knock them all over," Beth says, going for playful, though she can tell by Mother's frown that she's come off more petulant and anxious.

"You'll have fun. You might even meet someone special tonight."

Beth narrows her eyes. "I thought I was to go into this with a sensible head for a good match."

"There's nothing that says a good match can't be a love match," Mother says firmly.

"Only that I've just the four months to fall madly in love or we're dying in a hovel," Beth counters. Mother's frown deepens and her eyes turn downcast. "I'm sorry. I'm tired. Let's do the dress."

Mother steps in front of Beth, blocking her view of the mirror so Beth's left looking at her quietly devastated face. She really didn't mean to bring this up, tonight. She shouldn't beat a dead horse.

"I hope you find someone you *want* to marry. That is what I want for you."

Beth nods, biting her cheek as Mother takes her hands. "I know."

"And I'm very sorry. I hope you know that too," Mother insists, ducking her head to catch Beth's eyes.

"I know," Beth agrees.

It's not her mother's fault they're in this situation. And she's spent almost her entire settlement as it is for their dresses. Now it's Beth's responsibility to make sure her mother's sacrifices pay off. They need somewhere to live come the end of the season, and if Beth fails to find a husband—

"Let's get you into this beautiful gown, shall we?"

Beth nods, breaking eye contact. She raises her arms so Mother can lower the skirt their housekeeper, Miss Wilson, laid out before they shooed her away to rest for the evening. She watches as Mother adjusts the fabric until it sits comfortably over her hips and then helps slide her arms through the short capped sleeves of the bodice.

She does look nice, she supposes. The blue compliments her pale skin and dark hair. Her hair can't hold a candle to Mother's, but she always enjoys wearing a few of her mother's family jewels studded into her braided bun. Makes her think of when she and Mother used to get dressed up and throw their own fake balls when she was small—just the two of them alone in the country in their ball gowns while Father stayed in London for the winter season.

Mother finishes up the buttons and does the top clasp, settling the vee across Beth's shoulders. She pushes close and wraps her arms around Beth's waist, meeting her eyes in the mirror.

"I promise tomorrow we'll have hotcakes for breakfast and sleep until noon, all right?"

Beth smiles and leans back into her, gripping at her hands. "All right."

Gwen

"You're cheating!"

"*You're* cheating!" Gwen insists, glaring at her father through her mesh hood, as she teeters on the edge of the stone wall around the garden pond.

"You didn't riposte," Father argues, foil still pointed at her, waiting.

"You attacked twice," Gwen says. She backs along the uneven stones, one arm out for balance, the other hand still brandishing her foil. "And it doesn't become a man to quibble."

Father snorts and jumps up onto the wall in front of her, the two of them balanced precariously. They begin to trade attacks again. Gwen advances, but then retreats as Father bears down on her. She feints, trying to throw him off, but much as it rankles, he's got moves she can't hope to parry.

Instead, Gwen leaps suddenly from the wall, taking off toward the house at the opposite end of the garden, cackling. Father shouts behind her and gives chase. She twirls around, ready to return his next attack, when the foil is plucked from her hand.

"Hey!" she says, spinning to find their housekeeper, Mrs. Gilpe, frowning down at her.

"En garde!" Father yells, striking her in the back.

Gwen revolves, glaring as she pulls off her helmet. "Foul," she declares.

"Not so," Father counters, removing his own mask. "Mrs. Gilpe is but an obstacle. A true opponent would have kept up her guard."

"You're a filthy cheat," Gwen huffs, crossing her arms. Father grins at her, boyishly smug.

"You're both ridiculous," Mrs. Gilpe says, her voice fond but firm. Gwen turns to take in her unimpressed glare. "Get inside. The carriage will be here in an hour."

"One more round?" they exclaim together.

Mrs. Gilpe rolls her eyes, her narrow face still hard but her lips twitching. Father glances at Gwen and the two of them put on their best pouts. But nothing will sway Mrs. Gilpe today.

"If you want to attend the Halyard Ball drenched in sweat with matted hair, be my guest, but neither of you can really afford to start the season that poorly, can you?"

Gwen looks back at Father, who maintains his pout for a moment before his shoulders slump. "Cuttingly astute as ever, Mrs. Gilpe. All right, Gwennie, go up and let the girls turn you into a young lady again."

Gwen withers under Mrs. Gilpe's eager look. "Couldn't we just—"

"Mrs. Gilpe's right," Father says, adopting what Gwen considers his "stern father face." "Tonight is important. We can have a rematch tomorrow."

"Or you could admit you're a cheating cheater and we could match again now."

"The carriage will be here in an hour," Father says in a credible imitation of Mrs. Gilpe, who tuts.

"Like it matters if we're on time," Gwen says.

"Regardless of your feelings on the matter, we must still attempt to make this season count, no matter how onerous."

Gwen narrows her eyes at his tone. "Are you going to be a gentleman, then? Stand with all the fathers and ignore the debutantes this time?"

"I have never gone after a debutante," Father says quickly.

"No, no, just the opera singer, the dancer, the other opera singer, the widow Loughton, the widow Chastley—"

"The Dowager Pinches," Mrs. Gilpe puts in.

Gwen gasps. "You didn't!"

Father goes red, turning a glare on their housekeeper. He starts backing toward the house. "That was years ago. She wasn't the dowager then," he says, his voice cracking.

"Lord Havenfort's right," Mrs. Gilpe says mildly. "The late earl's mother hadn't yet passed."

"Father!" Gwen squeaks, hurrying after him. The Dowager Pinches is almost seventy.

"We waltzed a few times," Father defends, putting up his hands before slipping through the door to the solarium.

"Sure you did," Mrs. Gilpe says under her breath, holding the door for Gwen. "Come along."

"Father," Gwen protests, hovering just outside.

"It's time," he says, dropping his indignance. He hangs up his helmet and turns to her with a raised eyebrow.

Gwen reluctantly steps inside, tempted to keep arguing. She thinks she could wear him down, given enough time. They both hate balls, and the Halyards even more. The season is wretched, and neither is happy to be back at the London house for four months of tea parties and discomfort.

"I'll behave if you will," Father bargains.

Gwen tosses her helmet at him. She highly doubts that. "You get to drink and gamble. Hardly a fair trade."

"You're gambling," Father says, catching the helmet. "Think of every dance as a bet. Be charming and poised and the educated young lady I've raised you to be, and the payout could be enormous."

Gwen groans. "That's horrible."

Mrs. Gilpe tugs the door shut and nudges Gwen forward. Maybe he'll buy Gwen another pony if she keeps stalling. She did get her own landau last year as a consolation prize for ending the season without a match, again. Better yet, he could buy her a racing horse this year when she comes back husbandless. Surely after four seasons she deserves a racing horse. They could bet on it together.

"All kidding aside, you're a beautiful, accomplished young woman, and I'm proud of you," Father insists, taking her hand to drag her toward the foyer.

Gwen bites back a grimace. She hates when he gets sincere like this. Makes it so much harder to argue with him. "Father," she whines.

"Give it a real try this year, that's all I ask," he says. "You deserve a husband, and I know if you open yourself up to it, you can find one. Any man would be lucky to have you."

They reach the bottom of the stairs and Gwen hesitates. "You'll behave?"

Mrs. Gilpe steps up beside her, sighing impatiently.

"Cross my heart," Father says, starting to smile as her defenses come down.

"Fine," Gwen says, tugging off her gloves to whack them into Father's chest. "Let's get this over with," she says to Mrs. Gilpe.

Father gives her a playful bow, and Mrs. Gilpe takes Gwen's arm. Gwen huffs but lets Mrs. Gilpe guide her up the stairs, back to hoops and skirts and a frankly disgusting number of hairpins.

The Earl of Havenfort, Dashiell Fredric Bertram, may be the best catch of every season, dubious reputation and all, but the apple doesn't seem to fall close to the tree. For all Father's insistence that if she lets down her guard she'll attract a good husband, Gwen's not so sure. Beauty and poise and accomplishment she can fake, but deep down, she knows she'll make a horrid wife. She's sure they can smell it on her, like dogs do fear.

"Just remember, the Halyards have the crab puffs you like," Mrs. Gilpe says as she marches Gwen down the second-floor hallway to her room.

Gwen laughs, startled. "That's true. Want me to bring you some?"

Mrs. Gilpe purses her lips, reluctant to agree as they come into Gwen's room. Her lady's maid, Mrs. Stelm, is already waiting with the hoops and corset and makeup all laid out.

"Please do," Mrs. Stelm says. Mrs. Gilpe throws up her hands. "What, you don't want any?" she asks, grinning at Mrs. Gilpe, green eyes bright with mirth.

"You're all incorrigible," Mrs. Gilpe says, spinning Gwen around to strip her out of her fencing uniform.

"We try," Gwen says, winking at Mrs. Stelm, who giggles in return, ignoring Mrs. Gilpe's frown.

Gwen listens to them bicker as they dress her, transforming

her from the comfort of home into the puffed-up show bird of the opening night ball. And though the pink gown, stylishly braided blond updo, and dark lashes all complement her very well, Gwen's not sure at all that her curves and status will be enough to attract a suitor.

They certainly never have before.

CHAPTER ONE

Beth

She tripped on her entrance down the stairs. They called her name, she and Mother entered, and Beth tripped. Mother caught her and she's been swearing on all she can think of for the past ten minutes that no one noticed, but she's lying. Mothers all around the room are looking her up and down, judging, deciding, crowing.

Beth's by far one of the shortest girls here, a neck injury waiting to happen to any of their tall, stately-looking sons. Now she's clumsy on top of it. Her first night out is already a disaster.

"Darling, I need to go speak with Juliet."

"You cannot leave me here alone," Beth hisses, holding fast when Mother goes to pull away.

"I have to make the rounds and arrange our appointments," Mother whispers back. Both of them pause to smile at some acquaintance Beth can't remember, but who she knows comes from more money than they ever had when her father was alive. "You'll be fine. Just . . . mingle."

"Mother," Beth protests even as she releases Mother's arm from her death grip. She left indents with her fingers.

"I promise, you'll make friends. Just smile, chin up, shoulders back, and have a glass of wine." Beth feels her mouth fall open and quickly shuts it lest anyone think her unseemly. "One," Mother stresses. "For the nerves."

"Though fainting might not be a bad option either," Beth mumbles.

Mother frowns but Beth can tell she'd rather laugh. "One."

"One," Beth promises, noting Lady Berthshire waving Mother over. "Go, or she's going to put an eye out."

Mother leans in to kiss Beth's cheek before stepping around her and off to gather with her society friends. Beth watches, surprisingly envious, as Mother is eagerly accepted into their little circle. None of them made an effort to come see them in mourning; they're fickle friends. But at least Mother *has* friends here.

Beth stares out at the enormous Halyard ballroom, full to bursting with debutantes, mothers, and the eligible young bachelors of London's society. The vaulted ceiling and white walls with Greek columns give the space an almost endless feeling. The cacophony of voices is dizzying, and they're barely into the booze yet. It's all swirls of pastel colors, feathers, tulle, and coattails. She can't even imagine how claustrophobic it will feel once the band starts and the three hundred assembled begin to dance.

How can there even be space to dance? she wonders as she begins making her way across the room, eyeing the refreshments on the far side. She needs a glass of wine to make it through this evening, perhaps two. She can hold her liquor, despite what her mother thinks. Miss Wilson's been slipping her whisky for most of the last two years—in supervised amounts, but still.

She knows she needs to plaster on a smile, listen to some dull conversation, and begin making her own connections. Hopefully to the young gentlemen, but anyone would do. If she can make friends with any of the girls expected to marry this season, she can at least catch the eye of their castoffs. She's under no illusion that she's a prime match. A suitable one, surely, but she has no fortune to offer.

She'll bring her dowry and perhaps the small country estate, if her cousin James will deign to let them keep it once he comes of age. If her uncle, currently managing their affairs until James can inherit, is any barometer, they won't get a speck of her father's holdings. Just like he wanted.

It's so much less than almost any other lady in the room can offer. And on top of that Beth's short, clumsy, and unknown. Still, she's pretty enough, and Mother thinks she's delightful.

Beth wrinkles her nose, glancing up at the ceiling. She's really in a pitiful state if her mother is the only reference she can give for her charms. Father never thought much of her, and she barely got to know her uncle on his brief visit some ten years ago. She's never even met Cousin James.

Miss Wilson loves her. But who here would care about what their housekeeper has to say?

Beth takes a deep breath and forces herself to slow down, ambling rather than charging across the room, looking around for a friendly face. Debutantes and young gentlemen abound, but none of them seems the least bit approachable, and she's getting appraising looks from most of the clusters of friends. An oddity, daughter of the late Viscount Demeroven, kept locked away in the country with her . . . *energetic* mother.

Beth searches for an opening, any opening, but only manages to catch the eye of a graying older gentleman who gazes back at her with distinct interest. Beth breaks eye contact, trying to squeeze by a gaggle of mothers, knocking into their hoops with muttered apologies. She was looking for friends, not a man her late father's age. A man who definitely shouldn't be seeking out a wife of just twenty, much less one like Beth, who rarely looks her age, even made up as she is.

But try as she might, there's no escape. She's penned in by the groups of unfriendly guests. Her damn hoopskirt makes slinking away thoroughly impossible. The gentleman approaches her with what she assumes is his most winning smile.

It's slightly sinister.

"Miss Demeroven, isn't it?" the gentleman says, holding out his hand.

Beth hesitates just for a moment, reluctant to touch him, but propriety wins out. She didn't spend the last two years cosseted away with Mother for nothing.

"Yes," she says, extending her hand and clenching her jaw as he raises it to his lips for an uncomfortably long kiss.

"I'm Lord Psoris, a friend of your father's. A shame he couldn't be here. I know how proud of you he would be," he says, his voice rough and loud as he slowly releases her hand.

She pulls it back to her stomach as quickly as is polite. Father thought the entire idea of coming out was wasteful—uneager to spend his investment money on her dresses and activities. He'd planned to marry her off to an old friend. Oh, God, is it possible Lord Psoris is that friend?

Father wouldn't have blinked an eye. Mother was Beth's age when he married her, and he was twenty years' her senior then. But Lord Psoris is easily forty years older than Beth now. And his leer is anything but chivalrous.

"My condolences," he continues when Beth realizes she hasn't managed to find words.

"Thank you," she forces out, glancing around for salvation, but there's none to find. She's stuck here. "Have you been in town for the winter?"

"I have, I have. Parliament and some festivities, though of course we all eagerly await the season getting underway." Beth nods, taking a small step back as he advances. "I would be honored to have your first dance."

Beth bumps into the gentleman behind her as Psoris bears down on her. She squeaks, stumbling and trying to keep her hoop from belling outward. The man behind her turns and reaches for her elbow. Horribly embarrassed, she looks up at the tall, blond gentleman, her cheeks on fire. He glances from her to Lord Psoris, frowning.

"My apologies," she says meekly. What a little twit he must think her. "Felt a little faint."

"Then we must absolutely get you a drink. Excuse me, gentlemen," a young woman says, stepping out from behind the blond gentleman as if appearing from thin air.

The woman takes Beth's arm and effortlessly maneuvers them around the blond gentleman and away from the affronted Lord Psoris. They're yards away before Psoris can even splutter.

"He's a cad," the woman says, grinning at Beth, her blue eyes sparkling with mischief. Her hair is just as white blond as the tall gentleman's was, and there's a similar sharpness to their jaws and the broadness of their shoulders. "Father and I make rather a sport of saving young debs from his clutches. He caught you in his sights immediately, didn't he?"

Beth wilts, leaning into her savior. "Entirely. And there are so many people, I couldn't get away."

"Lucky you backed into us. Lady Guinevere Bertram. Gwen," she adds, squeezing Beth's arm against her side.

"Miss Demeroven. Elizabeth—Beth."

Gwen gives her an impressed look. "The prodigal daughter returns. You'll be popular."

"I'm not sure prodigal is really appropriate," Beth says, shaking her head.

"Oh, but you could play the part wonderfully. You've got the skin and the hair—perfect looks for a mysterious, triumphant season entrance. Pastel suits you, but I think you'd be captivating in something red. The right attitude, some wine, we could make an intrigue of you yet. Who doesn't love intrigue?"

Beth simply blinks up at her, allowing this strange, spirited woman to guide her around the room. Beth has no idea where they're going, or how they're not causing some sort of domino crash as they plough through people, but Gwen doesn't seem to worry. She walks with her head held high, smiling and nodding to people with an ease and grace Beth couldn't ever match.

"Here," Gwen says as they finally reach the refreshments.

Beth takes a glass of sweet wine gratefully. It's cool and mellow, with just the lightest taste of alcohol—though from the warmth at the back of her neck, there's plenty of alcohol in it. Beth takes another sip, desperate to relax even a little. Her run-in with Lord Psoris has put her on edge. Is this what it's like—overbearing men leaning over you when you can't get away?

"They get better," Gwen says, pulling Beth from her bleak perusal of the room. She takes Beth's elbow again and moves her toward the other side of the floor, away from where couples seem to be linking up for the first dance.

Beth can see Lord Psoris looking for her at the far end and curls closer to Gwen, who just laughs and nudges her. "You can always say no, you know."

"And risk insulting one of my father's oldest friends on the first night?" Beth says, her fingers worrying into her skirts. She wishes she'd brought a fan now, just for something to do with her hands.

"No one would begrudge you wanting to find someone closer to your age."

"I suppose," Beth says, glancing up at Gwen, who nods to their left.

Beth leans around her and notices a tall, gangly young man standing alone and looking as uncomfortable as she feels. "Him?"

Beth wrinkles her nose. "He's very thin, isn't he? And broody?"

Gwen purses her lips to keep from laughing. "Fair. All right, well, we should find you a good first dance. Come here."

She leads Beth over to the wall and together they sidle back until they're resting against it, out of the fray. Their skirts bump together and Beth feels her shoulders start to come down. She notices her mother across the room, still held in a circle of society mothers and looking bored to tears. Mother glances around and their eyes meet. Beth leans into Gwen to show she's managed to find at least one person to talk to, and Mother smiles, giving her a little nod before turning back to more gossip.

"What about him?" Gwen asks.

Beth follows her gaze to an enormous young man with wide shoulders, at least six feet tall. She turns to Gwen, incredulous.

"What?"

"How would that even work?" Beth asks, grinning as Gwen cackles.

A few heads turn and they both quiet down, snickering as they take sips of their wine. Gwen has a lovely laugh and such a bright, open face. Instantly captivating, really. Beth is surprised she's not on the floor already.

"He looks nice," Beth says, gesturing discreetly to a tall fellow with a trim beard and a prominent chin.

"Go say hello," Gwen says.

"For you," Beth corrects. "His height, your hair, you'd have lovely children." Gwen snorts. "What?"

"Well, his mother thinks I'm a menace, so that ship has sailed. And it's just as likely our children would be hairy as anything and tiny. His father's rather short, and my late mother had copious very dark hair."

"Hmm," Beth offers, trying to parse it all. "You've met then?"

"Two seasons ago we went on a few outings. It didn't end well," Gwen says, shrugging.

"Two seasons ago?"

"This is my fourth," Gwen says, meeting her eyes with a brash grin that's cracking at the edges. "I think if I make it to next season without a husband, I get a medal."

Beth allows herself to laugh along. Four seasons, she can't even imagine. And without a mother too. How trying that must be. "Maybe they just give you some land and let you run free."

"Wouldn't that be something," Gwen says. "Big plot of land, nothing to do but read and eat."

"Draw," Beth says.

"Paint. Swim."

"Oh, do you get a lake, or is that only if you make it to six?" Beth asks.

Gwen nudges her with her hip—at least, Beth assumes so from the way her skirts move. "If I make it to seven, I think maybe I get my own castle."

"Oh, well, you should hold out for that, then," Beth says. "Queen of your own castle surely beats a marriage to him." She gestures with her empty glass toward a scrawny young man with a patchy beard who's asking an equally awkward young lady to dance.

"That's Albie's younger brother, Bobby. Didn't think he'd be out this year," Gwen says with a frown. "Shame, he's a nice kid. Another few years, he'd probably be a catch."

"Albie?"

"Mr. Mason, my mother's elder nephew. If I spot him, I'll introduce you. Nice chap. Obnoxious most of the time, but a good lad."

"Lady Gwen!"

Beth turns, following Gwen's gaze. A young lady in a striking yellow gown hurries up to them, dragging over another young woman in blue. Both of them hold empty glasses of champagne, their cheeks pink.

"We've been looking for you for ages," the woman in yellow says, a pout on her round face. She looks Gwen over. "You don't have them!"

"Didn't have time," Gwen says with an apologetic shrug. She doesn't look very sorry for whatever's missing, Beth thinks, though both women look rather put out. "This is the Honorable Elizabeth Demeroven. Miss Demeroven, this is Lady Meredith and Lady Annabeth."

"A pleasure," Beth says, dipping in a curtsy.

Lady Meredith and Lady Annabeth curtsy with pleasant smiles before looking back at Gwen expectantly.

"Who's winning?" Gwen asks.

"We don't have the cards," Lady Meredith says indignantly.

"So?"

The women exchange a look before Lady Meredith grins. "I've spotted five heirs and two spares."

"I've only got three, but I swear it would have been four if I could have remembered the gray skinny one's name," Lady Annabeth says.

"Oh, Lord Frightan?"

"Lord Frightan!" the girls exclaim.

"That's four for me then. Tied with Eloise. We're about to sneak out to the gardens and meet up with the gents, do you want to join us?" Lady Annabeth asks.

Beth tightens her shoulders, preparing to lose her new acquaintance. How can she possibly compete with these glamorous ladies?

"I'm going to give Miss Demeroven the lay of the land tonight, but I'll catch the next game," Gwen says easily. Lady Meredith opens her mouth. "It's no real challenge if you have all the names on the cards, is it?" Lady Meredith and Lady Annabeth frown. "Father almost grounded me last year."

"Only because you followed him around to get all the heirs," Lady Annabeth says.

Gwen shrugs playfully. "Let me know who wins."

Lady Meredith rolls her eyes and Lady Annabeth winks before they curtsy and head for the back of the hall, presumably on their way to the gardens.

"You don't need to stay," Beth says perfunctorily, though she's rather sure if Gwen abandons her now she might hide in the washroom for the rest of the night.

"Honestly, if Father catches me playing Spot-the-Scion again, he really might confiscate my pin money."

"Spot-the—"

"Have to have fun at these things somehow," Gwen says with a shrug. "I usually make cards, but I couldn't be bothered this year."

"Cards?"

"To pin to the back of the dance cards. I usually put together a list. First one to spot them all gets bragging rights for the season. A little awkward if you end up dancing with one of the scions, but still," she says, eyes twinkling.

Beth considers her new, slightly eccentric friend. She has annual party games to play with numerous friends. Presumably some of them must be male, of marriageable age, and available. And yet here she is, four seasons deep, and clearly no interest in being on the floor. But surely a woman as stunning and charismatic as Gwen must have options.

"What?"

"Sorry," Beth mumbles, looking away. She was staring.

"You can ask," Gwen says more gently.

"I wasn't—" Beth starts before shaking her head. "So, do you not want to get married, or are you just really choosy?"

Gwen huffs. "I'm discerning."

"Can't be your looks that scare them away," Beth insists.

Gwen raises a hand to fluff at the dainty curls hanging down from her braided bun. "No, it's all the personality. I blame my father. Terrible role model."

Beth follows her look and spots the tall, blond man, Gwen's father, standing among a gaggle of wives and mothers, smiling with charm and poise. "Has he remarried?" Beth asks.

Gwen shakes her head. "Never. A perpetual bachelor, with an upstart daughter."

"Well, you both saved me, so I'll give you a good reference if you need one, whatever that's worth from me. My mother would too. At least she has friends here," Beth says, nodding across the room. Mother's facade is slipping. She's starting to list like she does when she's tired.

"Thank you," Gwen says, smiling as Beth looks back at her. "But it's you we should focus on. Find you a tolerable young man."

Beth shrugs. "I'd just as happily stay on the sidelines tonight. Get the lay of the land."

"Well, in that case, I think we'll need more wine, and perhaps the profiteroles?"

"Oh, absolutely," Beth says, chuffed that Gwen would rather spend her evening as a wallflower with her than with her friends outside. Gwen grins and takes her hand, leading her back toward the refreshments, the two of them giggling and chatting as the ball swirls on around them.

And though she's tired, and still a bit jittery, pressed against the wall sharing profiteroles and sips of Gwen's brandy, she's almost having fun. Not succeeding so much in garnering dances, but she's made a contact, and that feels like something. Maybe she's even made a friend, she thinks, as Gwen laughs in her ear, both of them flushed and a little tipsy.

"You should dance," Gwen says an hour or two later, when they're leaning against each other, sleepy.

"Next ball," Beth says. Gwen nudges her. "I can't leave you here alone."

Gwen arches a cool brow. "Think I'd waste away without you?"

Beth nods toward the broody, gangly boy, whose latest partner has clearly abandoned him. "I could always tell him you'd like a dance," she says, starting to raise her hand to flag him down.

"Don't you dare," Gwen hisses, grabbing her hand, eyes wide. Beth giggles in triumph and Gwen looks her up and down in light approval. "You're a little bit evil, aren't you?"

"Thank you," Beth preens.

"I'll get you back," Gwen says.

"We'll see."

Gwen wraps her hand into the crook of Beth's arm with a smirk and they fall into a contented silence, watching the whirl of the couples on the floor.

After a few minutes, Gwen sighs. "You should at least dance one. I'll hold your wine."

Beth shakes her head as Gwen opens her mouth to argue. "You didn't have to present today."

Gwen shudders in understanding. "God, the waiting in carriages is the worst, isn't it?"

"I needed the loo by the second hour, and then it was two more before we got inside, and forty minutes before I saw the queen. I thought I might pee on the drawing room floor," Beth admits.

Gwen snorts. "A girl did my year, actually. Not in the drawing room, but on the stairs. Horrid. Never came back."

"Oh, Lord, I can't even imagine," Beth says, feeling a pit in her stomach just at the thought. That poor girl.

"Father says my mother used to have dreams about it. Would wake up in a panic thinking she was late."

"Understandable," Beth says, watching as the couples twirl around the floor. There's not a lot of room with the newly fashionable hoops, so they're more swaying than anything. It's pretty. "Your mother didn't like the season either?"

"Father says she didn't," Gwen says, shifting a little. "Your mother?"

"I don't think so," Beth says, noting Mother fidgeting as well. This marble floor does nothing for the feet. "She and my father—I can't really imagine them courting."

"He wasn't romantic?"

Beth snorts. "Hardly. He'd hand her money to buy something nice for her birthday. Sometimes he brought home jewelry, but she never liked much of it," she admits, feeling a little heady. "Is your father romantic?"

"He's suave," Gwen says after a moment. "And utterly charming. I don't know if he's romantic though. Never seen him want to be."

"He hasn't courted at all?"

Gwen sucks on her cheek before glancing down at Beth. "You'll hear about his reputation soon enough, I think."

Beth nods once and looks back out at the floor. He has danced with a fair number of the debutantes tonight, but his face has always been affable, polite, charming. Nothing like the leer she's noticed Lord Psoris giving the girls. His look leaves her feeling slimy. But Gwen's father simply seems like a nice, handsome older man.

"But you like him," Beth says, noting Gwen's fond look as her father twirls one of the society matrons around.

"I do," Gwen says, shrugging. "He's fun."

"That's nice," Beth admits. Father was anything but fun.

The number ends and suddenly older gentlemen start to seep out of the crowd of onlookers, beckoning to the debutantes. Beth feels her eyebrows crease. There can't be that many unwed older bachelors. Mother promised men like Lord Psoris would be an anomaly.

Gwen waves to her father and Beth startles. Of course, the father-daughter dance.

"Are you okay alone here?"

Beth blinks and looks up to find Gwen watching her with perhaps too much understanding in her gaze. "Of course. Go, go," Beth says quickly, taking Gwen's brandy glass and nudging her toward the floor.

Gwen steps off, glancing back at her even as she reaches the floor. Almost all the girls seem to have someone to dance with and Beth slumps against the wall, hiding from the thought. Not that her father would have deigned to come tonight if he were alive. He would have said her name was enough; he didn't need to waste his time.

She watches the couples begin to dance to the lively waltz and swallows the last of Gwen's brandy. The warmth down her throat does little to fix the clench in her stomach. She doesn't miss him. But she's still sad.

Gwen and her father chat as they dance, both of them grinning. He keeps dipping her with a silly smile and Gwen looks delighted. Beth feels that knot moving from her stomach to her chest. She can't remember a single time her father looked at her that way, if he bothered to look at all. Not the son he wanted, that's all she ever was.

"I see you listened."

Beth jumps, turning to find Mother at her side, already plucking the brandy from her hand and frowning at Beth's nearly empty wineglass.

"I'm fine," Beth says. She is. Any remaining giddiness from the alcohol has faded. Now that Gwen's gone, all she feels is exhausted and melancholy. "How are your friends?"

Mother maintains her disapproval for a moment before sighing and leaning back into the wall with her. "Horrid. Yours?"

"She's nice," Beth says, nodding toward the dance floor. Mother tracks her gaze and then stiffens just as the waltz ends. "Mother?"

But she's distracted as she notices Gwen dragging her father toward them. Mother straightens up, grabbing Beth's wine and putting both glasses hastily onto a side table before adjusting her hair.

"Father, this is my new friend, Miss Demeroven, and this must be her mother?"

Mother just stares at Gwen's father, who's staring right back, both of them pale, eyes wide.

"Yes," Beth steps in, gently nudging her mother. "This is my mother, Lady Demeroven. A pleasure to meet you both."

"Yes," Mother says slowly, standing tall. "Yes. Lord Havenfort and I are acquainted already, actually. Though I've yet to meet your new friend."

"This is Lady Gwen," Beth says, watching as Gwen curtsies to her mother. Lord Havenfort is still staring like a gaping fish.

"We should be getting home. Lovely to meet you," Mother says, giving Gwen a forced smile as she grabs Beth's arm. "Lord Havenfort," she adds, nodding to the man.

"Lady Demeroven," Lord Havenfort says, his voice high.

Mother drags Beth away as she and Gwen exchange baffled

looks. "Mother," Beth protests, but she just keeps marching forward.

Beth would argue or hold her back, but she's too busy trying to avoid knocking anyone over. Mother bulls ahead, leading her through the throngs of avid partygoers, uncaring of who she bumps with her skirts, dragging Beth up and out of the ballroom.

"Mother," Beth insists as they clear the upper landing and hustle into the main foyer of the ridiculous Halyard estate. "What's the matter?"

"Nothing," Mother says tersely, nodding in thanks as the stewards open the front gates for them, revealing a line of waiting coaches. They must be some of the first people to leave. "We've calls to make in the morning."

"You said we'd have a lie-in," Beth says, frowning as Mother hurries her into the first hired carriage. "And I'd have liked more time with Gwen."

"I'm sure you'll have plenty of time to socialize with your new friend at the next event, though you should put more effort into meeting some of the young men, the whole reason we're here," Mother says stiffly as she settles into her seat and the coach takes off.

Beth just stares at her mother, utterly baffled. "Mother, what's—"

"I have a headache, darling, please," Mother says, closing her eyes, conversation over.

Beth watches her mother sit there, refusing to speak, head tilted back, breathing forcefully. She's never seen her mother this way outside of their home. Irritated, yes. Exhausted, yes, but this—this is panic. Whatever happened between her mother and Lord Havenfort before tonight clearly wasn't good.

CHAPTER TWO

Gwen

"Are you going to explain what happened?" Gwen demands as the steward shuts the door to their carriage.

Father looks over at her, unimpressed, and Gwen crosses her arms, tempted to throw a fit. It's been two hours since he froze like a deer caught in the crosshairs when Beth's mother showed up. Two hours he made them stay to avoid her questions. She had to dance with *both* Albie and Bobby. Twice.

"Father," she presses.

"Just an old acquaintance," he says with an uninterested shrug, looking out the window at absolutely nothing in the dark predawn.

"Who almost threw herself out of the party at the sight of you?"

"She always was a bit high-strung," he dismisses, feigning interest in his cufflinks next. "How was your evening?"

Gwen rolls her eyes. "As dull as the last three opening balls. Saw Meredith and Annabeth briefly, but most of my friends are married in the country now. And the only new friend I met is apparently the spawn of your arch enemy."

"Lady Demeroven isn't my arch enemy," he scoffs, glancing up to meet her eyes. "She's—no one. Her husband was an arse though."

"I got that feeling from Beth."

"Really?" Father asks, surprised.

Gwen shrugs. "She didn't say much, but it sounds like he was lackluster at best. How did you know him?"

"We sat in the Lords together. Awful man. Flatulent too."

Gwen wrinkles her nose. It's hard to imagine the glamorous Lady Demeroven with some overaged, gaseous man. She's so beautiful, it boggles the mind. "She must have had other options," Gwen says without thought.

Father's face tightens. "Yes, well, let's hope you do better this year, or perhaps you'll be Lord Psoris' next victim. Young Miss Demeroven got away all right?"

Gwen snorts. "Just fine. *She's* lovely. Funny."

"Cordelia had a sharp wit." Gwen watches as he seems to hear himself and then straightens up. "Well, time for bed."

The carriage pulls to a rough stop outside their manor. "Father—"

But he's out of the carriage and reaching back for her before she can blink, obviously eager to be rid of her questions. The sun's starting to come up as it is. They never stay this late; she could have been asleep hours ago. She isn't about to let this go.

"How do you know Lady Demeroven?" Gwen asks, following her father up the grand steps, holding her skirts higher than she should to keep up.

It's like he's actually trying to run away from her. He throws the door open and hurries into the foyer, only to skid to a halt at Mrs. Gilpe's unimpressed look. Gwen slides in behind him, covering her mouth against a laugh. Mrs. Gilpe scowls at her father, intimidating in her tartan robe and braided hair.

"It's nearly five," she says.

"And?" Father replies, going for dismissive but failing as his face splits in a yawn.

"You're never home later than two from these infernal balls. We were worried sick," Mrs. Gilpe says sternly.

"Father didn't want to risk running back into Lady Demeroven," Gwen says, diligently noting Mrs. Gilpe's slight reaction to the name. She must know more.

"I'm going to bed," Father says, shaking his head as Gwen opens her mouth. "And so should you. We've promenading to do far too soon."

"No, we're not actually going to promenade, are we? Can't we just linger in the parlor? It's so much less work for the same result."

"If I had to be up all night and then prepare a luncheon, the least you can do is walk around the park," Mrs. Gilpe puts in.

"See," Father says. "Can't go disappointing Mrs. Gilpe." He salutes them and then takes off for the stairs.

"You hate promenading!" Gwen calls after him. Father just shrugs dramatically and then disappears around the corner of the landing, leaving her protest hanging in the air.

"Come along, you can harass him later today," Mrs. Gilpe says, reaching out to take Gwen's arm and guide her up the stairs after him.

"Do you know who Lady Demeroven is?"

"Wife of Lord Demeroven, I'd imagine," Mrs. Gilpe says flatly.

"Really. To Father. He almost fell over when he saw her and she couldn't get away fast enough. She practically dragged her daughter, Beth, out of the room."

Mrs. Gilpe purses her lips. They clear the landing to the second floor and head down the hall. Father's door is already firmly shut. Gwen goes to prod, but Mrs. Stelm leans out of Gwen's room.

"Didn't die in a carriage crash then," Mrs. Stelm says gamely, grinning beneath her bonnet cap, a few of her ribbons half fallen out and framing her face.

"You weren't really worried, were you?" Gwen asks as Mrs. Gilpe ushers her into her room and the two of them get her situated to begin releasing her from the monstrosity that is her dress.

"Not really," Mrs. Stelm assures her. "Though Mrs. Gilpe was . . . concerned."

"For you," Mrs. Gilpe puts in, passing behind Mrs. Stelm with a nudge to her waist to begin unlacing Gwen's skirt. "Your father can stay out all night if he likes. You still have some honor to protect."

"Some?" Gwen exclaims. Mrs. Stelm slaps Mrs. Gilpe's arm.

"As long as your father was in eyesight, it doesn't much matter," Mrs. Gilpe says.

"Barely let me out of it for the second half of the evening," Gwen grumbles as Mrs. Gilpe finishes undoing her buttons. "It was like he thought if I turned away Lady Demeroven would somehow appear again."

"Lady Demeroven?" Mrs. Stelm repeats. They briefly disappear when they lift her skirt over her head. "They spoke?"

Gwen glances between her housekeeper and lady's maid as they exchange a series of narrowed eyes and eyebrow raises. "Who is this woman, what did she do?"

"No one," Mrs. Gilpe says firmly.

Mrs. Stelm rolls her eyes, laying out Gwen's skirt and bodice to air overnight.

"But—" Gwen says, looking to Mrs. Stelm.

Mrs. Stelm just shrugs and turns back to undoing clasps of her corset while Mrs. Gilpe undoes the hoop cage and lowers it to the ground.

"An old acquaintance, I'm sure he was just surprised."

"He was more than surprised, it was like—"

"Time for bed," Mrs. Gilpe insists as she deftly pulls the pins from Gwen's hair. "You need to look at least somewhat rested for this afternoon. You're not sixteen anymore."

Gwen gapes and Mrs. Stelm scoffs. "Mrs. Gilpe, really."

"Bed," Mrs. Gilpe says firmly, pushing Gwen toward her already turned-down sheets. "Good night."

"It's morning," Gwen protests, watching Mrs. Gilpe take Mrs. Stelm's arm and practically drag her out of the room.

"Sleep," Mrs. Gilpe says sternly, before shuffling Mrs. Stelm out into the hall.

The door shuts, and Gwen stands staring out at her slightly disheveled room completely nonplussed.

GWEN TWISTS HER hands together as she and Father trod along the walking path beside the Long Water. The clouds haven't lifted and the park is awash in a dull gray-hued light that does nothing for either of their moods. She barely slept, and Father doesn't look much better.

All her plans of subtly divining information out of him seem to fall flat against his listless mood. She stares around at the other families set up along the path, with their overlarge tea sets and tarps, the girls in bright colors, mothers equally done up. She feels a bit shabby by comparison in her dark navy dress and cape—but it's cold.

She can see one of the younger girls shivering. She looks back pleadingly, but her mother forces her to stand at the edge of their wilting picnic blanket to smile at the young men, who are more interested in the sculls on the lake than the girls along the path.

"We should have stayed home," Father mutters, taking her arm and leaning into her against a gale of wind that whips through the park.

"Agreed," Gwen says, tugging him closer as they continue to stroll. "We could play chess?"

Father smiles, nudging her. "You're on. Continue our wager?"

"Obviously," Gwen says with a grin. One of the lads tossing a ball on the lawn misses and goes tumbling into the grass. Gwen smothers a laugh.

Father has no such compunction and guffaws loudly, ignoring the scowls from the matriarchs on benches along the river. He shrugs at them, his charming grin thawing their disdain. Somehow when Gwen gives that grin when she's in trouble it never comes off well. But Father could smile his way out of an execution if he wanted.

"Shall we take the fork and walk you past the pitch?" he suggests as they come up on Carriage Drive, presenting them with the choice to stay along the lake or cross the park to wend toward the opposite boulevard.

Gwen hesitates. She does enjoy watching a game of cricket, and there's bound to be at least one on the pitches. But then she spots Beth and Lady Demeroven standing by the bridge. A much more engaging pastime, to be sure.

She begins leading her father in their direction without comment. He doesn't seem to see them, and Gwen holds her breath, hoping she can get within shouting distance to grab Beth.

Surely her mother would want Beth to promenade. Two young ladies attract more attention together than separately with their chaperones after all. Everyone knows that.

And that will leave Father with nothing to do but talk to the mysterious Lady Demeroven.

Beth spots her first and turns to wave. Gwen feels Father stiffen and automatically jerk to the side, as if he really does want to turn tail and run away. But they're far too close for that to be proper now, and Gwen withholds her grin. Beth drags her mother over, both of them physically hauling their respective parents together until they're all standing to the side of the walking path.

Beth and Lady Demeroven look wonderful, bright spots of pastel against the dreary day. Beth's light blue gown is fetching, highlighting her dark swept-up hair, while Lady Demeroven's lavender dress is appropriate but cheerful all the same. Beth grins at Gwen, while Lady Demeroven looks a bit like she's swallowed poison.

"You both look lovely," Gwen says quickly. Her father seems to stall now that they're within speaking distance. He looks like he's been struck in the stomach, actually.

"Mother, could I promenade with Lady Gwen?" Beth asks, turning her bright smile on her mother. "I'm sure Lord Havenfort would keep you company."

The adults exchange something . . . close to a look. Gwen's rather sure their eyes never meet. She can see Lady Demeroven searching for a rebuttal while Father splutters.

"Miss Demeroven and I could go walk by the pitch, pick a few lads to cheer for—start the season off as positive influences on them?"

Father shoots Gwen a look. She's never once cheered for a gentleman in a game. Jeered with Father, taunted Albie, but never offered the slightest encouragement. But Beth should give it a try.

"Please," Beth cajoles.

"Yes, fine, go," Lady Demeroven says with a sigh, releasing Beth.

Gwen grins and snags her arm, hurrying them a few steps away to walk ahead of their parents. Beth squeezes her arm and they set off at a slow amble. Their parents tortured them last night; it's time for payback.

"How was the rest of your evening?" Beth asks.

"Boring. Father forced me into a few dances, but they stopped serving food and it got hot."

"Any nice gentlemen?" Beth asks, her voice full of innocence. She doesn't know what she's in for this season, even with the slightly ignominious introduction she got last night.

"Of course not," Gwen says, laughing as Beth gives her a shocked look. "Remember, I have exacting standards."

"Apparently," Beth says, but there's no malice in her words.

"Picking a husband is serious business. Hard to get to know someone in all that commotion anyway," Gwen says, turning to look at Beth so she can glance back at their parents.

They're almost a meter apart, not looking at each other. Father's walking stiffly and it looks like Lady Demeroven may permanently damage her leather gloves with the way her hands are clenched.

"Did your mother say anything last night? Look at them."

Beth glances back in the guise of fixing her skirts. "Oh dear, Mother looks like she's about to break her teeth."

"She didn't tell you anything?"

"Nothing," Beth says, shaking her head as they turn toward the pitch. "Barely spoke at all this morning too. Did your father say anything?"

"Only that she was an old acquaintance. He tried to pretend of no importance, but clearly something happened."

Beth worries her lip, her arm still snug in Gwen's. It's helping with the chill of the air, and Gwen finds their height difference rather charming. Beth fits against her nicely.

"Did your father and mine spend much time together? He had a fair few enemies. Maybe he ran afoul of Lord Havenfort."

Gwen glances back at her father to make sure he's out of earshot. He's glaring so forcefully at the grass he probably wouldn't notice anyway. No need to scrutinize her when she's away from male company. Not that he tries that hard otherwise really. He's rarely had the need.

"He said they didn't get along, but that's not unusual with Father. He tends to rub people the wrong way."

"He seems lovely," Beth says softly. "And you two get along."

"We do," Gwen agrees, noting her new friend's downcast face. "I'm sure you could join us when we go riding later this week. He's always happy to have my friends come to visit. You could even stay over if you like. See if you're really the whist player you say you are."

Beth glances at her with narrowed eyes. "You doubt me?"

"I just think you haven't met your match yet."

Beth laughs. "I look forward to proving you wrong."

"This weekend?" Gwen suggests, already planning out treats to make with Mrs. Stelm, so she can trounce Beth and stuff her face all at once.

"I'd like that," Beth says, smiling up at her before glancing back at their parents. "Though I don't know that Mother would let me spend the night so early in the season. She's sure we're about to be flooded with visitors and wants me available first thing in the mornings from now on," Beth says, looking distinctly uncomfortable at the thought.

"Another time then," Gwen says easily. Beth nods, her smile slipping. "And I'm sure she's right. A beautiful girl like you is sure to be overwhelmed with suitors once they get their heads straight," she adds, smiling as Beth blushes. "In fact, who knows, you might find a suitor today. Run, boys, run!" Gwen calls out as they reach the edge of the pitch.

She hears her father snort behind them but pays him no mind. She doesn't want to see Lady Demeroven's reaction, even if Beth is giggling again, her face still a pretty shade of pink.

A gaggle of the ton's most eligible young men wrestle over the ball on the muddy field, already deep into a game of rugby. It leaves them sweaty, dirty, and high-spirited every time, and Beth and Gwen aren't the only girls watching. Huddles of pastel- and brightly clad debutantes stand around the field, waving handkerchiefs and giving modest encouragement. Gwen can already see their mothers glaring at her.

She's always been disruptive, but honestly, the boys seem to enjoy it.

"Go on, Mason, give it a try!" she calls, smirking as Albie glares over at her. He's sweating like a pig and covered in more mud than anyone else.

"Don't be mean," Beth says, nudging her. "He's trying very hard."

Gwen laughs. "Don't worry about Albie. It's my prerogative as cousin—he doesn't have sisters. The one next to him though, Lord Brightly, he's single, first in line to inherit, and not wholly irritating. And he's looking your way."

Beth stiffens next to her, her playful blush falling off her face as her smile disappears.

"Not your type?" Gwen asks, glancing over the other assembled gentlemen. "Too stocky?" Beth just remains still next to her. "Too tall?" Beth shakes her head. "Too—"

"It's his eyes," Beth says quietly.

Gwen feels herself frown. "His eyes?"

"They're cold."

Gwen looks over at Beth, but the woman doesn't meet her gaze, simply staring across the pitch at the other girls along the far side, all simpering and sweet.

"Men with eyes like that are cruel," Beth explains.

Chilled by her soft-spoken wisdom, Gwen pulls her closer and Beth relaxes. Gwen tries to shake off the pall and glances back, hiding her smirk as she spots their parents standing two meters apart now, watching the game with disinterest.

She's about to say that it seems their parents are mortal enemies when she notices her father isn't actually following the game. He's looking toward it, but every few seconds his eyes cut sideways to watch Lady Demeroven. And Lady Demeroven's face is not the stoic pale mask she thought it was.

"I don't think this has anything to do with your father," Gwen says.

Beth startles. "What?"

"Look at them." Gwen angles herself toward Beth so she can turn her head and consider their parents. Her perfume is lovely. "Something happened between the two of them. I'm sure of it."

"My mother's *blushing,*" Beth says, shocked. She looks back at Gwen. "I've never seen her blush like that."

Gwen grins and together they look back at the game, just as Albie takes a whapping hit to the back. He goes sprawling face-first into the mud and Gwen withholds her cackle. Beth covers her mouth, concerned.

"Is he all right?"

"He'll be fine. Get up, Mason! Show 'em what for!"

"Gwen!" Beth exclaims as Albie glowers over at them, his face dripping mud.

Father chuckles behind them and she can see Bobby, equally covered in mud, grinning at his brother's plight.

Gwen just shrugs, giving Bobby a thumbs-up before looking back at Beth. "Someone has to cheer for the poor thing." Beth frowns at her, but the corner of her mouth is tilted up. "I like rooting for the underdog."

"You're not rooting, you're heckling."

"Perhaps," Gwen agrees, glancing back at their parents. Lady Demeroven's lost her blush, but Father's looking a little pleased. "But I do like rooting for the dark horse, and I think my father is your mother's dark horse."

Beth looks over at her. "What?"

"I think maybe Father is a bit sweet on her."

"She couldn't have pulled me out of the ball fast enough," Beth argues, glancing back. "She's twirling her hair!"

"So?" Gwen wonders, looking over her shoulder again to see that the stalwart lady is indeed toying with her hair.

"She never does that."

"See?"

"I don't think that means they were sweet on each other," Beth says slowly.

"He's sweet on her. She's still an unknown," Gwen corrects. "But I bet we can figure it out." Beth hesitates as she watches another violent tackle. "Please? I need something to liven up this season. The balls and parties get boring otherwise."

"And this is more interesting?"

"Figuring out why they act as though they hate each other but look like smitten schoolchildren? Of course! It's a mystery. I love a good mystery. Promise you'll at least try and find out?"

Beth shifts, biting at her lip, unsure.

"It'll be fun," Gwen needles, thinking solving a mystery with Beth might be the perfect remedy for the drudgery of the season.

Beth snorts. "Fine. It couldn't hurt to talk about something other than hoop circumference over breakfast," she says.

"Excellent," Gwen says, jostling her arm just as Albie tumbles back to the ground. "Get up, Mason! Get up!"

Beth laughs and covers her mouth with her hand. Albie just rolls his eyes and stumbles up, lumbering back toward the scrum.

"See? Fun," Gwen insists, winking at Beth.

Beth can't seem to help herself and grins back, her eyes alight. "Fun," she agrees.

Chapter Three

Beth

"I look about twelve," Beth says.

Mother adjusts the light pink satin and lace gown over her padded and primped underlayers. "Pastels are all the rage this season."

Beth grimaces and shifts, frowning at her round, rouged cheeks. Mother can swear all she likes, but Beth would much rather look her age. While youth might appeal to men like Lord Psoris, she's proud of being twenty, not ashamed. Gwen's twenty-one and she looks just as desirable as she must have at eighteen.

"I want you to dance more this evening," Mother says as she circles Beth, reaching out here and there to adjust. "We should have had at least a few callers by now."

"It's only been a week," Beth protests, not liking the tightness of her mother's jaw.

They've attended eight teas and garden parties, promenaded every day, made unending morning calls, and been guests at four dinners. It isn't as if they aren't trying.

"I had at least five callers my first week in my season," Mother says as she adjusts the diamond necklace she's forced Beth to wear tonight.

"Gwen hasn't had any either," Beth argues.

Mother snorts. "I'm not surprised."

"Mother," Beth scolds, glaring.

"Your friend is a lovely young woman, but she's got a mouth on her and her reputation among the mothers is abysmal. She got in a shouting match with that Gentry girl."

"Miss Gentry was making fun of Gwen for not having a mother to teach her proper manners. Gwen should have punched her."

Mother frowns. Beth hasn't seen Gwen since the Jelison tea party on Thursday. And even though Gwen shook it off, she knows Miss Gentry must have hurt her feelings. How utterly callous. It's not as if it's Gwen's fault she has no maternal influence. And she's heaps more intelligent, witty, and charming than the other girls with their proper mothers anyway.

"You're determined to dislike Gwen," Beth says as Mother continues to frown.

"I'm not," Mother says. Beth narrows her eyes at her. "I'm not. She's a nice young lady, and I don't mind you being friends with her, but I won't have you looking at her as an example of how to behave in the season. She's been out for four years."

"I know," Beth says, her anger melting in the face of Mother's concern. "But I do like her."

"That's fine," Mother says, taking a deep breath. "Just don't spend all night with her, all right?"

Beth bobs her head. She hadn't really been planning on it . . . just all the time not spent dancing. But there's no reason Mother needs to know that. Instead, she should be leveraging this moment of détente. They come along so infrequently.

"You don't dislike Gwen just because of her father, do you?"

Mother blinks. "What? No."

"Because I know you don't think highly of him," Beth continues, watching as Mother sighs.

"I wish he'd been a better example to your friend, certainly," she says slowly. "But I don't blame her. You don't get to pick your father," she adds, meeting Beth's eyes.

Beth nods, refraining from mentioning that Mother did pick her father, and picked poorly. "Still, she's accomplished and kind. That must say something to Lord Havenfort's credit, right? As Miss Gentry said, it's not like she has a mother around."

Mother purses her lips and Beth waits her out, turning to her mirror to do a last check of her face. She looks ridiculous.

"Perhaps she's inherited some of Lord Havenfort's intelligence, but surely you can understand that having a man like that for a father doesn't give her a good example of how to behave in society. He's hardly a paragon of propriety."

"He's very nice!" Beth argues.

"Nice and respectable are separate things."

"He sits in the House of Lords," Beth says.

"The House of Lords hardly cares how many women a man has bedded."

"It's not like he's encouraging Gwen to do that. Gwen's honor is very safe."

"I'm sure it is," Mother says, holding up her hands. "I'm simply saying he's no example of proper etiquette."

"How do you know?" Beth insists.

Mother rolls her eyes. "I've known Lord Havenfort for a long time. His reputation precedes him."

"And you think he was like that when he was presented?"

Mother shakes her head. "He was . . . charming. And clearly that charm has gotten him rather far."

"So you knew him when you were in the market?" Beth presses.

Mother narrows her eyes. "We met in my season. He married his wife at the end of his second, as far as I know. And since her death he's gotten to know half of London's women biblically. That charm remains intact. Now, can we drop this?"

Beth sighs, tucking the information away, likely as much as she'll get her mother to admit tonight. Reluctantly, she spins for last looks.

"I doubt he's really bedded half of London," she says in lackluster defense. "It's not as if he could fall in love with that many women."

Mother smiles, laughing a little as she reaches out to fix a lock of Beth's hair. "I adore that you think that," she says gently. "And I adore you. I want you to have fun tonight. Just remember why we're here, all right?" Beth opens her mouth to defend her friend. "All right?"

"Yes," Beth says, shoulders sagging. "All right."

THIS BALL IS, absurdly, larger even than the last. The Kleisted ballroom could easily fit most of their London townhouse inside its cavernous three-story hall. Garlands of every type of flower imaginable line the walls, and Beth finds the entire effect dizzying as she tries to take it all in.

It's already very warm, and the press of bodies feels close despite the early hour. She feels even more ridiculous in her pink skirts and girlish makeup now. Mother wasn't wrong—many of the debs look softer tonight—but given how anxious her stomach feels in the face of all these people, she'd rather look her age and be able to glare them all down.

No amount of frowning can dampen the girlish charm pancaked onto her face tonight.

"I should begin scheduling our visits for next week," Mother says.

Beth sighs, glancing over at the society mothers. Always someone else to talk to, someone else's feelings to settle.

"You're beautiful, and smart, and any of them would be lucky to have you," Mother says, squeezing her arm.

That's the problem, Beth thinks, even as she lets Mother go with a false smile. Any of them might feel lucky to have her. But she doubts she'll feel as lucky in return to be had.

Beth stands at the edge of the room, her chest tight and breathing shallow. But she can do this. She's not about to let a lot of flowers and people cower her.

She starts to walk through the gathered crowd, keeping a wide eye for Lord Psoris, determined only to interact with young men she at least finds palatable this evening, if nothing else, when someone grabs her arm.

She turns, startled, and then relaxes as Gwen grins down at her. "You're finally here!" Gwen says excitedly.

Beth nods, a smile stretching across her face in response.

Gwen squeezes her arm. "Food?"

"You're a godsend," Beth says honestly.

Gwen laughs and tugs her across the room. Beth notices the looks they're getting now—the way mothers slightly sneer in their direction. Perhaps her mother wasn't totally wrong. It does seem Gwen has a reputation.

But when they reach the refreshments and Gwen passes her a glass of wine and a small quiche bite, Beth realizes her chest is no longer pulsing with anxiety. It hardly seems worth the upset to let go of her friend simply to appease a few mothers.

"Some house, huh?" Gwen asks, leading Beth over toward a less populated place along the entryway wall.

"It's amazing," Beth says, relaxing fully when her hoop brushes the wall, truly out of the fray. "Have you been here before?"

"They throw a few balls a season," Gwen says. "Have you been invited to the Yokely ball yet? They have the most amazing gardens, which is the only downside to this one."

"I don't think we have," Beth says, trying to recall the laundry list of events Mother has mentioned they'll attend. "Have I met the Yokelys?"

"They were at the Jelisons' tea party," Gwen says, not a lick of a frown on her face at the mention. "Lord Yokely is a portly man and his wife has a very pinched face."

"Oh! And the daughter is Lady Caroline?"

"Yes. The one with the nasal voice," Gwen says with a little grin.

"She was nice," Beth says, laughing as Gwen rolls her eyes. "She was."

"She's fine. Probably going to marry the Jackland heir."

"Really?"

"They've already been on two outings, just this week," Gwen says, shrugging as Beth gapes at her. "Some girls get lucky."

Beth bites at her lip. She's not had even one caller, and Lady Caroline is already courting?

"There's no competing with the Yokely fortune. I'm sure her dowry is immense," Gwen says, and Beth meets her eyes, trying to force her worry off her face.

"Right," she says, taking a sip of her wine to calm down.

"Don't worry. They just haven't had time to see how wonderful you are yet."

Beth blushes and takes another sip, trying to take Gwen's words to heart. She doesn't want to seem concerned about this, not with Gwen, who certainly hasn't danced with or been approached by anyone other than her cousins all week, and that was just so they could snipe at each other for sport.

"It's fine, I'm not—"

"Oh, here's one now. Damn, it's Freddie Highsmith, what a hawbuck."

Beth swallows hard as a tall, handsome young man with a strong jaw and thick brown eyebrows heads in their direction. Gwen slumps beside her, but Beth notices Mother across the room grinning. Beth thinks he's the son of an earl, if she's remembering correctly.

"Good evening, ladies," he says, his voice low and smooth. "Good to see you again, Lady Gwen."

"You too," Gwen says, dipping in a half-hearted curtsy.

Beth ignores her and gives the young man a formal curtsy of her own.

"And who is your friend?"

"This is the Honorable Elizabeth Demeroven," Gwen says, her voice much colder than it was a few minutes ago. "Miss Demeroven, this is Lord Clyson."

"Daughter of the late Viscount Demeroven, I presume? My

father was very sad to hear of his passing. A pleasure to meet you," Lord Clyson says, taking Beth's hand to give it an exaggerated kiss.

"A pleasure to meet you as well," Beth says even as Gwen sighs in her periphery.

"I wondered if I might have the honor of your first dance," Lord Clyson says, smiling at her. His face is pleasant enough to look at, and maybe only a few years older than her own.

"We were actually just—"

"I'd be delighted," Beth says, cutting Gwen off.

"Wonderful," Lord Clyson says, plucking the drink from her hand to give it to Gwen, who takes it with a frown.

That's a bit rude, of both of them, Beth thinks as she offers Gwen a weak smile. She lets Lord Clyson take her arm to lead her to the floor. They join the cluster of other couples setting up for the opening waltz.

Beth fights her anxiety as they square off, listening to the sounds of conversation around them and the last warming tones from the small orchestra settled on a large musicians' balcony. To have the money for architecture purely for music—

"How are you enjoying London?" Lord Clyson asks after they bow and curtsy.

His right hand comes to rest on her waist and his left fingers curl around her own. Beth fights the urge to fidget. It takes her a moment to get her words to work and keep her feet moving at the same time.

"It's lovely," Beth lies. She'd much rather be asleep in her bed in the country right now. But then she supposes she'd still be alone, and wouldn't have met Gwen.

Gwen, who's frowning at them as they dance.

"It is such a treat to be here each year. I get ever so bored at our country estate, you know? Though I am excited for the open season."

"You like to hunt?" Beth asks, trying to focus on what he has to say. His is a pretty enough face, but that can't be all. They'd need to connect on an intellectual level for it to be a potential match.

"I'm an excellent shot," he says.

"Pistols or bow and arrow?" She's a rather good shot with a bow herself. She used to win competitions when she was a little girl.

"Pistols, of course. Bow and arrow? Bit archaic, don't you think?"

Beth forces herself to move past it. "What else do you like to do in the country? I miss riding. The trails by our lands are marvelous."

Lord Clyson gives her what she assumes is an indulgent look. "I prefer to bet on horses rather than ride them through leisurely woodland trails, though riding is a lovely way to court."

Beth would shy away if she could. His look has turned a bit predatory, and all he's managed to do thus far is insult her interests. He could still grow on her, she supposes. She likes horse racing well enough. She's hoping she and Gwen can convince their parents to picnic together at Ascot.

"And what do you like to do, other than go for your rides?" Lord Clyson asks, and there's just something to how he says *your rides* that makes Beth think he's trying to toy with her.

"I read, and I enjoy needlepoint if I can sit outside. The weather here is rather dreary."

"It'll get better as the season progresses. I understand this is your first?"

"It is," Beth says, glancing back toward Gwen, who's practically glowering now. "It's been an adjustment."

"I see your friend is watching out for you. She's certainly got the experience," Lord Clyson says, following her gaze.

"She's lovely," Beth says firmly. She may take that kind of talk from her mother, but she won't stand for this man to slander her friend.

"Yes. She has her father's looks."

Beth frowns, not sure if he means it as a compliment. Either way, it rings hollow and callous. "She's equally charming."

"And does that kind of charm work on you?" Lord Clyson asks, his hand tightening on her waist. "I'd love to take you for a walk in the gardens later. They're small, but rather overgrown."

His grip on her waist and hand is painful now and Beth almost sags in relief when the waltz comes to an end. "No, thank you," she says as politely as she can manage. "I'd rather stay inside, and I'm thirsty, if you'll excuse me," she says, trying to pull away.

Lord Clyson resists for a second before letting go of her with a shake of his head. "Figures. Don't know why I thought one of Lady Gwen's friends would be a nice girl."

Beth holds up her chin. "Don't know why I thought a viscount might have more manners."

She turns, shocked by her own poise, and walks calmly off the floor, leaving the lout standing there alone.

She returns to Gwen and takes back her wineglass, fighting against letting any of her discomfort show. What a conceited, possessive, sniveling little man.

"Arse?"

"Arse," Beth agrees, taking a large swallow of her wine.

"I tried to warn you," Gwen says mildly.

Beth sighs and glances up at her. "You did. Thank you. I just thought—"

"I get it," Gwen says, waving her off. "We'll find you a good husband."

Beth takes another swallow, letting the wine warm away her discomfort. "Don't bother. If they're all like him, I'm not interested."

"They're not all like Clyson."

"Then why aren't you out there, dancing with them?" Beth asks, surprised by the bite in her voice. It's just that she thought the younger ones would be better, not their own horrible shades of awful.

Gwen gently takes the wine from her hand and places it on a side table before stepping closer and wrapping an arm around her waist. Beth forces herself to take a deep breath. Where Lord Clyson's grip was possessive, Gwen's touch is calming and lovely, and she lets her shoulders come down.

"Just because I think they're all arses doesn't mean you have to, and some of them *are* nice."

"'Nice' doesn't seem good enough to marry."

Gwen blows out a breath and Beth wilts. She doesn't mean to be a downer, but she thought—what did she think, she'd meet a pretty boy and suddenly she'd want to be married for the first time in her life?

"You're right. Most of them are horrible, and even marrying the nice ones is still giving up a hell of a lot."

"My mother always seemed so unhappy," Beth admits, noting

how her mother laughs across the floor, looking free and confident. Something she never seemed at home. "I'd rather be single and penniless than stuck in a marriage like that."

Gwen sighs. "Agreed. Though penniless looks different when you're really in it."

"I know," Beth says shortly.

Gwen squeezes her waist. "I don't want to be married any more than you do. Stuck with some boring man the rest of my life?"

"Would it be worse being stuck with your father your whole life?" Beth wonders.

At least Gwen has the choice to remain unwed. She'll have somewhere to live when the season's over.

"Oh, Father's hardly boring. He's fun, and funny, and I enjoy our house. You would too. I'm telling you, you should come stay sometime. You can't have my father—" Beth giggles, wrinkling her nose. Gwen grins, squeezing her hip. "But he could convince you some men are worth it."

Beth rolls her eyes, laughing as Gwen snickers. "Sure."

They stand for a moment, watching the dancing. It is pretty, even if it's the core of a ritual she wants no part in. Gwen nudges Beth and she follows her gaze, noticing Lord Havenfort standing across from them, his eyes tracking her mother as she dances with one of the elderly members of the House of Lords.

Lord Havenfort is full-on glaring at them. And when Mother spots him over the Lord's shoulder, she blushes and turns her look away.

Gwen stiffens beside her.

"What?"

". . . Nothing," Gwen says, shaking her head.

"What?" Beth insists, noting the calculating look in her eye and her rigid posture.

"It's stupid."

"Tell me, I could use a laugh," Beth presses.

Gwen sighs and looks back at her. "This is going to sound ludicrous," she cautions.

"Hit me."

"What if we got them together instead?"

Beth stares at her. "What?"

"Our parents. Clearly there's history there. Your mother is available, my father is available. He'd be very good to her, and kind, and clearly he already likes her."

Beth gapes at her new friend. Get their parents—"My mother hates him!"

"Does she?" Gwen asks. "She won't meet his eyes, but that doesn't look like hate to me," she says, jutting her chin so Beth looks across the floor to see her mother glowering at a young debutante who's making eyes at Lord Havenfort.

Beth bites at her lip. She doesn't think she could watch her mother in another bad marriage.

"He would be a wonderful husband," Gwen insists.

"Even though he's a rake?" Beth asks, wincing as Gwen raises an eyebrow. "Sorry, I didn't mean—"

"He's lonely," Gwen says. "And he can cure that loneliness in ways women can't. But he's an absolute gentleman, and I think for the right woman, he'd be an excellent husband."

Beth hesitates. It's intriguing, but—"We only have this season. Mother can't afford to present me again. I wouldn't want this to get in the way."

"If your mother married my father, we have enough money

for you to attend ten seasons," Gwen says immediately. "But if your mother married my father, you wouldn't even have to. They could have an heir."

Beth fidgets. Her mother, with child again? With an heir? She'd never have to marry if Mother had a son that could inherit. She could become the old spinster aunt she's always wanted to be.

No more balls. No more morning calls. No more leering men and grabbing hands and invitations for untoward trysts in the gardens.

"Come on. I don't want to get married. You don't want to get married. They're so clearly in love with each other, it only makes sense," Gwen says, clutching at her waist.

If it could get her out of an unhappy marriage and in return make her mother happy . . .

"Okay," Beth says, nodding as Gwen grins. "I'm in."

CHAPTER FOUR

Gwen

"Come on!" Gwen whines, standing in the foyer in her best pastel green dress, bonnet, and lace shawl. "We're going to be late!"

Father walks slowly down the stairs, messing with his cravat and looking distinctly uninterested. "I hate these things."

"I know."

"It'll be damp and warm and full of boring stuffed shirts."

"You need to fix yours," Gwen says, stepping up to him to straighten his vest beneath his frock coat. "You're wearing your good cufflinks? We'll be playing croquet, are you presentable under this?"

"Why will I be playing croquet? And yes, of course, I'm not a heathen."

Gwen frowns, looking him over. He looks decent—hair nicely coifed, shoes shined, coat pressed. Very handsome. Certainly handsome enough to turn Lady Demeroven's head.

"Shouldn't we be assessing you?" he asks, amused as she walks around him.

"Mrs. Stelm already did. What do you know of the current fashions, anyway?"

"I know that you never wear anything this bright unless she makes you."

"It's a garden party—I should look festive." That she's dressed well and plans to behave herself as a ploy to lure in Lady Demeroven doesn't matter. "I'm not a heathen either."

"No, but you're far too excited about this. You hate the Kingsmans."

"No, you hate the Kingsmans. I like Eloise," Gwen says as Mrs. Gilpe and Mrs. Stelm come down the stairs.

"You should have left already," Mrs. Gilpe says.

"Father took ages getting pretty."

"Told you she'd be done first," Mrs. Stelm says.

Mrs. Gilpe hands a quid to Mrs. Stelm. Gwen laughs.

"And how much more have you wagered on our young deb?" Father asks.

"Wagering on me? Whatever for?" Gwen says, trying to look innocent.

"As I understand it, the whole house has a bet on how many young men you can make cry playing croquet," Father says, grinning at her.

"Not how many suitors I come home with? I'm shocked," Gwen says, shaking her head as Mrs. Gilpe rolls her eyes.

"Put in two for me," Father says, handing two quid to Mrs. Stelm. "If I win, I'll order wine for everyone."

"Now, you've simply got to make a few boys cry," Mrs. Stelm tells Gwen.

Gwen snorts. "We've got to go. I'll make you all proud, one way or the other, now come on," she says, ushering Father out of the foyer.

She supposes she should be upset by their teasing. Absolutely no one expects her to come home with an interested suitor after an event like this. To be honest, she doesn't think any of them, including herself, expect her to make it out of this season with an offer, or even interest.

But now she just wants to see if she can make Albie cry. Though she's not sure Father will count that, since she regularly makes both Albie and Bobby miserable. Then again, she reminds herself as she and Father settle into the carriage for the twenty-minute drive across the park, making boys cry isn't the objective.

The objective is to get Lady Demeroven and her father to interact in a way that will force them into conversation. They're starting small. Get them to talk, that's all. And then rekindle whatever passion was there, and get both her and Beth out of this ridiculous marriage market.

But talking will be enough for today.

"You're absolutely too excited about this. What have you planned?" Father asks.

Gwen meets his gaze, giving him her most innocent smile. He narrows his eyes anyway, but her smile is practiced. That's probably what has him suspicious.

"I'm just excited to see Beth and play," Gwen says honestly. It's not the full truth, but any day she and Beth get to spend together is a good one. She's the perfect partner in crime. Sharp, witty, wily, and funny as hell—Gwen's never had so much fun with someone. And if their plan succeeds, they'll get to be together all the time. Well worth the potential loss of pin money should Father find out.

They ride in contented silence until they arrive at the Kingsman estate. They dismount from the carriage and head through the back gate to the already bustling party. They're not exactly late, but they're far from the first to arrive.

"Play nicely," Father murmurs as they're greeted by the Kingsmans, bows and curtsies exchanged and pleasantries extended until Gwen is ushered off to gather with the other "kids."

Gwen gives Father a toothy grin and hurries across the expansive back garden toward the gaggle of tulle and shawls by the small pond.

The Kingsmans may be sinfully dull people, but their gardener is a genius. The lush trellises of flowers and flowering shrubbery that encase the back garden are splendid. The blossoming spots of purples, yellows, oranges, and pinks among the green leaves brighten the slightly gloomy afternoon. Tables and chairs have been set up by the back patio, prepared for a formal tea to be served once everyone is in attendance. Benches line the sculpted walking path that wends its way through the yard. Each spot is intricately crafted to be the perfect place for polite conversation and staid courting.

An elaborate croquet course has been laid out for their amusement in the open space on the lawn. Because there's nothing the ton enjoys more than an excuse to get close passed off as a little competition. And there's no shortage of partners today. Every available chair, bench, and picnic spot is filled with the young and most eligible of the society set. They're all wildly overdressed for the humid afternoon, but eager to partake in this dainty mating ritual with finger sandwiches.

Gwen searches the milling crowd, smiling and nodding without engaging. There's only one person she wants to find, and she grins when she spots her chatting with Albie. Beth's wearing a lovely yellow gown that makes her hair shine and contrasts her rosy cheeks and dark eyes. Gwen can see Albie's at least a little bit entranced, even if their height difference is hilarious.

It's a shame Albie's father needs him to marry for money, not just status. She's sure Beth has a dowry to offer, but nothing large enough to help pull the Masons out of their increasing debt. Albie and Bobby never talk about it, but she knows the viscount's gambling weighs heavily on the whole family.

If Lord Mason didn't hate Father so much, there might be more they could do. But her uncle blames Father for her mother's death after childbirth, and they barely speak, though they at least allow the children to fraternize.

"Gwen!"

Gwen shakes off darker thoughts about her father's own reputation and hurries to join her friends. She wraps Beth in a quick hug and then punches Albie on the arm. He simply rolls his eyes in return and nods toward the drink station, ever the dutiful cousin.

"I've missed you," Beth says brightly, keeping hold of Gwen's arm as they turn to look out at the party together.

"You were supposed to promenade yesterday," Gwen says.

Beth sighs. "Yes, but Mother thought another round of morning calls was more important. Fat lot of good it did. Mr. Mason's the only one who would talk to me."

"Good ol' Albie," Gwen says as he lumbers back to them, extending a glass of wine for her before taking a decent slug of his own brandy. "You've cleaned up nice," she adds, looking him up and down.

He looks rather dashing, actually. But the grimace belies his true nature. "Father's set on this being the season now that Bobby's out too," he says glumly.

Gwen raises her glass to him. "It couldn't last forever."

He chuckles and taps her glass with his own. "I suppose so."

Gwen scans the assembled girls. Not just anyone will do for Albie. "Miss March?"

"I heard Dyfort's got his eye on her," Albie says with a shrug.

"So? Dyfort's an arse. You're sweet, and she's tall."

Beth snorts quietly and Albie laughs. "Tall is all you've got?"

"Well it's true! Didn't you say height differences were awkward?" she asks, looking to Beth, who sobers at her frown and nods seriously up at Albie.

"I'd have to climb on two apple boxes just to kiss your cheek. How embarrassing."

Albie rolls his eyes but bobs his head. "I suppose."

"Lady Meredith?" Gwen suggests, looking across the yard at Meredith, bedecked in a slightly garish magenta dress that accents every one of her curves and highlights her shiny auburn hair. "Penchant for color aside, she's very sweet and whip-smart. Great at duets."

"Perhaps," Albie says, and Gwen smiles, noting his interest.

"I'm a constant disappointment to Albie," she tells Beth. "I'm good on my own, but duets have never been my forte."

"You just don't like sharing," Albie fires back. "Maybe you two could practice together. Miss Demeroven says she and her mother play duets every day."

"We do," Beth agrees. "I much prefer them to playing alone."

"I suppose I could be persuaded," Gwen says, thinking that an afternoon letting Beth teach her duets would be much more enjoyable than Albie's frustration. She thinks Beth's likely to be a more amiable partner, and far nicer to look at.

"You're on. Mother might actually approve," Beth says.

"Excellent," Gwen says, bumping her shoulder to see Beth smile.

"What about you?" Albie asks, looking down at Beth. "Anyone caught your eye? If I wasn't such a fortune chaser I'd come to call, just so you know."

Beth blushes a little and shakes her head. "None so far. Mother's going a bit spare about it, actually," she adds, glancing back toward Lady Demeroven, who's making the rounds with the mothers clustered around the tea cakes.

The fathers are all seated on the deck, deep into the brandy already and smoking cigars. It's a small assemblage; most of them escape to the club if they can manage it, rather than suffer these events.

Gwen notices her father tracking Lady Demeroven's slightly frantic movement around the group as well. Perhaps she should put her plan into action sooner rather than later, before Father gets the chance to finish his glass and go for another.

"Well, we'll just have to make a little magic then, won't we?" Gwen suggests, turning back to her friends.

"How so?" Albie asks.

"I think a bit of couples competition is in order. If you'll excuse me," Gwen says, squeezing Beth's arm before throwing back the rest of her wine.

"What are you up to?" Beth asks.

"Shenanigans," Gwen says with a significant look, grinning as Beth's smile widens. Let the games begin.

She places the glass down on one of the tables and then walks to the center of the lawn, taking a deep breath. Time to turn on what little charm she has.

She goes for the youth first. "Gather around!" she calls, waving the friendly faces over to her, trusting everyone else to follow.

She may be no one's first choice, but she's known for her hijinks. She's made it a point to be the group director of morale since her second season. If she has to suffer it, she'll suffer it with fun.

"What will it be this year?" Eloise asks, dragging over Annabeth and Lord Prous along with her. Her voice carries an admonishment but the delight on her face says otherwise.

"I propose a tournament," Gwen says as the rest of the collected group gathers around her. "Of teams."

Intrigued looks all around. Gwen grins, meeting Beth's eyes with a conspiratorial wink as she sidles up along the edge of the group with Albie.

"First we'll pair off, ladies and gentlemen. The highest scoring three couples win. And then—" Gwen swings around theatrically to face the assembled parents, who are all watching their cluster.

Equal parts amusement, resignation, and disdain litter their faces but Gwen doesn't let it faze her. Father will back her up, at the least. She's counting on it.

"The mothers of the winning debs and fathers of the winning gentlemen shall have to team up in a fight for supremacy," Gwen announces. She hears the children laugh while the mothers and fathers exchange looks. "Such a nice way for potential future in-laws to become better acquainted, isn't it?" Gwen continues, all sweetness and light.

Father narrows his eyes at her, but she doesn't think he's caught on to her just yet. She waits, arms outstretched for the parental approval, and with a great sigh, Lord Kingsman nods and waves his hand for them to go ahead.

Gwen claps and spins back to the reason for this whole charade: matchmaking. That her real targets are of decidedly older age need not be mentioned.

"All right: Lady Eloise and Prous, Miss Blighe and Mort, Lady Annabeth and Johnson, Lady Meredith and Mason," she says, giving Albie a quick glance. His pressed-lip smile speaks volumes.

"Thorton, you're with me." She nods to the tall, strapping cricket player with whom she's shared a few lackluster outings. No worries of untoward feelings there, but she's sure he'll help her win. Competitive to a fault.

"Miss Susan with Haroldson, Miss March with Dyfort, and Miss Demeroven with Jacobson," Gwen completes, nodding Beth toward the Honorable John Jacobson.

He's a reedy, bashful boy, but she knows he's vicious on the pitch, and he's almost as competitive as Lord Thorton. He's also already promised to Miss Rose Anderson, but she's not sure he's gotten up the courage to tell his parents. Hopefully Lady Demeroven won't catch wind until later, or at least won't think ill of her for it. Most importantly, his father isn't in attendance today.

"All right, grab your mallets, line up, and let's play. We'll do expanded association, three teams per round!" Gwen exclaims, beaming as the kids scramble for the best equipment.

Lord Thorton ambles up to her, already having grabbed the best set. "What are you playing at, Lady Gwen?"

"These parties are sinfully dull. I thought watching our parents bumble around might be fun," Gwen says casually.

"Sure," Thorton says, and that's the last time they speak to each other.

Instead, they focus on decimating the competition. With

Thorton's edge and her years of playing billiards with Father, they're easily the best team on the field. Meredith and Albie give them a run for their money—they work perfectly together, as she thought—and Beth and Jacobson aren't far behind. They don't seem like they're having quite as much fun together, but they're equally focused and Beth has a surprisingly steady swing.

It works exactly as she thought it would. Eloise and Lord Prous spend the whole time too flustered by their proximity to pay any real attention to the game. Dyfort is an arse and barely lets Stephanie try. What a lout. Susie and Lord Haroldson are middling at best. And as she planned, Annabeth and Lord Johnson and Samantha and Lord Mort all do terribly, because they should have partners swapped. She feels a bit like an evil genius as the match comes to its end.

She raises Lord Thorton's hand, grinning at Beth as the rest of the debutantes wander away, commiserating on their losses. They head for the alcohol to settle in and watch what can only be an interesting match among the remaining parents.

Gwen leads the three winning teams up to the edge of the patio. The parents clap politely for them and they all bow and curtsy. Gwen pushes through the feeling of childishness that briefly descends on her. Like she's seven again and has just performed a dance for her father's dinner party, a little doll on show.

"Your champions," Gwen tells them, laughing as Father rolls his eyes and the mothers giggle. "That means Lady Harrington and Mr. Mason will be playing for Lady Meredith and Mr. Mason," Gwen explains, nodding to the prim lady and Albie's uncle.

Mr. Mason holds out his arm and escorts the reluctant, but clearly pleased, Lady Harrington from the patio and out onto the field. Albie and Meredith pass them mallets, and Gwen notes Albie's uncle patting him on the shoulder. It was nice of him to come for Albie today, given Viscount Mason would rather drop dead than attend a society tea. Nice, and convenient.

"Then Lord Lawson for Lord Thorton, and Lady Kingsman, would you mind very much stepping in for me?" Gwen asks, making her eyes wide and pleading.

Lady Kingsman glances at her husband, who waves his hand, shaking his head at Gwen's antics. Lady Kingsman nods and allows Lord Lawson to lead her out to Gwen and Thorton.

"I'll make you proud," Lady Kingsman promises.

Gwen grins and hands off her mallet. Though Lord Kingsman is a blowhard and a dolt, she has always liked his wife.

"That just leaves Lady Demeroven for Miss Demeroven, and Father, would you stand in for Mr. Jacobson?" Gwen asks brightly, giving the whole patio a broad smile.

Lady Demeroven goes stock still, and her father—oh, she hasn't seen a look like that on Father's face since the last time she broke a vase when she was ten. But there's no way they can refuse. Lady Kingsman, the host, just agreed to step in for her. They can hardly say no now, not without being terribly, terribly rude.

Still, even as Father rises stiffly and escorts a clearly uncomfortable Lady Demeroven from the patio and over to Beth and Jacobson, Gwen swallows thickly. She was sure when she started that this would go well. But the look on both of their faces as they take their mallets—the way he's holding her arm—

"Go on, go on," Mr. Mason says, clearly not noticing the discomfort that's fallen over two of the players. "Want a wager, Havenfort?"

Father seems to come out of his stupor and narrows his eyes at his younger brother-in-law. "Bragging rights aren't enough for you?"

"I was thinking perhaps the first shot in the season in August."

"At my manor of course," Father says.

"Indubitably."

Gwen winces as she and the other winning children back toward the refreshment table to watch. Beth leaves Jacobson to come to her side, slipping her arm anxiously through Gwen's.

"You sure this is a good idea?" she whispers.

"You're on," Father says. "Come, Lady Demeroven, let's give these people a show, shall we?"

"Oh dear," Gwen mumbles.

Father's got his competitive face on, and that's not a face that comes with manners, charm, or goodwill. Worse, it doesn't look like Lady Demeroven knows the first thing about croquet.

Gwen and Beth watch anxiously as Lady Kingsman and Lord Lawson take their first shots. Excellent, each of them. If Beth's mother has any skill at all, this might be a sporting game.

"Why didn't you tell me this was your plan? Mother has no coordination whatsoever," Beth whispers and Gwen sucks on her cheek, fighting the urge to chew on her nails.

Mr. Mason and Lady Harrington go next, and they're also wonderful, encouraging each other politely and grinning over at Albie and Meredith. Each pair must get both balls through the same wicket in order to progress, and her father and Lady Demeroven haven't exchanged a single word yet.

"Your turn, my liege," Mr. Mason says loftily.

"I'll make you eat your words," Father says gamely. "Come, Lady Demeroven, ladies first."

Beth tightens her grip on Gwen's arm as Lady Demeroven squares off her shot, bending awkwardly. Gwen can tell five seconds before she swings that she won't even hit the ball.

Lady Demeroven teeters before finding her balance to a smattering of polite laughter. She hesitates for a moment, her cheeks pink, and then rallies, turning to Beth and Gwen to give an exaggerated shrug. Beth laughs and Gwen gives her a supportive smile, but Father isn't having it.

"Come now, Lady Demeroven, you've more skill than that," he admonishes, stepping too close to force her to move aside.

She does, with as much grace as she can muster, but still trips and stumbles, further embarrassed. Father doesn't notice, too busy whacking his ball with too much force. His swing sends the ball on an angle, making it through the first but missing the second wicket.

"Blast," he exclaims.

Lady Demeroven scowls. Father shakes his head and grabs her arm, moving her none-too-gently aside as Lady Kingsman and Lord Lawson return for their next round.

"Ridiculous. You're able to play pianoforte and paint but can't hit a simple ball?" Gwen hears him mutter.

She grimaces. Beth turns to bury her forehead in Gwen's shoulder at her mother's snipped "Not like you did much better. I thought marksmen were meant to have good aim."

"What have we done?" Beth whispers as their parents continue to bicker, getting louder and louder while the other two couples play through, barely pretending to ignore them.

Gwen thought propriety would keep her father's competitive obnoxiousness to a minimum—that there was enough latent affection for Lady Demeroven that he'd be, God forbid, the charming man she's seen him be with other women. Instead, it seems she's unleashed an ugly monster.

By the time Father and Lady Demeroven step up for their second round, Father's glowering like he's just lost stock and Lady Demeroven is an unfortunate shade of puce.

"Go ahead, then," Father says gruffly, gesturing mockingly for Lady Demeroven to take her shot.

She glares at him and squares up. Father stays too close, egging her on from behind. When she swings her mallet back, it meets with more than empty air.

Father staggers backward, clutching himself between the legs and groaning. Lady Demeroven spins around, mouth agape, and accidentally whacks him in the knee, sending him sprawling.

Gasps and shouts fill the air as Father curls up there on the grass, staring up at Lady Demeroven through squinted eyes.

"My apologies, Lord Havenfort," Lady Demeroven says, dropping her mallet and falling to her knees, hands fluttering, skirt and hoop covering half of Father's body as he continues to wince. She does look genuinely sorry.

"No, no, stand back. Can't . . . trust your . . . coordination at all . . . no," Father manages, batting away her skirts and struggling to stand.

Without offering his hand to Lady Demeroven or a look to anyone around them, he stumbles off toward the house, leaving Lady Demeroven there on the ground, the party staring aghast. Gwen looks around and finds most of the girls now standing with their mothers, openly whispering.

Beth, horrified, hurries forward to help her mother up with as much pride as they can manage. Lady Demeroven takes her hand and together they get her to standing. The usually poised woman brushes herself off and offers a thin, guilty smile to the guests.

"My apologies for the excitement. I think Miss Demeroven and I should retire—I'm feeling a bit unwell myself. Lady Gwen, you'll make sure your father is all right?"

"Of course," Gwen says, meeting Beth's eyes, both of them shocked by just how astoundingly poorly that went. "Farewell, Lady Demeroven," she adds, curtsying.

That seems to jolt everyone out of their shock. Lady Kingsman steps forward to see the Demerovens out, while the party resumes otherwise. Gwen imagines this will be the talk of many a future garden party. Whether she or Beth will be invited remains to be seen.

She supposes she can kiss her afternoon of duets with Beth goodbye too.

"That went very well," Albie says, coming up to her side with Meredith in tow.

Gwen clenches her jaw and whacks his arm before stalking off, intent on finding her father and making their own hasty retreat.

Chapter Five

Beth

The sun beats down on the park and Beth feels a trickle of sweat making its way along the back of her neck. She's glad they'll at least have the evening to themselves tonight. She doesn't think her hair will have survived being under her bonnet all afternoon.

Mother wipes daintily at her face with a lace handkerchief and sighs. Beth glances up at her and then looks back out at the park, barely listening as Mother returns to her endless list of eligible young men and the family fortunes that come with them.

They didn't speak for the rest of the day after the croquet fiasco. And the next morning her mother came down to breakfast with an intensity toward Beth's courting that was frankly frightening.

Gone are their easy morning chats over the daily papers. Gone are the chess matches and even the duets.

Breakfast teas, midmorning teas, luncheons, morning calls, picnics, and dinners have filled every available speck of time so far this week. And all of them conspicuously missing Gwen's presence.

As if at the mere thought of her name, Beth spots Gwen across the green, stuck in a conversation with a few mothers. A chaperone, who must be her housekeeper, stands a few paces off to the side. Beth wants to walk across the park and steal Gwen away. Talk about anything other than teas and balls and courting. Ask her to finish her story about the time she and her father got stranded while boating on their lake until her housekeeper had to come get them. She got interrupted at the Gentry tea just at the part where her father had fallen into the lake, and Beth wants to know what happened. Wants to hear Gwen tell her, all the delight and mischievousness in her voice. Beth's pretty sure Gwen pushed him in, but won't know until she gets to talk to Gwen again.

But Mother won't see any time spent just with Gwen as valuable. Nothing Beth does can have just one purpose anymore. It all has to be for the cause, and Beth sighs, coming back to her mother's long tirade about—dear Lord, lace hems? Gwen catches her eye, looking woefully over at them, unable to get away and just as miserable, listening to what must be an equally boring conversation.

They can't let their plan peter out like this.

"Could we rest, Mother?" Beth asks softly, interrupting her explanation of the various intricacies of the Halyard fortune.

Mother looks down at her and takes in the flush that must be on her cheeks and her sweating forehead. The hoop beneath her petticoats and pale purple skirts lets in some air, but even that relief isn't enough today. The sun directly on her shoulders is starting to smart. She likely looks just as miserable as she feels. Surely a rest to recover her poise can be allowed.

"Here, darling, let's watch the boats," Mother agrees, guiding Beth over to the side of the lake, where they can stare out at the numerous couples out for a pleasant boat ride.

They all look about as hot and uncomfortable as she feels, but at least they're all wanted. She watches a blond girl throw her head back, laughing. The boy across from her looks delighted. And here Beth is, standing on the shore with her mother, invisible and happy that way. The boy's gaze looks pleasant, but she'd rather just be home reading inside away from the heat.

"What's the matter?" Mother asks, her voice soft.

Beth looks up and finds her mother's face cleared of its frenzied mission for the first time all week. Beth shrugs, looking back at the boats, not wanting to disappoint her, but desperate to be honest. Desperate for how it was at their manor up in the country, just the two of them and Miss Wilson, wreaking havoc and living in peace.

"I feel like livestock being measured up for sale," Beth admits, glancing behind them, noting the gentlemen who pass, giving them appraising looks.

Mother snorts quietly and Beth meets her gaze, surprised by the amusement and understanding on her face. "It is a lot, isn't it?" she agrees. Beth fights against gaping. "I don't remember doing quite this much with my mother. It seemed . . . easier when I was your age."

Beth considers her, thinks about the precision with which she's attacked this whole affair. The work and effort her mother is putting in, the nights spent calculating expenses and planning daily itineraries. There's makeup hiding her exhaustion too, and the effort to be cheerful and charming is wearing on her just as much as it is on Beth.

"I doubt that," Beth decides.

Mother laughs and pulls her closer, her arm squeezing Beth's. And though it's hot, she doesn't quite mind the proximity.

"It's dreadful," Mother admits, shrugging as Beth stares at her. "I only did one season and I can't tell you the relief when I finally married your father. I've had twenty-two years without this," she says almost fondly.

But she had twenty of those with Beth's father.

"Did you—" Beth starts, before biting her lip and looking out at the boats.

"What?" Mother asks gently.

Beth hesitates. She doesn't want to ask, but she wants to know. Has always wanted to know. "Did you marry Father just to escape this?"

She can't look at her mother. Can't stand to see the hurt she's caused with her curiosity, but she needs to know. Her horrible, dismissive, cruel father. Was twenty years beneath his thumb worth it just to escape the uncertainty of the season?

Her mother's hand curls over her elbow, gentle pressure. Beth sneaks a glance up at her and finds Mother watching her not with anger, but with understanding.

"I want to tell you it was love that forced my hand, but I can't," she admits, ghost regret on her face, but no pain. "I made a choice for security—so my parents wouldn't worry about me—so I could provide for the children I desperately wanted," she continues, reaching out with her free hand to brush a wayward hair from Beth's forehead.

"But he was so—"

Mother nods. "But I got you," she insists. "And this is not what I wanted for you. I want you to know that," she adds seriously.

Beth nods quickly. She won't complain about why they're here today, just that here is . . . unpleasant.

"And I'm sorry this is how it is for you too," Mother continues.

Beth breaks her gaze, turning back to the boats before sadness overtakes them too much. "Was any of it fun, at all?" she asks, going for wry and falling a bit flat.

But Mother rallies. "Some of it," she says, nudging Beth as she narrows her eyes skeptically.

"Like what?"

"The boats. I had . . . a gentleman friend before I met your father, and he was a wondrous dancer," Mother tells her.

"But only a friend?" Beth wonders.

She's often thought that there was no way her mother didn't have other suitors in her season. With her beauty, wit, and charm, she must have been the belle of every ball she entered. Beth is a pale imitation of how lively her mother was when she was younger. In truth, she's still a pale imitation of her now.

"He wasn't in line to inherit and didn't have the security of a title that Father wanted for my future," Mother says, staring off at the boats herself. "But we had fun for a while."

Beth watches the happy couple in the nearest boat, the girl bright and flushed, the boy beaming and bashful. She can't remember her mother ever looking at her father that way. Can't remember her father ever looking anything other than indifferent.

Did Mother blush like that when her first beau looked her way? Was she ever so happy and carefree? Was she ever in love, even once?

"My hope for you is that you meet someone who makes you laugh, and makes the endless formalities feel a little fun and silly," Mother says, turning her gaze back to Beth. "You've every chance of it this season, and I know it's onerous, but if you open yourself up to it, I'm sure you'll find a wonderful man."

Beth forces herself to nod, to appear as if she believes Mother's words. But if her mother, with all her various assets, couldn't fall in love with the right man, what chance does Beth have? The only company she's enjoyed so far is Gwen's.

"Shall we walk back toward home?" Mother asks, her false smile firmly back in place, all memory and melancholy locked away.

"Yes," Beth agrees, allowing her to lead them from the bank and back onto the walking path. "And you promise, no events tonight?"

"None," Mother assures her. "I thought we might play some duets after dinner?"

Beth smiles and leans into her. "I'd like that."

They walk on for a few minutes, and Beth manages to ignore the appraising looks from the men and mothers around them, bolstered by her mother's return, however brief, to normality. She's missed her, wild as it seems, when they've done nothing but spend time together for the past week. But she hasn't been *Mother.*

There's more than enough pretending outside of their house. They shouldn't have to keep pretenses up when it's just the two of them.

Beth's about to push her luck and ask if maybe they could play chess after duets when something thumps hard into her back. She stumbles, letting out a surprised yelp. Mother clutches at her to keep her from falling. They turn together to spot a rugby ball on the ground and a young man hurtling toward them, already shouting apologies.

Beth tries to reach around to rub at her back. Whoever threw that thing has quite the arm.

"I'm so sorry. I'm so, so sorry," the young man exclaims as he sprints up to them, coming to a halt just before he topples into them and sends them sprawling all over again.

"It's all right," Beth says automatically. She'd rather not have been hit with a wayward projectile, but he looks terribly upset.

It's only when he stands up tall and gives a little bow that she has a moment to truly take him in. Statuesque with a chiseled jawline and well-coifed but slightly askew chestnut brown hair—he's very pretty, for a boy.

"My sincerest apologies. I'm a terrible shot," the man says, looking at her askance. "And I, well, Viscount Montson, I am horrified to have caused you pain and ask your forgiveness, and your attendance to at least one dinner at my home, and a tea, and do you like pastries?"

"It's a pleasure to make your acquaintance, Lord Montson," Mother steps in, saving the poor boy. Beth's just dizzied by how many social engagements she's now required to attend for getting hit in the back. "Your father is the Earl of Ashmond?"

"Yes," Lord Montson says. "And he'll be thoroughly upset to hear what I've done. I believe you are Lady Demeroven?"

"Yes," Mother says, giving him a winning smile. "And my daughter, Miss Demeroven, is just fine, aren't you, dearest?"

"I am," Beth says honestly, though she doesn't at all like the gleam in Mother's eye. "You needn't go to any trouble over it. It really wasn't that painful."

"I am glad in this moment to be such a terrible shot with a poor throw," Lord Montson says with a grin.

Beth feels herself flush. "I'm sure you've a very powerful throw," she says quickly, wincing as Mother fakes a cough to cover a laugh.

"Well, I've certainly a powerful interest in your first dance tomorrow night at the Smith Ball," he says, and even Beth is impressed by how smooth that was.

"She'll be delighted to dance with you, won't you, darling?" Mother asks.

Beth winces. How embarrassing. "Yes, I would," she says, meeting Lord Montson's eyes. "Thank you, I look forward to it."

"As do I," Lord Montson says, holding out his hand to Beth.

She takes it after a moment of surprise, and then sucks in a breath as he raises her gloved hand to kiss the back of it. He has to bend quite a lot to manage. He's very tall.

"Until tomorrow night then, Miss Demeroven. And I give you much leave to step on all of my toes in retribution."

"She's quite an accomplished dancer," Mother says quickly.

"I'll do my best to cause us no further mutual pain," Beth says, smiling at him as he stands up. He still looks so concerned.

"Montson!" calls one of the other gents from his group.

Lord Montson looks over at them and nods before turning back to Beth and her mother, giving them a sweeping bow. "Farewell," he says, and then stoops to pick up his ball and jogs off.

They stand there watching him go. What just happened?

"We need to go home immediately, get your dress, and get to the modiste," Mother says after a stunned beat.

"What?" Beth exclaims, jerking into motion as Mother takes her arm again and practically drags her from the park. "But I thought we were playing duets and—"

"We've a future earl and his family to impress, and you've far too little lace on tomorrow night's gown," Mother says, ignoring Beth entirely. "We'll need to cancel that order of beef.

Miss Wilson can make something else for the weekend roast. Squash, perhaps? And we'll need to visit the cobbler for new shoes—yours are so drab," Mother mutters, rattling on and on as they hurry down the path.

Beth feels her shoulders come up as they stride out of the park, and it's not just due to the dull ache from being smacked in the back by Lord Montson's effusive throw.

CHAPTER SIX

Gwen

"Hold still, Gwennie, honestly," Mrs. Stelm mutters as Gwen stares at her reflection, bouncing her leg.

"I'm bored," Gwen admits.

Mrs. Gilpe snorts behind her, finishing off Gwen's ridiculous braided updo for tonight's ball. Mrs. Stelm pats a last bit of blush on Gwen's cheek and smiles encouragingly.

"You'll have fun tonight," Mrs. Stelm says.

Mrs. Gilpe nudges Gwen to stand and step into the hoop cage.

"What if Beth's not there?" Gwen asks, aware she's whining and unable to help it.

"Then you'll—God forbid—have to dance with a young gentleman. Or talk to the other girls," Mrs. Gilpe says, tying off Gwen's hoop.

"Mr. Mason will dance with you," Mrs. Stelm says. She motions for Gwen to lift her arms so they can guide her petticoat over her head.

"Albie's danced with Meredith all this week. I don't see that changing," Gwen mumbles.

"The other Mr. Mason then," Mrs. Gilpe says, rolling her eyes. She turns away to prepare Gwen's skirt.

"Hardly," Gwen says. Bobby steps on her toes.

"Then make another friend," Mrs. Gilpe says sternly.

"A boy friend," Mrs. Stelm adds with a wink.

Gwen watches herself wrinkle her nose before they lower her skirt over her head. "Please."

"Just like your father," Mrs. Gilpe mutters as the world briefly disappears in a flash of deep green fabric.

"What does that mean?" Gwen asks, looking between them once her skirt is settled.

"Oh, your father was a right pill his first season," Mrs. Stelm says, ignoring Mrs. Gilpe's look. "You started it."

Gwen pounces. "Father wasn't charming?"

"Oh, he was. Had all sorts of interest, but he was picky, like you," Mrs. Gilpe admits.

"Discerning," Gwen says, turning her nose up to make Mrs. Stelm laugh.

"He was all about the drink and dancing and playing rugby. Drove his father up the twist. Wouldn't make calls, wouldn't do anything he didn't think was fun."

Gwen can't fight her smile. Sounds like Father, and sounds like much more fun than being trussed up on show. "So he didn't court at all?"

"Well," Mrs. Stelm says, glancing at Mrs. Gilpe as she does up the buttons of Gwen's bodice.

"Please, I am *so* bored. I'll take twenty-year-old gossip," Gwen needles.

Mrs. Gilpe shrugs. "He didn't court, but he had a lady friend."

"A lady of the night kind of friend?" Gwen asks, squinching her face at the thought.

"Not then," Mrs. Stelm says, laughing as Mrs. Gilpe swats at her.

"Just a friend. They ran around like little hellions, not unlike you and your friend Beth, it seems," Mrs. Gilpe says.

That makes Gwen smile. "But they didn't court?"

Mrs. Stelm walks around Gwen, fussing with her skirt. "Not exactly, no."

"He didn't . . . they didn't get in trouble, did they?" Gwen asks as the thought passes through.

"No," Mrs. Gilpe and Mrs. Stelm say immediately.

"No, she broke his heart," Mrs. Gilpe admits.

Gwen stares at her. Father, heartbroken? "But you said they didn't court."

"No, they didn't," Mrs. Stelm agrees. "Doesn't mean he didn't want to."

"But why not?"

"Your father wasn't the heir to this title," Mrs. Gilpe says with another shrug. She reaches out and settles the vee of Gwen's bodice across her shoulders.

"Who was she?" Gwen asks, trying to keep her tone casual despite the pickup of her pulse.

"Oh, who can remember all the names," Mrs. Stelm says blithely.

"You know. Of course you know," Gwen insists. "Was it—"

"We're going to be late," Father says, pushing into Gwen's room without so much as a knock.

All three of them look over at him, caught out. Gwen frowns. He's well dressed, but there's still exhaustion on his face. He's been out drinking every night this week, and God knows what else.

"Ready?" he prompts.

Gwen nods, glancing back at Mrs. Stelm and Mrs. Gilpe even as she lets Father lead her away. One minute longer and she'd have known. If Lady Demeroven broke his heart, no wonder they can barely speak to each other.

It would explain how a woman so beautiful and accomplished ended up married to such a lout. Gwen can't imagine exchanging her father for Beth's. She should hate Lady Demeroven for hurting her father, but even with a broken heart, Father surely got the better end of their exchange.

"You look lovely," Father tells her, and Gwen forces herself to smile as he hands her into the carriage.

"Thanks. You look nice too," she says. He settles on the opposite bench and they head off toward the Smith house. "Did you have fun last night?"

Father meets her eyes with a sardonic smile. "I did."

"Too much fun."

He laughs. "I'll be well-behaved tonight. A man needs his freedoms."

"Be nice if a lady could have the same," Gwen grumbles.

"You will never, ever, have those freedoms," Father says quickly.

Gwen blinks. "I—"

"I meant," he starts, taking in what must be the outrage blooming on her face. "You are an honorable, civilized young woman. I would not want you to know the worlds I have passed through, and certainly would never want you to look for solace in them."

Gwen stares at him, insulted and touched at the same time. "I can take care of myself."

"I pray that you never have to," he says firmly. "Which is why we're here, isn't it?" he adds, trying on a smile. "To find you a fabulous husband."

Gwen laughs despite herself. "Couldn't we find you one instead?"

Father snorts and Gwen relaxes, letting her discomfort go.

"You don't think it would further tarnish my reputation?"

"If he was a nice husband, why should I care?" Gwen returns. "Lord Bletchle is quite handsome."

"Oh, yes, he's a beautiful man, but far too much of a snob for my liking," Father says lightly. "And I'd like someone more strapping."

Gwen can't fight her giggle, imagining her tall broad-shouldered father as the little man, held in the arms of a goliath. "We'll find you a kind giant, then."

Father smiles and then looks out the window, their strange tension finally passed. It's not that he's been unkind to her since the croquet match, but it hasn't been . . . this. It wasn't her fault that Lady Demeroven can't swing a croquet mallet to save her life, but it was also entirely her fault. Orchestrated by her own hand.

She hasn't come up with a good second plan to force Father and Lady Demeroven together without them coming to fisticuffs. But she hopes she and Beth can steal away tonight. It's been a long, unpleasant week without her friend, and she's desperate to get some good time in with her tonight.

As soon as they're in the respectably sized Smith ballroom, Gwen cranes her neck, looking for Beth. It's really annoying how she disappears into a crowd, so petite.

"They're over there," Father says, nudging Gwen so she turns to spot Lady Demeroven and Beth waiting just to the side of the foyer, near the curved entrance staircase. She missed them on the way in.

"Will you come say hello?" Gwen asks.

Father shakes his head. "No, no, you go. I've business to attend to this evening. The Matrimonial Causes Act has to pass, and I've palms to grease."

Gwen just nods, letting him step away. He looks practically gleeful, heading for whatever statesman he thinks he can fell to his will.

But Gwen's not interested in the rights of divorce tonight. Tonight, she's going to sweep Beth away and they'll plot their next attack, and hopefully get gloriously drunk in the meantime. It's been such a long week.

Gwen scurries over to Beth and Lady Demeroven. Beth spots her and taps her mother's arm where their elbows are linked. Both women look beautiful. Beth's in a gorgeous blue gown, her dark hair piled atop her head with stylized curls falling to frame her face. There's lace all over her dress and she's wearing higher heels, her forehead almost at Gwen's cheek for the first time.

Lady Demeroven looks equally stunning in a darker navy gown, a black sash still around her waist and accented in her gloves. But she hardly looks the brooding widow. In fact, she looks a bit . . . crazed, watching every entrance to the hall in turn. Gwen's rather afraid her neck might snap.

"Hello," Beth says as Gwen finally muscles her way up to them.

"You look beautiful," Gwen tells her, laughing as Beth flushes. "As do you, Lady Demeroven."

"Thank you, dear," Lady Demeroven says. "You look lovely as well. Green becomes you far more than those pastels. Such gorgeous hair."

Gwen blinks, surprised. "Thank you, my lady."

Lady Demeroven gives her a quick smile and then continues craning her neck. Gwen takes that as a dismissal and steps to Beth's side, leaning in so they can talk more quietly as the party bustles around them.

"Who is she looking for?"

"Lord Montson," Beth says, edging away from Lady Demeroven as much as she can with their arms still linked.

"Whatever for?"

Beth frowns, looking up at her. "You don't like him?"

Gwen hesitates. There's nothing wrong with Lord Montson. Not much great about him either. He's entirely . . . neutral as a person. "He's fine," she hedges.

Beth seems to relax. "Good. He's asked for my first dance after hitting me in the back with a rugby ball."

"He hit you?" Gwen asks, grabbing Beth's hand.

"With a rugby ball," Beth repeats, loud enough that this time Gwen catches the whole thing. "Terrible shot, apparently."

Gwen snorts. "And your mother's letting you dance with him?"

"He asked, and invited us for dinner. Mother thinks it's a chance at a match," Beth explains, shifting to rearrange her hoop so they're closer together.

"I see," Gwen says, looking out at the overpacked room. "That's . . . good."

"Yes," Beth agrees, though Gwen hears little enthusiasm there. "So we're waiting for him to arrive. I think Mother's worried if I wander off they won't ever find me."

"You are tiny," Gwen agrees, laughing as Beth drops her hand to whack at her arm. "Adorably so." Beth purses her lips, but Gwen can tell she's trying not to smile. "Montson's tall."

"I know," Beth says, her smile falling. "I might actually have to dance on his shoes."

Gwen laughs and takes back Beth's hand.

"Do you think she'd release you just long enough to get some wine?" Gwen asks, watching as the hall continues to fill, more than enough people to get lost in.

Beth shrugs and leans back into her mother. Gwen can barely hear their conversation but meets Lady Demeroven's gaze as she looks Gwen over.

". . . right back as soon as Lord Montson arrives."

"Yes, Mother," Beth says, nodding seriously before turning and hustling Gwen away, dragging her across the room for a change. "Never thought she'd let go," Beth admits as they snake their way along the wall, edging around clusters of parents and debutantes alike.

Gwen watches Beth move confidently through the crowds. It's like something new has come over her, a confidence she didn't have before. Gwen hopes it's not just because Montson asked her to dance.

"Was it awful?"

Gwen startles. They've made it to the refreshments already. Beth passes a glass of wine into her hand; it's her favorite, from the back of the table. She didn't even have to ask.

"What?" Gwen asks inelegantly.

She swigs back a large sip.

Beth is here to get a husband. That's the point. It shouldn't be anything but good that she's found a dancing partner. Though it does mean now Gwen will have to relinquish her, for most of the night if Lady Demeroven has her way.

"Was your father badly hurt?"

"Oh," Gwen says, laughing a little. "He's recovered. Your mother?"

"Only wounded pride on her end," Beth says, taking Gwen's elbow to lead them to the opposite side of the hall. They can clearly see Lady Demeroven still standing by the steps, now roped into conversation with Lord and Lady Barthelmis. Poor woman, they're sinfully dull.

"Was he very angry?" Beth asks, and Gwen's thoughts slow as she catches the concern on Beth's face.

"No," Gwen says quickly, watching as Beth's shoulders relax. "No, he wasn't pleased, and he was pissy, but not mad at me, not really."

"Good," Beth says. "I had wanted to call, but Mother wouldn't hear of it, and then you weren't at any of our teas or garden parties."

"I spent most of the week trailing after Albie," Gwen admits. "Father wasn't angry, but I think he was a bit put off the social events. Meredith's fun to talk to, at least."

"She is," Beth agrees. "And Mr. Mason?"

"Absolutely smitten," Gwen says, smiling at the thought. "Bumblingly so, actually. It's very funny."

"That's sweet," Beth says, nudging Gwen as she laughs. "He deserves it."

"He does," Gwen agrees. "And you? Exhausted by all the merriment?"

Beth nods seriously. "It's been like she's possessed," Beth says, glancing over at Lady Demeroven, who looks ever so bored. "But I did find out that she had a suitor, I think, in her first season."

Gwen hesitates. "Oh?"

"A friend, she called him. But the way she looked when speaking about him—I think she fancied him. But her father forbade her from marrying him. I don't know if he ever proposed."

Gwen sighs as the whole terrible portrait settles into place. She can't hate the woman then, can she? She could hate Beth's grandfather, she supposes, for forbidding the match.

"She seemed rather sad about it, actually," Beth says.

"I think it was my father," Gwen says quickly, pushing it out in a rush.

"What?"

"My father had a friend his first season too. Mrs. Gilpe thinks she broke his heart, but he said it wasn't of any importance, just a friend."

"My mother broke his heart?" Beth asks, eyes wide and dismayed.

"It's not her fault. You said your grandfather said no."

Beth nods slowly. "He wanted her to marry a fortune and title. My father—" She breaks off abruptly, tracking Lady Demeroven across the room.

"He gave her a title and a fortune," Gwen completes, noticing her father eyeing Lady Demeroven as well from the other end of the wall. "So they couldn't be together."

"He used to mention Mother's other suitor," Beth says softly.

"Who?"

"My father. He'd tease her when she was writing letters,

would ask if she was writing to her other suitor. Mother always played it off, but I think it made her sad."

Gwen bites back the comment that wants to tear up her throat. How utterly callous. But Beth is upset enough. And here Gwen's been thinking of this entirely for herself—that Father marrying would give her grace to forget the marriage market, at least for a while. Give her and Beth a chance to have some fun this season.

But now—now they must get them back together.

Because if their seasons were anything like Gwen's have been, they deserve some resolution after all these years. She wants Father to be happy—to have someone. God forbid she does get married someday, what would he do all alone, rattling around their manor? He may enjoy politics, but even that can't sustain a man forever. He deserves a chance at love too.

"We have to fix this," Beth says firmly.

"Agreed." Gwen loops her free arm through Beth's. "We'll just need to think of activities that require no coordination."

Beth laughs and leans into her. "If you'd told me your plan, I could have told you Mother's hopeless."

"Yes, well, my being the only conspirator works in our favor. She won't suspect you. Me, I'm going to have to be very cunning to get anything past Father now."

"Hmm. We discussed Ascot," Beth says slowly.

"That's ages away though," Gwen says, watching as Father moves about the room, conducting business but always oriented toward Lady Demeroven somehow. She's never seen him like this before. It's sweet, really.

"Riding?" Beth suggests.

"We could do that with other chaperones," Gwen says. "Does your mother like to ride?"

"It's our favorite thing to do at our country home," Beth says, her voice a bit lighter at the thought. "She's excellent. We could race?"

"Oh, I'd like to see you two try and beat us."

"You think we can't? We had nothing but time and land my whole childhood. I bet I could canter circles around you."

"Father taught me to trick ride," Gwen counters.

"That must have been fun," Beth says, looking so genuine that Gwen can't help but smile.

"It was. I could show you sometime. There are loads of tricks we could do together." Beth's eyes light up. "Maybe we convince our parents to supervise?"

Beth sighs. "I think Mother would have a heart attack if I did that in front of her."

"So only secret trick riding lessons then?"

"Afraid so," Beth says solemnly.

They both laugh.

"Maybe theater?" Beth suggests, pulling Gwen from thoughts of steadying Beth on the back of an enormous horse, of the two of them in breeches.

"Oh, that has promise," Gwen agrees. "We'd have to make it seem like a coincidence though, have our seats together. I'm sure I can arrange something."

"Excellent," Beth says, grinning up at her, her cheeks a bit flushed. She's had a lot of her wine already. "I love the theater, but we've rarely attended."

Gwen's about to suggest a few upcoming performances when

she notices Lady Demeroven looking around wildly for them. She sees Montson and his mother descending the stairs.

"Damn, I guess I've got to go," Beth says, slowly disengaging from Gwen.

Gwen pastes on a smile. "Dance pretty," she says, trying to be supportive.

"You talk to your father—pick a play. I'll be back," Beth promises. "I'd much rather drink with you," she adds as she passes over her wineglass before scurrying across the room.

Gwen watches her go and sidles back to lean against the wall, out of the fray as couples start lining up to dance. She can see Lady Demeroven and Beth bowing to Montson and his mother. Countess Ashmond's face seems perpetually set in a frown, but Montson looks delighted to see Beth. Who wouldn't be?

Gwen swigs the last of her wine and places it down on a side table, slouching into the wall to begin nursing the rest of Beth's glass. So much for a fun evening.

She watches as Montson brings Beth out onto the floor. They're an absurd match in height, but with his sharp jaw and her cheekbones, she supposes the children wouldn't be terrible to look at. They'd at least have some chance at height.

The band begins to play and she follows the couple as they waltz around the room. Beth's very graceful, and Montson's no slouch. He's no great talent either, though, and Gwen sighs, swallowing the last of Beth's wine. Beth deserves so much more than mediocre Lord Montson. His fortune may be suitably vast, but she'll be bored to tears. Beth, with her love for Shakespeare, and duets, and chess, and riding, cooped up with his dyspeptic mother up north—what a waste.

The Ashmond lands are something to behold, at least. She remembers stopping once on a trip with Father. He got along with Lord Montson's grandfather, the late Earl of Ashmond. They hunted while Gwen and Montson roamed around the gardens. She thinks Father and the late earl used to take meals together in town, even. Of course, when Lord Montson's father took over the seat in parliament, he completely reversed every single one of the late earl's positions. They never visited the estate again.

It makes Gwen uncomfortable, watching Beth and Montson talking, even laughing. Beth looks for all the world like she's having a wonderful time. God, but what if she really likes him? What if, to Beth, Lord Montson is a true catch? With only her horrible father as reference, Gwen could understand how Montson might seem more than adequate.

"That's a shame."

Gwen jumps as Father slips in beside her. "Announce yourself," she grumbles. He plucks the empty wineglass from her hand. "And what's a shame?"

"You said Miss Demeroven's quite the conversationalist. She'd be bored to death with the Ashmonds."

"Yes," Gwen agrees.

"It would be a good match for her though," he says, leaning back into the wall beside her. "She could do worse."

"She could do better," Gwen says tightly, unnerved by the clutch Montson has on Beth's waist.

She knows rationally that it's simply that Beth has a tiny figure and Montson is a broad man. But it looks like he wants to possess her—like he could squeeze the life right out of her if he wanted to.

She looks across the room and notices Lady Demeroven watching the pair with a gleam in her eye. She's sure Beth's mother will do everything possible to ensure a match. Gwen supposes it's what any practical mother would do. Even still—

"She'll be well taken care of," Father says softly.

"She could be happy instead," Gwen argues, glancing up to find her father looking across at Lady Demeroven. "Wouldn't you rather I was happy than secure?"

Father blinks and then meets her gaze. "I'd rather you be both," he says seriously.

Gwen swallows at the look on his face. "I'll try," she says after a moment. He nods and looks back out at the room. "Could you have been happy, with Lady Demeroven?"

Father stills at her lack of tact. She bites her lip and turns her gaze back to the floor. The waltz ends and Montson brings Beth over to their parents, his hand still on the small of her back. Beth glances over her shoulder at Gwen and Gwen takes a step forward, thinking rashly she might join their little circle.

Father's hand snags her own and pulls her back. Gwen looks up at him and sees more on his face than she's sure he means to show.

"Happiness is not the only thing that matters," he says, his voice tight.

"But—" Gwen says, glancing back at Beth.

"Lady Demeroven has a solid head on her shoulders, as did her father. I was no prize at the time."

"But you are now," Gwen insists.

Father smiles and pulls her in to wrap his arm around her shoulders as they watch the next round of dancers pair off. "I appreciate that."

"If she'd just had some faith," Gwen mutters.

Father shakes his head. Both of them watch as Lady Demeroven laughs at something Lord Montson has said, every movement choreographed and practiced. "Faith doesn't pay bills," Father says softly.

Gwen looks up at him and watches him shutter something away. It looks a lot like heartbreak—the crease of his brow, the arc of his frown, the sheen on his eyes.

They have to fix this. They can't let the end of their parents' story be this heartache.

She and Father can't *both* end this season heartbroken. One of them deserves a happy ending.

"Ah, Albie," Father says, and Gwen blinks as Albie steps up to them, blocking her view of Beth and her mother, and the handsome, dull viscount who may vie for Beth's hand. "Why don't you and Gwen take a spin, if you think Lady Meredith won't mind."

"Of course," Albie says, holding out his hand for Gwen.

She takes it, her chest still tight. Why should she be heartbroken by the end of this season? Beth getting married would be the proper outcome, after all.

Chapter Seven

Beth

Beth holds her mother's arm as they shuffle beneath the white columns outside the Adelphi Theatre, trying to stay together despite the push of the crowd. Their skirts are buffeted this way and that and Beth hears Mother cursing under her breath. It's only more crowded when they finally make it from the hazy street outside into the narrow entry of the theater.

The dark red velvet walls and golden tassels make the space seem even smaller, and amid all the hoops and top hats, Beth forgets about their plans, simply following Mother as she charges through the crowd and up to the first mezzanine. The ton is all atwitter, excited for the benefit performance, many of the men crowing about how much they've donated in honor of Céline Céleste. Mother and Beth were the surprised recipients of two tickets donated by the Harringtons. Meredith is at home with her mother, who's taken ill.

Beth has no idea how Gwen managed that, or if chance really did just fall into their laps. But she promised she'd arrange it, and arrange it she has. Now it's Beth's job to situate them in the right seats, if they can ever squeeze their way through. For all its benefits, the hoopskirt is rather impractical in a press of bodies, and even without a load of petticoats, by the time they get to their section in the mezzanine, both of them are sweating and heaving for air.

"I don't know why you talked me into this," Mother mutters as Beth guides her down to their thankfully empty row.

"Yes, this was my plan," Beth says, shooting her a look before coming to a stop. "This is us," she announces, motioning Mother forward. They shuffle between the seats all the way across the row, leaving Mother beside the lone empty seat at the end.

"Thank God," Mother says as they finally plop down, or at least try.

Two minutes of shifting and they've settled their skirts around their legs, twisted to provide as much room on either side as possible. It's still too close for comfort, but Beth forces a smile, determined to make the most of this.

Her enthusiasm for the evening is mostly about her plans with Gwen, but there's a small thrill at the thought of seeing live theater. Father used to take them once every long while, but such good seats at such a lavish premiere would have been unthinkable. Certainly if it had been their money on the line, they wouldn't be here tonight. She'll need to thank Lady Harrington for the honor.

"Does this say what the play is about?" Mother wonders aloud, flipping through her crinkled program.

Beth leans over to get a look, having lost hers in the shuffle, and then spots Gwen and Lord Havenfort across the seat block. She waves, noting Mother looking up in her periphery. That frown doesn't bode well.

Gwen gamely begins scooting between the seats, her demure navy skirts curled expertly to allow her room to maneuver. Clearly Gwen and Lord Havenfort frequent the theater. Gwen's grin is contagious, and Beth beams back. She laughs when Gwen plops dramatically down beside her.

"Horrid getting up here, isn't it?" Gwen says, before glancing back at her father and rather obviously checking the seat number. "Oh dear, Beth, are you in Father's seat?"

"She isn't," Mother says immediately before tightening her jaw. That came out rather hard and fast.

"We checked," Beth says apologetically, glancing up as Lord Havenfort reaches Gwen's side. "What's your number, Lord Havenfort?"

"Ten," he says, glancing at his ticket.

"Oh, that's next to Mother," Beth says sweetly, ignoring Gwen's not-so-subtle nudge.

"We can just scoot down," Mother says.

Beth bites her lips, glancing over at Mother, but she's struggling already to move her skirts. The group waits a beat, and Beth holds her breath, fearing that Mother will manage to free herself and their plans will be dashed. But their lack of theater experience in the new hoopskirts seems to prevail and Mother huffs, entirely stuck.

"Why don't you sit beside Lady Demeroven," Gwen says innocently, looking back up at her father. "It'll take all three of us ages to move our skirts."

Lord Havenfort frowns, looking down at them, squished into their seats, hoops only just settled into place. "Yes, all right. Don't bother, Lady Demeroven, really," he adds, nodding to Mother before turning on his heel to exit the other end of the row.

"These preposterous skirts," Mother hisses, shifting in her seat. "Ridiculous."

"We'll get better at them," Beth placates.

"I suppose, but one can't even move. Your father shouldn't have to do acrobatics simply to take his seat," Mother says, leaning around Beth to look at Gwen.

"He doesn't mind," Gwen says, smiling brightly back at her. "And he'll be much better behaved with you. He heckles."

"What, you don't egg him on?" Beth returns, swatting her arm and laughing as Gwen blushes.

"She's worse than I am."

They all turn to find a slightly winded Lord Havenfort standing at the other end of the row.

"And whose fault is that?" Gwen says.

He rolls his eyes and sits down next to Mother. "Mrs. Gilpe's," Lord Havenfort says.

"An aunt?" Mother asks, and Beth has to clench her jaw to keep from laughing at the surprised look on Mother's face, as if the question just popped out on its own.

"Housekeeper. You met her once," Lord Havenfort says idly, flipping through his program.

"Yes, with your maid. Lovely women," Mother agrees, staring straight ahead.

But Lord Havenfort doesn't seem to notice. "Oh, blast, I didn't realize this was a Webster role."

"Really?" Gwen asks, slumping beside Beth.

"What . . . do you have against Benjamin Webster?" Beth asks, glancing between them. "Isn't he the talk of the ton? They had a benefit for him earlier this year too."

"He's an absolute cad," Lord Havenfort proclaims.

Beth looks down at her lap, lip between her teeth. The Havenforts certainly are more worldly than they are.

"You would know," she hears Mother say under her breath.

Beth winces and Gwen huffs as the lights begin to dim.

"Would you like to hit him with a croquet mallet too, then, or was that just for me?" she hears Lord Havenfort whisper.

"This was a mistake," Beth hisses to Gwen, slipping her arm through Gwen's amid the coughing and rustling of program pages.

"Give it time," Gwen says, her elbow squeezing Beth's to her side a little jerkily before she shifts, slouching down beside her so their heads are at the same height.

"Intentionally hitting a man with a croquet mallet would be battery, wouldn't it? I can't abandon Beth to the season alone."

Beth turns, staring at her mother with wide eyes. Gwen stifles a laugh. Lord Havenfort gapes at Mother, who simply flips a page in her program as if she's commented on the weather. But Beth can see a little tilt to her mouth.

"That's your only hesitation, Miss Demeroven's season?"

"And prison, I suppose. Though they might let me off with a warning, don't you think?" Mother wonders, glancing at Lord Havenfort. The scandalized look on his face cracks her and she laughs.

He frowns before shaking his head. "You've always been incorrigible."

"One of my better charms," Mother agrees.

"Despite Father's opinion," Beth mutters to Gwen.

Gwen nudges her. "My father clearly thinks it's charming."

"What are you girls whispering about?" Lord Havenfort asks while the final stragglers make their way into the hall, muttering excuses.

"Beth thinks it'll be a morality play. I think it will be a murder," Gwen says smoothly.

"Mmm, I vote both," Lord Havenfort says. "Lady Demeroven?"

"Oh, I hope it's not a morality play," Mother says. "Dreadfully dull."

"Sometimes they're fun," Beth argues. "If there's enough that's exciting before the moralizing kicks in."

"Gwen, I think you've found a good friend," Lord Havenfort says. Gwen grins.

"What did I say?" Beth wonders.

"Gwen is all for the blood sport and scandal, and then she'll suffer a morality play. I find them interesting without."

"Only because you like to deconstruct the story. You've no more room for morals than Benjamin Webster," Mother says stiffly.

"Time has not dulled your edge, has it?" Lord Havenfort asks.

Mother shrugs and Beth settles back in her seat, dejected. It had seemed it was going rather well. Sportingly, but well. But Mother has her mind set on disliking the man, it's clear. And once her mind is set it's impossible to move her.

The lights go down to their lowest and the curtains open below them on the proscenium.

"I should not have shouted at you. The competition brought out the worst in me," Lord Havenfort whispers.

"It did," Mother agrees. "I didn't intend to hit you with the mallet, for what it's worth."

Lord Havenfort chuckles. "That's something."

Mother sits up primly, the matter apparently settled. The two studiously avoid looking at each other and turn their attention to the production.

Gwen sighs and Beth shifts closer to her. "Not as bad as it could have been?" she whispers.

"I suppose," Gwen agrees. "Toe to toe though."

Beth nods, leaning into Gwen and forcing herself to focus on the stage rather than their quarrelsome parents.

It's not a murder, and the morals are rather obvious, but Beth enjoys the characters and relationships of *George Darville*. Despite Lord Havenfort's opinion of the man, Benjamin Webster gives an excellent portrayal of a man driven to despair by guilt. And Céline Céleste is radiant as Marion. Beth finds herself captivated by Céleste's expressions—the way she turns from joy to grief, moves through anger and betrayal—it's incredible.

"She's beautiful," Gwen whispers.

"Yes," Beth agrees, a little awestruck. She's never seen a woman embody a character so completely before. "It feels so real."

"I'd like to clout him," Gwen says.

"Trip him down the street."

"A croquet mallet to the family jewels might be warranted," Gwen returns.

Beth giggles, biting at her lip as Mother shushes them. Gwen snickers next to her.

"Incorrigible, you are," Gwen whispers.

Beth swats at her knee and Gwen nudges back. Beth's smile doesn't leave her face for the rest of the performance, and they continue to whisper throughout. Gwen's delight is infectious.

When the curtain goes down, the audience explodes in

applause. Beth and Gwen struggle to their feet, tugging at each other's skirts to stand with the rest of the assembled. They clap enthusiastically, beaming. Gwen even whoops.

Beth glances over at their parents only to find them in a heated debate already.

"Oh dear," she says, reality crashing back in on her. She elbows Gwen, who leans around her in dismay.

"I just don't see why she had to die," Lord Havenfort exclaims.

"It's not a tragedy without a death," Mother replies.

"Why not make her a Lady M? A coconspirator. Wouldn't that have been more entertaining?"

"At one of the premiere theaters, you expect a modern Lady M? It would be a scandal."

"Better a scandal than a moralistic, heavy-handed, self-aggrandizing—"

"Does nothing please you?" Mother returns, her voice ringing around them even through the applause.

"Father, people are staring," Gwen hisses.

Lord Havenfort puts up his hands. But he and Mother continue to glare at each other. They turn back toward the stage, grudgingly clapping along.

"Though he does have a point," Gwen mutters to Beth as she leans back into place.

"She should have taken the money and run. Far too good for him," Beth agrees, shifting away from Mother lest she hear.

She can't imagine Mother approved of Céline Céleste's character dying, just that she's aware that making her complicit in the long-term con of using stolen money to improve her husband's station wouldn't sit well with the society set. Honestly,

Lord Havenfort's proposal sounds like a much more interesting play. Not that this was bad, by any means. But really, the woman dying of grief because her husband gave her a good life, even if through dubious means?

The curtains close on the bows, and Beth turns her attention to trying to squeeze her way through the seats. Gwen bends down and helps Beth twist her hoop. Beth smiles and takes her hand gratefully as they clear the seats and scurry up behind their parents. Gwen's palm is sweaty in her own. They shuffle along, exchanging winces in the push of the crowd.

"Just say you agree with me."

"I will not."

Beth groans and Gwen squeezes her hand. Their parents continue to bicker all the way down the stairs and into the lobby. Even as Lord Havenfort gallantly takes Mother's arm to lead her onto the street, he's needling her, insisting she agree.

"Dogged, isn't he?" Beth wonders. They follow through the open lobby doors and onto the street, traipsing down to join the line queuing for hired coaches.

"Decidedly," Gwen agrees with a sigh. "But speaking is better than not. I think your mother enjoys it, really."

"Possibly," Beth says, scrutinizing the clench of her mother's jaw—whether that's all anger and indignation, or her trying to hide a bit of a smirk. She does like to argue.

Beth and Gwen spend a pleasant few minutes watching the crowd and exchanging thoughts on the play. It's the freest Beth's felt in days, and it's glorious. Even if their parents aren't quite getting along, this is far better than anything else they've done this week. And surely far better than any time spent with Lord Montson.

Gwen's hand is warm in hers and their cheeks are both pink from laughing as they whisper about Céline Céleste. Beth thinks it's possible Céline and Webster are having an affair; their passion was so real. But Gwen's convinced Céline is far too good for him and would never stoop to sleeping with a cad. Beth nudges her and Gwen just grins, bright eyed and standing as close as she can against the wind.

"All right fine!" Mother exclaims.

"Hah!" Lord Havenfort grins. "You're far too intelligent to enjoy something so patronizing."

Mother rolls her eyes and pulls her arm from his. Beth's not sure how they made it to the front of the queue so quickly. She's been too distracted, giggling with Gwen and making up an increasingly exciting romantic life for Céline Céleste. She wants to stay in this peaceful, playful moment longer.

"You're a horrible snob, you know," Mother says as she reaches back for Beth.

Beth holds on to Gwen, not eager to be parted just yet. They've barely had any time together as it is. "Mother, couldn't we—"

"You've an important promenade in the morning. Come along, we'll leave your friend to her father's boasting. My apologies, Lady Gwen."

Gwen snorts and then covers her mouth. Lord Havenfort laughs and steps back to take Gwen's arm. Gwen holds on to the tips of Beth's fingers and squeezes, before letting go with a chagrined smile as the two of them are pulled apart by their parents.

"Good evening, Lady Demeroven, Miss Demeroven," Lord Havenfort says, tipping his hat.

Mother simply rolls her eyes, but Beth smiles back and then lets Mother tug her to the front of the line. Mother steps up first, smiling demurely at the footman helping everyone into the carriages, as if she hasn't just spent the last ten minutes sniping at one of the most titled men in the city.

Beth glances back at Gwen, who gives her a subtle thumbs-up, and then lets herself be handed into the carriage after Mother. They settle onto opposite seats and the carriage lurches forward.

"What a horrid, smug man," Mother says, brushing at her slightly disheveled curls.

Beth nods absently, watching Mother look out the window. It may not have been a roaring success—no moony looks, no simpering or flirtation—but Beth thinks Mother doth protest a bit too much.

IT'S HOT AGAIN. The sun beats down on them and even her bonnet can't quite keep the light from her eyes. Beth has to squint every time she looks up at Lord Montson. And since he won't stop talking about his racing horses, she's forced to stare into its brightness over and over.

Beth nods at the right moments, faking a smile, even as she'd like to interrupt to request they take a seat anywhere at all. The grass. On the riverbank. Even right here on the path would be nice. But Lord Montson doesn't seem to notice. She glances over her shoulder at their mothers, following them at a discreet distance. But the two women look utterly unaffected by the blinding sun and the rising heat, avidly watching the pair of them.

Beth sighs quietly and hums as Lord Montson describes the last race his champion stallion won. She thinks maybe he said its name is Racepoint. Rather on the nose, really.

It's not that promenading with Lord Montson is wholly unpleasant. Other than his obsession with racehorses, he's polite and interesting enough. And he seems rather taken with her, all things considered. This is their second promenade this week. Her feet hurt.

Lord Montson chuckles at his own joke, something about divots, and smiles as he glances at her. She wishes she could talk to Gwen. Their evening at the theater seems months ago, even if it was only a few days. In the interim it's been all trips to the modiste, and the florist, and morning calls to mothers in Lady Ashmond's circle to get their approvals. No time for purely social calls or friendship or anything fun.

Beth just wants to sit down with Gwen and ask how on earth she's supposed to survive more of this. Every single interaction Beth has is discussed with her mother ad nauseum. She must think about her laugh and her posture and the stories she can tell. Everything must be enticing and alluring, and God forbid she show any true human emotion or exhaustion. Ladies are nothing but grateful for male attention.

It doesn't seem to bother Lord Montson either. He's affable always—the picture of easy countenance and good disposition. Though Beth supposes it probably doesn't matter much to him. He'll be earl one day, whether he marries her or not. Beth, on the other hand, has just one shot at being his countess, as Mother has reminded her every single morning this week.

"My apologies, Miss Demeroven. I've gone on about my horses for quite a while, haven't I?"

Beth looks up at Lord Montson, shaken from her broody thoughts. "It's interesting," she lies.

He smiles at her. He is a very handsome young man. She wishes it inspired more in her. But though Mother has teased her about her exhaustion, suggesting it's because she's up at night daydreaming about Lord Montson, she's felt nothing but indifference about him since the ball.

Even Mother seems to feel more for Lord Havenfort when they argue than Beth does for Lord Montson on a lovely stroll.

Shouldn't she be swooning? He's swoon-worthy, she can tell. But there's no swoon in her.

"Tell me, what could you discuss for hours?" he asks.

"I'm sure nothing of interest," Beth says immediately.

"I highly doubt that," Lord Montson says, giving her an encouraging look. "Young ladies are so accomplished—much more accomplished than I could ever hope to be. After all, I simply own the horses—the jockeys have all the skill. You must have something you enjoy. Please, it's your turn to go on."

Beth laughs a little at that. "I quite like chess, I suppose," she admits.

"You do?"

He looks so surprised. Is that not something young ladies often enjoy? "Mother and I usually play at least one game a day, and duets as well. I'm decent at needlepoint."

"I've never had the dexterity for needlework," Lord Montson says seriously.

"It would hurt your back," she says solemnly.

He snorts. "I suppose. What's your favorite thing you've ever done in needlepoint?"

Beth looks across the lake, surprised by the question. The

true answer—what she'd tell Gwen—is a profane limerick that had Mother shouting for almost thirty minutes. Of course, Mother then promptly hung it in her drawing room behind the chaise, so she could look at it and laugh without Father knowing.

"I've done a few of the view of our gardens," Beth says instead. "And the forest. I don't race horses, but I do quite like riding, and I've memorized more than one of the trails."

"I love forests!"

Beth meets his eyes, trying not to laugh at the pink in his cheeks. "I do too."

"They're so peaceful," he says, his voice lower and more serious even as that flush creeps up from his collar too.

"I always wanted a secret tree house," Beth says, feeling like she owes him some admission as well.

"Really?" Lord Montson asks, his embarrassment fading in light of what seems like genuine interest. He's a sweet boy.

Beth shrugs as she fiddles with her gloves. "There were a few spots on our lands that would have been perfect, but Father was never home long enough to see it commissioned. I'd still like to do it someday," she continues, thinking of that dappled little clearing with the enormous oak tree. "Of course, they're not my lands anymore."

"We could do it on mine," Lord Montson says.

Beth looks up at him, surprised. "Oh?"

"I can think of a few good spots. Would be nice for the children."

That makes her chest tighten and Beth forces a smile. She's not sure at all that she wants his children, nor that she wants her fabled tree house on his lands. Never her lands. She won't have her own lands after this at all, even if they do marry. Even if he comes into a thousand acres, they won't be hers.

Just then, Mother and Lady Ashmond catch up to them. Beth curtsies as Lady Ashmond makes their apologies. Lord Ashmond has a dinner for some of the sitting Lords, and they must get back.

"So much fuss about this silly Matrimonial Causes Act," Lady Ashmond says to Mother. "As if we need to change the whole shape of marriage."

"Mother," Lord Montson admonishes.

Beth remembers Mother mentioning how in favor she is of the act. Yet another thing they'll have to hide from the earl, along with the dire state of their fortune, and her own intense dislike of herring.

"I'd much rather walk another few miles with you," Lord Montson tells Beth.

Beth smiles, and it almost doesn't feel forced. She accepts his kiss to her hand and then watches as he takes his leave, bowing to her mother before escorting his own away.

"That went well," Mother says as she steps up to take Beth's arm.

Beth leans into her and they head in the opposite direction. "Did it?" she wonders.

"He looked genuinely regretful of leaving you," Mother replies.

Beth shrugs. She thinks her company is certainly better than most of the Lords', at least the ones who used to visit Father in the country. They weren't in favor of the act either, if she remembers. None of them seemed to think a woman might have any reason to leave a marriage unless she was being beaten bloody, and therefore they saw no reason to remove arbitration from the church's clutches.

"Do you think if the Matrimonial Act had been passed you might have—"

"The viscount seems a lovely young gentleman. Tell me, what did you discuss?"

Beth purses her lips as Mother stares straight ahead, walking just a bit faster than before. Heaven forbid they talk of anything but Lord Montson.

"He's nice," Beth allows.

"He seems far more than nice," Mother says, prompting her with a little nudge.

"He's fine," Beth says, a little louder than she means to. A few older mothers look their way and Beth blushes. "There's nothing bad about him."

"A glowing review."

"I don't know, Mother," Beth clips back, frustrated by her own disinterest.

There's absolutely nothing wrong with Lord Montson. And yet there's just . . . nothing there. She feels empty, like she's observing herself be courted from afar.

They walk silently for a long while, crossing most of the park. She's coming to hate this place, even with the pink flowers blooming on the shrubs and the thick green of the leaves that throw intricate patterns onto the manicured grass. She wishes she could ride through their forest paths instead.

"Should it feel like more?" she asks, thinking of Lord Montson's kind offer to build her the tree house she's always wanted. How hollow it left her.

"More?"

"He's perfectly lovely," Beth admits. "Just . . . it's only pleasant. Should it feel like more than that?"

"Pleasant is more than many women ever get," Mother says immediately, before turning pensive.

"So I should be happy with my lot," Beth deduces, swallowing against a rush of disappointment.

Mother opens her mouth a few times, but doesn't seem to come up with anything to say as they walk the few blocks back to their townhouse. Beth sags against her, a deep melancholy settling over her shoulders. She should be grateful, but she just feels cross and disappointed.

As they head inside and remove their bonnets, she considers her mother. Surely she wants more for Beth. Surely she wanted more for herself.

"Was it ever pleasant with Father?" Mother stills, her hand curling around her gloves, knuckles going white. "Were you satisfied with just pleasant? Should I be grateful he doesn't yell, like Father did?"

"Beth," Mother says, her voice taking on that edge that comes with exhaustion and exasperation.

"Gwen says Lord Havenfort's never cross like Father was. That even when he's mad, he's kind about it. Could you tell that Father would be frightening? Was he pleasant before he turned into a brute?"

"Beth," Mother snaps, her voice hard.

"Shouldn't I at least make sure Lord Montson will be kind? Even if he's a rake, Lord Havenfo—"

"Of course he isn't," Mother lets out, her voice ringing around the narrow foyer. "There isn't a mean bone in Dashiell's body. He's affable, and kind, and frighteningly fair."

Beth stares, lost for words. Mother runs a hand through her hair, tugging it down from its sweaty wrap so her hairpins fall and ping against the floor.

"And I'm sorry that I couldn't model the ideal marriage for you, and that my choices continue to be a disappointment. But Lord Montson is a kind boy, whose father, while a blowhard, has no reputation for the kind of drinking yours did. You'd be lucky to marry into the Ashmond family. It's more than I could ever have hoped for. Be grateful," she insists, before turning on her heel and storming up the stairs, leaving Beth alone in the ringing silence left behind her.

Beth spends the next few hours on the precipice of tears, unsure whether they're for herself or her mother. All she knows is a pervasive sadness has settled over the whole household. Even Miss Wilson can't quite muster a smile or idle chatter as she helps Beth dress for dinner.

If her mother really did love Lord Havenfort, and was forced to marry her father instead, then she left love for psychological torture. She always says Beth was worth every cruel word her father uttered, but that can't be true.

He was horrible. Vindictive. She never *saw* him hit her mother, and Mother's never discussed it, but she knows there was occasional violence. He never struck Beth, though she thought he might more than once. What would he think, to see her so conflicted over such an advantageous match?

Beth shakes herself as she enters the lonely dining room. Mother's already seated at the head of the table, frowning down into her fish. What her father would think doesn't matter, but what her mother thinks still does. She suffered a lifetime for Beth. Beth can suffer the next few months, can't she?

"I'm sorry," Beth whispers as she sits down on Mother's left.

Mother looks up and meets her eyes, her own slightly bloodshot. She made her mother cry.

"It's all right, sunshine," Mother says, reaching out to squeeze her hand. "This is hard."

Beth nods, a lump in her throat. "I'm still sorry."

"So am I," Mother says softly. "Now, eat up. I don't know about you, but I think I sweat my body weight on that walk. My goodness, can that woman blather on."

Beth laughs despite herself and reaches up to wipe at her watery eyes. She takes a large swig of wine, and nearly chokes. She looks down into the glass and realizes it's a full tumbler of brandy.

"I raided your father's liquor cabinet. Thought we needed it," Mother says with a shrug.

Beth coughs and then takes another sip, letting the burn of the alcohol wash away her melancholy. "Could have done with some on the walk," she says, smiling as Mother snorts.

"I'm sure Lord Montson's much more engaging than his mother."

"He is," Beth agrees. "And I—you're right, I should be—I am grateful, that he's interested. I'll try my best." She says it willingly, but the knot in her stomach twists tighter.

A boring life with Lord Montson wouldn't be the worst thing in the world. And perhaps she and Mother could still ride together daily. If Mother could stand seeing Lady Ashmond that often.

They sit quietly for a few minutes, focused on forcing down their fish. Beth fights against a gag. She wishes they hadn't had to let their cook, Mrs. Mildred, go. Miss Wilson's the best housekeeper in the world, but cooking isn't her forte, especially when it comes to fish.

Beth glances over at her mother, struck suddenly with the vision of her eating alone in an even emptier house. If Beth does marry Lord Montson, surely they'll see each other often, but Mother will end up somewhere else. They won't dine together anymore. Beth will be dining with Lord Montson and the earl, and Mother will dine alone, in another house with the rooms draped in sheets, closed off and unused.

"Do you ever think about it?" Beth asks, the question popping out of her mouth before she can stop herself.

"Think about what?" Mother asks, glancing up at her and then straightening at whatever look has overtaken her face.

"Getting married again. After I'm settled. You're eligible now." Mother gapes at her. "I just—if you found someone wonderful—not just someone fine or kind. Would you marry again? If it was for love?"

Mother swallows and blinks at her, her gaze turning far away, truly considering her question. Beth buries her eyes back into her undersalted fish, unable to watch the emotions play across Mother's face. Maybe it was cruel to ask, no matter what she and Gwen hope could happen—maybe she shouldn't even dangle the thought into the world.

"I've already had my great love," Mother says a few minutes later.

Beth looks up, startled, and finds Mother regarding her softly. Was it Lord Havenfort? Beth's afraid to ask.

"You," Mother says with a little smile.

Beth forces herself to return it, to thank Mother and squeeze her hand. But it breaks her heart, to think her mother can't even imagine finding love again. Or is it perhaps that she can't imagine finding it for the first time?

She and Gwen have to succeed. Forget whether Beth marries Lord Montson or not. Her mother deserves to have love at least once in her life. And Beth—Beth will be *fine*.

Chapter Eight

Gwen

"It's dry."

"Just eat it."

"I'm telling you, it's overbaked."

"So go in and tell them, then, and get your money back."

"I cannot go and complain that my scone is overbaked."

Gwen glares across the table at Albie, who glares right back. "Then at least go and ask for more cream if it bothers you so much," Gwen says.

"Only if you admit these are as dry as sandpaper."

Gwen refrains from sticking out her tongue, but only just. They're supposed to be sitting primly out front of Patisserie Violette, eating little overpriced delights together, demure companions. Instead, they've been kicking each other and taking turns hogging the cream for their scones and their tea and generally making a nuisance of themselves.

Father, seated a few tables away, keeps chuckling while pretending to read his paper.

"I'm not hungry anymore," Gwen decides, slouching just a bit in her seat as Albie snickers. "I bet you'd get more cream for Meredith."

"'Course I would," he says immediately. "But she'd say please."

"Give her a year," Gwen says, waving off his proud little grin.

He and Meredith have been on nine outings and he's probably a month away from a proposal. He's doing Gwen a favor, sitting out with her. Albie doing favors for her instead of her doing favors for him, how the tables have turned.

It rankles.

"Here, eat the rest of this if it'll stop your pouting," Albie says, sliding his scone, smothered in cream and jam, across the table.

Gwen takes it without complaint, popping it in her mouth and savoring the cream, even though the dough is horribly dry. This is supposed to be the best patisserie in the city, but Mrs. Gilpe's scones could dance circles around these pathetic crumbly things.

"I could speak with Grish," Albie says softly as Gwen slumps back in her seat, the momentary pleasure of sweetness giving way to her melancholy.

"Grish is a drip," Gwen says immediately.

Albie frowns and glances back toward Father, who's thoroughly engrossed in his paper now. "He's not . . . that terrible."

"You got to wait until you found someone you actually like. Afford me at least that courtesy," Gwen says gruffly.

Albie sighs. "I just—I'd like to see you happy," he says, and she looks over to find his face laid bare, honest.

"I'm fine," she says, sitting up, prim and proper and pasting on a smile. She can't let Albie start feeling bad for her now. Not *Albie*.

"It's just—"

"What a pleasant surprise."

Gwen turns, delighted to find Beth hovering at her shoulder.

Lady Demeroven frowns lightly down at them, but Beth's bright smile has Gwen's focus.

"Hello!" Gwen chirps, her bad mood vanished. She stands to kiss Beth's cheek and curtsy to Lady Demeroven. "Will you join us?"

Beth glances at her mother. Lady Demeroven looks around, taking in the packed outer tables. "Ten minutes. I'll find you somewhere inside—keep on the lookout for Lord Montson."

"Yes, Mother," Beth says demurely.

Lady Demeroven gives Beth a significant look and heads inside. Gwen notices her father watching over the edge of his paper, quickly ducking down again when he catches her eye. Gwen snorts and pulls a chair around for Beth so they can squish together at her little table with Albie.

"Miss Demeroven," Albie says, nodding to her.

"How are you, Mr. Mason?" Beth asks, her cheeks a pretty shade of pink, light green skirts rustling. She looks a bit like a pastry.

"I'm well," he says.

"He's going to propose to Meredith," Gwen says conspiratorially, just to see him roll his eyes.

"Oh, how exciting! She'll be so thrilled," Beth says. Her hand snags Gwen's in an enthusiastic squeeze. Gwen can feel the warmth of her palm even through both of their white kid gloves. "She was telling me yesterday how much she enjoyed going boating with you."

"Didn't you fall in the lake?" Gwen asks, clenching her jaw against a frown. She and Beth haven't attended a single mutual event all week.

Albie glares at Gwen.

"Were you hurt?" Beth asks.

"You should be more like her," Albie grumbles toward Gwen. "And no. Gave Mere a good laugh though."

Beth smiles and then turns and meets Gwen's eyes. "How are you? It's been ages."

"I know," Gwen agrees, squeezing the hand she hasn't yet released. "Montson's keeping you busy?" she asks, scooting a bit closer to savor the time they have together without him.

"Yes," Beth says. "My mother and his have scheduled so many events, it's exhausting."

"I assume he's meeting you here?" Albie asks.

"That's the plan," Beth says. "Though it's awfully crowded. Mother wanted to make sure we'd be seen," she adds to Gwen.

"You can join us at worst," Albie says gamely. "I see her all the time."

Gwen does stick her tongue out at that, just to hear Beth's high, bright laugh. The sound makes her smile.

"What have you been up to?" Beth asks.

Gwen shrugs, tangling their fingers together. Nothing's felt as good as sitting here with Beth, soft and close and thrumming. "A few boring tea parties, a few small dinner parties and dances. Bobby's getting better," she adds for Albie's sake.

"Good. Awkward chap," he says, taking a sip of his tea.

"Did you ever finish *Madame Bovary*?" Gwen asks Beth. "I couldn't stop thinking about it after the performance."

"Yes!" Beth says, turning to face her more fully. Gwen basks in her excited regard, warmth spreading through her chest. "It was almost like a role reversal. I just lent it to my housekeeper, I hope you don't mind—"

Albie raises a hand, breaking Beth from her thoughts.

Gwen follows his look and spots Lord Montson approaching them, looking thoroughly handsome and affable. Immediately all their cozy loveliness disappears, like being drenched in a bucket of ice water. Gwen sighs quietly as Beth stands up, dragging Gwen up with her, her hand still a vise around Gwen's own.

"Hello, Lord Montson," Beth says, her hand slipping from Gwen's so she can dip into a pleasant curtsy.

Gwen follows suit, tugging discreetly at Beth's skirt so she doesn't get tangled up when she sits back down. Montson smiles at her and then looks at Beth, that smile blooming into a look of fondness that twists unpleasantly against Gwen's gut. Her empty hands curl into fists in her skirts.

She shouldn't be anything but happy for her friend, and yet she feels as if she'd like to stamp her feet in frustration. She doesn't want to give up her moment with Beth just because Montson's here. She wants to shout that Beth should stay at her table—tell Montson to sod off with his perfect hair and teeth and obvious wealth. Beth has books to discuss, with her.

Lady Demeroven exits the patisserie, looking harried, and spots Montson with their little group. Gwen notes the tightness in her jaw as she walks over. She feels herself getting jittery, anxious in her sudden desperation to find a reason to forestall Beth and Montson's date.

Lady Demeroven curtsies. "Lord Montson, lovely to see you. I'm sorry to report there are no free tables available. I've ordered tea for you and Miss Demeroven, but—"

"They can join us," Albie says, standing to greet Lady Demeroven formally. Gwen could kiss him. "I don't think we've been introduced. The Honorable Albert Mason, Lady Gwen's cousin."

"Charmed to meet you," Lady Demeroven says, dipping in another shallow curtsy. "I'd hate for Miss Demeroven and Lord Montson to interrupt your tea," she adds quickly.

Gwen opens her mouth, eager to explain just how much she'd like for Beth to keep interrupting—

"It will give us time to get reacquainted," Montson says gamely. "It's been at least a year, hasn't it, Mason?"

"More," Albie says with a little grin. "That boxing match, I believe, near Oxford?"

"Oh, that was a set, wasn't it?" Montson returns, sliding into the seat beside Albie as Albie plops back down.

Gwen blows out a relieved breath. For once, she's glad that men are so utterly predictable. She turns to see Lady Demeroven and Beth exchanging a series of pointed glances. Albie and Montson might be content, but Lady Demeroven seems hell-bent on keeping Beth's date intact. Gwen bites at her cheek to keep from glowering at the woman, a possessive irritation clawing at her chest. They'll suffer the intrusion of Montson, isn't that enough? Do they really have to be parted too?

Gwen casts about, searching for another excuse. It would be far from ideal, but perhaps if Lady Demeroven could join them too, she could lose that sour look—

"I believe I can offer some assistance," Father says, stepping up behind Lady Demeroven. Gwen chokes back a laugh. The woman's hat hid him from view. "Lady Demeroven, would you join me for a spot of tea? Leave the children to their chat?"

Beth's cheeks lift hopefully as Lady Demeroven considers it, looking apprehensively up at Father. Gwen finds she's almost vibrating with anticipation, pleading silently with Lady Demeroven to just for once give in, even a little.

"If you really don't mind," Lady Demeroven says softly.

Gwen nearly deflates in relief. She grins over at Beth, bouncing on her toes. Beth beams back.

Father simply smiles at Lady Demeroven, winking—how cheeky.

"But let me at least buy tea," Lady Demeroven says. "I did . . . injure you the last two times we saw each other."

Father frowns. "Only the once."

"The second time was a wound to your ego."

Father puts a hand to his heart as Gwen stares, shocked, at Lady Demeroven's little smirk. Father starts laughing and Gwen shifts her gaze to the pink on his cheeks and the full-bellied delight that pours forth. Dear Lord, he's still smitten. She socked him in the jewels and insulted him, and he's like a lovesick schoolboy even still.

Honestly, she can hardly blame him. Lady Demeroven's blush is nearly as pretty as Beth's. And if he's as excited for an afternoon with Lady Demeroven as Gwen is with Beth, how could he not be just a bit dopey? Not that it's the same, of course, but they are charming, these Demeroven women.

"My pride is more than intact. However, I'll let you pay for tea if we get those Florentines you used to devour by the basketful," Father says.

"They still make those?" Lady Demeroven asks, all hesitance forgotten.

"Mrs. Chutsky will, for me," Father says with a little grin.

Lady Demeroven laughs. "All right. But we're getting two sets then."

"Glad to see your appetite hasn't changed a bit." He looks over their table, nodding to Albie and Montson. "We'll send your biscuits to you when they come out. Enjoy your time, ladies. Boys, behave."

"Thank you, Lord Havenfort," Beth says, managing to find the words Gwen can't seem to push out around her own eagerness and shock.

Father nods at her and then winks at Gwen before gently taking Lady Demeroven's arm as both Albie and Montson salute him.

That went astoundingly well for something they didn't plan.

Beth giggles and grabs Gwen's hand to tug her back down to their seats. Gwen threads their gloved fingers back together, a rush of excitement coursing through her at the prospect of a true afternoon with Beth. Even if she does have to share her with Lord Montson.

They settle in together, all four of them crowded around the table, too close and a little too warm. But she's sitting at the table with Beth, poised for a whole afternoon with her, their knuckles knocking together, shoulders brushing. Her cheeks are starting to ache from smiling.

Albie ends some story about another boxing match and then the boys turn back to them. Montson seems to return to propriety and smiles at Beth. A brief, awkward silence descends on the table and some of Gwen's joy slips away.

"Miss Demeroven, I meant to ask, Lady Gwen says you can best her in chess. Is that true?" Albie asks.

"It is," Beth says quickly.

Albie whistles. "That's a feat," he tells Montson. "Lady Gwen can best even the most senior Lords in the House."

"Oh dear, and you can beat her?" Montson asks, looking at Beth. "I'm ruined."

Gwen sucks on her cheek, her chest tightening to see Beth's attention turned to Montson, that pretty blush coming out for him too. She goes to pull her hand back, telling herself it's to give Beth the best advantage in flirting, but Beth's grip tightens. Perhaps she's not as comfortable as she appears. She's become a better actress in the last two weeks.

"I'm sure you can still beat me at archery," Beth offers. Gwen can't help but scoff. "What?"

"You're a perfect shot," Gwen says, giving Montson a sympathetic look as he playfully slumps in his seat. "You'd have to teach her something new. She's annoyingly good at everything."

"That's not true at all," Beth says, even as she goes further scarlet.

"You're not tall," Gwen allows.

Beth huffs. "Well, you're very pale."

"You're paler!" Gwen argues, grinning as Beth's eyes sparkle with challenge.

"Lady Gwen's terrible at group dances," Albie puts in. Gwen shoots a glare his way. "I am too. We were the worst at lessons."

"Abysmal," Gwen agrees, eyes still narrowed. "But I can stay in a boat."

"She made me laugh!" Albie exclaims.

"You fell out of a boat?" Montson asks.

"Courting Lady Meredith," Gwen says, smiling as Beth leans into her, giggling. It sends a little spark through her chest, that laughter just for her.

"A lovely girl," Montson says, clapping Albie on the shoulder. "What's a little embarrassment for love?"

"Nothing," Albie says, holding his chin high. "Though Father almost had my hide. The suit was new."

"I'm sure he'll forgive you," Montson says seriously. "The chance for grandchildren forgives so many sins."

Beth blushes, and Albie snorts. Gwen forces a polite chuckle, but the very thought curdles in her gut. She doesn't want to consider Beth taking tea with Montson, let alone having babies with him.

Montson blinks and then goes scarlet. "I'm sorry, that was rude."

"Funny," Albie finally says, when neither Beth nor Gwen has offered something else. Albie glances over at Gwen, raising an eyebrow. She tightens her jaw, searching for something respectable to say to be polite.

"I'm sure Lady Demeroven would forgive Miss Demeroven for falling into a lake as well," she pushes out, forced sweetness in her voice.

"Oh, never," Beth says, picking at the lace of her dress. "The money and the hours hemming this? She'd make me sew a new one."

"Could you?" Montson asks, genuinely curious. Gwen laughs, how ludicrous. "What?"

"I suppose I *could*," Beth allows, her thumb stroking against Gwen's wrist. The sensation almost makes her shiver. "But it would take ages, and the material—"

"I absolutely could not," Gwen puts in, a little overloud. "Clumsy fingers, me."

"You said you do needlepoint very well," Montson says, still somehow confused.

"Not as well as a modiste would," Beth explains.

Gwen fights the urge to roll her eyes as Beth gives a more detailed explanation of what goes into a season gown for Montson.

All the while, her thumb continues to draw hypnotic patterns against Gwen's pulse. She wonders if Beth can feel the way her heartbeat is jumping through her gloves.

Lady Demeroven and Father exit the patisserie, balancing baskets of biscuits with a pot of tea and cups, followed by an employee who walks a truly mammoth platter of goodies over to their table. Gwen keeps an eye on Father and Lady Demeroven as they head to their table, but it is difficult with Beth's fingers between hers and the absurd array of baked goods placed down before them.

They've pulled out all the stops here—biscuits, cakes, canapés, and sandwiches, with a full tea set. She hopes Father at least persuaded Lady Demeroven he could pay for this. Gwen knows that Beth's success with Montson is important, but this is . . . excessive.

"Excellent!" Albie says, grinning eagerly with Montson.

Beth smiles and then looks over at Lady Demeroven, her eyes lighting up. Gwen follows her gaze, watching as Lady Demeroven laughs at something Father says while they bicker over the biscuits, and squeezes Beth's hand.

"Going surprisingly well, isn't it?" Beth mutters.

"Yeah," Gwen agrees, leaning in to whisper in her ear. The scent of her lavender perfume pervades Gwen's senses, sweet and lovely. It's a moment before she can find her words. "Maybe group outings are the way to go?"

"We'll have to plan some more surprise encounters, I think," Beth whispers back, turning her cheek to catch Gwen's eye. Gwen swallows hard and nods, her breath catching as their eyes meet, close and secret. Between the perfume and the sun and *Beth,* she's a little bit dizzy.

Beth's fingers curl against Gwen's and Gwen feels herself shiver in anticipation. The promise of more intrigue and scheming and time simply spent with Beth flutters through Gwen's chest. She feels her cheeks pinking with pleasure and is about to make another suggestion when Lord Montson passes Beth a plate piled high with sugar and crème and biscuits.

"What are you two whispering about?" he asks.

"Nothing," Gwen says quickly, leaning back into her seat with regret.

"I was telling Lady Gwen about my tree house," Beth says instead, her hand slowly slipping from Gwen's.

Gwen feels the loss of her touch like a cold draft, all that warmth and comfort and fun sliding away. Beth uses her newly freed fingers to pluck the pistachio macarons from her plate to slide onto Gwen's, as if in consolation.

"Tree house?" Albie asks.

"Miss Demeroven wants to build a forest tree house," Montson explains.

"I've wanted one since I was small," Beth admits.

"Oh, there's a marvelous spot on my father's estate. We could put yours next to mine," Gwen says eagerly, a little pride surging through her as Beth turns back to her, eyes alight.

"You have one?" Beth asks.

"Father and I helped the staff build it one fall," Gwen says, glancing over toward Father and Lady Demeroven, who are *laughing*. "Maybe you can come see it later in the summer. We could bring books and spend the whole day up in the tree."

"I'd like that," Beth says, beaming at her.

Gwen feels an answering grin spread across her face as she

frees two profiteroles from the croquembouche to place onto Beth's plate—her favorites.

"If her grove is too perfect, I'll happily supply your wood," Montson says.

Gwen glances his way and finds him watching Beth's excited nod fondly. Gwen bites back a quick retort that she and Father have more than enough wood. If it means Beth's tree house will be on her land, she can allow Montson the expense.

"I didn't know you and Lord Havenfort built that yourselves," Albie says, looking rather impressed.

"We had some help," Gwen admits. "But Father insisted we do as much as we could. Nearly broke all of our fingers and I fell out of a tree, but we managed. It was fun."

"Lord Havenfort's a good man," Albie says with a smile.

"The best," Gwen agrees.

"You should come hunting with us," Albie adds, drawing Montson in, though Gwen notes Montson's interest is tepid at best. "The Havenfort lands are wild with game, and Lord Havenfort always stocks his lake to the brim. Has to have the whole village for the open or it never empties."

"That's generous of him," Montson says with a tight smile.

Gwen wonders what hesitation lies under his placid look. Her father's never been anything but kind to him, even though they do both think he's boring.

Beth taps her knee and glances toward their parents, both of them flushed and laughing, making rather a spectacle of themselves even. Gwen suddenly wishes she could share in the joke. Wishes she and Beth could simply sit at their own table, pressed up close. Wishes she could spend the afternoon with Beth's gloveless fingers tangled in her own, cheeks pink, breathless from laughter.

Instead, a stilted tension falls over their table, and Beth pushes biscuits around on her plate. Lord Montson begins describing everything they do on the *Ashmond* estate each summer, and how Beth will adore it.

Gwen's appetite disappears altogether. She fights the instinct to insist Beth will be too busy visiting her to see much of Lord Montson.

FATHER'S SMILE LASTS the whole evening. He returns from the kitchens with their desserts, chuckling to himself and brushing flour from his jacket, thoroughly engrossed in some private joke. Probably something Lady Demeroven said. Gwen watches as he sits and attacks his cake, still looking pleased as punch—a wholly different man to the acerbic Father she left with this morning, teasing her about Albie and Meredith.

"You look absolutely smitten," she decides finally, unable to rein it in any longer. He looks like a child.

Father rolls his eyes. "No worse than you do."

Gwen stills. "Excuse me?"

"You and Miss Demeroven, thick as thieves. I'm surprised Montson got a word in edgewise."

"He talked the whole time," Gwen returns, feeling a blush climb up her cheeks for absolutely no reason.

"And yet it was you two sharing sandwiches, and he spent more time making plans with Albie than with Miss Demeroven as we left."

"I don't know what you mean," she says, taking a bite of cake to avoid his eyes.

It was all fun and games on the carriage ride home, talking about Montson's faults, and the jokes Lady Demeroven told, and how lovely Beth looked. But now he has his game face on. Father dearest about to give a life lesson. And for the first time perhaps in her life, Gwen wants to run away.

Because that gnawing feeling in her gut is still there. Has been since the ball. It only got worse as the tea went longer, and even with Beth beside her, she couldn't quite shake it. Or perhaps because of Beth beside her. She doesn't want to think about why.

"Be careful, Gwennie, that's all I ask."

Gwen feels her brow crease. "Careful with . . . what?" she asks, hushed, like she's little again.

Father considers her. She waits, watching him open and close his mouth a few times before he shakes his head.

"What?" she asks, her shoulders coming up. He's never bashful about his opinions, never shies away from a frank conversation. With no mother at home they've had more than one.

"Just remember why you're both here, that's all I ask," he says finally, reaching out to squeeze her hand that's turned into a fist on the tabletop, her nails digging into her palm.

"Of course," she says, searching his face. She doesn't know what he means—or maybe doesn't quite want to know.

Gwen watches as he considers her for a moment longer before standing. He comes close and bends to kiss her head.

"Why don't you take these into the kitchen," he suggests gently, nodding to the dishes. "Mrs. Stelm and Mrs. Gilpe are baking—I'm sure they'd appreciate it."

He leaves her with a pat to the shoulder. Gwen sits there, rolling his words over in her head. Careful—careful of what? Of wanting her friend close? Of interfering in Beth's relationship?

Lord Montson might not be good enough for Beth, but she's not about to upend Beth's courtship or something ridiculous like that. She might run interference more, find ways to get them apart, save Beth the exhaustion of the courting season as much as she can. But there's nothing to be careful of.

She stands and clears their plates mechanically. The dishes clatter in her grip. Father's reading something into this that isn't there. Something strange and worrying, but that's just Father, overprotective and—

Gwen swings the door to the kitchen wide and then stops cold, staring at Mrs. Gilpe and Mrs. Stelm, pressed up as they are against the counter, covered in flour and kissing like they're drinking oxygen from each other's mouths.

It takes her longer than she wants to unstick her feet and back through the door. It swings closed on Mrs. Stelm giggling as Mrs. Gilpe leans her back over the counter, both of them flushed and grinning.

Gwen stumbles back to the dining room, depositing their plates with a clatter before sinking shakily into her chair.

She knew. Of course she knew—has known since she was small. They never discuss it, but the women share a room and trade affections with little disguise. But she's never—in all her years somehow she's never seen them together. She supposes they're more careful in the country with more staff about. The London house has fewer people in it in general. Father—who insists staff take the night off, who keeps the household small and close and secretive—

Is that why he had her clear the plates? He wanted her to see?

Does Father think she's so inclined? Think she wants to be like Mrs. Stelm and Mrs. Gilpe—happily living together in secret beneath their roof since she was small? Loving, caring, adoring women who've helped her grow—does Father think that she feels—that she wants—that—with Beth?

Gwen stares blankly at the wall. She can't—she likes Beth. She thinks about her a lot, of course. And the days are better when they get to be together. And when she's dressing for balls now she thinks more of what Beth might think of her gown than what any of the young men might. And holding Beth's hand today made her feel more than she's ever felt dancing with anyone, even the prettiest, nicest boys.

But surely that doesn't mean—they're *friends*. Shouldn't she love her friend?

Gwen blinks, the image of Mrs. Stelm and Mrs. Gilpe burned there behind her eyes. She's never much liked to see courting couples kissing, finds it intrusive and showy, and it always looks a bit like they're eating each other's faces.

But Mrs. Gilpe and Mrs. Stelm looked . . . happy. Playful and fun and bright. Beautiful.

Is that what Gwen wants? Is that what she wants with Beth? The gnawing in her gut, the unsettled feeling of jealousy—is it because she wishes it were them on that countertop, giggling and flushed and kissing?

And Father—Father what? Approves? Worries for her?

Gwen blows out a breath, sinking further down in her chair, a heavy weight settling over her chest while her mind whirs dizzily.

Father wasn't mad. He wasn't disgusted. He wasn't judgmental. But he saw it. Sees it. Sees what she's been telling herself she doesn't feel for weeks—feelings she shouldn't have. Feelings society won't want. Feelings she's sure Beth won't want either.

Feelings that could get them both terribly hurt.

CHAPTER NINE

Beth

Beth glances around under the guise of stretching her neck. She and Lord Montson are seated on one of the Bloughtons' benches at their second tea of the week. Lord Montson's still prattling on about his father's bets for the regatta next month, but Beth's barely paying attention.

She knows Gwen is around here somewhere. She came in with her father and Beth saw Mother greet them. Mother and Lord Havenfort are standing on the patio now, speaking quietly, Lord Havenfort leaning in to hear her mother, smirking at what must be witty commentary. They're becoming awfully chummy, though Mother still won't say a word about their tea earlier in the week. Beth wishes she felt half as content sitting here with Lord Montson as Mother seems loitering with Lord Havenfort, swapping jokes and gossip, shoulders close.

Gwen was supposed to come save her from this. They agreed after Lord Montson left that she would run some interference so Beth would get a little relief. Lord Montson's lovely, but he's becoming increasingly intense, and honestly looking up at him is hurting her spine and her brain. She really could use one of Gwen's dirty jokes right now.

"So if the LRC wins, he really might go spare," Lord Montson says.

Beth hums and reluctantly gives him back her attention. "Has he placed any other bets?"

"He's got a pool going on some law making its way through the chambers," Lord Montson says dismissively. "But it's the sporting events that really get him going."

"Seems to be the way with men," Beth says, forcing a smile.

"Do you bet on cards or anything like that?"

She does, but she's not about to admit to it, especially since it's always just been with the staff. "A lady would never," she says.

Lord Montson chuckles. "I do some small wagers, but nothing like my father. I'd hate to think what could happen if you get in too deep, like Lord Mason."

Beth fights a wince, spotting Mr. Mason and Meredith across the way, giggling together as they sit on a picnic blanket that's strewn with fallen blossoms. Lord Montson shouldn't speak so openly about the Masons' misfortune. Gwen's told her some of it, and it seems Mr. Mason's lucky to have any fortune to offer at all, and that's mostly down to Lord Havenfort stepping in.

"You'll just have to stick to the smaller games then," Beth agrees tightly.

Lord Montson nods and then waves. Beth looks over and sees his mother gesturing for him. "I suppose my time is up, but you and your mother will join us on the boat tomorrow, yes? My mother's so looking forward to having a companion, and I promise to teach you to steer if you like."

Beth nods with the best smile she can muster. She's rather

sure she'll be seasick, but he's so excited to show her his father's boat, she can't ruin that for him.

"Excellent. Then I'll take my leave," he says, snagging her hand to raise it to his lips for a prolonged kiss.

Beth keeps her smile wide across her face, lowering her eyes as if in pleasure. She's desperate for him to leave. She wants to speak with Gwen—wants just a few minutes of freedom from the ritual of all of this. But Lord Montson takes his time, releasing her hand slowly and standing to look down at her as if she's something special.

She wishes it made her feel more. She doesn't know what's wrong with her, other than that something certainly must be. She's being envied around the garden, she can see it.

From no one, to one of the most coveted matches in the season—she should be crowing, giddy, excited. Instead, she's simply grateful when Lord Montson finally takes his leave with a little bow, smiling his pretty smile as he saunters off to join his mother.

Beth stays seated, watching them go, her leg jumping beneath her skirts. She waits until they're out of sight to light off the bench. She heads for the refreshments, trying not to look relieved. Trying not to look like she's desperately searching for Gwen.

She notices Mother and Lord Havenfort seated on the opposite side of the patio now, talking with a few other guests, making polite connections. Though as she stands there watching, they keep turning to continue some other conversation between themselves, more interested in each other than whatever news is being shared by the other adults. Their casual impropriety bolsters her and she gives in to a little desperation, moving through the party with purpose, searching for her friend.

She spots Gwen along the far edge of the hedgerow, standing alone with a glass of champagne like she'd like to slink into the shrubbery if she could. Beth feels the tension of her conversation with Lord Montson finally let go. She snags her own glass, taking a grateful sip, and hurries to join Gwen, mostly out of sight, thoroughly out of mind.

"You were supposed to come spring me," Beth announces as she slips in beside Gwen, their skirts rustling together.

Beth likes the play of her pale purple against Gwen's deep green satin. It looks like spring.

"Sorry," Gwen says stiffly before taking the last swig of her champagne. "Excuse me."

Beth blinks and then shoots her hand out, catching Gwen's elbow. "What's the matter?"

Gwen hesitates, pulling lightly against Beth's grip on her arm. "Nothing. I need more champagne."

"You don't," Beth observes, noting the flush already creeping up Gwen's neck, the slight fray of her blond curls around her face. "Chat with me awhile. We can make excuses to get more drinks later."

Gwen's shoulders slump, but she lets Beth pull her back to their shelter in the shrubs. Beth takes her in, watching the way Gwen won't quite look at her—the way her eyes scan the party instead, as if in indifference.

"What happened?" she presses, concerned.

"Nothing," Gwen says, twirling her empty glass in her hands. "How's Montson?"

"Fine. We're boating tomorrow," Beth says tiredly, releasing Gwen's elbow to thread their arms together, but Gwen pulls away. "Are you all right?"

"Fine, just warm," Gwen demurs, stepping a little away from her. "Is he going to wrap his arms around you and teach you to steer the ship?" Beth blushes at the mocking lilt in her voice. Gwen glances at her and rolls her eyes. "Predictable."

Beth frowns, taking in what seems like . . . scorn, on her face. "I guess. He's excited though. And so is his mother, to mine's chagrin."

"Yes, I'm sure they'll be bosom friends by the end of the season. She could even live with you and them," Gwen says.

"I think Mother would rather die. Did you see though? She and your father have been talking all day. And laughing."

Gwen nods, turning to look back at the party, disinterested. Doubt creeps into Beth's chest. She can't think of anything she's done to disappoint her—to insult her. "Are you mad at me?" she asks, ashamed of how meek she sounds.

She's a grown woman, and they're both far too old for schoolyard quibbles.

"No," Gwen says, glancing at her before looking back at Mr. Mason and Meredith, who have joined a group about to set up for croquet. "You and Montson would have won."

Is she—"Are you jealous of me and Lord Montston?" she asks before she can censor the thought.

"Please," Gwen says, scoffing as she steps away, marching toward the drinks.

Beth purses her lips and follows, tossing back the rest of her champagne. She scurries up beside Gwen. "You're being awfully rude."

Gwen huffs at her and strides around the side of the house, as if that might throw Beth off. But she's not about to lose her only friend over something as stupid as Lord Montson.

"It's not like I want to marry him," she hisses. They clear the side of the manor and head for the open wine cellar door. "You were supposed to come interrupt over an hour ago. I'd much rather have been with you."

Beth hesitates as Gwen continues straight down into the wine cellar. She glances back, but no one has followed them, and the pull of the dark and quiet is too strong to fight. More than that, maybe with some privacy, Gwen will get this stick out of her arse and explain what's wrong.

Beth descends into the dim cellar, lit only by the open doors at the top of the stairs, and a small window along the same wall. It's dusty and close, but wonderfully cool and calm. Gwen paces in front of a stack of barrels, her black slippers kicking up dust that swirls in the limited sunbeams from the grounds above.

"What is the matter with you?" Beth demands, coming to stand a few feet away. Gwen doesn't look up, just keeps pacing. "Has something happened with your father?"

"What? No," Gwen says, shaking her head with only a dismissive glance Beth's way.

"I'm sorry I had to spend time with Lord Montson. It's—God, this is why we're here. You can't actually be mad at me. If you tried even at all you'd be swarming with suitors, and I wouldn't be acting like you are," Beth lets out, frustrated.

Something else creeps up her chest at the thought, but she pushes it away, channeling her anger and disappointment and sadness toward Gwen and her indifference.

"I don't want this any more than you do, but I have to—I don't have a choice, and Lord Montson's not terrible. Gwen, please, I know we sort of made a pact, but I need him, whether I like it or not."

"He's not terrible," Gwen admits, glancing up before turning back to the racks of wine bottles along the walls. "But he's a dullard. You could do better."

"How?" Beth exclaims. "If you can't get one, how on earth am I supposed to?"

"Because you're beautiful and bright and you can smile and curtsy and look like you mean it," Gwen spits back.

"That's—that's hardly anything," Beth says, watching in fascination and annoyance as Gwen finally faces her full on. "I'm lucky Lord Montson's interested and I should—I should be grateful."

Gwen's look hardens. "You deserve a hell of a lot more than Lord Montson."

"What do you want from me?" Beth demands, fisting her hands into her dress. "I'm not going to do better than him and I thought at least I'd have you while I had to accept that."

"I want you—" Gwen says, breaking off with a hiss.

Something's changed and Beth wishes she knew what it was. How they went from holding hands beneath the table to . . . this.

"Want me to what?" Beth insists. "What should I be doing better?"

"That's not—" Gwen cuts herself off again, glaring at Beth.

"You've had three goes at this and you haven't done it. What am I doing so wrong that you can judge me for it?" Beth demands. "How can you be jealous when you're not trying?"

Gwen scowls and stalks forward. Beth stumbles back, surprised. Her hoop hits the stack of wine barrels. But Gwen doesn't stop. She comes right up against her, their stiff corsets nudging together, skirts pushing to either side, breath mingling between them. Her hands bracket Beth's waist, squeezing tight enough Beth can feel it beneath all the layers between them.

"I'm not jealous of your *beau*," Gwen mutters.

And then her lips crash onto Beth's. Beth gasps against her mouth, frozen in shock. Her mind goes totally blank.

Gwen, kissing, wine, jealous—oh. *Oh*.

Gwen goes to pull back but Beth's hands shoot out, quite of their own accord, clutching at her waist, anchoring Gwen against her. Beth rises on her toes, pressing their lips back together, the warm, soft pleasure of it trickling through her. This is what it's supposed to be. This is what it's supposed to feel like. Swoony and bright and everything.

Gwen sighs against her lips and Beth parts her own, sucking on Gwen's bottom lip. Gwen hums and Beth's whole body tingles. Gwen's waist between her hands, Gwen's chest pushing up against her, pressing Beth into the barrels behind her—it's overwhelming and wonderful and so much, so much. Gwen moans softly, dragging her hands up to cup Beth's jaw, angling her head to deepen the kiss, and Beth goes willingly.

It's like being lit on fire and doused with cold water all at once. Goose bumps rise on her arms and shoulders. Heat blossoms through her chest and down her belly. She tugs Gwen closer, leaning back to take more of her weight, wanting more than they can have with these stupid dresses between them.

Gwen breaks from her mouth, both of them heaving in air. She trails languid kisses down Beth's jaw. Beth pants, looking up at the ceiling, the aging wooden beams barely visible in the dim light. It's just the two of them here, secret against the world. She squeaks when Gwen nibbles on her earlobe, the sound hanging around them.

She didn't know anything could feel like this. Hot and soft and hard and fierce and beautiful. She wants to stay like this forever, her hands twisted into Gwen's skirts, Gwen's stroking at her collarbones.

She groans, turning her head to capture Gwen's lips again, sucking on her bottom lip before she slicks her tongue across it. They both shudder as Gwen meets her, tongues and teeth and open-mouthed kisses that are all hands and neck and sweet and raw—

Laughter penetrates their bubble and Gwen rears back, turning her head to stare at the stairs up to the lawn. Beth clutches at Gwen's skirts, unwilling to be parted from her even with the threat of discovery looming around them. She'd let the whole world watch for another minute pressed against these aging barrels with Gwen's lips on hers.

But no one comes down. Gwen slowly looks back at her and they stare at each other. Her hands are still on Beth's jaw, both of them flushed and breathing heavily.

Beth struggles to find the words—*more, please, soon*—can't explain how desperately, how ardently she wants to stay like this forever. What's never made sense before—how everything has crystalized into this moment—how they should run away right now, forget the balls and boating and parties and just lie beneath trees in the woods like this forever and always.

"Your mother is probably looking for you."

Beth blinks, startled. Gwen's hands fall from her face. Beth grips her tighter, refusing to let go even as Gwen tries to step away. "She's with your father. I'm sure they don't care."

"You should prepare for tomorrow, pick out your dress, don't want to get blown off the boat."

"Gwen," Beth beseeches, but Gwen shakes her head, gently prying Beth's hands from her waist and stepping back.

"Have fun," she says, and even in the low light, Beth can see the anguish on her face. She turns and hurries out of the cellar, leaving Beth splayed there against the barrels.

BETH STARES OUT at the choppy gray water beside the boathouse where they've retreated to take tea and get out of the misting rain. It's fittingly gloomy outside. Matches the catch in her chest and the gripe in her gut and the knotted ache at the base of her skull.

"Are you all right?" Lord Montson asks as she pours herself a fourth cup of tea while Mother and Lady Ashmond continue their never-ending discussion of proper tablecloths for dinner events.

"I didn't sleep well," Beth admits before taking a scalding sip.

The heat of it makes her push her tongue to the roof of her mouth, which careens her back to her kiss with Gwen yesterday—the press of her hands, the slick of her mouth, the clenching pleasure of—

"I hope sailing was invigorating at least."

Beth forces a smile around the rim of her cup. "Very," she admits.

The cold sea breeze and horrible weather were certainly a distraction, though not the kind she's sure he was hoping they would be. The press of Lord Montson against her back as they steered the ship did nothing for her. Nothing like the jolt she felt holding Gwen, being held.

"Is everything all right?" he asks again.

Beth forces herself to shake off the exhaustion and melancholy. She's here to be a lively, enticing partner. She'll have more than enough time awake alone tonight to replay her kiss, to mull her confused emotions, to plan exactly how she can next get Gwen alone.

"I think I simply had too much champagne yesterday in the heat," Beth says, attempting to look self-deprecating.

Lord Montson nods sagely. "I know that feeling well. The trick is to drink as much water as you do champagne."

Beth doesn't roll her eyes, but it's a close thing. How inspired. Whyever didn't she think of that?

Perhaps because she was so shocked and flabbergasted and utterly intoxicated that she threw back four glasses after Gwen ran off. Mr. Mason and Meredith let her sit there, stunned, on their picnic blanket until Mother was ready to take her leave. She talked all the way home about her conversations with Lord Havenfort around the upcoming season events. Then it was what she'd learned from the other mothers about the Ashmonds, and all the excellent courtship activities they'd suggested.

Mother didn't notice that Beth barely spoke all night. Didn't think a thing of her retiring early. Didn't see her sitting on her window seat until it was nearly light again, reliving the kisses, wondering what happens now. Wondering how to do it again. Wondering what kind of life she could lead that would give her Gwen.

"My father swears by a large piece of steak," Lord Montson

continues, and Beth strains to give him even half of her attention. "Butter basted, of course."

"Of course, for the fats, I assume?" Beth asks in a shockingly calm voice given the tap dance of her pulse.

"Naturally. Mother often simply has another drink with breakfast," he adds, leaning close into her space to whisper it to her.

Beth notices Mother smiling at them, obviously thinking he's whispering sweet nothings. But his breath against her neck inspires no such curl of desire in her belly, no tingle in her toes, no lightheaded rush.

"Perhaps that's the best way," Beth decides, smiling as Lord Montson pulls back, looking amused. "Simply remain lightly intoxicated always. You'd be very merry."

"But dead rather young, I think," he says with a laugh. "You might experiment with less sweet drink. Wine or beer."

Beth nods in false thanks. Both get her far more drunk more quicky, too easy to swallow. Too easy to just keep drinking and drinking, like her father used to do. Drinking to excess therefore isn't usually her style, unless she's just been kissed silly, apparently. She's seen what it can do to a person.

But she knows most men aren't so careful. "What's your poison of choice?" she asks, hoping to entice Lord Montson into one of his longer monologues so she can turn off her brain again and simply keep track of the rain sliding down the windows.

Lord Montson delivers, allowing Beth to sink back into a light stupor. What future could she and Gwen possibly hope to have? There's no mechanism for them to own property separately, hardly more than that together, and not enough money between them to make any kind of go of it.

They could be infrequent companions, like the women who sometimes visited her mother on country trips. Beth stills as Lord Montson prattles on about the distinctions of various whisky labels. Mother and her friends never—

No, no, she would have known, wouldn't she? She would have been able to tell.

But then again, she had no idea until yesterday that the affection she feels for Gwen translates to such . . . ardor. That the tingle of their hands touching or her admiration of Gwen's face was anything more than natural observation.

But now—now thinking about her smile, her touch, her laugh—it sends butterflies fluttering against her stomach. How could she have misunderstood herself so badly? Has she always felt this way—always wished to kiss her friends, always wished for their touch, their affection, their passion?

No, she thinks. She hasn't felt anything like this before. It's wonderful and devastating and all-consuming. Like Gwen lit a spark that didn't exist until yesterday, until their lips touched and the possibility of more presented itself like an explosion. An explosion that cannot be undone.

There's no going back from that moment. What she feels for Gwen she will never feel for anyone else. It is singular, and beautiful, and she wants more of it. More of Gwen's hands and her lips and her time and her affection and—

She glances at Lord Montson, speaking passionately now about hops, and those excited butterfly wings develop razors, lodging at the top of her stomach in a burning ache not likely to disappear anytime soon.

There's a future being built for her here, filled with luxury and security and Lord Montson. It's the best promise of stability and protection a woman can hope for. She knows well it's no guarantee of kindness, but at least until his death, she'd be provided for. It's a future that's as stable and solid and expected as it can be. A future that should be her singular focus.

A future that is the whole reason she met Gwen in the first place.

She's here for the season, and this season only—make a match, get a husband, live happily ever after. Her mother is counting on her, Miss Wilson is counting on her. A match with the Ashmond heir, that's the goal.

But how is she to settle that in her head, when she feels nothing for Lord Montson and everything everything everything for Gwen?

Chapter Ten

Gwen

Gwen sits at the pianoforte, slumped and listless. She forces herself through her scales, making intentional mistakes. But it doesn't help. It's been two days since she's seen Beth and it feels like she could crawl right out of her skin.

She knows she should regret it. The position she's put them both in, the impropriety, the sin of it—but all she wants is to be back in that dim, dusty cellar pressed against her best friend, devouring her mouth like it's the end of the world.

Gwen groans and lets her head drop to rest against the fallboard. There was part of her that really thought if she just got it out of her system, that would be the end of it. The end of the confusing thoughts, and yearnings, melancholy, and frustration. Instead, she's made matters ten times worse. And now she'll have to watch Beth marry Lord Montson knowing—

Knowing what? Knowing what it's like to have something she can never have? Knowing how it feels to hold someone she actually cares about? Knowing what it's like to be in love?

Is she? In love?

Gwen rolls herself back up, staring blankly out the window

at the steady misting drizzle. Is what she's feeling love? This all-consuming thought? The heated tickle across her skin when she thinks of their kiss? The thought of Beth's smile bringing one to Gwen's face? Is that love?

Would a man think himself in love after one kiss? Surely she can't have fallen so hard so quickly, much less for a woman she's only known for two months.

But the butterflies in her stomach tell a different story. They may have only known each other for months, but Gwen's never felt so close to anyone before, man or woman. The day doesn't seem as bright without Beth in it.

But Beth might not feel the same way. She was so caught up in the heat and press and flesh of it all, maybe she imagined Beth gripping at her hips, pulling her closer. Maybe Beth was repulsed and too surprised to pull away. What if Beth doesn't feel like this? What if she's just waiting for the next tea party to politely brush Gwen off?

Gwen sucks on her cheek, worrying a sore into her bottom lip. What if Beth doesn't feel the same way? What then?

And somehow, both worse and better, what if she does?

"There you are."

Gwen nearly jumps off the bench, a hand to her heart as Father strides into the room, his cheeks flushed and hair damp. He wasn't supposed to be home until late afternoon—some meeting of parliamentarians at the club.

Gwen blinks, noticing the time on the clock over the mantel. It's nearly five already. Has she really just been sitting here in a strop all afternoon?

"Go up to your room and put on a gown," Father says.

Gwen stares, feeling like his words are traveling through fog. "What?"

"Go and get dressed. I'm taking you, Miss Demeroven, and Lady Demeroven to the opera to celebrate."

Gwen's stomach drops. "Celebrate what?"

"We're going to pass the Matrimonial Causes Act," Father says, his grin nearly splitting his face.

"That's . . . wonderful," Gwen manages, trying to return his joy. She knows how hard he's worked for this—how much it means to him—but the feeling of dread clutching at her chest makes it hard to smile.

"I've sent Mrs. Stelm up to lay out your best dress. We'll have dinner at Wilton's and then ride to the theater. Box seats, best in the house."

Gwen swallows past her unease when his smile just doesn't fall. "You're very excited."

He laughs. "Yes. Now, go and get pretty, and I shall do the same."

Gwen giggles despite herself and lets him guide her from the parlor, listening as he prattles on about the various business dealings and negotiations that created this magnificent assurance of votes. Of course, that quorum needs to survive until the vote, but they've done it.

He leads her up to her room and passes her over to the preparations of Mrs. Gilpe and Mrs. Stelm. Gwen's stomach twists. Images of the two of them pressed together in the kitchen swarm her head as the pair move around her, helping her out of her housedress and into her fresh shift and corset.

Did their stomachs somersault like this the first time they kissed a woman? How did they even come to realize they could? And find each other? How did they decide together to risk everything to lie in the same bed each night?

"Are you quite well?" Mrs. Gilpe asks as Mrs. Stelm adjusts Gwen's corset.

"How did you—" Gwen blurts, stopping just shy of shouting it like a demand.

Her housekeepers exchange a confused look and Gwen balls her fists, feeling so exceedingly uncomfortable and twisted up.

"Is something bothering you?" Mrs. Stelm asks gently, her rounder, more open face easier to consider than Mrs. Gilpe's assessing stare.

She knows they both love her. Mrs. Stelm has just always been the softer of the two. Because they've always been a pair. Even if Gwen never thought on it much—even though it's never discussed or brought up, they're a pair. A team. A . . . couple.

"How did you two meet?" Gwen ventures, trying to look disinterested, though she can tell from both of their faces that she's easily overplayed her hand.

"Mrs. Gilpe's been with your family since she was born," Mrs. Stelm says slowly.

"Right, I know," Gwen mumbles, feeling foolish.

She knows *how* they met. Mrs. Stelm was hired by Father's mother on recommendation from a local seamstress. And of course Mrs. Gilpe's lived with the Havenforts since she was small, because her father was the groundskeeper. So they met at the country estate, and have been working together for Gwen's entire life.

She doesn't know how to ask what she really means. How do two women decide to . . .

"I thought I heard you come into the kitchen a few nights

ago," Mrs. Gilpe says idly. She bends to raise the hoop cage, stepping behind Gwen to secure it. "Your father asked you to bring in the dishes?"

Gwen nods slowly, watching Mrs. Stelm's eyes widen. The two women exchange a knowing glance between them. It makes her blush. Why is it everyone in her household seems to have seen this before she did? She's no child. She's been out for four seasons, is . . . seasoned in the ways of courtship. Why has this hit her like a speeding carriage?

"Was there something you wanted to ask?"

Mrs. Stelm smiles at her, gentle and open, like she used to when Gwen had questions as a little girl. *How do bees sleep? Why is the sky blue? Why do trees lose their leaves?* But her question now feels too big for her tongue.

"You looked happy," Gwen says, letting the words fall free even though she can't seem to pluck up exactly what it is she wants to ask.

"We are," Mrs. Gilpe says firmly, like it's an easy, given fact.

"I'm sorry if it upset you, to see us like that," Mrs. Stelm adds.

"No!" Gwen exclaims, wincing as they both jump. She doesn't want them to think—"It's not that at all. No, I'm . . . I'm glad. I mean, I knew, but I'm—it looked . . . nice," she trails off, her cheeks going scarlet.

Mrs. Gilpe and Mrs. Stelm share another knowing look and Gwen wants to melt into the floor. *Nice.* She saw them in flagrante and all she can say was it looked *nice*? How—she shouldn't even be commenting on it. She bites at her lip. If one of them were a man, it would be a scandal.

And she certainly wouldn't think it nice. A man pushing you into a solid countertop, nosing at your neck, scrabbling at your waist—it would look barbaric. But what she saw was anything but. It was giggling and blushing and just . . .

"It was," Mrs. Stelm says, withholding a laugh. "Nice."

Gwen groans. "I don't—"

"If it's consensual, two people touching that way should always be nice," Mrs. Gilpe adds.

Mrs. Stelm does giggle then. Gwen watches her reflection as her blush crawls from her chest to the tips of her ears. She looks like a tomato.

"Don't know how many kisses you've had—though of course it should be none," Mrs. Gilpe continues, fixing Gwen with a stern look before she cracks and laughs herself.

Gwen stares. She's rarely seen the woman so open. "Only two—well, three," she corrects, her face going further red as memories of her moment with Beth flit through her mind. "I just, I—How did you decide to . . . be like this?" She ends on a whisper, feeling embarrassed and ashamed for her curiosity.

She wouldn't ask if one of them was a man. No one need ask when one is a man. That's simply how it's meant to be. You're born a girl, you grow up to be a wife, then a mother, then more than likely a widow, and then you pass, hopefully with a smattering of male heirs.

You don't grow up to kiss your best friends and become a spinster.

"I had more than my share of kisses as a lass," Mrs. Stelm says.

Mrs. Gilpe strides to firmly shut Gwen's door. Gwen swallows as full privacy surrounds them. She's not sure she truly wants to know this. It feels like there's no turning back, like somehow this conversation will cement a reality she's not sure she wants to face. But she's already started it. Already pressed herself to Beth and taken her mouth—would have taken more if she could.

"And none of them felt the way I'm betting it did when you kissed that new debutante you're always talking about," Mrs. Stelm says.

Gwen sways in place. How do they just *know*?

"Oh, sweetheart, it was all over your face when you came home from that garden party," Mrs. Stelm says.

"Like you'd been socked in the gut and slapped in the face, and then given a new pony," Mrs. Gilpe adds, chuckling as Mrs. Stelm whacks her arm.

"Felt like that," Gwen whispers, something releasing as she meets their eyes in the mirror—speaking it into the world is like breathing that clutching panic right out of her chest.

"Once you've been kissed like that, it's hard to go back to other kisses," Mrs. Gilpe says frankly.

Gwen feels her shoulders droop. She knows it won't ever feel the same with a man. It's not that the kisses of her first seasons were terrible, but they weren't . . . Beth's. "And you never thought of getting married anyway, either of you?" she wonders.

Mrs. Gilpe and Mrs. Stelm glance at each other for a long moment. Gwen watches their silent conversation in newfound interest. She's seen couples at parties look at each other this way, silently discussing something before giving an answer.

"It was our wish to find a way to be married together," Mrs. Gilpe tells her, meeting her eyes in the mirror. The two of them step close behind her. "But, and this is the only time in your life I'll say this, it was simpler for us as commoners than it will ever be for you."

Gwen lets out a startled laugh. "Oh?"

Mrs. Stelm smiles. "Though you know we sleep in the same room and call us Mrs. despite neither of us having husbands, how often have you really thought about our situation?" she asks.

Gwen bites at her cheek, unwilling to say she's never, not once, thought on it. That's just how it's always been, even though she knows there are more than enough servant's quarters for them both to have a suite of them should they wish it.

"Which is exactly as we expected it to be. And as your father takes as little interest in our love lives as he does the others', it's never been an issue," Mrs. Gilpe adds.

"But, to be fair, your father is no ordinary lord. Certainly in another house we would not have survived. Your mother never caught on," Mrs. Stelm adds after a moment.

"Oh, she would have had us both thrown in the asylum," Mrs. Gilpe says with a snort. "We were simply careful."

"Why would she do that?" Gwen asks, the question popping out like she's an innocent child.

She knows her mother was anything but saintly. A vicious tongue Father pretends was merely witty, but Gwen's heard enough stories to know there was cruelty behind the beauty. But to have two women thrown into the asylum for the crime of happiness?

"Your father is a good man. You mother was a woman of her time and station. It would have offended all that she knew," Mrs. Gilpe says easily.

"Was she really that awful?" Gwen wonders, staring at her reflection.

What would her mother have thought of her, then, fantasizing of kisses with her best friend?

"I think she was very unhappy," Mrs. Stelm says softly, reaching out to squeeze Gwen's shoulder. "Unhappy people are often cruel to avoid the cruelty within."

"Regardless, you are a lovely young woman, and anyone would be lucky to have you. Whether or not it's as you'd wish it to be, there are arrangements that can be made," Mrs. Gilpe says.

Gwen meets her eyes in the mirror. "What do you mean?"

"There's many a young wife who has a constant companion, or one who visits often throughout the year. And many more a husband and wife who sleep separately. You can live your own life, should you find the right match. Your station could put you in a good situation to orchestrate a lifestyle."

Companions, nothing more, stealing what time they can while their husbands are away in parliament or sleeping in the opposite wing.

"But, tonight, all you have to do is put on your gown and enjoy a dinner and evening at the opera with your father and your friend," Mrs. Stelm says, sneaking in to tickle Gwen's side and wipe her face of concern.

It half works.

"Yes, he did seem very excited to take Lady Demeroven out on a date."

Gwen's head swims for the second time. "This is a date?"

"Oh, you are rather hopeless, aren't you?" Mrs. Gilpe says.

Gwen glares as the women laugh, helping her into her gown. But their smiles are soft, and she loves them so dearly. More dearly than she even thought she could—sisters in some other world than they are in now.

CHAPTER ELEVEN

Beth

Sitting beside Gwen in the opulent carriage is shockingly nerve-wracking. Their parents are all chatter, Mother trying to tease out their dinner reservations and getting increasingly competitive as Lord Havenfort refuses her at every guess. Lord Havenfort looks pleased as punch, obviously taken with Mother's gorgeous gown, and hair, and besotted face.

Were Beth not excruciatingly aware of every minute movement from Gwen beside her, she'd be very excited that their parents seem so happy. That Mother even accepted the invitation was monumental on its own, but now she's here and acting so girlish. Beth should be doing high kicks. But she can barely focus.

Gwen shifts in her deep navy skirt, her hands clasped tightly in her lap, and Beth feels the resulting wobble of her hoop like an earthquake. She risks a glance at Gwen, but Gwen's staring out the window, lip between her teeth. Beth picks at her gloves, wrapping her own hands into her lap to stall the impulse to adjust the lay of Gwen's skirts.

It's been days since they've seen each other, and she can't even push a hello out of her mouth without feeling like every confused, hopeful, desperate thought she's ever had will come tumbling out at once. She feels silly, and overheated, and anxious like she hasn't been since the first ball of the season. Worse, actually.

Because it's *Gwen*. She kissed Gwen. Well, Gwen kissed her, and she kissed back, and then Gwen ran away and the whole world has turned upside down and now she's just sitting there—

The carriage comes to a halt and Lord Havenfort promptly hops out and extends a hand back to Mother, who eagerly climbs out behind him. Beth thinks maybe he finally said where they were, but truth be told everything sounds a little like buzzing to her ears right now.

"You next."

Beth nearly jumps out of her seat, startled as she meets Gwen's amused expression. "Oh," she says dazedly, following Gwen's nod toward Lord Havenfort's waiting hand. "Right."

She takes his extended palm with numb fingers and climbs out of the carriage, staring up at the whitewashed walls of Wilton's, which calls itself the premier oyster bar in London.

She's never had an oyster before.

"This is the best seafood establishment in all of London," Lord Havenfort tells them while he ushers their group toward the entrance.

Beth feels her pulse accelerate as Gwen's hand brushes the small of her back to gently push her inside after her mother. The contact sends shivers up Beth's spine. She hopes Gwen can't tell.

The walls are lined with green velvet booths divided by white-linen-clothed tables with candles flickering at the center. There's a broad oak bar along one wall, and servers in full uniform wander among the tables, dispensing plates of fish and crustaceans.

It smells like the ocean—close, salty, and a little sweet.

"Lord Havenfort, of course, right this way," the host says, guiding them toward the back corner where the largest booth has been reserved.

Beth tenses, watching her mother and Lord Havenfort enter the booth on the same side, leaving Beth and Gwen to settle opposite. Their skirts press together again, shoulders touching. It sends a current up and down her arm, and Beth hopes no one can see her flaming cheeks in the flickering candlelight.

"I brought your mother to Wilton's twenty-two years ago," Lord Havenfort says, and it takes Beth a moment to realize he's speaking to her.

"Really?" Beth wonders, trying to focus enough to enjoy the thought—trying to keep her head on straight enough to realize this is a *date*. He brought them here because it's special to her mother.

"It was just a stand back then," Mother adds, her face lit up at the memory. Beth hasn't seen her look this lively in such a long time. "We ducked out of, what was it, dance lessons?"

"Badminton, maybe?" Lord Havenfort wonders. "Something organized. I convinced her to take a carriage with me to Great Ryder Street and we wandered up and down the shops. We got oysters here—"

"And then ice cream and pastries down the way. Do you think it's still there?"

"Gephino's, was it?" Lord Havenfort asks, and Beth watches as they lean their heads in, naming old restaurants back and forth.

"Maybe we should duck out of our next tea," Gwen mutters, her voice close to Beth's ear, and Beth starts violently, bumping their skirts together.

Gwen winces as Beth finds enough fortitude to meet her eyes, to act like she's not thoroughly undone just by sitting next to her. "We should," she agrees, her voice tight and high. "I doubt we could just hire a coach though."

"We'd have to convince Albie—dreadfully inconvenient, really," Gwen agrees, her words a little halting. "He'll never leave Meredith."

"Meredith might be game," Beth says, picturing the four of them ditching their high tea, in all their finery, to walk around the fish markets and buy street food. "It could be fun."

"It really could be," Gwen agrees, her smile tentative. "I'd buy you gelato."

Beth feels some of her hesitation melt away. This is easy—familiar—planning hijinks with Gwen. Even with all the . . . kissing, they're still friends. At the very least, whatever else, they're still friends.

And something as simple as browsing a fish market sounds so fun because Gwen would be there. She makes everything fun. Everything is better with Gwen, from the kissing to sitting here listening to their parents bicker.

Her mother laughs loudly and Lord Havenfort playfully shushes her, chuckling. Not so much bickering as . . . flirting? It seems it's a family trait, making the mundane into fun.

"Comport yourselves," Gwen chides, laughing.

Her father gives her a false scowl and Mother straightens up, wiping at her eyes. Beth doesn't even know what they were laughing at. She's about to ask when a man in a green velvet waistcoat arrives at their table. He has a large mustache and a mop of curly brown hair, both of which only complement his beaming smile. His jacket matches the booths.

"Mr. Wilton," Lord Havenfort says, attempting to stand and nearly falling over as his feet get caught in Gwen's and Mother's skirts.

"Sit down, sit down," the man says. Lord Havenfort plops back into place and Beth hides a laugh. "It's been too long."

"It has," Lord Havenfort agrees. "Do you remember—"

"But of course!" Mr. Wilton says, beaming over at Mother. "Miss Paulson."

Mother smiles. "Lady Demeroven, now. It's good to see you."

Mr. Wilton frowns briefly over at Lord Havenfort before giving Mother a gracious bow. "A pleasure to see you again, my lady. Well, I imagine this calls for the chef's special," he says, looking back at Lord Havenfort.

"And that would be—"

"Everything!" Mr. Wilton says gleefully. "For you, Lord Havenfort, we do the whole menu. I hope you ladies are hungry," he adds, bowing lightly to Beth and Gwen before he disappears back into what must be the kitchens.

"You're in for a treat," Lord Havenfort says.

"Everything, Dashiell, really," Mother says and Lord Havenfort laughs.

"Not up to the challenge?"

Mother demurs for a moment before glancing at Beth. "What do you think, darling, can we eat these two under the table?"

Beth gapes at her mother for a beat before the challenge in her eyes and Gwen's snickering get the best of her. "Oh, absolutely."

"We might think to plan enough time to walk to the opera," Gwen suggests, laughing as Lord Havenfort reaches out to squeeze her shoulder.

"You are my daughter."

Another waiter comes over with glasses of sparkling champagne. He dutifully passes them around, his eyes lingering on Gwen. Beth feels her gut clench, a fast, hot roll of jealousy surging through her.

She blinks as he turns and walks away, no one at her table any the wiser. Lord Havenfort raises his glass. She follows suit with Gwen and Mother, utterly baffled by the extreme range of emotions she's felt in just the past thirty minutes. She's never been this upended before. Thinking about Gwen now is utter emotional chaos and butterflies and—

"To the health and safety of women everywhere, and the good health, happiness, and cheer of the three beautiful women I have with me tonight," Lord Havenfort says.

Beth raises her glass and then takes a sip, letting the fizz of the bubbles against her palate attempt to ground her back to earth. Her mother is making eyes at Lord Havenfort and he's turning his head to mumble in her ear, like they're—

"Going rather well, isn't it?" Gwen whispers.

Her breath against Beth's ear makes her shiver. "Yes," she manages.

This is what they've wanted, and it's—it's like it's working.

She puts her glass down shakily. Gwen seems to relax beside her, her hand landing on the bench seat between them. Beth can feel the delicate weight of it against her skirts—the lightest pull of fabric. She could so easily reach down and touch Gwen's hand—hold it, even, and who would know?

She thinks Gwen would like that too—thinks about all the times they've held hands in the past weeks—of the way it always made her feel safe and just a bit tingly and she never put it together. She could feel like that now if she just—

Mr. Wilton appears from the kitchen with a frankly enormous platter, placing it down onto their table with a flourish. All thoughts of illicit touches fly out of Beth's head as she stares down at the excessive spread. Crab and shrimp and toast points. Tureens of sauce. Skewers of cheese. And what must be oysters there all around the edges, swimming in butters and sauces and brines.

Mr. Wilton spends a few minutes explaining each dish, but Beth can't quite keep up. They've been eating mostly vegetables and soup with lean meats, and now here's a platter of abundance just for them. She's salivating.

"Beth?" Gwen asks.

Beth blinks. Mr. Wilton has left them and Lord Havenfort and Mother are already taking their first samples.

"I . . . don't know what to try first," Beth admits softly, overwhelmed by all of it.

Gwen smiles. "Oysters first, then we'll do crab. Ooh, gosh, Father, did he say that was caviar?"

"It is," Lord Havenfort says around a mouthful of something. Mother whacks him and Beth laughs, coming back to herself.

"Which kind is best?" she asks Gwen, gesturing to the oysters.

"Try the garlic butter first," Gwen says, reaching out to daintily pluck one of the dripping oysters, offering it to Beth.

Their fingers brush as Gwen passes her the oyster and Beth nearly fumbles it into her lap, her cheeks flaming. But Gwen only smiles, reaching out for her own oyster, and Beth forces herself to focus. She needs to observe, since she doesn't know how to eat it. Do they really just—

She swallows hard as Gwen slurps her oyster from its shell, tipping her head back to get the rest of the sauce. The bob of her throat and the line of her neck and the way her tongue snakes out to rim her lips—dear God, that was perhaps the most arousing thing Beth's ever seen.

"Go on," Gwen says, laughing softly.

Beth shakes herself and tries to sip her oyster as gracefully as Gwen managed. It's a bright pop of salt and brine and the tang of the garlic. Slightly slimy but pleasant all at once, it bursts in her mouth and glides down her throat. She hums, delighted.

She opens her eyes and finds Gwen staring at her, flushed, eyes wide. Beth smiles, surprised. It sends a surge of something through her to know Gwen's as undone by all of this as she is.

It wasn't an aberration, a champagne-fueled mistake. Gwen wants her, just as much as Beth wants her back.

Her mother groans and Beth drags her gaze away from Gwen to find Lord Havenfort feeding her mother an oyster, both of them looking rather heated.

Is this some kind of illicit adult pleasure she's never heard of before—feeding oysters to a—what, exactly? What are they all to each other now?

"Good?" Gwen asks, her voice tight and low.

"Ye-es," Beth says, blinking and looking away from their parents. It feels like she's intruding somehow.

And yet, she suddenly, desperately wants to feed Gwen an oyster. It's improper for Lord Havenfort to do it for her mother; it would be beyond scandalous for Beth to do that with Gwen. But she *wants* to.

She wants to spoil and savor and touch and kiss and dote on Gwen the way she sees Lord Havenfort doing for her mother. She wants to *be* with Gwen, in all ways. Slurping oysters, and exchanging kisses, and going on walks, and reading quietly in the library. Just—living with her.

The thought is big and bright and broad and Beth reaches out mechanically for another oyster, wanting the sensation of it to wash away the burning desire to haul Gwen into the back and kiss her senseless.

It sort of works. The salty brine chased by a horseradish reduction certainly brings her back to the current moment. And then she and Gwen are tasting all the options. She's trying caviar for the first time, in its bursting brine with smooth goat cheese on a toast point. She's cracking crab clumsily while Mother, Lord Havenfort, and Gwen seem to do it with poise. But she doesn't care. She's swimming in butter and laughter and lust, and if she could stay right here forever, she just might.

Her mother giggles at something Lord Havenfort whispers in her ear. The four of them clustered around oysters is the happiest she's seen her mother in—long enough it would be sad to consider too closely.

And she finds to her surprise it's the happiest she's felt in quite some time too. Everything is better with the Havenforts, she decides, laughing as Gwen noisily slurps butter off her crab leg.

Everything is better with Gwen.

Chapter Twelve

Gwen

It's exquisite torture.

Sitting beside Beth in the darkened theater, bodies pressed together and skirts rustling between them, hands resting demurely in their laps lest they bump together on the armrest. All night it's been heated glances and suppressed blushes fueled by oysters and champagne and their parents' delighted laughter.

Somehow, while they've been . . . falling for each other? Their parents have fallen deeper. This is absolutely a date, and it's going exceedingly well.

Gwen glances over and watches with fascination as Father drops his hand below his seat and Lady Demeroven quickly meets it with her own, their hands clasping out of sight, gloveless and intimate.

Gwen swallows hard and turns her attention back to the stage, even more aware of her extremities. Of how she could so innocently touch Beth's foot with her own beneath their mountain of skirts.

Of how easily she could slip her hand between them, taking Beth's own. Or how she could splay her hand on Beth's knee, hidden in the fabric of her skirts. She takes a chance to sneak a look at Beth and finds her equally flushed, but her eyes are still resolutely settled on the stage. Gwen watches her for as long as she dares before looking back at the performance.

Don Giovanni is serenading, but she can't focus. She's restless and a little overwarm, and her father is whispering on her other side. If anyone is watching their private box, the widower and widow Havenfort and Demeroven are certainly getting cozy.

Their daughters, however . . .

Gwen nearly groans, slouching in her seat. And then she jerks forward, straight-backed again. Beth's gloveless fingers brush at her knee, glancing against the bend beneath her skirts. Gwen sucks on her cheek, trying to continue looking unaffected even as she holds her breath, slipping off her own gloves. Her heart hammers as she lowers her hand.

Their fingers tangle together instantly, warm and tight and wriggling, and Gwen feels heat rise all the way from her belly button to her scalp. Such a silly, simple, innocent connection feels like a lightning bolt, like frisson, like fire. Beth leans toward her and Gwen slowly shifts to do the same so they're shoulder to shoulder in their seats, their hands disappeared between them, tangled and gripping.

Time seems to expand and contract at once. The show continues below them, haunting and melodic and epic. But there in their seats, everything is narrowed to their point of connection. Gwen forgets entirely to pay their equally flustered parents any mind, focused only on the feeling of Beth's hand in hers.

Beth's wide eyes and flushed chest at dinner soothed her

worries, but now, with their fingers threaded together, knuckles knocking, shallow breath rising and falling almost in tandem—Beth *wants her back*.

Myriad fantasies explode across Gwen's mind. She could pull Beth from her seat, run to the lavatory. They could crowd behind a pillar and kiss until the show ends. Or better, they could run out of the opera house and never look back at all. Escape to Gwen's country estate and live in her tree house. Or they could escape all the way to Paris, work menial jobs and live together in a boardinghouse. Two seamstresses unconcerned by society, unnoticed by the rich, living in peace together, lying together every night.

Gwen's so caught up in her imagination and the stroke of Beth's thumb along the side of her hand that she nearly misses the end of the performance. People are standing and clapping below them. Her father and Lady Demeroven have separated to stand and clap as well.

But Gwen doesn't want to let go of Beth, and Beth seems to feel the same, the two of them rising carefully, secretively, still pressed close. They don't clap, but they smile, hands still hidden between their skirts. They sneak furtive glances throughout the long bows. There's a world outside and around them that won't abide even the holding of their hands, but it doesn't much seem to matter in their little box.

Gwen doesn't want to think about anyone else—doesn't want to leave this stolen moment for the practicalities of their actual lives. She wants to savor the feeling of Beth's palm tight against her own—a quiet, private pleasure. Of course, eventually the applause dies down and they're forced to separate, forced to turn and smile, following their parents out of the box and into the press of people exiting the opera house, as if nothing has happened at all.

Gwen at least takes the opportunity to press up against Beth, hand on her hip to keep them both steady as they descend the stairs. Lady Demeroven is chattering to Father about the orchestrations and the vibrato on the actor playing Don Giovanni. Gwen catches Father's smile, the way his hand glances off the small of Lady Demeroven's back much in the same way Gwen is using the tumult to touch Beth.

How strange to see it this way—as if they are suddenly alike in this somehow. Sneaking touches and secret smiles. He does look happy. Surely some of it is the drink, and the lingering excitement of securing the votes—his pride and excitement shouldn't be discounted. She watches the soft look he gives Beth's mother as they're jostled about in the atrium, all four of them pressed close and gripping hands to stay together. It's not quite as romantic now that they're all claustrophobic and sweaty.

But then they burst outside into the cool early summer air. A gust of wind rustles their dresses and musses Father's hair before he can get his top hat onto his head. Lady Demeroven eyes him fondly and Gwen takes in their clear relaxation. Father hates crowds as much as Gwen does, but seems to hate them distinctly less with Lady Demeroven underfoot.

Gwen sees a golden opportunity bubble up and gives it no more than a passing thought before opening her mouth. "Father, might Beth stay over tonight? We've barely gotten to discuss the opera at all and haven't seen each other all week."

Beth goes still beside her, her fingers curling into Gwen's elbow, gripping hard. But Gwen ignores it—ignores the broader implications and the butterflies in her stomach—ignores the impropriety teetering at the edge of her thoroughly rational request.

"Of course, if Lady Demeroven doesn't mind," Father says after a moment, turning to smile at Lady Demeroven.

"Beth?" Lady Demeroven asks.

"Please," Beth says eagerly, stepping closer to Gwen so they can both smile serenely at their parents. "I promise I can be home for breakfast."

"Oh, why don't you join us for breakfast instead, Lady Demeroven," Father says smoothly. "We'll drop you off at yours and my driver can pick you up in the morning, then perhaps we can all head to the game?"

Right, there's a cricket match they've agreed to attend, together, somehow. After a week of no time at all, suddenly their families are the closest of friends.

"Perfect," Lady Demeroven says, allowing Father to escort them toward the street, where their carriage waits among a sea of others.

Beth and Gwen trail behind, arms curled tight together. Gwen glances at Beth, who meets her gaze and then skids her eyes away, a blush climbing her cheeks. There's nothing innocent about the invitation, is there? She can hardly believe Father's allowed it.

Then again, perhaps he doesn't truly mind. What is affection between female friends, to him? Especially between two friends who can never be more than that—never more than passing companions.

But Gwen won't think on it tonight. Tonight is like an evening out of time, ethereal and fleeting. Magic seems to float on the air as they pile into the carriage, Father and Lady Demeroven pressed close on one bench, Gwen and Beth on the other. They're all pink cheeks and giggles, even Father.

What a strange collection they make. But Gwen sinks into the camaraderie as best she can, gripping at Beth's hand beneath their skirts. They chat with their parents about the opera. Well, their parents chat. Gwen notices Beth has as little to say about the quality of the production as she does.

Somehow, though she knows Father and Lady Demeroven had their own exchange of subtle caresses, they were still able to pay attention. Perhaps it comes with age, or practice, or they're better liars than she or Beth will ever be. She doesn't remember if the main soprano had a vibrato or not. It could all have been utter drivel, and she wouldn't have noticed.

Then they're at the Demeroven house, and Father hops down to take Lady Demeroven to the door, leaving Beth and Gwen alone in the quiet, dark, close carriage.

Gwen breathes around a rush of nerves while they both peer out the window. Is her Father going to *kiss* Lady Demeroven?

"Tonight went well, didn't it?"

Beth's voice is like a shock to Gwen's system in the quiet of the cabin. She swallows around her suddenly dry throat and manages a nod. "Good show, whatever you did to your mother."

"I didn't do anything," Beth says, glancing back at her.

All other thoughts die on her tongue as their eyes meet. Gwen hesitates a moment before bringing her other hand up to brush at Beth's cheek. They stare at each other, coming closer, pulled like magnets, and then the carriage door jerks open.

They split apart, their hands separating to fiddle anxiously with their skirts as Father climbs back into the carriage. Gwen barely notices there's lip stain on his cheek as he smiles at them. She attempts to look unruffled, at ease, casual.

She's invited Beth to spend the night. Oh, God, but what does that *mean*?

CHAPTER THIRTEEN

Beth

The Havenfort London home is massive. Gwen's always spoken about it as this standard, boring manor, but the foyer on its own could fit half of Beth and Mother's townhouse. The floors are marbled and gleaming, all of the sconces lit and throwing shimmering patterns along the columns that rise up the walls. She's sure the price of the paintings alone could rival her dowry, just in this room.

"Come on," Gwen says, laughing as Beth slowly spins on the threshold, oblivious to Lord Havenfort removing his hat and coat beside them. "Let me show you around."

"Don't stay up too late," Lord Havenfort says, and Beth blinks, allowing Gwen to turn her to meet his false-stern expression.

"You don't stay up too late daydreaming about Lady Demeroven then," Gwen tosses back.

Beth stifles a gasp at the impertinence. She can't imagine ever saying anything like that to her father. But Lord Havenfort just chuckles and shakes his head.

"That's enough of that. Do you have everything Miss Demeroven will need?"

"Of course, more than enough," Gwen says quickly. "Sleep well."

"You two try to get any sleep at all," he counters, and Beth feels a flush rise up her cheeks, thrown back to the reality that she's probably not just here as a friend.

"Good night, Father," Gwen says firmly, but there's a lilting playfulness to her voice.

Beth watches as Lord Havenfort shakes his head and turns on his heel, loping up the stairs with an informality she never saw even once from her father.

"Don't mind him, sometimes he acts like I'm still about twelve," Gwen says, turning back to Beth. They're alone in her cavernous foyer.

"My mother's the same way, sometimes," Beth says absently, gripping at Gwen's hand as she swivels to continue taking in the space. "Some house."

Gwen laughs and pulls her in, looping her arm through Beth's to lead her toward the grand winding staircase with its carved banister and shining steps. What would Gwen think of her tiny little home? Beth has been thinking all this time that she and her mother fit into this society they're presenting her to, but how can they really, when this is Gwen's house?

How could Mother's father ever have thought Lord Havenfort wasn't a suitable match, even without the title?

"Father's father bought this place almost seventy years ago. It was one of the first homes built along the square," Gwen rattles off. Beth turns her head, trying to take in each massive portrait and painting. "Father doesn't like to spend any longer here than he needs to, but as I understand my mother enjoyed being in London more than at our country estate, and his mother was much the same."

"But it's so crowded here," Beth says softly, stumbling as they clear the first landing. The artwork is just so massive.

"Harder to see friends though, when you're away in the country," Gwen says with a little shrug. "I've never minded, but it could get lonely."

"I suppose," Beth agrees, following her up the next flight of stairs. She hadn't truly appreciated how tall the townhouse was from the outside, preoccupied as she was with the true nature of this visit.

That thought settles heavy in her stomach as they come up on the second landing and Gwen begins to lead her down a long broad hallway full of closed doors and landscapes. This must be her . . . wing.

Gwen's arm slips from hers and her hand trails down to catch Beth's fingers, squeezing. They come to a stop at the last door on the hall and Beth wonders if Gwen can hear the slam of her heart.

"This is me," Gwen says, opening the door.

Beth hesitates there at the threshold, eager to move forward, terrified too. She peers into the room, smiling at the clutter and the few petticoats and sets of gloves scattered all about.

Gwen tugs gently on her arm and Beth shuffles forward with her into the room, staring around as Gwen softly shuts the door behind them. Their beds are so similar—white and piled high with a comforter and blankets and a mass of useless pillows. Gwen's four-poster curtains are green, while Beth's are blue, but there's something comforting in the familiarity.

The rest of her furniture is a pristine white—vanity, armoires, and even a small bookcase stacked high with books and knickknacks. There are pieces of clothing just about everywhere, though Beth can tell someone's been in by the pile of folded skirts and petticoats sitting out on the armoire.

"It's messy," Gwen admits, stepping close, their hands still clasped.

"It's lovely," Beth counters. It's lived in, she thinks, smiling as she turns to meet Gwen's look.

Gwen's sucking on her cheek, face a bit pink, and looking about as awkward and unsure as Beth feels. "I can have Mrs. Gilpe set up the guest room if you'd prefer, but you're—"

She's not sure why she does it, or from where she gets the gumption, but the door is closed, and they're alone, and she will absolutely not spend the night—their only night?—sleeping down the hall.

Instead, she leans in and presses her mouth clumsily to Gwen's, using her free hand to cup her cheek and pull her in. Gwen startles, but recovers almost instantly, deepening their kiss and releasing her hand to take Beth by the hips and pull her closer so they're pressed up against each other, a clash of lace and tulle and hoops at awkward angles.

Beth smiles against her mouth and turns them, backing Gwen into the door. Gwen laughs and Beth grins, arching onto her toes to apply a little pressure. It's not a wine barrel, but it will have to do for retribution, even if since Beth's the shorter of the two it's not quite so domineering, especially with all the skirts between them.

Gwen allows it anyway, sighing as Beth breaks from her mouth to lave kisses down her jaw and throat, like Gwen did days ago to her. She's soft and warm against Beth's lips, her perfume pervading her senses. Beth skates her lips around to the other side and moves up to nibble on Gwen's ear. She's been thinking of it all week when she lies in bed—the feeling, the sounds, the press of hands and lips and teeth.

"So you don't want the guest room, then?" Gwen asks, breathless.

Beth pulls back to meet her gaze. "Did you invite me over to put me in the guest room?" Beth asks, surprised by the strength of her voice. Her whole body feels like melted chocolate.

"Not on your life," Gwen says, yanking at her hips to pull her close before she pushes them both further into the room. "There's more than enough bed for both of us."

"Good," Beth says, tugging her down with the hands she has cradled around Gwen's jaw until they're kissing again in the middle of the room. It's heady and splendorous and the longer they kiss the better it gets, like they're both learning and advancing and chasing the same inexorable pleasure.

"God, get this off of me," Gwen mumbles into her mouth.

Beth pulls back, laughing and stunned. Gwen's lips are plumped and red, her cheeks flushed, blond hair falling from her elegant updo to frame her face in whisps. She looks beautiful and a bit debauched, and Beth finds her hesitance sliding away altogether. Gwen is letting Beth see her this way—make her this way. Everything beyond this room tonight no longer matters. It's just them together, and Gwen's right, the skirts absolutely must go.

"Spin," Beth says, smiling as Gwen grins at her.

She turns in Beth's arms and Beth tries to make quick work of undoing her eyelets, but her hands are shaking. She takes a deep breath, trying to steady herself. This is Gwen, beautiful, funny, kind Gwen. She needn't be nervous. But damn, these things are small.

"Jesus," she mutters as she fumbles at another clasp.

Gwen snorts. "Do you need more light?"

"I'm perfectly capable," Beth says, managing two eyelets in quick succession before getting stuck on the third. "How much do you like this dress?"

"Do not rip it," Gwen says on a laugh, her body quaking beneath Beth's hands. "Honestly."

"Fine," Beth says, bending down to peer at the clasp and work it until she's able to separate the hook from the seat and make her way to the end of Gwen's bodice. "Success," she crows, helping Gwen slip her arms from the capped sleeves and then lift the bodice and skirt up and away from her hoop, petticoat, and corset. Gwen tosses them toward the vanity, where they land in a heap. They both giggle.

"Your turn," Gwen says, reaching out to take Beth gently by the hips and spin her so she can work her way down the row of buttons at Beth's back.

Beth shudders as Gwen's fingers trip along her spine, deft and quick. She'd be embarrassed by her own fumbling fingers if Gwen's fingertips against her skin didn't send little zips and tingles flitting across her body.

"I love buttons," Gwen murmurs as she undoes the bottom one and then slides her hands beneath the back of the bodice, wrapping around Beth's middle and pulling her back into Gwen's chest. She plants a wet, languid kiss to Beth's neck, sucking gently on her pulse.

Beth moans, eyes opening wide to take in the picture they make in the vanity mirror: Gwen in her underthings, wrapped around Beth as her dress slowly falls off her stays. Beth works her arms from her sleeves so she can wrap her hands around Gwen's arms, leaning back into her and meeting Gwen's eyes in the mirror.

They stare at each other, curled close, cheeks and chests flushed, hair in ruins already, mouths rubbed raw, smiles on both of their faces. She wants to sear this moment into her mind forever.

"Off," Gwen whispers, regretfully stepping back to gather Beth's skirt.

Beth raises her arms, shivering as the satin glides up and over her head, brushing against every heightened nerve ending. Gwen tosses Beth's dress with equal glee so it lands atop her own. Beth grins, moving immediately to wrap her arms around Gwen's waist and undo her petticoat and hoop. Gwen does the same. They share a few delighted minutes of breathless kisses and tugging strings, petticoats tossed over their shoulders.

Beth grunts triumphantly as she manages to release Gwen's hoop first, grinning against her lips as it clatters to the floor. Not to be outdone, Gwen's fingers make fast work of Beth's and it follows with a whump, the two of them left standing in the innermost circles of their hoop cages, arms around each other even as their hips remain two feet apart.

They separate and stand straight, taking each other in for the first time. It's just them in their drawers, chemises, and stays, and Beth feels a change in the air. Gwen holds out a hand and together they step out of their hoops and shuffle close to the bed. Gwen leans in and sips a gentle kiss from Beth's lips, her fingers slowly undoing the clasps of Beth's corset.

Beth shivers at each small jerk, the playfulness of the past few minutes dropping away to the import of this moment. Gwen reaches the last clasp and gently peels the corset from Beth's chemise, tossing it onto their pile of skirts. She deepens the kiss, hands immediately starting to wend around Beth's waist. But Beth's desperate to keep them at the same level, petticoat for petticoat, stay for stay. She sucks on Gwen's bottom lip as she roughly tugs open the front clasps on Gwen's corset, smiling at Gwen's startled gasp and laugh.

She didn't know women could be rough together, could be playful together, could be heated and wanting and clutching together until Gwen kissed her at the party. And now, now she's about to know all the other things they could do together. Where she was content to sip kisses and tug at skirts minutes ago, now she wants them both together on Gwen's absurdly plush bed. She wants to know what Gwen tastes like everywhere.

The thought startles her as she throws Gwen's corset behind her. She pulls back and they stare at each other, heady, both of them in their thin chemises and drawers, nothing else between them but two layers of cloth. They teeter there, something crackling between them, and then there's a knock on the door.

It splits the silence like a gunshot and they wrench apart, stumbling over their skirts. By the time the door opens, Beth's across the room and Gwen's leaning against the armoire by the door. They're the picture of suspicion and the tall, imposing woman who steps into the room with a heating pan and a pitcher of water looks between them with raised eyebrows.

"For the night," she says simply, handing Gwen the pitcher before striding to the bed to place the pan beneath the comforter. She turns and surveys the mess of their dresses and hoops and clicks her tongue. "You might think of hanging those so they don't wrinkle and you don't trip to your death overnight," she offers before exchanging a look with Gwen and leaving the room.

The door shuts with a firm snick behind her and Gwen and Beth stare at each other. Gwen clutches at the water pitcher, her cheeks stained bright red, while Beth fiddles with her chemise. Could the housekeeper tell? Is it normal to enter and find skirts all over the room, or will this stand out as strange, make people ask questions?

Gwen slowly puts the pitcher on the bedside table and then plops down onto the edge of her bed, looking out at the shambles they've made of the room. Beth takes a shallow breath, suddenly desperate for a way to distract herself from her racing thoughts.

She hurries forward and begins gathering up their dresses, spinning with both in her arms for somewhere to hang them. Gwen snorts and stands, guiding her toward the armoire and opening it to hand her two hangers. Together they wrestle the delicate dresses into the armoire and then turn to the rest of their discarded skirts.

They move as a team, sorting their hoops into organized piles by the armoire and picking up petticoats. They lay them over the vanity chair. Such a simple action, but Beth feels like it speaks volumes, their underthings there, together, atop each other.

They stand staring at the pile of their skirts. Beth can feel the brush of Gwen's chemise against her own, close but not close enough. But where she felt confident a few minutes ago, the appearance of the housekeeper has swallowed up her nerve and she doesn't know how to return to their little bubble—to banish thoughts of what the housekeeper might think, or Lord Havenfort, or Mother for that matter.

"You're shivering."

Beth shudders as Gwen's hand glides down her back. "Oh," she says, blinking at her own stupidity.

Gwen merely smiles, guiding her toward the far side of the bed and throwing back the covers. She turns Beth and nudges at her until she sits down. Beth laughs as Gwen pulls the covers over her, tucking her up tight, before scampering around the bed to crawl in on the opposite side.

And then it's not so funny, both of them there beneath the covers, warmed by the heating pan, nothing but their chemises and the mounds of feathered down to separate them. Beth lies still for a moment, unsure and wanting and nervous, and then Gwen's hand reaches out to take hers, squeezing. With the press of her fingers Beth feels the surety she felt in the wine cellar, the desperate yearning to follow Gwen and pounce on her—to chase her into the garden and press her into the hedgerows.

And with nothing else to do, and no more graceful ideas, Beth gathers her courage and does just that.

Chapter Fourteen

Gwen

Gwen squeaks as Beth lunges at her there amongst her blankets and sheets and pillows. But the sudden press of her body isn't at all unwelcome. Gwen happily settles beneath her, accepting her weight and her kiss and making use of their hideaway beneath the blankets to run her hands everywhere, everywhere she hasn't been able to yet.

Where they were both playful before, now they're equally desperate, hands and teeth and tongues, grabbing and pulling and squirming against each other frantically, as if there isn't a single second more and they're to be ripped from each other in the next moment.

The thought slows Gwen's pace. They're safe alone in her bedroom, everyone else asleep, and they've nothing but time. As much as the desperate, feverish kisses stir in her belly and warm her from toes to ears, she doesn't want this to be some fumbling mess between them.

She doesn't want to think about tomorrow—about how this could be the first and last time they're together this way. But she allows herself to know that this matters, and they must make the most of this moment, not toss it away in fraught panic.

And so Gwen sucks in the deepest breath she can amid all

the teeth and tongue and fabulous sensation, and slides her hands purposefully, one still cradling Beth's jaw as they kiss, the other skimming firmly down her side. Beth gasps at the pressure and her legs contract, straddled on either side of Gwen's hips, pressing down tight. Beth pulls back just far enough for them to meet each other's eyes.

"Um," Beth says, lips plump and red, hair in disarray. They never bothered to try taking down their hair.

Gwen laughs, reaching up to smooth one of the dozens of flyaways from her face. "You're beautiful," she says.

Beth blushes further, lifting one of the hands braced by Gwen's head to trace the line of her jaw. It shoots tingles up and down Gwen's spine. "*You're* beautiful," she counters.

Gwen smiles and then lowers her hands, rucking up Beth's chemise, raising a brow. Beth's flush deepens but she nods, shivering as Gwen slides it up her torso, her fingers trailing along forbidden, newly freed skin.

And then the damn thing catches on Beth's hair. They groan and laugh, stuck there beneath the blankets, Beth's head lost in her chemise, pins poking them both.

"Christ," Gwen mutters, giggling as Beth squirms against her, the sensation as playful as it is arousing. "Here, sit up."

She maneuvers them both up so Beth is cradled in her lap, the blankets curled around them. She has enough room now to carefully lift the chemise away from Beth's artfully piled hair. She tosses the garment away triumphantly and then looks back at Beth.

The candlelight glints off her skin in a soft glow. Gwen takes in the small swell of her breasts, the long line of her neck, the peak of her nipples, the dip of her navel. She's like a goddess, and she's there, in Gwen's lap, staring back at her. What on earth does she do with her *hands*?

Gwen curls her fingers at her sides, itching to reach out, to run her fingertips everywhere, and trail them with her lips, taste every inch of Beth's exposed skin until she's a moaning puddle of want and mess and desire. But she can't quite seem to move.

Beth blows out a little laughing breath, and Gwen startles as hands cup her jaw, guiding her mouth up. The press of their lips unfreezes her and Gwen lets her hands come to rest softly on Beth's hips, delighting in the juxtaposition there between her drawers and the satin of her skin.

Beth sighs against her, lips parting to suck on Gwen's bottom lip. Gwen finds her hands moving of their own accord, tracing upward. She trails her palms along Beth's flanks, drinks in her slight shudder and the shifting of her hips against Gwen's own. She slowly glides her hands around to rest against Beth's stomach, swirling her fingers around Beth's belly button.

Beth giggles against her lips but doesn't break their kiss, and Gwen files her ticklishness away for later, too intent to explore the rest of her to settle there, despite the beauty in her laughter. She takes a deep breath against Beth's mouth before raising one hand to cup Beth's small rounded breast, her other gliding around to anchor on her back.

Beth arches, pulling away from her mouth only far enough to rest her forehead against Gwen's. Gwen traces the edge of her nipple, squeezes, strokes, watching every reaction, repeating anything that makes Beth gasp or twitch or wriggle. It's intoxicating, seeing that pleasure play across her face, feeling the aching softness of her skin, knowing that she can do this to Beth, can give this to Beth.

She wants to know what more she can do, what more she can elicit from this woman. So she leans Beth back, nosing down the line of her throat, pressing kisses to her soft skin. Beth moans as she lays a kiss against the top of her other breast. Gwen looks up, waiting until Beth meets her eyes before lowering her mouth to her nipple, glorying in the cry that escapes Beth's lips.

Her skin is soft and slightly rough at once, and the *sounds* she makes—Gwen could settle here, stay just like this for the rest of her days if she could simply live in the press of Beth's hips and the arch of her back and the soft delight of her flesh beneath her tongue.

But all too quickly Beth is pulling away, rucking Gwen's chemise. Gwen tries to lean inward, not ready to relinquish this moment, this discovery.

Beth huffs at her. "Off. I want to touch you too."

Her look is insistent, and though Gwen could spend the whole night simply learning the pleasure of Beth's body, she can feel her own want growing. She can't help but lift her arms, suddenly eager for more than the press of flesh against her mouth. Eager for the hips grinding into her own and the promise of them completely bare together.

Beth's hands are careful but quick. Gwen laughs as she watches Beth toss her chemise high across the room before turning back to take her in. Gwen feels like perhaps she should be modest, but now that she's known what it's like to touch

Beth, all she wants is to know her touch in return—can't be shy when she wants those hands on her so desperately.

Beth doesn't disappoint, immediately trailing her fingertips from Gwen's clavicle down to her navel. Gwen shudders, but nothing tickles. There's only a tingling pleasure and overwhelming sensation as Beth learns the planes of her chest. As those smaller hands curl around her breasts, touching her in ways she's only ever touched herself. It's different, and new, but utterly, gloriously wonderful and Gwen finds she's making her own sounds now.

Their mouths crash back together as they squirm against each other. Their breath is hot and loud between them. Gwen finds her hands migrating down to Beth's hips of their own accord, tugging at the laces of her drawers and loosening them until she's able to shimmy them down her hips.

Beth lowers her hands to do the same, groaning when both of their drawers get caught against their thighs. Beth breaks from her mouth and shuffles off her. Gwen feels her loss both in warmth and the press of skin and hurries to copy her as Beth triumphantly tosses her drawers away. Gwen does the same and suddenly they're fully naked.

Beth's skin is beautiful, flushed and lovely in the firelight. They sit facing each other, chests still heaving as they look one another over. Beth's small breasts and narrow hips fit her small frame, the curls at the apex of her thighs as dark as those falling from her half-pinned hair. The contrast of light and dark is bewitching and Gwen shifts closer without thought, running a hand up Beth's leg.

The soft hair rasps against her palm and Gwen looks up to

meet Beth's eyes as she settles her hand on Beth's hip. Beth's eyes are blown wide, her lips plump, her cheeks pink. She looks so utterly beautiful it's almost painful.

"You're so pretty," Beth whispers.

Gwen shakes her head. "You are."

Beth giggles, blushing, and Gwen leans forward, pressing her lips to Beth's neck and breathing her in. She slips her hand down, down, down from Beth's hip. Beth shudders, her hands coming to grip Gwen's waist, jaw going slack beneath her lips. Gwen hums at the warm wet between Beth's thighs and gently pushes to lay her down against the sheets, the comforter now a lump in the middle of the bed.

She continues her exploration, mapping all the places that make Beth gasp, circling her fingers and making delicate patterns against the top of her. She delights in the squeaks and moans, in the flutter of Beth's eyelids, in the little flare of her nose, in the wide, searching pupils that meet her gaze.

She sips kisses from Beth's lips as she slips a single finger inside her, both of them stilling. Beth pants against her mouth. Gwen marvels at the feeling—to be so intimate, so close as to be inside another person, inside Beth. To see her unraveled this way, to hear the way her breath hitches as Gwen circles with her palm and slowly curls her finger, searches for the place inside Beth that she's found before within herself. Finding that she can know her, can know what will make her happy and give her pleasure.

Can watch in fascination and joy as Beth tips over that crest of pleasure, back arching, legs shaking, breath coming in short gasps. She slowly pulls back her hand and Beth's hips fall back to the bed, her body going lax as the wave passes.

Gwen watches Beth's eyes flutter back open. She tips her head forward again to meet Gwen's gaze, eyes heavy-lidded. Gwen smiles and leans down to press kisses to Beth's face, taking a moment to wipe her hand on the sheets before using both palms to cradle Beth's jaw.

The smell of her lingers between them and Gwen hums as Beth shifts in her hold to catch her lips in a kiss. Beth seems to regain control of her hands and suddenly they're everywhere, skimming up and down Gwen's sides before one slips between her own legs. Gwen nearly falls onto Beth in surprise, a shudder consuming her body, a herald of what's to come.

Beth smiles against her mouth and uses her other hand to shift herself upward, flipping them slowly until Gwen is pressed beneath her in a full reverse. She squirms against the sheets as Beth does her own study. Her hand is smaller, different; the rhythm, the movement, the feeling of her fingers inside of Gwen is strange and new and exhilarating. Pulsing pleasure lights up in her belly, her legs shaking, brought so close already to the edge by touching Beth and kissing Beth and feeling Beth atop her and inside her and around her.

She tries to prolong it, doesn't want this to end so soon, but Beth's finger crooks inside of her, her palm hard against the top of her, and Gwen falls over that cliff of pleasure, tight and pulsing and raw and magnificent. Gwen clutches at Beth's back, gasping as Beth continues her ministrations. The pleasure lasts, waves crashing upon waves as her hips jerk and her back tenses and her belly clenches over and over until it's so much she has to push Beth's hand away.

She blinks her eyes open only in time to see Beth's fingers slide from her mouth. She groans at the very thought—to have missed it, for it to have happened. The smell of them mingles all around and Gwen tries to come back to herself, to summon romantic words, something, anything.

All she manages is "Holy hell."

Beth snorts and falls down onto her, pressing a smacking kiss to her lips before cuddling into her, her face buried in Gwen's neck, legs laced between hers. Gwen breathes her in, wrapping her still-tingling arms about her back, hands splayed wide against her shoulders.

"That was wondrous," Beth whispers, her lips brushing Gwen's pulse.

It sends yet another shudder through her and Gwen wonders how anyone ever leaves their bed, if this is what it is to know someone else, to give and receive pleasure, to kiss and squirm and sigh. Why do they leave at all? Why not simply live like this forever?

"I love you" slips from her tongue.

Both of them still and Gwen clenches her eyes shut, mortified.

She does, she thinks, love Beth. How could she not, after what they've just done, after how it just felt, after how it feels now to lie with her here, skin cooling, pulse calming? When Beth is the first person she wants to speak to, first person she wants to see, and whose smile made her heart flutter long before they kissed? And now—the look Beth gives Gwen as she arches up, propping herself up with her arms on either side of Gwen's head—it makes Gwen's stomach flip, her toes curl.

"I love you too," Beth whispers, leaning down to press her forehead to Gwen's. "I want to stay right here forever."

Gwen grins and leans up to catch her lips, cradling her face between her palms, content to do just that. The morning will come, with its light and its reality. But now, here in the cocoon of her bed, in their love, with nothing between them, is a perfection she's never known, and she intends to savor it for as long as she can.

CHAPTER FIFTEEN

Beth

"Stop it," Beth says, laughing. Gwen continues pressing up behind her, lips skating kisses along her throat, hands on her hips, as Beth tries to finish her hair. "This is hard enough without you distracting me."

Gwen snorts and pulls back, batting Beth's hands away to place the final pins to keep her sleep-and-other-activities-mussed hair artfully piled on top of her head. Gwen's hands are gentle and precise, doing an admirable job that just makes Beth want to push her back down to the bed. But then they'd rub the makeup hiding their tired eyes into Gwen's white sheets. She already feels strange enough that they'll be laundered as they are, smelling of a mix of the two of them.

"There," Gwen announces, stepping around her to look at her hair straight on. "Perfectly acceptable."

Beth rolls her eyes and reaches up to adjust Gwen's hair as well. Her blond curls have better recovered from their tousle, but both of them still look windswept. Hopefully Mother and Lord Havenfort won't ask questions. They can simply assume Gwen and Beth were up talking all night. Which they were, of a sort, in between all of the . . . decidedly not talking.

Beth feels herself blush, images of the previous evening flitting across her mind, hot and joyful and heady.

"Stop it."

"Stop what?" Beth asks, blinking the thoughts away before she meets Gwen's eyes.

"Thinking about last night."

Beth huffs, noting the flush climbing Gwen's neck as well. "You stop."

Gwen laughs and pulls her in for a kiss. Beth squeaks, a little ungainly in her hoop after an evening in nothing but her skin. And though it's less than they were able to have in bed, it's still lovely, Gwen's hands on her cheeks, her hands gripping at Gwen's skirts. Gwen's mouth is hot against Beth's and she thinks maybe they should skip breakfast altogether, pretend to have a lie-in. Maybe actually have a—

"Lady Demeroven has arrived."

They jump apart at the firm rap on the door. Beth presses her hands to her cheeks, as if someone could tell just by looking at her what they've been doing. But the door doesn't open, and she hears footsteps retreating down the hall.

"I guess," Gwen starts.

"Right," Beth agrees, dropping her hands and forcing her shoulders down.

Time to return to the world.

She hesitates, not quite ready—unwilling to consider the greater reality, that this is likely the first and last—no, no, she can't let herself go there, or she'll weep into her breakfast.

Gwen reaches out and takes her hand, twining their fingers together. She opens the door and confidently guides Beth down the hall. It isn't so strange, to hold hands with a friend. They can get away with at least that through the halls. And so Beth focuses on the knock of their knuckles and the warmth of Gwen's palm. She lets herself be led down the staircase and through the grand entryway to the dining room.

Gwen comes to a halt so suddenly Beth bumps into her back, the two of them teetering there in the doorway to the massive dining room. She'd marvel at the enormous mahogany table set and chandelier, but it's the sight of her mother and Lord Havenfort cozily ensconced at the far end, chairs close together and hands a breath apart on the tabletop, that steals her focus.

Her mother is giggling while Lord Havenfort watches her so fondly it almost makes Beth's chest hurt. Father never looked at her mother that way, and Mother never looked that free in their own dining room. The only time she's ever been that at ease around food is in the kitchens, baking with Mrs. Mildred or taking breakfast with Beth, far from her father's reach.

Gwen's hand grips at Beth's as they watch their parents interact. Their parents, who they want to get married, so they could become—Beth swallows hard, her throat tight. They were meant to be getting their parents engaged, not engaging in . . . it themselves. Suddenly their silly plan seems to have manifested, but everything's been turned upside down.

"There you two are," Lord Havenfort says, grinning when he catches sight of them. "Come in, come in. Lady Demeroven and I were just setting the terms of our wager for the match today."

Gwen slowly drags Beth into the room, guiding her around to sit opposite Mother and dropping her hand as they get to their respective chairs. Beth feels the loss of her fingers keenly, barely able to meet her mother's happy eyes. If Mother knew what they'd done—

"Lord Havenfort seems sure that the UEE will win its match against the AEE, which I highly doubt."

"Doubt to the tune of five pounds?" Lord Havenfort teases.

"I wouldn't take that wager, Lady Demeroven," Gwen says as her father passes her a trivet of eggs. "Father wins all his cricket bets."

"Just because his father went to school with Jemmy Dean doesn't make the upstarts on the UEE good players," Mother replies primly, smiling over at Beth. "Beth and I always root for the AEE."

"Oh, do you?" Gwen asks, and Beth swallows at the playful glint in her eye. It's the same one she had before the infamous croquet debacle. "Care to make a wager of our own?"

Beth glances over at her mother, still feeling at sea. But Mother's look brooks no surrender, and she's not about to let Mother get ganged up on, even by their respective . . . whatever the Havenforts are to the Demerovens these days.

"Five pounds," Beth says, nodding as Gwen gapes. "George Parr's got the lineup all settled, and they've won every match so far this year."

"George Parr wouldn't know strategy if it bit him on the arse," Gwen returns.

"Gwen," Lord Havenfort interjects, laughing even as he tries to frown at his daughter. Mother snorts.

"He wouldn't!" Gwen defends.

"Well, no of course he wouldn't, but don't let me catch you using such language at the match. Miss Demeroven, I'm counting on you to keep her in line. You've heard her at Albie and Bobby's games."

"Oh, no, you don't heckle at the first-class matches, do you?" Beth says, hearing the whine in her voice. Mother begins to blush. "Mother does too."

"She does?" Lord Havenfort crows, grinning over as her mother slouches. "I never."

"I learned it from you!" Mother exclaims, making all of them laugh.

Beth settles in to listen as their parents bicker and explain the matches they attended twenty years ago. How they were almost expelled once for poor behavior and Mother was kept on the world's shortest leash for the next week by her governess. Beth and Gwen eat, exchanging easy smiles. It almost feels . . . normal. As if nothing happened the night before—as if their plan is simply going swimmingly, and they could all be eating at this table, taking bets and teasing as one big happy family.

But as they all sidle into the stands together hours later, freshly dressed and trussed up for a public outing, that ease disappears. In public, in the face of all that they've done, Beth feels distinctly uncomfortable.

Can people tell that they've lain together? That the way Gwen presses up against her is less than innocent? That her body still tingles with the memory of the previous night, and the blush on her cheeks has nothing to do with the heat and her skirts, and everything to do with the hand Gwen slips into her own?

Mother and Lord Havenfort pay them little mind, sitting too close together on their own and nudging back and forth as the teams step onto the field for the captains to shake hands. The stands are full to bursting, the whole ton out to see this auspicious match. The AEE under new management, the UEE still considered an upstart even five years later—the crowd is wild and she can hear more than one wager being made around them in absolute excess.

"You're going down," Gwen says firmly as the teams begin to take their positions.

"Oh, please," Beth replies, squeezing her hand. Gwen nudges her shoulder. "The UEE couldn't outsmart George if they consulted mathematicians. They've got nothing on our speed and Mortlock can hit circles around Clarke. You're doomed."

"Father swears by Clarke. I think you'll be disappointed."

"Well, he can't be right about everything," Beth counters, glancing over at Gwen's father, who's whispering to Mother in much the same way, though Beth can tell Mother's giving no quarter in return. "And he's wrong about this."

"We'll see," Gwen says, leaning against her. "If we win, you have to stay over again tonight." Her fingers slip down to skate against Beth's pulse.

"I thought the wager was five pounds," Beth says, fighting against a shiver.

She shouldn't be able to affect Beth like this, in public, with just her fingers on her wrist. But the thought of what else Gwen's fingers can do, and vivid memories of where they were just a few hours ago have Beth shifting in her seat and Gwen grinning smugly.

She doesn't know if they can manage another night together. Though with the way their parents are sitting, cozy and close, Beth thinks suddenly it might not be impossible. They simply need to get them together for a nightcap and feign exhaustion. She couldn't *possibly* haul herself all the way across the square, can't she just bunk with Gwen again? The thought makes her equally bold and she's about to lean back to Gwen and suggest their wager be exchanged for a promise of larger acts when someone taps her on the shoulder.

She turns and nearly falls out of her seat when Lord Montson appears there at her side, dapper and grinning with his top hat beneath his arm. He plops down beside her and takes her other hand, kissing its back. Gwen grips at her concealed palm.

"So glad I found you," Lord Montson says, dropping her hand to lean around her. "Lady Gwen. Lady Demeroven, Lord Havenfort," he adds.

Gwen manages a brusque nod and Beth hears Mother saying something, but she can't quite make it out around the ringing in her ears. Or maybe that's the starting pistol as the game begins reverberating around the pitch.

Lord Montson's here. Beside her. Her suitor. Likely to propose within the month. He's here, next to her, sitting there all tall and handsome, while Gwen grips at her hand with fingers that have been inside her and lips still slightly plumped from her fervid kisses and other—

Beth swallows against a massive lump in her throat. She can't escape. She just has to sit here as Lord Montson goes on and on about the AEE and their superiority. Suddenly she wants to switch allegiances. Wants to root for Gwen's team just to spite him, though he's done absolutely nothing wrong.

"I'll give you that Mortlock has the batting average, but Clarke is faster and more agile, and the UEE plays in worse conditions regularly. They'll have no trouble on a day like today. See?" Gwen says, leaning around Beth as Clarke hits over the boundary and evades all the AEE fielders to run the wickets.

Beth blinks, hasn't even been paying attention to the conversation or the game. She hadn't realized Gwen had picked up where she had failed. She's been talking amicably to Lord Montson for ten minutes, as though absolutely nothing is amiss. Their hands are still tangled together beneath their skirts, fingers gripping too hard, almost painful. But Gwen looks for all the world like everything's perfectly normal.

"That's just luck that Adams is on the bench, is all," Lord Montson tosses back. "What do you think, Miss Demeroven? You think Clarke's got them all?"

Beth struggles to find her voice, feeling Gwen's thumb brushing over her pulse again. She glances at Gwen, who simply looks back at the game. But Beth can tell from the tension in Gwen's jaw and shoulders that she knows what she's doing. Toying with her with Lord Montson right beside them.

"I think Mortlock will win us the points back on our inning, and Clarke will trip up eventually. No one can run a perfect game."

"Agreed," Lord Montson says happily, his arm brushing her shoulder as he slips a bit closer, sandwiching Beth between himself and Gwen. "We had a chap at school who would run a perfect game all the way to the end of the second inning, and then fumble, every single match. Drove us all to drink."

"I could use a drink now," Gwen whispers, turning her cheek to whisper in Beth's ear under the guise of stretching her back.

Beth just squeezes her hand and they sit and watch the match, ignoring their parents' pleasant bickering. Lord Montson comments now and then, but Beth is happy to lose him to the match's intrigue. It's a close game. AEE looks set to win, but she couldn't care less about the wagers—can't imagine how they go back to their carefree disregard for the world now, not with Lord Montson's physical presence weighing them down like an anchor.

How foolish she was to think they could just live in their happy little bubble. Reality has crashed back in and it feels like someone has sat down on her chest, squeezing the happiness and breath from her until every movement makes her jolt and she could cry from the confusion, frustration, and heat.

"You see?"

Beth startles at Lord Havenfort's bombastic crow, glancing his way to see him beaming proudly at her mother. Mother grudgingly hands him the wager, but she's still smiling. Gwen doesn't extend her hand, choosing to keep their tangled fingers beneath the mountain of their skirts instead. She doesn't boast or brag either, both of them simply sitting there, sapped of energy. Lord Montson chuckles beside her.

"Well, that was invigorating, wasn't it?" he asks. Beth manages to nod, glancing at him with a tight smile he doesn't seem to notice. "I'll send our carriage for you and your mother first thing tomorrow then."

That brings her back to the moment. "Oh?"

"For our riding outing," he adds, smiling softly at her.

"Oh, of course," she manages. "Sorry, the excitement of the game. Yes, we're looking forward to it," she continues, forcing cheer into her voice. She'd entirely forgotten they were supposed to survey his London property tomorrow. How had she forgotten that?

"Lady Demeroven, my father and mother are most excited to take tea with you while Miss Demeroven and I ride," Lord Montson adds, leaning around Beth to catch her mother's eye. "Father has much he wants to discuss."

Beth's stomach drops as Mother gives her proper excited agreement. Beth watches more than feels Lord Montson turn back to her, kiss her free hand, and tell her he looks forward to the following morning. She nods, but can barely hear him. It's like everything is moving through fog. He sets off with a jaunty grin before she can even unglue her mouth.

"Sounds like you'll be getting a proposal," Gwen says softly, her voice flat. Her fingers slip away from Beth's so she can fold her hands tight into her lap.

Beth can barely swallow, barely blink. She can't even chase after her hand. She can't move. A *proposal*.

"Oh, this is most exciting. My sincere apologies, Dashiell, but we'll need to postpone your victory dinner. Beth and I must get to the modiste, add some decor to that riding dress."

"Of course," she hears Lord Havenfort murmur. "But you must let us know how it goes. Perhaps dinner tomorrow, if you're not too tired."

"That would be lovely," Mother says, even as Beth's stomach sinks down to her feet. To go from a proposal to Gwen's dining room, after losing every last bit of joy she could have—

"Come, darling, we've no time to waste. Good day, Lady Gwen," Mother says as she slips in front of them, reaching down to take Beth's frozen hand and pull her to standing.

"Good day, Lady Demeroven, Miss Demeroven," Gwen says, her face entirely blank. Beth stares down at her.

"Gwen," she manages before Mother pulls her away.

She goes, stumbling behind her, feeling weightless and detached, as if her legs and feet and body are moving without her. She's still caught in the stands, staring into Gwen's empty eyes.

Chapter Sixteen

Gwen

The carriage ride back to their townhouse is silent. Gwen stares out the window, trying to make sense of the cacophony of thoughts in her head. Her horror, her pain, her sadness, the overwhelming feeling of guilt and regret. And yet, all she can truly focus on is the feeling of Beth's hands on her skin, and the complete peace of the two of them together. How can they give that up for *Montson*?

Father leads her from the carriage and up into their foyer. She stands there, thinking of the previous night, of taking Beth's hand and dragging her upstairs. Of how she'll never get to do that again, how last night was it. Forever.

She turns and finds herself enveloped in Father's arms. She grips at his waistcoat, burying her face in his chest, soaking up the smell of his cigars and pomade—of home and safety and childhood. It makes her wish she was still small, that he could wipe the pain away with a kiss and a sweet. That he could swing her about by her arms and make her feel like she was flying and banish all bad thoughts away.

When it was just the two of them in her heart, and she needed nothing else at all. No one else.

He pulls back after a long moment and holds her by her

shoulders, ducking his head to meet her eyes with a sad smile. "It'll be all right, you'll see."

But she's not four anymore, and he can't fix this with a smile and a promise. "It won't."

Father sighs, considering her. "There can be more space in a marriage. You'll remain friends. He'll have to spend much of his time in London, and when he does, you can visit Beth in the country. It's . . . normal for ladies to have companions. You'll see her more than you think."

Gwen watches his face, sees him trying so hard to make this right for her. But is that what she wants? To be a spinster—to be in love with someone married to another, kept as a dirty secret—a *companion*? To be known to the world as the sad little friend who keeps company in the country? To be only a friend, forever?

"Would you do it?" she wonders.

Father blinks. "What?"

"If Lady Demeroven had married her husband and kept you on as a companion, to visit and lie with her when he was away, would you have done it?"

Her father's face hardens for a moment, anger coming over him, before he takes a deep breath. He can be mad at the insinuation all he likes. She wants to know. Would he be content with this arrangement—to be a tawdry secret behind closed doors, second to a wife or a husband?

She knows that it's her only option. Even were Beth financially settled, even if Gwen herself could inherit her father's title, there's no place for them together in the ton. No place for them together in the country, or anywhere. Two women cannot run a house, own land, live together and lie together in public view. Companions, yes. But there is no marriage for two women.

She doesn't want to be a secret, to be second to *Lord Montson* of all people. To know Beth has felt his touch. To lie in the bed she's lain in with him.

"Would you do it?" she asks again.

"No," Father says softly.

"Then don't ask me to," Gwen says, pulling from his hold.

She can't take the look in his eyes, the heartbreak on his face. She doesn't want to make him hurt for her, when he's been hurt enough by the Demerovens himself.

Instead she shuts herself up in her room. She stares at her crisply made bed, linens changed. At her tidied vanity, rearranged from the mess of last night. The pins she and Beth took from their hair are mixed together in her late mother's dish. She doesn't know which belong to her and which to Beth. She falls heavily onto the chair in front of the vanity, staring at this stupid pile of metal.

She knew the risks when she kissed Beth. She knew this was a pain charging at them when she invited her to stay last night. Knew it when they kissed, and undressed, and touched in her bed. Knew it as they came to know each other more intimately than she's known anyone else—more intimately than she thinks she will ever know another person.

But knowing doesn't make it easier. It feels like someone is prying her chest apart, ripping her open from the inside out and burrowing at her innards. Like a weight has settled upon her shoulders and the world has grown dimmer in just a few hours.

Gwen growls at herself and stands, ripping pins out of her hair for something to do with all of her hurt.

She wrestles her way out of her dress. Tosses her petticoat across the room. Undoes her hoop and leaves it in a pile on the floor. But the sight of her clothes, rumpled and scattered, just like her things were mixed with Beth's last night, makes her stall out.

She stands there torn between heart-wrenching sadness and a deep, pervasive feeling of emptiness. Like all the good feelings she's ever had have left and now there's just a hollow pit in her chest.

How does she move on from here?

The door opens, but she can't quite tear her eyes away from the pile of clothing on the floor—from the dress she was wearing when the sky caved in.

It's only when hands gently loosen her laces that she seems to come back to herself. Mrs. Gilpe turns her by the shoulders, wrapping her up tight, and Gwen presses her face into her shoulder. Mrs. Gilpe sways them side to side, like she used to when Gwen was small. She's always been stern and uncompromising, but in these moments, she's soft and warm and so so safe.

"Come, let's get you into something comfortable. Sally's bringing up your favorite biscuits."

Gwen feels a genuine smile spread over her face and lets Mrs. Gilpe help her put on a fresh petticoat. They layer an old housedress on top, comfortable and worn. And by the time they've gotten her hair down, Gwen feels like she can breathe again.

Mrs. Stelm slips into the room with a tray of warm biscuits and tea for three. Bless both of them. "Your father thought you could use some comfort," Mrs. Stelm explains as she places everything onto the bedside table and shoos Gwen onto her bed.

Gwen smiles as Mrs. Stelm and Mrs. Gilpe climb up as well, reminding her of when she was small and they would tell stories. Mrs. Gilpe rarely joined them, but it was always so lovely when she did. Comfortable and close and like family.

Mrs. Stelm holds out a biscuit, and Gwen takes it, biting into the buttery shortbread and spilling crumbs onto her dress. She feels her shoulders come down as she chews and gamely takes another one when offered. The food does help. After a few minutes and some gulps of tea, she feels almost human again.

The sadness hasn't lifted, but she feels like she's back inside her own head now, can feel the rise and fall of her chest and the soft mattress beneath her. She sinks against her pillows, pulling her knees up to her chest as she looks at Mrs. Gilpe and Mrs. Stelm, who simply watch her with glum smiles.

"A little better?" Mrs. Stelm asks.

Gwen nods. "Thank you."

Mrs. Gilpe smiles and holds out a hand for Mrs. Stelm to pass her a biscuit. Mrs. Stelm rolls her eyes, grabbing three and passing only one to Mrs. Gilpe. Gwen laughs.

"Spoilsport," Mrs. Gilpe mutters.

Mrs. Stelm giggles and breaks the third cookie in half, passing that over as well. Mrs. Gilpe grins and leans in to kiss her cheek. It's so fast Gwen could have missed it, but Mrs. Stelm blushes a little, the two of them sitting closer than she realized. They're happy together, serving and sleeping together. Living this life they've found a way to share.

There must be a way she and Beth could be together like this, always. *Companions* she hears in her head and frowns. She doesn't want them together around Montson. She just wants them together.

"Do you regret it?" Mrs. Gilpe asks, the question loud against the quiet room.

"No," Gwen says, the answer immediate and firm. She wouldn't give up last night for anything. To know that joy—even if this is the heartache she feels forever as a result—it's worth having known it even once.

"Then it's worth the pain," Mrs. Gilpe says easily.

"You'll know happiness again," Mrs. Stelm adds. "Companions can build their lives as they please. Your father would surely finance a few more years for you before you find a match, and perhaps you could settle close to Miss Demeroven."

Gwen feels her stomach clench. It's one thing to grapple with the idea of Beth and Montson together. She doesn't think she can bear the thought of herself with a man. She doesn't think she could ever—the way Beth touched her, the way it felt—she couldn't do that with a man, couldn't feel that with a man.

"There are worse ways to live a happy life," Mrs. Gilpe adds.

Gwen sighs. "It's not fair," she says, wincing at how petulant and petty she sounds. She's no child. *Fair* is not something she's ever expected out of the world.

But she didn't expect Beth either. Didn't expect to feel this way. To know that beyond simply being a woman—second class, chattel, property—she could feel even less like a person in the eyes of society. These wants, these new needs, no one will respect them, save the women on her bed and her father.

"Your father loves you," Mrs. Stelm says. "And we love you. And no, it isn't fair. But you won't be thrown in prison."

"That's a grim silver lining," Mrs. Gilpe agrees.

Gwen blows out a breath, trying to find her resolve and her fortitude. Tries to find some gratitude that this only costs her

her happiness, not her life. But all she wants to do is rail at God for the injustice of all of it. Of a title she can't inherit, of a husband she needs for security, of a love that cannot exist and a lover who will belong to someone else in far too many ways.

She searches for words and comes up short, exhausted and overwhelmed by it all. Mrs. Stelm smiles softly and hands her another biscuit, waiting until Gwen takes her first mouthful.

"So was it wonderful?"

Gwen chokes, spluttering as she coughs. Mrs. Gilpe whacks at Mrs. Stelm, all three of them laughing.

"It was . . . lovely," Gwen manages when she can take in air, wiping at her crumby mouth.

"We'll have to gussy you up for that dinner tomorrow, see if you can't get a repeat performance."

Gwen blushes even as she winces. She doesn't know how they could lie together with the specter of Lord Montson's proposal over them. But she also wouldn't want to give up the opportunity.

"She's awfully short," Mrs. Gilpe says.

Gwen blinks at her. "What?"

"She's very short, and small. Just saying."

"So it doesn't matter if it's a man or a woman, you're going to judge them either way, hmm?" Gwen says.

Mrs. Gilpe grins. "Of course, dear. It's our right."

"Yes, we don't care who you're kissing. It's the kissing we must tease about," Mrs. Stelm adds.

Gwen groans.

"And you did quite a lot of that," Mrs. Gilpe says, reaching out to turn Gwen's cheek, exposing the love bite she hid with makeup this morning. "My goodness, you're grown women. Keep those where they can't be seen."

Gwen laughs and pushes her away, blushing up to her ears. Mrs. Stelm and Mrs. Gilpe start going on about the mess from last night and how cute Gwen and Beth do look together.

And even as she knows it cannot last, and even as the grief of tomorrow looms ahead of her, Gwen lets herself be briefly lost in their lighthearted teasing—in the idea that Beth could be someone they tease and toy about, who they can embarrass her about, like aunts crowing over a man. She should take her happinesses as she can, for she knows they'll be forever fleeting. But at least she'll have them.

CHAPTER SEVENTEEN

Beth

Beth stares out at London, watching the distant carriages rumble along the city outskirts and the smoke rise from untold numbers of chimneys. The city stretches out before them like a winding industrial labyrinth and Beth finds herself wishing she could simply escape into it and never return.

Because the Ashmond lands are gorgeous. Apparently the estate by the Peak District is five times as large, with its own lake and farmland and orchard. But the estate just outside of London is splendid enough. Miles of riding trails both on and off the property they're given leave to use, and with the trees in full bloom and the greenery, it's absolutely stunning. She'll admit she's entirely taken by the land.

Lord Montson's been gentlemanly to a fault all afternoon, accommodating and cheerful. She's listened as he details the land, the value, their normal schedules, and everything to do with his family. Part of her mind has dutifully noted down the various aunts and uncles and relations she should know, kept track of every detail. But the larger part of her has been off in a daydream, wishing it was her and Gwen out riding instead.

Wishing she's simply fallen asleep in Gwen's arms and this is all just a nightmare. For though the berm on which they've stopped provides a wonderful view, and though Lord Montson is a lovely man, and though she'd be richer than God and have every luxury, Beth wants nothing to do with any of it.

She can hear their chaperones behind them, a pair of stable hands tasked with following at a discreet distance. They're chatting about crop yields, she thinks. She'd rather discuss that than continue to discuss the Ashmond family as if it's about to be her own.

Because it is. Their parents are at the house, and his father is discussing the terms of the arrangement with Mother now. Taking tea in the vaulted library with its massive shelves—two months ago, Beth would have happily said yes based on the books alone. Lord Montson *is* a kind man with land, and titles, and status, and security. He is everything—*this* is everything they wanted, and more than she and her mother could ever have hoped to get.

"What do you think?"

Beth looks over and finds Lord Montson waiting eagerly, arms outstretched at the view. "It's amazing," she says honestly.

He grins, so pleased by her approval. He's charming and kind and seems genuinely interested and invested in her opinion. He's perfect, and she still feels thoroughly empty inside about him.

"When I can see it like this, it always makes me long for the country, with nothing around for miles."

"But then you can't see the hustle and bustle and be glad you're not in it," she returns, watching as he chuckles.

"Entirely fair. Do you think you'd miss it?"

"The city?"

"Of course, I have to spend some of the year here, but I do

prefer the country. Would you miss the city, staying north for most of the year?"

"Not at all," she says quickly. "I don't enjoy London, much less the season. But I would miss my friends," she says, her chest aching at the thought of calling Gwen something as mundane as *friend*.

"They could come visit," he says gamely. "Anytime you wish. And then you could even stay at home when I return for the parliament season if you liked."

"You wouldn't mind?" Beth asks, her breath catching at the thought.

"Not at all. My father is always at the club making deals and negotiating. It's dead boring for my mother. I wouldn't want to subject you to that unless you had friends in town as well."

"That's very kind of you," Beth says softly, her stomach clenching.

She could keep Gwen.

They could spend much of the year together at the estate. Avoiding Lord Montson's mother, she supposes, but still. The two of them, cosseted in the country, away from prying eyes. Running across the magnificent Ashmond lands, rolling through the forests, splayed out in enormous beds—

"And of course, there would be space for your mother. She could live in your wing, if you both agreed, or there are a few guesthouses that could be staffed for her. I don't know if you'd want to bring any of your staff as well."

"Miss Wilson, certainly," Beth says softly, a leaden weight starting to lift from her chest.

They set off at a slow amble back toward the house. Lord Montson returns to prattling about his various relatives and their massive estates. Beth's mind whirs dizzily. She could have some kind of life with Gwen.

They could be near-constant companions. There's nothing else for them to be, really. And with this arrangement she'll have the money to spoil Gwen silly. To build up a corner of the world just for the two of them.

She'd so much rather marry Gwen, even if it meant their ruin. But she has Mother to consider. This sets Mother up. This provides for them both. It's not the future she would choose, if she had the choice. But given what she has . . .

Hope fills her heart as they wend back through the house. She and Gwen are good at scheming. They'll find ways to spend nearly all their time together. She'll architect a life that contains as little of Lord Montson as possible, and fill all the empty space with Gwen.

She'll get to have Gwen. She could almost do cartwheels.

She's pulled from her plans when Lord Montson throws open the doors to the massive library. Beth breathes in the scent of the books, almost giddy. But then her shoulders rise, spotting Mother with the earl and countess. Lord Montson's tall, but Lord Ashmond is even taller and broader, a beast of a man. She wonders if his wife finds that attractive, or if she too feels intimidated, and even a little threatened when he looms over her.

Lord Montson guides Beth into the room and they come to stand at the end of the low table that separates his parents' two armchairs from her mother's settee. Beth dips in what feels like a very unsteady curtsy and smiles as brightly as she can manage.

"I hope Harry showed you the best of the grounds," Lord Ashmond says, his deep voice reverberating around them.

"He did," Beth says, looking between Lord and Lady Ashmond. "Your lands and your home are so beautiful."

"We're delighted you approve," Lord Ashmond says. "Unfortunately, Harry, we must be going. But, we have arranged for the two of you to meet in four days' time. That should be more than long enough to have everything finalized with the solicitor. Say your goodbyes, son, and we'll take our leave. Lady Demeroven," he says, nodding to Mother, who curtsies.

Lord Montson takes Beth's hand and kisses it, grinning at her. "I'll see you soon," he promises, looking so absurdly cheerful.

She nods, keeping that pasted smile wide on her cheeks as he and his father leave the room. Their footsteps gradually disappear. Even Lord Ashmond's tread is heavy.

Beth turns back to her mother and Lady Ashmond. Four days? That's all she has?

But she'll have Gwen. She just has to keep reminding herself, she'll have Gwen. She can live through anything if it will give her nights and days and sunrises with Gwen.

"We should be going as well," Mother says softly. "Thank you so much for your time, Lady Ashmond."

"You must call me Bess," the woman says, smiling absently at them both. "And of course, of course. I'll have a messenger sent over with details for the weekend. Have a good evening, both of you."

"Thank you," Beth manages, dipping in another curtsy before she takes Mother's extended arm.

They walk slowly from the room, polite and courtly. Concerningly, Mother doesn't say anything once they're in the hall. She should be grinning, beaming. She should be ecstatic at the match they've just secured.

Instead, her face is curiously blank and their retreat from the estate is silent. Even once the carriage doors have shut, Mother doesn't give anything away. Beth opens her mouth, but Mother shakes her head and closes her eyes, leaning back against the seat.

Beth vibrates with anxiety, forcing herself to breathe as she looks out at the passing city. It's nearly a thirty-minute ride home from the Ashmond estate. But Mother won't budge.

By the time they've arrived at their townhouse, Beth is ready to scream. This is her life they're not talking about. She's about to be married off for an estate and a title. She deserves to know how, and what for, and under what conditions. She deserves to know how to start planning her future.

Mother practically leaps from the carriage when they come to a stop. Beth struggles to unfold her skirts and climb down after her, hurrying up behind her even as her mother vaults up the stairs. She only manages to catch her arm once the front door slams behind them.

"What happened?" Beth demands, holding fast even as Mother tries to pull away.

It's like she wants to run from Beth, and if either of them should have that right, Beth thinks it should be her.

"Lord Ashmond said it was all arranged. Did something go wrong—are they not agreeing?"

"Everything's fine," Mother says, still turned away from her, her shoulders high.

"Mother," Beth insists.

But when she turns back, Beth wishes she hadn't. There's something wrong there on her mother's face, something broken and bruised. She looks the way she did the only time Beth recalls Father hitting her. She didn't see it, but she heard the slap when Mother tried to argue Beth should be presented early, to give her a season to get used to the ton. Father said that they needn't waste money on Beth that way. Mother said Father wasted money on frivolities every day; how could he be so cruel and capricious about Beth? And he slapped her.

Her face looks the way it did when she walked out of his study and found Beth in the hallway. It's a cracked look, like the worst of the damage is below the skin. And Beth remembers how Mother retreated into herself after that, for months and months. How she lost her sparkle and slowly turned into this version of her mother, with her single-minded focus and intensity.

"What happened?" Beth presses.

"Lord Montson will propose on Saturday. You'll have all the land you could ever want, a fortune for generations, and they'll put me up somewhere lavish, I'm sure."

"Isn't that what you wanted?" Beth asks. "What *we* wanted," she corrects quickly.

She gets Gwen. She can live through any of it if she can have Gwen.

"It is," Mother agrees.

"Then—"

Mother closes her eyes, taking a deep breath. When she opens them, they're harder. "We cannot see the Havenforts anymore."

It's the absolute last thing Beth expects to hear. She thought maybe someone was dying. "What?"

"Dashiell has been instrumental in garnering support for the Matrimonial Causes Act, and Lord Ashmond is vehemently opposed. Apparently there's been some bribery, I'm not sure on whose side, but the blood has gone bad between them. It was his one demand."

Beth stares at her mother. "He demanded it?"

Mother nods slowly. "I planned to find a gentler way to break it to you. I know how fond you are of Lady Gwen."

"That's absurd," Beth says, her voice ringing around the room. How petty and vindictive and absolutely ridiculous—

"If we continue consorting with the Havenforts I am certain he will rescind his approval and that will mark you for the rest of the season," Mother says.

Beth just stares at her, her eyes stinging with rising tears. Mother steps forward, obviously able to see the brimming anguish on her face, but Beth steps back.

"I'll stop seeing Dashiell as well," Mother says, like it's some sort of consolation that they'll both be miserable.

"I can't give up Gwen," Beth says, her voice raw, fists clenched. "I won't."

"Beth."

"And you," she adds, swiping at her cheeks and shaking her head. She won't, she won't believe this. "You can't just stop seeing Lord Havenfort. You like him so much. He makes you smile."

"I'm not worried about—"

"He makes you happy. You've never been happy!" Beth exclaims roughly. "And you want to give that up just so I can marry someone?"

"What else are we supposed to do?" Mother snaps, her voice a dampened shout that reverberates around them. "Your uncle wants the residence as soon as the season's over. He's already arranging for deliveries to the estate. We're about to be out of a house and what's left of my settlement won't get us through six months. We cannot throw away our one chance for stability for—"

"For what?" Beth shouts back. "For love, friendship, meaningful connection?"

"You'd rather we be on the streets than marry the heir to the Ashmond fortune?" Mother returns.

"We wouldn't be on the streets. I'm sure we could stay with the Havenforts."

"And seal your fate away to be a burden of charity on your friend until you die? We would never survive the scandal," Mother says firmly.

"I don't care," Beth says.

"Lord Ashmond will ensure there isn't another offer for you if you refuse his son. Not this season, not next, possibly not ever," Mother continues, like Beth hasn't even spoken.

"I don't care," Beth yells, her words bouncing around the room. "I can't—we can't just give them up because Lord Ashmond is angry about some stupid act!"

Mother opens her mouth and then shuts it, jaw clenched. She raises a hand to rub at the back of her neck. She must be getting a headache. Beth feels one coming on herself. But they will stand here until Mother is disabused of this ridiculous notion that they have to give up their only happiness—that Beth has to give up *Gwen* for some stupid fight Lord Ashmond has with—

"Lord Montson is a nice man," Mother says, so much more than exhaustion in her voice now.

"What?" Beth asks, ripped from her own sinking thoughts.

"He's a nice man. He dotes on you. He'll be kind to you, give you everything you could want in life."

Beth hesitates. Of course Lord Montson is nice. But he's simply that, nice, nothing more, nothing less.

"You'll have a safe, happy marriage. What more is it you want, Beth? Explain it to me."

Just because her mother has given up doesn't mean Beth has to.

"I want to be loved," Beth says without hesitation. "I want to feel more than bland fondness for the man who'll be in my bed and own me."

Mother steps toward her. "You could grow to love him."

"Like you grew to love Father?" Beth spits back, watching as Mother stops cold, the burgeoning look of understanding sliding from her face.

"The man we have found for you is gentle and kind. If you cannot grow to love him, you will be secure knowing he will never hurt you. It is so much more than most girls get to ask, and he's throwing it all at your feet."

"So it doesn't matter if I never love him," Beth says, fists curling into her skirts as she stares at her mother.

She sees it so clearly now. Love has never been part of the equation in her mother's mind. A happy accident, possible, but never the goal, not ever, not once. All those platitudes, all those apologies, and she never expected Beth to have it. Because she's never expected it for herself.

"It is the most we can get and you should—we should both be grateful," Mother says, stepping forward to hold her by the shoulders, ducking her head to catch Beth's eyes. "You'll be safe."

Regret lives in her mother's gaze and she steps forward, sliding her hands around to pull Beth against her. Beth holds stiff in her arms, fighting against her comfort.

The one true hope for her mother's happiness will have to be shoved aside just as Beth's will. Theirs will be a strangely mutual grief and loss, as they depart for a life beneath another thumb. It should make it hurt less, the solidarity. But it just makes her angrier.

"You could grow to love Lord Montson," Mother whispers, stroking at her back like she used to do when Beth was small. "Affection can blossom over time. You haven't felt love yet, you might be surprised."

"I know what love is," Beth says, feeling the words like a slap against her face. She pulls back so she can step out of her mother's arms. "Like mother, like daughter."

"Beth," Mother says softly.

"I need to lie down. You'll have to tell me what you told Lord Havenfort last time. I can say the same to Gwen."

The heartbreak on her mother's face should give her some kind of victory, but all it serves to do is make her own chest ache as she skirts around Mother and marches up the stairs. Her body is heavy and her head hurts. When she finally makes it to her room, she hasn't even the energy to slam the door.

Instead, she lets it snick shut behind her and stumbles over to her bed. She slides to the floor to brace her back against the footboard, poked and prodded by her hoop and buttons. Her skirt is a mound of cotton and starching around her. She stares at the empty wall and then leans her head back to look blankly up at the ceiling.

She had convinced herself she could live with all of it if it meant she could have Gwen. *Companions*—such a meager word. But it was a word. It was a relationship. It was something.

It was her one chance at love. And now it's gone in one brutal strike.

In this room that isn't hers, this house that isn't hers, she sits with a life ahead that won't be hers either, devoid of all happiness and desire. No love, no hope, no Gwen.

There's no way out but forward. Like mother, like daughter.

Chapter Eighteen

Gwen

The Harringtons have embraced extravagance. Flowers seem to burst from every corner of their expansive back gardens. Ribbons and streamers have been artfully draped around the topiaries as well, with beautiful, enormous floral centerpieces on each of the two dozen round tables laid out along the lawn.

Half the ton must be attending and Gwen wishes for the fifth time that she and Father had been able to come up with a viable excuse. Lady Demeroven and Beth declined their last two invitations for dinner, and neither has heard a thing from them since the dreaded meeting with the Ashmonds. Lady Demeroven begged off with a light cold both times, but neither Gwen nor Father quite believes it.

But there's no way Lady Demeroven would miss this tea and the opportunity to talk up her daughter's most fortuitous match. For though they haven't seen the Demerovens, the news that there's an impending proposal certainly has reached them.

Gwen's stomach feels permanently knotted. She sucks on her cheek as she looks around the garden, half desperate to speak with Beth, and half determined to avoid her at all costs. She doesn't know if she'll be able to smile brightly and congratulate her. Not when she knows it dooms them both to a half life without each other.

She's been trying, she has, to convince herself that a half life is better than none, but the idea still settles sour in her mouth. Father's been giving her extra attention—chess matches, fencing, even some low-level horse gambling ahead of the Ascot opening next week. But it hasn't been enough to distract her. She's horrible company.

And now she has to smile and nod and look at least passably interested as they approach the guests. It's all she can promise, despite the fact that she and Father really should be ecstatic for the whole event. She feels Father start to pull away and holds fast to his elbow, unable to let go of his quiet steadiness.

"It'll be fine," Father murmurs, raising his other hand to squeeze hers in the crook of his arm. "Go and find Albie and Lady Meredith. Focus on them."

"And watch them make mooning eyes at each other all afternoon until the big event?"

Father snorts. "You could spend the afternoon interrupting any time alone they get instead, wouldn't that be fun?"

Gwen wrinkles her nose. It should be cruelly entertaining, but it's not—she'd rather sneak off for her own time alone. The Harrington gardens are expansive and wending. Surely she can find an opportunity to steal Beth away to a quiet corner, at least to talk. Or to see how far she can press her into a hedgerow without damaging her hair.

Father nudges her shoulder and then pulls away, heading for the cluster of fathers once again on the deck. There are two distinct factions today; likely more to do with the MCA. When he hasn't been trying to goad her into anything childish, it's all

Father's spoken about for the last week. And she understands the import—would and perhaps will be grateful someday for the ability to seek an end to an unhappy marriage without needing to approach the church—but the politics of it all is fretfully boring.

Gwen allows herself a brief hesitation, teetering there on the edge of the lawn, before she settles her mask into place, all confidence and swagger. Just because her best friend and . . . lover is about to marry the season's most eligible bachelor doesn't mean she can't still walk tall. She'd rather curl up in a ball and sob, but that's as forbidden here as her relations with Beth.

She strides purposefully through the party, nodding to the happy couples at tables and on picnic blankets, pretending she has somewhere to be while desperately looking for a familiar face. She finally spots Albie and Meredith by the drinks table and hurries their way.

They look nauseatingly happy. Meredith's a mountain of pale green tulle and lace with a comically large bonnet, but her smile is bright and her cheeks are fetchingly pink. Gwen's never really noticed before how nice a blush looks on her. Albie is similarly flushed and grinning, looking as happy as she's ever seen him. It's almost enough to make her veer off for the gardens, but Albie spots her and waves her their way.

With a forced polite smile, Gwen steps up to join them, gratefully taking the flute of champagne Albie passes her way.

"Lovely party, isn't it?" Albie offers.

Gwen nods and takes an overlarge sip, trying hard not to look like she's searching behind them for Beth. "Have you been here preparing?"

"About an hour," Albie says. "You and Lord Havenfort are fashionably late."

"My apologies," Gwen says, giving Albie a look before meeting Meredith's gaze. "Father got caught up in some politics. It's a wonderful spread. Your mother should be very proud."

"Oh, Mother had nothing to do with it," Meredith says with a laugh. "It was all me and our housekeeper."

"Then you should be proud," Gwen insists.

Much as it's not at all her scene, and she finds the entire notion of planning parties abhorrent, it is a lovely picnic. The gardens are resplendent. Care has been taken, it's clear.

"Well, I wanted to make sure everything was perfect for today," Meredith says, glancing up at Albie, who beams back at her.

Gwen forces an excited smile, unwilling to spoil whatever tension lies between them—whatever anticipation. She doesn't want her displeasure to show, that she'll be obligated to stay to the bitter end, with her cousin getting engaged in the middle. No ducking out early.

"Miss Demeroven went for a walk in the topiaries, if you'd like to see her," Albie says, offering it casually, though she can see some glimmer in his eye. Is it obvious to everyone how attached they've become?

"I wouldn't want to miss anything," Gwen says slowly. Her whole body nearly vibrates with the urge to throw herself toward the maze of hedges at the back end of the garden.

"I think you're safe with an hour or so of wandering," Meredith says with a shrug, glancing up at Albie. "Wouldn't you say?"

"An hour and a half, even," Albie hedges. "We're expecting a few stragglers."

"Of course," Gwen says, barely keeping from shaking her head at their obvious delight. "I'll see you later then."

"Bye," Meredith says vaguely, and the two are lost again in each other's eyes.

Moony lovebirds, the two of them, Gwen grouses as she glances toward the open doors to the solarium. She can just see Lady Demeroven pulling her father aside. He grins at her and ducks his head to listen. Gwen bites at her cheek, unable to watch them so happy when her own insides feel so twisted.

She skirts the large hedgerow until she gets to the back of the garden, where the Harrington property opens up into a maze of green topiaries, flower bushes, and fountains. Hardly appropriate to roam on her own were it evening, but she thinks she can get away with it in daylight, especially if it's in search of a friend.

Or whatever it is she and Beth are to each other.

She walks down the central row and then pauses at the first fountain, unsure which way to check first. Unsure if she truly wants to find Beth here. For now that she's alone among the flowers, she's not confident at all that she'll be able to keep her cool when she sees Beth, nor that she'll be able to keep her hands to herself. And while this was exactly her fantasy upon entering the party, she finds the longer she wanders the hedges the more that fantasy turns to knots in her stomach.

By the time she comes around another endless corner and discovers Beth loitering at a dead end, nail between her teeth, Gwen's broken out in a cold sweat. She stares, watching Beth pace.

Beth is radiant in a pale blue dress with low-capped sleeves and a plunging vee across her collarbones, bareheaded and bare-armed—her bonnet is on the ground a few feet behind her, along with her gloves. The entire effect is wonderfully fetching and pretty and so beautiful it actually hurts. Gwen thinks she could watch Beth for hours—could think about pressing her lips to every inch of her exposed skin—could fantasize about leaning her back against the hedgerow and climbing beneath her skirts to make her moan.

"Oh!"

Gwen startles as Beth jumps, spotting her with a hand to her heart. "Sorry," Gwen manages.

"You scared me," Beth says, her voice rough.

Gwen shrugs guiltily and finds her feet moving of their own accord until she's an arm's length away. She wants to grab Beth by the waist and pull her in for a kiss, but Beth steps back, worrying her hands together.

Gwen rocks on her heels, balling her own hands into her purple skirts. She watches Beth, notes the way she's biting at her lip.

"So, how was it?" Gwen asks, wincing the moment the words come out.

"What?"

She sighs. "The—riding with Lord Montson. His grounds are something, aren't they?" she continues, going for interested and genuine. She can be supportive. She can. What other choice does she have?

"They're . . . fine," Beth says. "They're—a lot."

"Good view of the city," Gwen agrees.

"Yes. Nice to be out of it at the least, I suppose," Beth says with a listless shrug.

"Was it the perfect spot for a proposal?"

Damn it, why is her mouth like this? Beth's face falls and Gwen falters, trying to find the words to repair it.

"It's not some trivial little thing," Beth hisses.

"I know," Gwen says quickly.

"It's sacrifices and planning and paperwork," Beth rattles off. "So much arranging, and discussion."

Gwen blinks, feeling as though her heart has fallen all the way to her toes. "Did he really ask you already?"

Beth meets her eyes, surprised, and shakes her head. "Not yet."

"But soon," Gwen surmises.

"By the end of the weekend," Beth says, both their voices suddenly low and hushed.

Gwen can distantly hear the party, but it's nothing to the thud of her pulse against her ears. "That's before Ascot. I guess you'll be in his enclosure then, rather than on the grounds with us?"

She tries to say it lightly, but the hunch of Beth's shoulders proves her words still carry a bite. She's trying, she is, but it's like her chest is cracking in two.

"Probably," Beth says. "But I can't—" She pauses, and Gwen watches her knuckles go white from the strain of her fingers together.

"What's wrong?" Gwen asks, feeling the distress on Beth's face like a grip on her stomach.

She steps forward, unsure of what she can offer, but wanting to offer something. Beth steps back again and Gwen pauses, watching as she shakes her head.

"Mother's going to find your father."

"Oh," Gwen says, confused. "She found him. Is she feeling

much better?" Beth shakes her head again and Gwen takes another step. "Is she all right?"

"She's fine," Beth says quickly, brought out of whatever state she's in enough to recognize Gwen's concern.

"Then what's the matter?" Gwen asks, her tone as light and airy as she can manage.

Beth's face only crumples further. "Your father's gathered support for the Matrimonial Causes Act."

Gwen blinks. "He has."

"And he's had to make some agreements, move some stock options to entice votes," Beth continues.

"I suppose." Beth stares at her, looking so forlorn Gwen takes another step toward her. Beth goes to step back yet again, but she's already up against the hedge. "Beth, what's happened?"

Beth takes a shuddering breath, and it's only now that they're a few feet apart that Gwen can see the tears on her cheeks. "We won't be able to make our dinner," Beth says softly.

"Oh, all right," Gwen replies, reaching out to snag one of her hands, worried now for her cuticles. "Is that all?"

"We won't be able to reschedule," Beth says, her chin quivering.

"Is Montson taking you to see his country estate or something?" Gwen asks, trying to smile through it.

Beth shakes her head. "No. No, it's—" She takes a shaky breath, using her free hand to wipe at her cheeks even as her other clutches at Gwen's fingers.

"Has something happened? Are you and your mother all right?"

Beth slowly meets her eyes. "If I marry Lord Montson, I can't see you anymore," she pushes out in a rush.

Gwen stills, her hand a too-tight vise around Beth's. It's like wind is rushing by her ears though the day is thoroughly lovely around them. "What?" she asks, inelegant and overloud.

"The deals your father's made, the stocks he's had picked up—he apparently bought Lord Ashmond out of a huge investment and he's livid. His one condition on the marriage is that we break contact with you and your father."

Gwen blinks at her. She hears the words, but they don't make sense, sloshing around in her head. "You . . . to marry Montson, his father is insisting you promise not to see me anymore?"

"And Mother can't see your father either," Beth says quickly.

"That's absurd," Gwen says firmly. "Montson doesn't care."

Beth lets out a startled laugh. "Of course Montson doesn't care," she says, her words hard. "But his father does. And we'd be living with them. We won't—if I don't say yes, we won't have anywhere to live," Beth says, voice turning brittle. "I don't want to, but I don't have a choice."

Gwen just stares at her, trying to comprehend it—this ridiculous, petty demand. How can it matter who they see, how can it jeopardize a match simply to spend time together?

Beth's hand grips at hers and Gwen finds her footing, meeting Beth's eyes as her own fill. "So that's it?"

"I wanted to come to dinner," Beth says desperately. "I wanted to come to dinner, and stay the night, and tell you alone—to have—" She tugs hard on Gwen's arm.

Gwen stumbles forward, breath hitching. Beth wraps her arms around her, their skirts bumping, awkward and full of angles. She stiffens, thoughts whirring, her body warring between outrage and heartbreak. But Beth holds on tight, shivering into her.

"I wanted one more night," Beth whispers into her neck.

Heartbreak wins and Gwen wraps her arms around Beth, turning her cheek into the side of Beth's face, staring at the leaves of the hedge, almost too close to see distinctly. Or maybe that's the tears in her eyes.

She thought she'd at least get to keep half of Beth—all this time convincing herself that she could live that phantom life, sneaking happiness in snippets and snatches. That they could live together among the hedgerows, secret and illicit. Never what they should have had, but so much more than nothing. And now—

There's nothing she can offer that would stop this match. Their only solution has been struck down by the earl. Their parents won't marry, so that Beth can. And Beth has to marry Montson. She has to be married by season's end.

Gwen's been living in a fantasy—clinging to a childish, stubborn belief that they could outplay the odds, could create a fairy-tale ending.

But it's not to be. Like a knife to the heart, Gwen has to let her go. She loves her too much to hold on, to damn her to the mercy of friends and family. And even if she could—if she could twist destitution into romance, Lady Demeroven would never allow it. Beth will marry Lord Montson.

"I can't," Beth murmurs into her neck.

Gwen sucks in a breath, turning to press her lips to Beth's slightly sweaty head. "He'll—" She pauses, dragging the words up her throat. "He'll be good to you."

"I don't care."

"You'll have money, and time, and children," Gwen continues, staring blankly at the fuzzy leaves.

"He won't be you," Beth says, lips against her skin.

Gwen shudders and pulls back, wanting one moment to savor, one moment to remember. "We'll write letters," she says.

"Stop comforting me," Beth exclaims and Gwen blinks.

"What?"

"You should be yelling," Beth says, voice stuffed but eyes blazing. "You should be angry."

"Of course I'm angry," Gwen says, able to feel her rage beneath the brimming sadness. "But what do you want me to do? Go punch Montson or his father?" Beth snorts wetly. "Run away and be a seamstress?"

"You can't sew," Beth reminds her.

"You want me to be mad? Want me to yell at you? Want me to tell you you can't, and that I hate you? Is that how you want this to go?"

"No," Beth says roughly.

"Then what?"

She stumbles as Beth surges forward, taking Gwen's face in her hands to drag her down into a searing kiss. Gwen gasps, her body going slack in shock, before instinct takes over and she's gripping back. Beth spins them and pushes her into the hedges, just as Gwen dreamed of doing to her. She clutches at Beth's waist, drinking from her lips, their breath in hot pulses between them as they kiss. Heady and illicit and forever forever forever.

Just as she begins to think maybe they could stay like this, in a liminal, timeless eternity, there's a cough that seems to echo through the hedges. Beth jerks away from her, stumbling backward, both of their eyes wide and horrified—if anyone saw—

"We must be going now."

Gwen wilts in relief when she spots Father standing at the mouth of the dead end. He looks utterly reserved and unruffled at finding his daughter pressed up against the leaves by her lover, his first love's daughter.

"Right," Gwen manages, standing up tall and smoothing out her skirts. Beth blushes and wipes at her face, bending quickly to grab her bonnet. "Miss Demeroven."

She dips in a clumsy curtsy, can't think of anything else to do or say—any true way to say goodbye.

Beth stares back at her, anguished, before stooping in her own curtsy as she wipes at her eyes.

"Lady Gwen."

They stand for a moment, just staring at each other. Gwen tries to memorize how the sunlight hits her face, sparkling against the tears she's missed. How Beth's breath still hitches after their kisses—the pink in her cheeks and the flush on her neck. She'll remember her this way, lightly debauched and tearful after a blissful, horrid, beautiful goodbye.

Father coughs discreetly again and Gwen tears her gaze from Beth to turn on her heel and walk as calmly as she can to her father's waiting arm. She doesn't hear Beth move behind them and Gwen lets Father lead her from the hedgerow. But he doesn't take them back to the party yet, winding them instead deeper into the far side of the maze.

Gwen sniffles gratefully and Father tugs her to a gentle stop halfway down another dead end. He takes out his handkerchief and cups her cheek to wipe her tears. Gwen meets his eyes, finding nothing but a twin sadness and understanding staring back at her.

"Break your heart, don't they, the Demerovens?"

Gwen nods, shattered. "I'm sorry."

"Oh, sweetheart, me too," he says, pulling her in for a hard hug. She buries her face in his chest, taking solace in his arms for a few long minutes.

If she cannot have her happiness, at least they are grief-stricken together.

"Ready to watch Albie get engaged?"

Gwen groans and shakes her head, even as she knows she has to stay. Has to gather herself and paste on the first of what will be many an empty smile. Albie has stood by her through thick and thin; she must put away her heartache to be happy in the face of his joy.

"If it helps, Lady Demeroven is going to collect Miss Demeroven and go home. I left her a few rows back and told her to wait for Miss Demeroven to come to her while I found you."

Gwen pulls back to look up at him. "Does it ever stop?"

"The heartache?"

"Yes," she whispers.

He smiles so sadly she thinks she could fall back to pieces. "No. But we'll find you someone someday who will take some of the pain. And at least you had this much."

Gwen forces herself to nod, like this much is even halfway to enough. At least she had this, that's what she'll have to tell herself for the rest of her life. At least she had one brief moment of love and joy and affection before a life without.

Chapter Nineteen

Beth

Beth stares at her reflection as Miss Wilson finishes pulling the last of her laces. She steps blindly into her hoop cage and barely feels Miss Wilson raising it and securing it about her waist. Cares little for the petticoat she layers over it, nor the embroidered bodice and skirts that go over that in their pale pink loveliness. None of it matters. She looks as beautiful as she probably ever has, but it's utterly hollow.

She thinks there's no way Lord Montson won't see it. That he'll know, by looking into her empty eyes, that this isn't what she wants. She's desperate for him to see it—the aching sadness that she thinks permeates every inch of her face—she wants him to see it, to acknowledge it, to take back his promises.

But she knows he won't. She's getting engaged in a matter of hours; she should be a mess of anticipatory nerves. What woman wouldn't be a bit nervous? And what woman would refuse such an offer?

She has to smile, and pretend to weep, and gush, and celebrate this joyous day.

Instead it feels like her stomach might fly out of her mouth at any moment, with her heart following after.

"You look wonderful," Miss Wilson says as she settles the last of Beth's skirts and tucks everything into place.

"Thank you," Beth manages, her voice a whisper around her tightened throat.

"Do you want the earrings?"

Beth follows Miss Wilson's pointed finger, feeling like she's moving through water. Mother's left her bridal earrings on the vanity in what Beth assumes is a peace offering.

"No," she says, forcing a smile for Miss Wilson. "I wouldn't want to overgild the lily."

"More of a rose, don't you think?" Miss Wilson asks, working so hard to stay cheerful. She goes on, filling the silence with a prattle of floral comparisons. Beth hums vaguely in her direction.

She and Mother didn't speak at all in the carriage home from the Harrington tea. Mother didn't mention Beth's smudged lips or frayed hair. She doesn't know if Mother even noticed; she'd clearly been crying herself. She should care about her mother's happiness—be sickly grateful she's given up yet another chance at love for Beth's security and marriage.

She should care. She should be grateful. She should be kind and wear the earrings. But all she wants to do is scream, at Mother, at Lord Montson, at Lord Havenfort, at the prime minister and the queen.

"It's a beautiful day, don't you think? Memorable. Not a cloud in the sky," Miss Wilson continues, fluffing at her skirts for something to do with her hands.

Beth clenches her jaw against a retort that she'd rather it were raining, since she doesn't want to remember this day anyway. But Miss Wilson doesn't deserve her nerves, so she just shrugs.

This is the mess her father left for them: no provisions for their well-being, no savings for another home. His two women destitute and at the mercy of her callous uncle, followed by a cousin she's never met.

She should scream at her *father,* that's what she should do. Make Mother stop the carriage on the way there to go and hurl insults at his grave.

"It's time."

Miss Wilson's chatter dies away. Mother stands in the doorway to Beth's room, severe in dark mauve with black accents—the perfect widow.

"You'll be great," Miss Wilson says, squeezing Beth's shoulder.

Beth watches as she hurries out around Mother, taking the last dregs of normalcy with her.

Mother stares at Beth in her pale pink dress, the model of an expectant bride-to-be, and utterly miserable. She opens her mouth, but doesn't seem to find the words.

Beth doesn't need them. She knows what she has to do. Knows who she has to be, today.

"We should go," Beth says, her voice a rasp against the unnatural quiet.

"Yes," Mother agrees, stepping back to lead Beth down the hall.

There's so much they could say, but their ride in the carriage is quiet. The words stick in her throat, too many and too much to fit into the thirty-minute journey. Instead, she clenches her hands and breathes steadily, counting the houses as they pass.

By the time they're being led through the Ashmond mansion, her stoicism has left her. Her stomach is all knots, that anxiety rising heavy and fast. Her pulse is hammering and she can feel sweat dripping down her back and into her drawers. She's never longed for the barrage of petticoats before. What if she sweats so much it pools beneath her?

They reach the large glass doors that lead from the solarium and out onto the patio that sits at the base of the expansive gardens. The porter steps through, and Mother goes to follow, but Beth stands rooted to the spot, clutching at her arm.

She can't do this. She can't walk out there and—

"You'll be fine," Mother says softly, leaning into her. "Breathe, smile, and if you can work up to it, which I bet you can, give a good cry."

Beth shudders. She shouldn't need coaching on how to properly react to a proposal, but given that her instinct is to turn tail and sprint away, she'll take it. She squeezes Mother's arm, dragging in a few rapid breaths.

"Go on."

There's a beat where it feels the world stands still, all the air sucked out of the sky. A moment where she teeters, the life she wants with Gwen behind her, this life she hates ahead. A brief hesitation, as if to say goodbye.

And then the world starts turning again.

She forces herself to step through the doorway, toward her new, empty life.

Chapter Twenty

Gwen

As she stands squished between Albie and Bobby, listening to Meredith prattle on about their upcoming wedding reception, Gwen considers choking on her remaining profiterole.

The Johnson ball is in full, boisterous swing. What seems like a thousand candles twinkle overhead, sparkling against the jewels that dapple every floral arrangement and hanging garland. The room is a swirl of pastels and fans, dancers twirling on the floor. Servers with hors d'oeuvres meander through the crowds milling on either side of the expansive dance space.

It's a massive spectacle, though nothing compared to the upcoming Yokely ball. At least at the Yokely estate she can disappear off into their gardens. Here she's trapped on the edge of the floor, unable to escape the talk of weddings and engagements. She's been desperately trying to slip away, but Albie keeps hold of her elbow, and Bobby's pressed tight on her other side. She thinks Father may have something to do with it and both resents and appreciates his forethought.

If she were able to get away, she'd be stealing multiple bottles of wine and getting drunk in the servant's corridor. And while it wouldn't be good for her image, she'd much prefer it. Because of course, now that she's suffered two hours, the true excitement of the ball has just entered, and it feels like her stomach is a piece of lead fighting to sink to her toes.

Beth, looking as glorious and beautiful as Gwen has ever seen her, descends the massive staircase down to the ballroom on the arm of her equally glowing fiancé, Lord Montson, and Gwen just wants to die.

"I need the lavatory," Gwen mutters, trying to pull away from Albie.

"Meredith can go with you when she's done with her aunt," Albie says, holding fast to her arm.

"I can use the—"

"The very last thing you want to do is flee the room when the Ashmonds enter. Your father would never forgive you. Aren't the two of you playing cool with the Demerovens?"

Gwen glares up at Albie. "It's none of your business."

"He told me to look after you—that includes keeping you from making a spectacle of yourself," Albie says, angling his body away from the commotion of Beth and Montson's entrance to meet her eyes, face serious. "You should be happy for her."

"Right," Gwen says tightly. "The pride and joy of the season. I should sing her praises and send thanks up to the gods of love?"

"It might not hurt to put some good energy out into the world," Albie says with a little shrug.

"Just because you're coupled up doesn't mean the rest of the world needs to be all about roses and ceremonies," Gwen says, hearing the bite in her voice, but unable to protect Albie from her misplaced anger. It has to go somewhere. "Two months ago you would have been teasing her with me. Montson's a drip."

"He's a good lad," Albie says seriously. "Jealousy isn't a becoming color on you, Gwennie."

She curls her free hand over his on her arm and pinches him. Albie grunts and releases her. "I'm not jealous."

"Right. Clearly. My mistake," Albie says, rubbing at the back of his hand. "Mere, Gwen could use the lavatory, would you go with her? Don't want her falling in with the wrong crowd."

Meredith nods, giving Gwen a bright smile. Gwen sighs, allowing Meredith to take her arm and lead her away and down the corridor off the dance hall. She wonders what Albie has told her of the Havenforts' "falling out" with the Demerovens. Wonders whether Meredith has had cause to speak with Beth since she got engaged.

Gwen hasn't been to a social event since they heard. Father let her sulk for one day, and then they spent the following afternoon fencing, taking out their mutual anger in sword fighting and footwork. But Meredith and Albie have been to four teas in the past two days.

"So what's got you in a knot?" Meredith asks as they come to the lavatory chamber.

It smells sickeningly of lavender and Gwen swallows against the nausea that's been roiling in her stomach all night. She wants to simply push into the water closet, continue her ruse. But Meredith's giving her quite a look, and for all that they've really only ever been society friends, she is about to be family.

"Beth's mother and my father rather . . . fell out of sorts. And the Ashmonds are violently opposed to the MCA. We haven't spoken in the past few days, that's all."

Meredith frowns. "That's a shame. She's such a lovely girl. Though I will say, for the belle of the ball, she's been downright dour since the engagement. Even Lady Ashmond's noticed. I heard her reprimanding Lady Demeroven about Beth's demeanor."

Gwen leans back against the wood-paneled wall, sucking on her cheek. It seems neither of them is a very good actress. "I'm sure she's fine. It's an adjustment, is all. Lots of responsibility coming her way," she pushes out, trying hard to sound casual and disinterested.

"The planning is brutal," Meredith agrees, shrugging a little as she leans back into the wall as well. "I can only imagine it's ten times worse for a marriage to an Ashmond."

"Probably," Gwen agrees, taking a deep breath to push down the rise of bile that comes with the thought of Beth in a white dress beside Montson. "How are you holding up?" she asks, forcing herself to meet Meredith's eyes.

She could use the distraction, and despite how much Albie's on her nerves, she likes Meredith, and she should be making more of an effort. She can't quite manage excitement, but she can pretend at interest, at least.

"I'm excited," Meredith says, smiling. "And exhausted. But I love Albie so I know it will all be worth it. I feel very lucky."

Gwen considers her, pleased by the honesty in her voice. It's clear to look at Meredith and Albie that they do actually love each other. A rare, fatefully lucky match, indeed. She and Beth could be just like Albie and Meredith if the world were different.

"Albie's the lucky one," Gwen says as brightly as she can manage. "You're doing him a kindness."

Meredith snorts and reaches out to slap her side. Her hand hits Gwen's hoop and her whole skirt shudders. They both laugh.

"He's a wonderful man."

"Yeah, he is," Gwen agrees. "A brat, but a wonderful man,

and I'm sure he'll be a good husband. He's always looked out for me, even if I pretend it's the other way around." Meredith beams at her. "Please never tell him I said that."

"Oh, I'll pick my moment someday," Meredith says, waving off her frown. "I'll use it for good, promise. One day when he's very angry at you, I'll tell him you actually love him very much and he's your most favorite cousin. It will be fun to watch his head explode."

Gwen gives Meredith a slow once-over. "You suit each other."

"I know," Meredith says with a little grin. "Now we just need to find you a good man."

Gwen pushes off from the wall. She won't be roped into any matchmaking this late in the game. She's failed another season in the eyes of the ton; no need to add insult to injury. No one will ever know that she, too, found a love match. So let them all think she's a failure.

"I'd rather support you and Albie," Gwen says, adjusting her skirt and picking at imaginary lint.

"Oh, but you must have someone to dance with for the reception," Meredith says quickly.

Gwen starts back for the ballroom, striding up the corridor. Meredith scurries behind her, trying to catch up.

"I'm sure Bobby would dance with me," Gwen says over her shoulder.

"Bobby's actually—"

Gwen stumbles, arms pinwheeling as she collides with another body. She manages to stay standing, turning to give the inconsiderate blighter what for, only to find a horrified Beth staring back at her and gripping at her waist.

"I'm so sorry," Beth says.

She's even prettier up close. Her cheeks are flushed and eyes a little wild, whisps of hair falling from her intricate braided updo. Her off-white gown only highlights her dark hair and lashes. Gwen lurches backward and out of her hold, unsteady.

"Miss Demeroven, lovely to see you," Meredith says as she steps up next to Gwen.

"And you as well," Beth replies quickly, curtsying. "Lady Gwen."

Gwen manages to nod, but it feels like her head is disconnected from her body. Her tongue feels too big for her mouth. And it makes her angry.

She shouldn't have to feel like this, not when Beth's chosen someone else. Not when Beth and her mother tossed the Havenforts aside like trash in the face of some money.

And protection, and stability.

Gwen finally unglues her tongue. "I'm surprised to see you without your fiancé."

Meredith winces beside her. Beth meets her gaze. Gwen forces herself to keep their eye contact, even though the subtle hurt in Beth's eyes makes her want to shrink back.

"I was looking for the lavatory. We were stuck in traffic on the way here."

"Of course, it's just down there," Meredith says kindly, pointing down the hall while she takes Gwen's arm. "Congratulations, by the way."

"Thank you," Beth says softly, her hands twisting together, that giant engagement ring glinting in the gaslight.

"Your mother must be overjoyed."

"She is," Beth says, smiling at Meredith, though Gwen can

tell it's forced. "And congratulations to you. I don't know if I've said. Mr. Mason's a lucky man."

Meredith grins. "I know."

They stand for a moment in stilted silence. Maybe Meredith expects Gwen to offer some pleasant congratulations of her own, but she can't. It's either keep her mouth shut or say something truly horrible, and she's already done enough. Anyone could walk by. Meredith doesn't deserve the scandal.

"I should . . ." Beth says, nodding toward the lavatory.

"Of course," Meredith says, pulling Gwen rather roughly aside so Beth can shuffle past, all of their skirts bumping awkwardly in the narrow hall. "Have a good evening."

"You too," Beth says, smiling at her before cutting her eyes to Gwen's.

"Don't trip" is what falls out of her mouth, and she winces as Beth's eyes dim.

"Thanks," she mumbles before hurrying off.

"Honestly, it's like you were raised in a barn," Meredith mutters, yanking on Gwen's arm to steer her back to the ballroom.

Gwen lets herself be dragged along, feeling utterly awful. It's not Beth's fault. It's not Gwen's fault. It's horrible circumstance and society and their stupid parents—but she needs someone to be angry with or she has nowhere for all the hatred in her heart to go. If she doesn't do something soon, it's going to eat through everything and she'll be weeping at the side of the ballroom.

"Drink." She blinks and finds Meredith pressing a glass of champagne into her hand. "And for goodness' sake, try and look less like your puppy has been strangled."

Gwen swallows around a snort, coughing as the champagne hits the back of her throat and fizzes up to her nose. "Excuse me?"

"Whatever's going on between you and Miss Demeroven, you need to buck up. You're attracting attention," Meredith says firmly, all that bubbly gentleness gone from her voice. "Bobby's going to ask you to dance in a few minutes, and then we'll get you another drink, and you won't have to do anything but look vacant, all right?"

Albie appears at Meredith's side and Gwen deflates. "Yes, all right."

"And then you're going to eat something, and then you can have another drink," Albie says quietly, leaning in to meet her eyes. "It'll be fine, Gwennie. Try and enjoy yourself."

"You enjoy yourself," she mumbles, rolling her eyes as he laughs and Bobby appears at her elbow.

"Bottoms up," he says, swigging back his own glass of champagne.

He's becoming a handsome kid. There's the shadow of a full beard on his face and he's coming into his cheekbones. He's still a bit gangly and awkward, but he's far more confident tonight than he was at the start of the season. Seen a few things, flirted with a few women; he's growing up.

"You're not terrible at this," she decides thirty minutes later as they sway through their fourth dance.

"You're horrid," Bobby says without remorse. "But Albie says you're sad, so I'll let it slide."

Gwen glances back at Albie and Meredith, twirling slowly a few couples away. He wouldn't have told Bobby why she's sad—not the real reason. She's not entirely sure Albie really understands, though she thinks he might. He told her once the boys at Eton sometimes snuck off to the bushes and didn't seem as repulsed as most people would.

What anyone does in the privacy of a bedroom, or shrubbery, should be their business she thinks. Even so, she's not sure she wants this gawky young man to know she's been rolling in the sheets with Miss Demeroven, the belle of the ball being spun around now by Lord Ashmond. She keeps wincing, like he's stepping on her toes.

Gwen yearns to go save her—pull her away like she did months ago at the first ball—play the dashing stranger. But Beth isn't hers to save anymore, and her toes will just have to get used to being stepped upon. She's in for a life of it.

"I could use another drink, couldn't you?" Gwen asks.

Bobby glances over at Albie, who's thoroughly wrapped up in Meredith, gazing soppily into her eyes. Disgusting, the two of them. Bobby looks back at her and gives her a sneaky grin.

"I'm thinking something harder than champagne."

"You're on, little Mason."

Bobby takes her hand to lead her off the floor and over to the drinks station. And though Meredith and Albie seem intent on keeping her demure and acceptable to the ton, Bobby has no such hesitations. He grabs a bottle of scotch and two glasses and leads her over to one of the small tables by the large narrow windows that look out on the lawn.

And there they stay, knocking back swigs and giggling, exchanging courting horror stories. It seems Bobby is as miserable as she is, and she wonders why she's never bothered to give him the time of day before. She loves Albie, but he's no longer her partner in misery. He's a success, now. Worse, he's Meredith's. Won't have time for her for much longer at all.

Bobby will have to make a fitting substitute.

"I'd rather recite the whole Bible in Latin than attend another tea," he says, hiccoughing a bit.

Gwen snorts. "I'd rather prick myself with a hundred embroidery needles than sit through another picnic."

"I'd rather run over hot coals than promenade," he counters.

She grins. "I'd rather wear eight petticoats than watch another cricket match."

"Really? I enjoy the sporting events at least. Will you be at Ascot?"

"Of course," Gwen says, raising a hand to wipe her sweating brow. "You'll attend with Albie, won't you? Father's got us all tickets for the main stands."

"Excellent," Bobby says, his cheeks dangerously red. "Albie says you're a betting woman."

"You want to wager, Mason? Because we can wager. I've a dowry no one's using."

Bobby laughs a little too loudly, attracting stares from the back half of the room. Gwen shrugs and takes another swallow, enjoying the burn of the alcohol against the back of her throat and the warmth spreading up her chest. Who cares what the mothers think. She's relaxed for the first time all evening.

"There you are!" Father exclaims loudly, stepping up to their table, his own cheeks rather red, smile broad and friendly, glass empty. "Bobby, how are you?"

Bobby blinks up at him. Even though Bobby's lanky, he's got nothing on Father's height, and especially when inebriated and lilting, Father makes quite an impression.

"I'm well, sir," he says as Father reaches for the bottle and pours himself a sample. "And yourself?"

"That's good," Father says after he swigs back the swallow. "And I'm well. Glorious, in fact. I just had a large return on a recent investment. Gwennie, how would you like to own one of the Ascot horses?"

Gwen stares up at him. "Really?"

"Why not?" he says, grinning down at her. "We've money and opportunity and the whole of the ton to impress. We'll make our picks tomorrow and then cheer the jockey on next week, what do you say?"

"I say that deserves a toast," Bobby says, gamely refilling all of their glasses.

"The fastest one?" she asks Father.

"The fastest one," he assures her, his hand falling to her shoulder as he sways in place. "To your good health and a happy marriage, Bobby," he adds.

Bobby laughs and they sloppily clink glasses. "And to your good fortune," Bobby says, pouring another round.

"To your growth spurt last summer," Gwen declares, reaching out to grab the bottle only to send it toppling to the ground in a spectacular crash. She jumps at the sound and manages to knock into the vase at her back, sending that sprawling as well.

"Damn," Father exclaims, loud enough to attract the half of the room that didn't turn at the sound of shattering glass.

"And that's enough for the three of you," Albie says, stepping up to block them from view. He plucks the glasses from their hands and slams them none-too-gently onto the table. "I think it's time the two of you headed home, and Bobby, you can see yourself out."

"It's early yet," Father argues, his voice bouncing around them.

Albie steps in close, completely blocking Gwen from view. She's never seen his face like that—dark and brooding and just a bit intimidating. It's not a word she's ever associated with him.

"You are making a spectacle of yourself and your daughter," Albie says, his voice low and hard.

"Nonsense, I—"

"I would hate for you to end such a triumphant night as the ton gossip. Gwen has enough against her this season without your behavior playing in. Now, I'll escort you and your daughter out."

Father locks eyes with Albie, pulling up to his full height. "I am your uncle, young man—"

"And you've taught me better than this," Albie cuts him off. "Now come on, both of you," he says, reaching out to tug Gwen up.

She stumbles, the whole room tilting beneath her feet. She's drunker than she thought. Everything's hazy and spinny.

"Grab onto your father. Bobby, you get her other side, discreetly," Albie hisses.

As an awkward group, they skirt the side of the ballroom, moving slowly. Heads turn as they pass, mothers gawp, fathers shake their heads. She can see the other girls tittering, but she hardly cares. And drunk as she is, it isn't until they're nearly at the grand entrance that she thinks to try and look for Beth.

But turning her head makes the sloshing, swaying room worse and it's all she can do to keep moving, Father and Bobby holding her up as Albie escorts them up the stairs. When they reach the top and step into the foyer, Gwen groans, feeling her stomach swirling.

"Do you realize what a spectacle you just made of us?"

Father demands as Albie ushers them outside and raises his hand to hail one of the waiting coaches.

Albie turns to meet Father's eyes head on. "No more of a scandal than you loudly boasting about your bets and your bribes. Half the room is against the MCA—you know that. And you getting drunk and sloppy, rubbing it in their faces, won't make you any more beloved. Your methods are just short of shady."

Gwen lists into Bobby. Her mouth is dry and stale, her stomach sour, and her legs feel unsteady. She's never seen Father look quite so indignant or drunk before, now that she thinks of it. His hair is a mess and his cravat is askew. What goes on in the parlors during these dances?

"You have no right," her father says around a hiccough.

Albie's look hardens further just as the carriage pulls up to their side. "I'd hate to see you become my father, sir. It's hard enough with one in the family, don't you think? For Gwen's sake?"

Father glowers but doesn't argue. Instead, she's roughly passed up and into the carriage, Father vaulting unsteadily in after her. Albie shuts the door with a sharp bang. They both wince. Albie taps the side of the carriage, setting them off at a lurching rumble that's destined to steal what little she ate for dinner.

Did she eat? She should have.

She could have eaten Beth. She looked like a flouncy dessert.

"Albie's grown a pair, hasn't he?" Father asks, sitting at an angle in his seat as Gwen clutches at her head. "How much did you drink?"

"Too much," Gwen moans, her shoulders curling as bile rises up her throat.

She slams her hand against the top of the carriage and they have just enough time to stop and for Father to throw open the door before she's on the carriage floor, vomiting onto the street. She hopes they're far enough away from the Johnson estate for only the coach hands to see her.

"Gwennie," Father sighs, sinking to one knee to rub her back as she heaves.

Sadness, and whisky, and self-loathing spatter onto the cobblestones beneath the carriage. Some triumphant evening.

CHAPTER TWENTY-ONE

Beth

Beth shifts uncomfortably, wiggling in her damp corset to try and coax a bead of sweat away from the itching on her back. The air is staid and humid, and the smell of horse manure doesn't help. They can heap all the flowers they like along the railings of the royal enclosure behind them; it doesn't do a damn thing.

"Stop twitching," Mother mutters.

Beth looks over at her and then jerks back as their lacey broad-brimmed bonnets knock together. The third day of the Ascot races is no laughing matter. Beth feels like she's weighted down by petticoats again with how many layers of lace and silk they've piled onto her hoop. Never mind the itching at her ankles from what she thinks might be ants. No hope of checking, the way they're all packed in, hoops bumping awkwardly as they continue to wait for the opening shot. There was a lot of laughter and shrieking at the start. Now they're all too tired and trying desperately to keep up the ruse that anyone wants to be under the hot sun waiting to watch a horse race they'll only be able to see for moments each lap.

Lord Montson's consumed with talk of betting beside her. She tried to join in, at the start, but one look from her mother and another from Lord Ashmond quelled any interest in inserting herself into Lord Montson's conversations. She's here to look like a trussed-up, melting dessert, nothing more. She glances to her right and left, but she's trapped where she is, no friendly faces.

She's long since finished the drink Lord Montson braved the crowds to get for her. She can't bring herself to ask him to go again, not when he tripped and almost ruined his new pressed white trousers. He nearly lost his top hat too.

"Do you think they plan to start the races, or is there some sort of hat competition of which I wasn't made aware," Beth wonders, glancing at Mother.

Mother goes to scold her, but the woman on her other side steps closer, bumping Mother's hoop into Beth's. Beth watches in dismay as some of Mother's last sip of champagne sloshes from her glass and onto the packed dirt ground.

"I dearly hope so," Mother says, wiping her dripping glove onto her lavender skirts. No one will notice, just as they all politely ignore the sweat stains marring everyone's clothing. "This is dismal."

"It really is," Beth agrees.

She glances across the track and starts, bumping her mother again. Mother doesn't even huff, just grabs her arm to steady them both and then knocks back the last of her champagne.

"I'm going to get us something to drink, damn the skirts," Mother says.

Beth's too distracted looking over at the inner track lawn to care, even as Mother's effort to turn around jostles her, creating a domino effect around them as hoops bump and clash.

Beth stares across the track at the crowd of onlookers making raucous merry on the other side. They've space, and ample drink and food from their personal picnics. And in the center of the crowd, right against the railing, she sees Gwen, Meredith, Lord Havenfort, and Gwen's cousins having a wonderfully good time.

Gwen looks enchanting in her bonnet, which only has a demure lace lip, nothing like the heavy monstrosity on Beth's head. Gold ringlets cascade out of it, and Beth can see her green dress has a much more practical hoop below it, allowing Gwen movement, and air, and the freedom to enjoy a glass of champagne and the sandwich Meredith hands her.

Beth watches as Gwen carries on two conversations, chatting with Meredith while clearly placing bets with her father and cousins, turning at intervals to bark numbers at them without missing a step with Meredith. No one seems to care that they all look a bit undone. No one seems to care that they're being loud and rowdy. There across the track, Ascot is fun, social, and exciting.

And instead of being there with them, as they planned, picnicking and getting their parents to fall in love, Beth is stuck here in the royal lawn enclosure, listening to Lord Montson blather on and on about the horses and the odds.

That feeling of hopelessness that's been sitting on her chest for a week constricts further and Beth sighs, trying to breathe through it. So Ascot won't be fun; they won't have to attend every year. And at the least the inn Lord Ashmond has put them all up in is lovely. The meat pies in the pub are good, and she and Mother have been taking advantage, eating to their heart's content. Her stomach's full, which is something. And once they're no longer trapped like livestock for this race, she might even get to wander the grounds a bit, see the gardens they're cultivating on the other side of the grandstand.

It won't all be a total loss.

"Be grateful, I nearly took down a countess, I think," Mother says, bumping Beth's hoop as she shuffles back to her side and extends a flute of champagne.

"At least that would have been some excitement," Beth mutters, smiling a little as Mother snickers quietly.

"It's distasteful," says a voice to Beth's right.

Beth turns, glancing at the couple standing just beyond Lord Montson and his schoolmates, who have taken up a post behind Beth and Mother.

"It's supposed to be an event. Really, it's not that untoward."

"He's got that girl as drunk as he is. And as loud. I can hear her from here."

Beth glances across the track as a cackle splits the rowdy atmosphere. She'd know that laugh anywhere. It's Gwen, gloating at Mr. Mason for something while Lord Havenfort eggs her on. Incorrigible, the two of them.

"I'm sure there's a young lad here who would find her charming. A man could do with a wife who enjoys a good sport."

Beth glances at the couple and finds the woman glaring down into her wine. Her husband tips back his beer. She hears Gwen laugh again and looks over to find her waving something under Mr. Mason's nose as Meredith tries to snatch it back.

They *are* making rather a spectacle of themselves, though she supposes the man beside her isn't wrong. Today isn't a day for staid conversation and appearance, unless you're on her side of the track, here to see and be seen. The inner lawn is for fun and cheering and betting with abandon. And though the ton might look down their noses at anyone who didn't manage an invitation to the royal lawn enclosure, Beth thinks those on the other side made the better choice.

"Of course the act shouldn't go to the floor," Mother says, dragging Beth's gaze from Gwen's bright face.

She turns and finds Lord Ashmond standing on Mother's other side, his wife crammed between them, her skirt and Mother's knocking enough to set Beth tilting. She grabs the railing in front of her and takes a too-large sip of her champagne. But of course no one's paying her any attention.

"The very idea that it's gotten this far is abhorrent," Lady Ashmond says.

"We'll find a way to reverse it if Havenfort and his ilk manage to pass it through," Lord Ashmond says, his boom of a voice grating even amongst all the others.

"I thought Lord Havenfort all but had it locked down," Mother says, and Beth can tell by the hold of her jaw that she's trying not to let her true colors show.

This must be about the Matrimonial Causes Act, again. It's all anyone talks of these days. Even Lord Montson's friends were lamenting its imminent passage, like the act isn't there to protect women from monsters and marital brutes. How must they treat their fiancées behind closed doors if they're so worried they'll be able to convince a court of abuse?

"There's still a few weeks until the vote, more than enough time to find the right palms and make the right exchanges," Lord Ashmond says firmly, as if all Lord Havenfort's machinations and work might be waved away with enough money.

Beth hopes not. If Mother could have petitioned a civil court—left her father—

"That's something then," Mother says tightly.

"I'll be bringing Harry into the final rounds as well, train him up. We've got to keep the party going, and our children are the future, aren't they?"

"Of course," Mother says.

"Your Elizabeth would never—" Lady Ashmond begins.

"My Beth will be an excellent wife and your son an excellent husband, so the matter need never be discussed," Mother says firmly.

Lady Ashmond nods and Lord Ashmond turns to a gentleman on his left to continue the conversation, leaving Beth and Mother alone, pushed up against the railing.

"Are they all afraid their wives will divorce them given the chance? Doesn't say much for their marriages," Beth mutters as Mother sidles as close as she can.

"Change makes most people nervous," Mother says, taking her own overlarge gulp of champagne. "And this isn't polite talk."

"But it is when the earl does it?"

"Hush," Mother says, shaking her head and looking across the track.

They're starting to line up the horses. At least there will be some excitement soon. There ought to be, after two hours in this infernal heat and press of bodies.

"Does it bother you?" Beth asks, tracking Mother's gaze across to Lord Havenfort, who looks not at all concerned that his plans may come crashing down.

"Does what bother me?" Mother asks, sounding lofty. It falls a bit flat, with the clear exhaustion at the edge of her voice.

"Pretending."

"Not now," Mother mutters.

"Does it?" Beth presses. "You can't really support that infernal position."

"You know I don't," Mother hisses, leaning close under the guise of fixing a lock of Beth's sweaty hair. "But this is neither the time nor the place. We're here to drink, smile, and be seen. You can seethe and rail later."

Beth purses her lips. She's tired of being cosseted and patronized, like her discomfort is an aberration when she knows Mother is equally uncomfortable, in this box, in this life, with these people.

"You could try making other friends. Brooding is only going to give you wrinkles."

"I don't need other *friends,*" Beth returns, scowling as Mother rolls her eyes.

Gwen isn't her friend. She's so much more than that, and to hear Mother dismiss her pain like it's something as mundane as a season alliance—

"How did you do this?" Beth asks, frustration pouring out of her.

"Do what?" Mother asks.

"Live like it wasn't crushing you to death."

"It is rather pressed in here, isn't it?"

Beth jumps, turning to face Lord Montson as he grins down at her. "Oh, well, I—"

"Here," he says gamely, stepping a scooch in front of her, so his leg presses lightly into the bell of her skirt. It pushes her skirt back, shifting the front close to her legs and forcing the back out behind her, creating just a modicum of space.

Lord Montson winks. Mother smiles at him, but Beth catches

the warning in her eyes. They'll continue their argument later, when the doors are closed.

In the meantime, she'll smile and curtsy and encourage the misunderstanding. It does feel less congested now, which is . . . something.

"Thank you," she says honestly.

"See, partnership comes in many forms," Mother says, smiling at Lord Montson even though Beth hears the bite in her words. "How have your bets been taken, dear?"

"Oh, well, well," he says easily. "We're rooting for Skirmisher," he tells Beth, as if she couldn't possibly have an opinion.

She doesn't, but it still raises her hackles. Mother narrows her eyes as Lord Montson leans around them to look at the starting line, and Beth nods. She won't take that one out on Lord Montson; it would be beyond petty. Still.

Biting her tongue, Beth turns back to the track. The horses and jockeys are finally lined up. She watches as the starting gun is loaded, and with a great bang, they're off. Cacophonous screams and cheers fill the air, and Beth's too preoccupied with trying to keep herself from being crushed against the railing to care much about which horse is winning. It's absurd, especially given that even though they're the best racehorses in the country, it still takes close to a minute for them to reappear around the track for any meaningful view.

She would try and squint across the inner lawn to the opposite side of the track, but every time she does she gets distracted, watching the way Gwen is clutching at Meredith. Absurd possessive jealousy rises in her chest, even knowing full well that Meredith is happily promised to Mr. Mason. But she's felt those hands on her, inside her, and the thought of Gwen's fingers on another woman's arm . . .

It's like she's doing it to spite Beth. Pretending all day she hasn't noticed they're right across from each other, waving her free, merry life in Beth's face. Like Beth *wanted* this and deserves to be tortured for the choices she's had to make. Like seeing Gwen so happy and carefree isn't ripping Beth apart inside minute by minute.

Like it's Beth's fault and Gwen alone has the right to be angry.

And maybe she does. This isn't Gwen's fault; the rage in Beth's heart, the fire in her lungs, the desperate twist in her gut have nowhere to go. If she could talk herself into hating Gwen, she would. But she can't.

And much as it's tearing into her heart, it gives her a sick satisfaction that at least if Gwen is punishing her this way, it means she's still thinking about Beth.

Lord Montson whoops and Beth realizes she's spent the whole race staring at Gwen. Skirmisher's the winner. They won.

How utterly meaningless.

Hands wrap around her waist and she squeals in surprise as Lord Montson lifts her up. He takes her shock for joy and then all of a sudden, he's kissing her, right there in the royal lawn enclosure.

It's rough, and hard, and he releases her just as quickly, leaving her breathless with shock and the coarse press of his shadowed beard against her cheeks. His lips are chapped. He puts her down and turns without a word to cavort with his friends. She's been kissed in broad daylight, and no one here seems to care.

All the talk of appearances, of decorum, and it doesn't matter. She's no more than something to kiss when things go well. Not good enough even for conversation.

"Well, he'll have the funds for an extravagant honeymoon," Mother says, and Beth slowly turns to find her bracing herself on the railing, her knuckles white.

"Perhaps we should have placed our own bet, doubled my dowry," Beth says dryly.

Mother laughs, glancing at Beth for a brief moment like they're home alone in the parlor. "Next year."

"And then what?" Beth wonders.

"You and I can have a grand adventure while your husband is here for the winter, maybe," Mother says with a shrug. "Go to the Continent."

Beth stares at her mother, the slight slump of her shoulders, the lines by her eyes. Exhausted, just like she is.

"We could go now," Beth says softly. "Run away."

Mother stands up tall again, that brief open expression gone from her face and eyes and smile. "I should make some rounds," she says, barely even looking at Beth before she begins the arduous process of fighting her way through the cluster of bodies and hoops.

Beth stands there, bereft. So much has been lost, none of it tangible. She glances across the track and finds herself at last under Gwen's gaze. They stare at each other for a long moment before Gwen takes a slug of something and turns away, back to her father and friends and family, while Beth stands alone, surrounded by people.

CHAPTER TWENTY-TWO

Gwen

"I did not!" Gwen insists. Father fumbles with his key to unlock their front door, scraping it against the panel twice before managing to insert it into the keyhole.

"You most certainly did," Father says, crowing when he gets the lock open and pushes into the foyer, dragging Gwen with him. "You count your cards. Where did you learn to do that?"

"You!" Gwen says before slapping her free hand over her mouth.

"I knew it!" he shouts. "You're a cheat."

"No more than you. You had cards up your sleeve," she shoots back, letting the door slam shut behind them.

"How would you know?" he asks.

"Because I spent hours learning to do it before you told me women never wear coattails and they've done away with the long sleeves. It's a travesty."

Everything's a bit fuzzy, even Father as she turns to regard him, rumpled but grinning in the middle of the foyer. The room is brighter than she would have expected. It's very late, she thinks, or possibly very early. Mr. Mason had port, and it was good port. She cleaned up, even if she did count her cards a few times.

"A lack of sleeves wouldn't stop a true cheater," Father says, laughing when she tries to scowl at him.

Her face feels a bit numb, now that she thinks of it.

"You're finally back."

They both swing around, unsteady, and find Mrs. Gilpe standing in the archway to the dining room, glaring at them with bloodshot eyes.

"It's only, what?" Father says, twirling around to squint at the clock above the mantel.

"It's nearly gone five," Mrs. Gilpe says, marching into the foyer, her slippers making a definite smack against the marble floor. "We thought you'd crashed or fallen down into the Thames."

"We're nowhere near the Thames," Gwen says before an enormous belch surprises her. It rings around the room. Father snickers.

"You've gone and gotten her pissed again," Mrs. Gilpe deduces, glaring at Father. "Did anyone see you?"

"We were just at Albie's," Gwen says, trying to look demure and contrite even as she sways on her feet. She'd quite like to go to sleep now.

"No one saw us," Father says, rolling his eyes. "Go on back to sleep, Mrs. Gilpe. I'll get Gwennie upstairs."

"I haven't been to sleep," Mrs. Gilpe says loudly. Gwen and Father wince; the loudness hurts her brain. "No one has been to sleep. We've been worried sick."

"Whatever for?" Father exclaims. "You cannot decide we've died every time we're not home before one."

"Home at two would have been fine. But three, four, five? What respectable lady is out until five in the morning?"

"I was just at Albie's," Gwen repeats, confused by her housekeeper's ire.

Father's face darkens. "With her father? A proper chaperone?"

"You're in no state to be considered a proper chaperone," Mrs. Gilpe says tightly. "Gwen, go to bed," she snaps, turning her hard look on Gwen.

"But I—"

"Now. Mrs. Stelm has left water by your bedside. Drink a full glass, then go to sleep."

"It really isn't his fault, I wanted to play—"

"Bed," Mrs. Gilpe insists, pointing toward the stairs.

Gwen looks to Father, but he just sighs and nods, waving her away, like she's a child. It's *her* reputation they're fighting over.

But she can't quite make her mouth form the words in her head, and her soft bed does sound inviting, and she's actually quite parched. So she goes, leaving Mrs. Gilpe and Father bickering behind her as she slowly climbs the stairs with her leaden feet.

"It's unconscionable that you would be this reckless with her already difficult position. We've had no morning calls all season."

"What did you expect?" she hears Father ask. "She's not a show pony. None of them are good enough for her."

"Well they're all you've got. The poor thing's heartbroken enough without ending up thoroughly alone."

"I'm here!" Father returns.

Gwen rounds the bend and continues up the stairs to the second floor. It's not like she's pathetic. She's fun. She's a hoot. The life of every party. And so what if Beth's about to be married off? She's not going to get married just to soothe her ego—or whatever she's been telling herself isn't an utterly broken heart.

"And was Samantha's father enough to keep her out of trouble?"

Gwen pauses, heart in her throat.

"It's not the same," Father says gruffly.

"No? Your heart was broken," Mrs. Gilpe counters.

Gwen slowly slides herself down to sit on the stairs, head pounding.

"It's not the same," Father repeats. "Gwen isn't me."

"No, she's both of you. Samantha made choices as well. I'm telling you to be careful."

"Gwen's not going to get in trouble," Father insists.

Gwen covers her mouth, her other hand clenched into her skirts. She's always suspected, but never knew. No one talks much of her mother, only that she wasn't what any of them would have expected for Dashiell Bertram. Now she knows why.

But Father's right. It's not the same. She can't get in trouble, because the only person she'll ever sleep with is Beth, and that's no longer an option. The thought sends a stab of pain through her heart and she starts to cry.

Beth's are the only arms she ever wants around her. She's not about to drown her sorrows in a man, in a fumble, in something painful and stupid and dangerous. The very last thing she wants is to be saddled with a child in addition to a husband.

Her stomach roils as her tears turn to sobs. She heaves in air, her heartache rising in her chest like a rapid tide, with an enormous wave now waiting to come in behind it. Is that what happened to her father? He was saddled with a wife, and a child, all dreams of love and happiness gone, because of one moment of recklessness?

"You're drinking like a fish and letting her do it with you. You turn your back in the wrong place and who knows what could happen," Mrs. Gilpe says.

"Gwen isn't interested—she would never," Father spits.

"If she's blind drunk she won't know up from down, and you'd best hope there's no young man trying to forget his own heartache with her."

"How dare you—"

Gwen's stomach tightens without warning and she vomits all over her dress and the stairs, snot and tears running down her face as she gags. She hears footsteps as she tries to right herself, tries to aim her heaves away from her dress, tries not to slip down the stairs, her narrow hoopskirt shifting this way and that as she squirms.

"Sweetheart," Father says softly, kneeling on the step below her to brace a hand on her back.

"Serves you both right," Mrs. Gilpe says tartly, stepping around Gwen to hurry up to the hall for towels to clean her up.

Gwen gasps in air as her stomach finally calms. Vomiting in a corset and hoopskirt is something else. She supposes at least there aren't layers and layers of ruined petticoats now. Just her silk brocade skirt and lining. She wipes at her mouth with the back of her hand, feeling woozy and horrible.

Father gives her a soft smile and takes out his handkerchief to wipe off her face, like he did when she was small. When he was alone with a little girl to raise. No wife. No comfort. Just crying and begging and annoyance.

And here they are again, alone together.

"No more port for you," he says and Gwen laughs, startled.

"You're not sick," she says, going for a whine that comes out more like a hoarse whisper.

"No, but I'm taller and I've much more experience. Maybe this will teach you not to try and keep up. You're impressive enough at two glasses, you didn't need five."

"You let her have *five* glasses?" Mrs. Stelm asks, appearing at their side with a towel. She pats over Gwen to mop up most of the mess.

"I'm sorry," Gwen tells her, even as she lets Father and the disgruntled Mrs. Gilpe get her up to standing.

"He should be sorry," Mrs. Gilpe mutters.

"And you do know better," Mrs. Stelm adds.

Gwen could hug her for at least admitting she has fault in this mess. She knew she was drinking too much. But it hurt less to drink than to listen to Albie's uncle wax poetic about Meredith and the upcoming wedding and how they're all heading for the country immediately afterward. She's not a child. She's a stupid, hurting adult, and she's gotten what she deserved from this, heartache and painful family revelations and all.

Father wraps his arm around her waist to steady her. "I'll help Gwennie to bed. Thank you for taking care of us. We promise not to worry you again, don't we?" he asks, nudging Gwen gently.

"We promise," Gwen parrots.

Mrs. Gilpe simply stares at them blankly before taking the soiled towels from Mrs. Stelm. She marches around them and down the stairs toward the laundry. Father sighs, rubbing at the back of his neck.

"A bottle of whatever has you both sloshed wouldn't go amiss," Mrs. Stelm says, winking at Father before following Mrs. Gilpe.

Gwen sags against Father's arm and he blows out a breath. "All right. Let's get you to bed," he says.

Gwen nods and together they shuffle their way up the next staircase and down Gwen's hall. She's breathing heavily, ribs and stomach sore, throat raw, and he's not particularly stable, but they're both much more sober than before. She doesn't know how he does it, but losing whatever was left in her stomach helped, disgusting as it was.

They make it into her room without killing themselves. Gwen looks around, noting the folded clothing on her dresser and vanity, the rearranged makeup and hairpins, the orderly bed—a maid came in and cleaned. It didn't look this way when she left last night. It was a sty. It's been a sty for weeks.

"All right, let me do the laces and such, and then I'll turn around," Father says.

Gwen turns to allow him to undo the eyelets at the back of her relatively simple frock. The silk may be fine, but it's a boring navy that's now dotted with—ugh, better not considered.

Father steps back and busies himself pouring her a glass of water as she slips out of her overdress and wrestles herself clumsily out of her hoopskirt. She hears Father snickering as she bumbles around and has half a mind to toss the soiled overdress at him. She lays the dress over her vanity chair and lets the hoop collapse by the armoire.

She makes clumsy work of her corset and then slips into her housecoat. She does up the sash before falling gratefully into her bed.

"Decent?" Father asks.

"Yep," Gwen says, glancing over to find he's chugged half her pitcher of water. "Hey, I want some of that."

He laughs and passes her the glass before sitting down at her hip where she's propped up in bed. "Are you feeling better?" he asks.

Gwen takes a few swallows and places the glass down with a wobble. "Yes," she says, though it's clear she's not fully sober yet. Her limbs feel uncoordinated.

"We'll do better," Father says, laying his hand on her calf on top of the comforter. "Find some activities that involve less alcohol, hmm?"

"Agreed," Gwen says softly. "Though, if you still want to go to the club, you can, you know. You've been home a lot," she says, watching as he frowns. "Not that I mind."

"I suppose I haven't felt much like talking politics, but I should check in, round up the yea votes one last time. Perhaps if you'd like to attend a few teas with Lady Meredith?"

Gwen nods, even as the very idea gives her a headache. But they both have their roles to perform. "I'll be better, I promise."

He smiles and leans in to brush her cheek. "You're perfect just as you are. Don't let the society mothers tell you otherwise. And when you're not so drunk you're vomiting, you're a delight. We'll find you someone someday. I'm sorry it couldn't be Miss Demeroven."

"Me too," Gwen admits, her chest hitching.

Father nods and leans back, patting her leg again. "All right, I say we sleep until noon, and then take a promenade, looking our best and brightest."

Gwen blinks. "Won't—only if it's cloudy?"

Father grimaces. "Good thought. Better yet, we'll sleep until one and then spend the rest of the day in the library. Bribe Mrs. Stelm with some of that port to get her to make your sick-day soup and play chess. And tomorrow we become respectable members of the ton again. Deal?"

"Deal," Gwen says, shaking the hand he extends before he stands.

He smiles down at her and then turns and leaves the room, closing the door softly behind him. Gwen stares at the door, half wanting to follow after him—to ask, to know—did having her ruin his life? His mistake—was it worth it?

But her head is still swimming a little, and he loves her, that much is clear. However she happened, however he married her mother, he did it. And it's them against the world. She'll live up to her bargain, be a polite society lady for the rest of the season, only mildly tipsy and making sober mayhem.

So she'll be a failure four times running. Maybe she'll really get a medal, or a plaque.

FOUR NIGHTS LATER, as she stands with Albie and Meredith in the grand Yokely ballroom, she desperately wants to renege on her promise. Meredith and Eloise are going on about ribbon colors and taper heights, and Albie's been talking to Prous for the past ten minutes about locomotives, with Bobby chiming in on his other side.

All Gwen's had to do is stare around at the crowded ballroom. Of course it's grand, with its massive chandelier and shiny marbled floor. The white-paneled, two-story walls make the space feel endless, and she supposes all the flowers are beautiful. She's been itching to slip out into the gardens for about an hour, but Albie won't leave Meredith, and Bobby's already tipsy. She doesn't think Father would approve of her getting drunk with him a second time.

At least not here, at the ball of the season. Everyone who's absolutely anyone is here. The dancing never seems to stop, and the mothers all have a crazed, predatory look in their eyes. They're approaching the last month of the season, and it's eat or be eaten now.

She's glad at least to be with friends. When she entered, she was forced to dance with two of Father's compatriots from his smoking club before she could excuse herself and steal away.

She promised Father she wouldn't drink. But when Beth Demeroven steps up to their circle with Lord Montson, greeting Eloise, Meredith, and Annabeth with smiles but giving Gwen only a brief flick of the eyes, Gwen decides to sod her promise. She's about to take Albie's drink when he nudges her and she realizes in her desperation to numb the pain, she's missed Montson addressing her head on.

"Apologies, I couldn't hear," Gwen says, dipping into a short curtsy.

"I asked if you were quite recovered," Montson says and Gwen swallows, tightening her jaw.

Apparently after the last public ball Albie began a rumor that he dragged Gwen and Father out because they were both ill with food poisoning. How he managed it, Gwen doesn't know, given that they were both clearly drunk and not at all poisoned. But it seems to have stuck, and she's been waving off concerns all evening.

"Quite," she says, keeping her voice light.

She can feel Beth's eyes on her but can't meet them. Instead, she goes to step back, eager to excuse herself. Only Albie's grip on her elbow stops her, preventing her from being rude to one of the highest-status young men in the room, even if he has stolen the love of her life. Blasted Albie.

"Was it the fish?" Beth asks.

Gwen feels Albie's hand tighten around her elbow and she turns her gaze to meet Beth's. "No. I think it was the chicken," she says as politely as she can manage.

"Funny, I had the chicken and I was perfectly fine," Beth continues.

Why is she pushing this? "Well I'm glad. No one should be put through food poisoning. Dreadful business. Lady Meredith, you mentioned your uncle once served a rancid trout but the dog got to it first, didn't he?"

She turns to find Meredith staring back at her, a bit agog. "Um, yes. It was horrid. We had to put him down, actually."

She'd forgotten that the end of the story was tragic. "Right."

"Good thing we don't do that to people, eh?" Montson puts in.

The group titters as they all shift uncomfortably. She's sure no one knows exactly why the air now feels so heavy, but it's clear they can all sense the tension.

"It is a good thing we don't murder the ill, yes," Albie agrees, elbowing Bobby when he lets out a startled laugh. "Though I suppose the practice is more to ease suffering than punish animals for falling sick."

"Wouldn't that be a world," Montson says.

"Actually, they did used to murder people for being sick. It's a large part of how the plague was eradicated," Beth chimes in.

She shrinks a moment later when all of the eyes in the circle swing to hers. Gwen fights against laughing. Beth is just so stupidly funny and charming. It's terribly unfair.

"Quite right," Montson manages, looking a bit alarmed at his future bride. "We should all be grateful there's no longer a plague."

Beth opens her mouth, and Gwen oddly hopes she's about to go on one of her rants about plague isolation islands. But this isn't a month ago, and they're not tipsy and pressed up against the wall. "I'm glad you're feeling better," Beth says instead, meeting Gwen's eyes. "You've been ill a lot recently. I do hope you're firmly on the mend."

Gwen meets her look, that momentary hope seeping out of her. Is that a veiled reference to her drinking? "Thank you. I'm sure I'll get over the last of it soon enough," she says, feeling a swell of both pride and pain as Beth's look hardens.

"As long as you stay away from the source, I suppose that's the natural way of things," Beth says.

"The source stays far from me now," Gwen returns.

Albie's hand slips higher up her arm, squeezing, but Gwen's attention is firmly on Beth's disapproval.

"Are you being stalked by a disgruntled, diseased chicken?" Montson wonders.

Gwen forces a laugh for his sake. "No, no, just . . . sometimes it seems while I'm avoiding further disease, it's actively seeking me out, like it's drawn to me, somehow."

"Perhaps it can smell weakness," Annabeth puts in.

"That must be it," Meredith adds quickly.

"Or that I'm ready to fight it when it comes," Gwen counters, not liking the insinuation that she's at fault here.

Lord Montson and Beth approached her circle, after Beth

made it so abundantly clear that any association with her would ruin her engagement. Is she supposed to take the high road, when Beth's flaunting her new, happy life in her face?

"And how would you fight it?" Beth prompts.

"Oh, I can think of a number of ways to—"

"Montson?"

Montson turns and takes the hand of a tall, mustachioed man. "Rodgers, good to see you."

"Your father sent me to fetch you, if your lovely fiancée can spare you for a bit," the man says.

"Yes, of course," Montson says immediately. "You'll keep Beth entertained, won't you?" he asks the group.

There are nods around the circle. Montson smiles before setting off with Baron Rodgers without even a glance at Beth. Beth watches him go and then looks back at them, putting on a brave, unbothered face. But Gwen can see the cracks. Her world has narrowed now to just Lord Montson, and without him, what does she have? Who does she have?

It makes Gwen feel just a little bit mean.

"I'm sure it's very important, whatever they're talking about," Gwen says, and even she can hear how snide she sounds.

"Yes, it's about the Matrimonial Causes Act, I'm sure," Beth returns. "Lord Montson's working hard with his father to see that it doesn't pass. Your father is desperately trying to hold on to his votes, I expect?"

Gwen curls her fists into her skirts, even as Albie keeps hold of her arm. She knows Beth supports the act. Remembers her saying everything could have been different if Lady Demeroven could have escaped her father's hold. How dare she throw it around so casually—like the act passing wouldn't also protect her from the miserable life she's bound to have with Lord Montson. The man just abandoned her to a group of people his father has forbidden her from speaking to. Hardly a great protector.

"He certainly hasn't struggled to get them. The lives of unhappily married women and women to be unhappily married depend on it, don't you think?" Gwen tosses back.

"All right, I can't do this anymore. Let's go to the gardens. It's stifling in here," Albie says, a little overloud.

"I need the lavatory, actually," Meredith says, exchanging a very unsubtle look with Albie before grabbing Annabeth and Eloise and marching them off.

"You two, outside, now," Albie says gruffly, nodding to Bobby to escort Beth while he all but manhandles Gwen around and toward the open patio doors.

"What are you doing?" she hisses as he marches her outside and into the cool night air.

"You and Miss Demeroven are going into the gardens and you're going to have whatever this is out. We'll distract Montson if he shows back up. It's dark, no one will notice, and I'm frankly sick of you either being drunk or depressed."

Gwen gapes up at him as he hauls her to the mouth of the hedge maze, more expansive and grander than the Harringtons'. The very sight of it sends shivers down her spine with memories of the last time she and Beth—she can't do this.

"You can let go," she hears.

She turns and finds Bobby looking awfully sheepish while Beth shakes out her arm. "Sorry," Bobby mumbles.

"In, both of you," Albie directs, waiting with his arm outstretched toward the high green walls. "Come back when you can be civil."

"I can't," Beth says, looking a bit pale.

"We'll tell anyone who asks that you're in the lavatory, and then with Meredith. No one will know," Albie insists.

"And if I won't?" Beth challenges.

"Yeah," Gwen adds. "Suppose we all just stand here until Lord Ashmond spots us, what then, Albie?"

She means it as a taunt to her cousin, to highlight the futility of his ruse, but Beth groans and strides straight into the hedge maze. Albie grins and gestures for Gwen to follow. That wasn't the outcome she wanted.

Albie raises an eyebrow and Gwen gives her own frustrated sigh, stalking after Beth. Who is she kidding—of course this is what she wanted. She's just not sure what to do with the opportunity now that everything's so horribly broken.

CHAPTER TWENTY-THREE

Beth

Beth wends through the hedgerows, stomping a bit and listening to Gwen shuffle along behind her. She's not ready to face her yet and so keeps winding them deeper into the labyrinth. Lord Montson abandoned her, and Gwen was goading her, and she's trussed up and hot and tired and she just wants to keep storming away until she fades into these stupid hedges forever.

"Beth, Jesus, stop."

She whips around, startled by Gwen's hoarse whisper, and finds the other woman only feet away. She's slightly sweaty and a little disheveled by now, but utterly, wrenchingly gorgeous. Her blond hair has fallen in whisps around her face with the rest of it piled up in a twisted braid on her head. Her collarbones catch the moonlight above them and her eyes seem bigger and darker here, alone in the hedges.

She's so beautiful, and so wonderful, and there just in front of her, and Beth can't have her. The frustration makes her itch to punch something. "No champagne for the hedges?"

She feels vicious, like if she jabs Gwen hard enough maybe she can pull her down into her pit of despair. Because while Beth's been miserable and alone, it's looked like Gwen's been having a marvelous time being "ill" with drink, cavorting with her cousins and father, one big happy family.

"I'm refraining," Gwen says tightly. "I'm surprised you let Albie force you in here. You must have people to talk to, invitations to give out, flowers to pick."

"Well we can't all gamble and drink our feelings away. Some of us have responsibilities."

"Yes, like condemning decades of women to unhappy marriages. Can't let that one go by."

"Don't talk politics now," Beth says quickly. "I'm sick of it. It's all they talk about."

"You weren't sick of it in the ballroom," Gwen counters. "More than happy to take Montson's side now, aren't you?"

"What else am I supposed to do?" Beth exclaims, her voice rising above their heated whisper. "If it's not talk of the wedding, it's talk of that stupid act. You get to drink and run wild, and I'm trapped with them all the time."

"I haven't been running wild," Gwen argues.

"You've been having a gay old time forgetting about me, and I'm trapped in hell," Beth spits back.

"You think I'm having fun, watching you parade around with Montson? You think this isn't ripping me apart? You left me, like yesterday's trash," Gwen says, stepping closer, her face dark and tight. "You threw me away, threw my father away, and you want to judge how we're coping while you're the talk of the ton?"

"I didn't throw you away," Beth says quickly, the fight sapped out of her now that she's this close to Gwen. Now that she can see the tears running down her lover's face. Now that she can see she's lost weight, can see the bags beneath her eyes.

"You get this big life, with the pride of the ton. Luxury and happiness. And I'm stuck watching you have it while everyone else around me goes off to their stupid happy endings. And I'm just standing there with no one. You don't think it's killing me?"

Beth finds herself reaching out before she can think about it, cupping Gwen's jaw in her hand and stepping forward until their skirts press together. "You look worse than Mother," Beth whispers, searching Gwen's eyes.

"What?" Gwen asks, the word soft, her whole body gone slack at Beth's touch.

"She's been taking laudanum," Beth admits, all her anger and hurt dissolving to a quiet peace now that they're together here, alone, just for a moment. "And even then she's barely sleeping. But she won't talk about it."

"Why?" Gwen wonders.

Beth almost smiles as Gwen's hands settle on her hips, too many hoops and skirts to feel more than the pressure, but it's there. "You think it's all happiness and wedding planning, but I envy you. *Mother* envies you and your father, laughing and drinking while we're trapped in this waking nightmare with these terrible people that just . . . goes on forever," she says, wrapping her other arm around Gwen's neck until their foreheads press together.

"So we're in mutual misery," Gwen murmurs, curling closer until her hands meet behind Beth's back.

"I miss you," Beth admits, looking up to meet Gwen's eyes, almost too close, a little blurry.

Gwen nods and leans down, pressing her lips to Beth's in a chaste kiss. In the moonlight, at the back of this hedge maze at the biggest ball of the season, it feels like they're in a moment outside of time. A détente from all the pain and acrimony and separation.

"I miss you too," Gwen says. She pulls back so they can see each other. Even the moon is helping, unusually bright. "Maybe you could see Meredith sometimes, and I could happen to be there, and no one needs to know."

Beth sighs, the moment shattered. It's not enough.

"I don't want that," Beth mumbles. Gwen goes to pull away, but Beth shakes her head, sliding her hand to cup the back of Gwen's neck. "I don't want just that," she amends. "I want—this is so stupid. All of us miserable, and for what?"

Gwen sighs. "So we don't end up destitute with our parents ruined."

Beth blinks. Their parents.

The proper marriage presented itself, and Beth just . . . accepted defeat. Submitted to this terrible future because her mother told her they should—told her it was the only way. She trusted that her mother knew best. That she had truly considered every possible option. But her mother was *wrong*.

This—all of them devastated and heartbroken—can't be the only way out. Beth refuses to believe it. Refuses to stand by and watch them all suffer forever because they weren't brave enough even to *hope*.

If Mother could just open her eyes—could believe she's worthy of Lord Havenfort's affections—if Beth can just make her see reason, they can change this. She and Gwen had a plan, and they just—

"We surrendered!" Beth exclaims, wincing as the sound bounces around their little hedgerow.

"What?"

"Our parents. We—God, Gwen. We just gave up. We could still—would your father still propose, do you think?"

Gwen gapes at her. "Would my—you want to get our parents together, now? We tried, it was a miserable failure," she says slowly.

Beth shakes her head. "It wasn't though. In the beginning, maybe. But once they started talking again—Mother cried all the way home the day we had to break off our friendship with you. She was so happy before that. They were in love, I'm sure of it." Gwen stares at her. "Your father's been drunk as a skunk for weeks. Is that normal behavior?"

"Well, not normal, exactly—"

"And my mother, taking laudanum? I've been telling myself it's just exhaustion and resignation—the Ashmonds really are quite dull and their opinions—but she's sad. She's heartbroken, just like I am."

Gwen blinks down at her, head cocked to the side, and Beth surges up in renewed joy, pressing a hard kiss to her mouth. She pulls away before Gwen lists into her, sliding her hands around to take Gwen's so they can see each other fully.

"We can still do this, can't we?" Beth slots their fingers together until they're clutched knuckle to knuckle.

Gwen hesitates. "I'm not sure."

"Can't we try?" Beth insists. "The wedding is in three weeks. We could still do it."

Gwen sucks on her cheek, considering her. Beth fills up with hope, planning already. They'll force their parents together. Everyone gets to be happy.

"Do you think your mother would allow it?"

"Allow what?" Beth asks.

"The scandal. You dumping Montson will inflame tensions that are already there. And my father's votes for the MCA are so precarious—"

"You're really citing that damn act as a reason not to do this?" Beth exclaims, gaping at Gwen and trying to tug her hands free. "You can't be serious."

"I'm not saying we can't try," Gwen says, holding tight and sighing. "I just—you're about to marry one of the most influential men in the whole of London. Breaking your engagement is no small matter."

"I know that," Beth snaps back, unnerved by Gwen's calm, detached tone. "But if it would make our parents happy, and us happy, what does it matter? Your father can pass the bill. Lord Ashmond wouldn't be blustering about it if he wasn't worried."

"I suppose," Gwen says slowly.

"So sod it. Get your father to propose and I'll break it off with Lord Montson and they'll vote and we can leave London, the four of us together."

Gwen gently pulls her hands from Beth's. "You know it's not that simple. We got lucky before. I'm not sure we'll get lucky again."

Beth curls her empty hands into her skirts, the hope deflating in her chest. But she's not going to give this up without a fight again. She's not going to let Gwen become a drunk and let herself become a broodmare for Lord Montson.

It wasn't just luck. There was something there. There had to be. They can change this.

"Does your father not love my mother anymore?"

Gwen meets her eyes, startled. "What?"

"I can still see it, the way he looks at her. Like you're looking at me right now," she adds, appealing to what she knows Gwen is trying to hide. What she herself has been trying to hide for weeks. "If he thought he stood a chance, would he try again?"

Gwen shifts her shoulders, glancing around their little hideaway. "Would your mother say yes?" Beth hesitates for a moment. "Because I won't put him through this a third time."

"I can convince her," Beth says firmly, though it sounds weak even to her own ears.

Can she convince her mother to give up the security of an alliance with the Ashmonds? Can she convince her that the four of them would withstand the resulting scandal? Convince her that Lord Havenfort would never leave them in the situation her father did?

Because Beth doesn't care if there's insecurity down the way. This stolen, fraught moment with Gwen is the best she's felt in weeks. Like the aching loneliness has been punched out of her chest, leaving nothing but joy in its wake. And if having Gwen means being invited to fewer balls, all the better. If it means watching her mother relax, watching her be treated well, watching her be loved? After more than Beth's lifetime of sadness, isolation, and abuse, Mother deserves some happiness, whatever the cost.

"Can you really?" Gwen presses. "I'm not going to get his hopes up again. I can't—I can't get my own hopes up again."

Beth resolves then that it's happiness or bust. They'll make this work. They'll get their parents to admit their love, to commit to each other, and then she and Gwen can walk into the sunset together. Society will no longer care about them, daughters of two joined empires.

"I'll convince her," Beth says again, pushing all her hope

and desire into the words. "All you need to do is convince him there's hope."

Gwen considers her for a long, painful pause. Beth pulls herself up to her tallest, her most confident. They can do this. She's sure.

At least, she's sure she wants to be sure.

"All right," Gwen says.

"Really?" Beth asks.

Gwen laughs softly and steps back up to her, wrapping her in her arms. Beth buries her face in Gwen's shoulder, careful of her gown, and breathes her in. She smells like lilacs and sweat, sweet and tangy.

"If you're convinced, I'm convinced," Gwen tells the side of her head. "I'm really not strong enough to lose you again."

"That makes two of us," Beth says, pulling back to meet her eyes. "So we'll try?"

"We'll try," Gwen agrees. She glances over her shoulder to confirm they're still alone and then looks back, her gaze distinctly more predatory. "How long do you think we've been here?"

"Ten minutes, maybe?" Beth posits, stepping back toward the hedges and tugging Gwen with her. "We could stand another ten, couldn't we? We got lost."

"Terribly lost," Gwen agrees, following Beth and dipping her head down to skate her lips up Beth's throat.

Beth sighs when her back hits the hedge. Gwen grunts as she's momentarily knocked away from her.

"These damn skirts," Beth growls, tugging Gwen in and bumping her hoop off to the left while hers shifts to the right.

Gwen hums in approval and crashes their mouths back

together. And then they're lost in the heat of lips and teeth and tongue. In their private sighs and moans. In their mutual frustration of all the layers and the silks and that no, neither of them can get on the ground right now, and there's not a bench, and, God, did no one think about the poor ladies itching to—

Well of course they didn't.

They content themselves with ten minutes of fiercely traded kisses until even the heat of each other's hands can't distract them from their responsibilities inside.

Gwen steps back first, her lips too plump and bodice askew. "We should get you back to Lord Montson. He'll have had time to miss you now."

"Shut up," Beth says, shaking her head as she rights her own bodice and gingerly touches her hair. "All right?"

"You're fine. I think you did a number on mine though," Gwen says, patting at the braid Beth accidentally tugged down from her updo.

"Oh, damn, here, let me," Beth says, stepping forward just as Mr. Mason appears at the end of their hedgerow.

"I've got her. You need to get back." His eyes flick over them and Beth tries to step into the shadows so he can't see her flushed cheeks and kiss-raw lips. "You're more than invigorated enough by the air."

"Mr.—Albie, it . . . isn't," Beth starts.

"You two made up?" he asks, cutting her off with a knowing look.

Beth glances back at Gwen, who just rolls her eyes. "Um, yes," she says slowly.

"Good. Gwen can fill me in. Bobby will escort you back to Meredith, who's waiting to bring you back inside."

"Thank you, I—" Beth starts, stepping toward him with a final glance back at Gwen—beautiful, disheveled, so kissable Gwen—

"Hurt her again and I won't be the one hauling you out of the bushes," he says lowly as she reaches his side.

"I'll do my best," Beth says honestly, reaching out to squeeze his arm before hurrying through the maze. Because now that she knows at least Gwen's cousins approve, there's even less calling her to return to her fake life.

They just have to survive the next few weeks, convince their parents to marry, and then undergo the scandal. That's all. Easy.

CHAPTER TWENTY-FOUR

Gwen

It's a short walk from the Tudor-style Henley-on-Thames locomotive station to Henley bridge, but it takes nearly an hour of pushing and shoving to do it. By the time they've hauled halfway across the bridge, Father's new white linen suit and top hat look a bit dusty, and there's mud on Gwen's deep blue gown, the white edging almost invisible beneath the muck.

Gwen stares out at the river, wondering how the sculls will even race with so many other boats littering the water for an up-close view. She thinks it might be nice some year to get here a few days early and have a boat. Wake up at the crack of dawn and just row out. Maybe she and Beth could do that. No one would look twice at them in a little boat.

Not like the scrutiny they'll face today beside the Steward Enclosure. The royal tent is already packed full when they finally shuffle past. Gwen wonders if she could even see the queen if there were fewer people, tiny woman that she is. If she's here at all. Hard to tell, honestly.

Instead, they arrive at the third tent along the water, stepping gratefully into the shade and out of the hot summer sun. White linen cloths cover a series of picnic tables, and members of the ton mill about in a crowd that's still more than claustrophobic enough to make Gwen wince. They may not have as many guests as the royals do, but it's still a press.

Gwen subtly shunts her father toward the northern edge of their tent, pointing to two suspiciously empty seats at the front where they can gratefully collapse. Gwen plunks down, ignoring that her right arm is fully in the sun. Father sits beside her, loosens his cravat, and rests his hat in his lap with a sigh.

"Finally made it, did you?"

Albie leans around Father to wink at her. Did he reserve their seats? How would he even—

"And that's further proof that the common folk can't be trusted. Just look at the blockage there," a voice booms disparagingly to their right.

Gwen glances over, and low and behold there stands Lord Ashmond, surveying the commoners along the river with disgust. Behind him, Beth and Lady Demeroven sit stone-faced while his wife titters along. Beth looks wonderful in a light pink froth of a gown. She's fanning herself manically and Lady Demeroven beside her looks ready to melt already.

They might actually pull this off.

Father grunts as Lord Ashmond continues to bloviate about things that should be kept silent, or at worst, muttered under one's breath. How his entire tent hasn't already pushed him into the river is anyone's guess. They've clearly been there for an hour longer than anyone in Gwen's.

"Here."

Bobby appears on her other side with two flutes of champagne for her and Father. She grabs hers gratefully, taking a large sip. Bobby settles into the chair behind them, downing his own glass.

"Horrid, isn't he?" Bobby says, nodding toward Lord Ashmond, who has now attracted a small horde of equally low-minded parliamentarians.

"Quite," Father agrees. "Now, who are you rooting for, Bobby?" he asks, turning to regard her younger cousin.

"Oh, the London Rowing Club, for sure. They're going to trounce the Leander Club. Apologies—I know you had said they're your favorite, Raverson," he adds to a younger gentleman next to him.

"Oh, I'll take a skirmish, no matter who wins," the man says, smirking at Bobby. His deep brown eyes are quite striking. "I don't think we've met," he adds to Father.

"Lord Havenfort," Father says, extending an awkwardly angled hand. "And this is my daughter, Lady Gwen."

"A pleasure," the man says, nodding to Gwen so a lock of almost-black hair falls over his face. "Viscount Raverson."

She feels she should probably think him quite handsome. But he pales in absurd comparison to Beth and no amount of straight white teeth and broad shoulders will sway her on that fact.

"Ah, I knew your father. I'm sorry for your loss," Father says quickly. "Will you be joining the Lords in his stead?"

"Thank you," Viscount Raverson says rather flatly. Gwen gets the feeling he doesn't harbor deep grief over the loss. "I will. It's actually why I'm here today. I wanted to get your opinion on this Matrimonial Causes Act. Father was vehemently opposed as you know, but I'm not so sure."

She watches in resignation as Father's face lights up. "Of course, of course. Help me gather food for my lovely single daughter, and we'll discuss," he says, winking at Gwen as he stands.

She only just refrains from swatting him. She wants no part in his matchmaking, especially not when it's taking him decidedly away from her own plans. She slumps in her seat as he and the viscount make their way back toward the catered buffet at the rear of the tent. She looks out over the water and spots Montson entering one of the sculls, along with a crew of three other young men. She hopes the LRC trounces them viciously.

"Want to make it interesting?" Albie asks.

Gwen sighs and digs in her skirts, pulling out a few pounds and handing them over without looking at Albie. "Put that on the LRC on top of whatever Father's bet."

"Don't worry. Raverson seems malleable," Bobby says as Albie turns back to Meredith, pocketing Gwen's money. "He may be a handsome face, but I didn't get the sense he has any real interest."

"I suppose that's good," Gwen mumbles. Bobby leans onto Father's chair, his face level with her own. "Do you know him?"

"He was a year above me at Oxford, I think. Didn't get to know him well. But if your father can convince him, that might be the deciding vote."

"Perhaps I should have made more of an effort," Gwen says, glancing back at them. She may not be swayed by the man's smile, but she could help in gathering votes. Men have some uses, after all.

"I think we should focus on whatever it is you and Miss Demeroven have planned."

Gwen goes still. "What?" she manages inelegantly.

"You've been glancing at her every minute or so, and she's been staring at you for the past five. Her mother looks awful."

Despite herself, Gwen flicks her eyes over to the next tent.

Lady Demeroven does look like she's only a few minutes from passing out. "Beth and I are just . . . acquaintances," Gwen says slowly, dragging her gaze back to meet Bobby's, so close he's almost blurry.

Far too close for comfort.

Gwen stands up, tugging her own fan from her skirts. She fans herself and leans out of the tent under the guise of watching the lineup. They're pushing off from the docks, so the first heat can't be too long now.

"Do you need a distraction?"

"Do you mind?" she asks Bobby, leaning around him to get a look at Beth.

He grins, rocking back and forth on his feet where he's sidled up beside her. "What's the aim?"

Gwen sighs, glancing behind him to try and catch Albie's attention, but he's thoroughly engrossed in conversation with one of Meredith's cousins now. She doesn't want Bobby underfoot for this, but she can't make too much of a fuss. Father may be at the back of the tent, but it's not that far, and his hearing's too good.

"You promise not to say anything?" she mutters.

"Cross my heart," Bobby says eagerly. "I'm at your disposal."

Gwen sighs and tugs Bobby further out of the tent, like they're trying to lean over the bank to get the best view. "All right. We're hoping my father might come to her mother's aid should she need to go into the boathouse and out of the sun."

Bobby blinks back at her. "That's all?"

"What?"

"That's your whole big plan to get Lord Havenfort and Lady Demeroven together?"

"Who said—"

"Albie's been onto you for ages. Thought it was a good laugh, and then whatever ugly business happened with the Ashmonds and you've been downright dreary."

Gwen feels a flush rising up her neck. Has she been that transparent? And when did Bobby start paying any attention to her goings-on, or her father's for that matter? And when did he get so tall? She has to look up at her little cousin now and it's rather infuriating.

"So what's the strategy—just hope she faints?"

Gwen groans softly into her fan. That sounds so stupid when he says it out loud. "Beth's been pushing champagne on her."

"And that's enough?"

She takes in Bobby's unimpressed face. "Well, you try wearing all the layers and moving around in a hoop in this heat. It's no picnic."

Bobby glances at the picnickers across the river, who are using the day for exactly that, and who look far more comfortable than they are. Gwen shifts, enjoying the light breeze that wafts up from the river and settles beneath her skirts. Would that she could wear linens like Bobby.

She thinks she might look dashing in a suit. Maybe she can get Father to tailor one for her someday. If she and Beth don't succeed, maybe she could at least get a whole rack of them as consolation presents.

Gwen shakes herself. They're going to succeed, Bobby's dubious concern aside.

"And how are you planning on distracting Lord Ashmond long enough for your father to need to step in?"

Gwen wrinkles her nose. "We're winging that bit."

"Great. Good strategy. Excellent," Bobby says.

"Could you be less of a brat, please?" she hisses.

"For two such smart women, this is a dreadful plan."

Gwen glares back. Her fierce need for this to work is the only thing keeping her going, because their track record is admittedly terrible and their options severely limited. They know it's a dreadful plan. She doesn't need Bobby rubbing that in her face on top of everything else.

"How about this—we wait until Montson's run his first race. They'll probably win."

"Wait, I thought the LRC was a given. Have I just blown my money?" Gwen asks, momentarily distracted.

Bobby laughs. "They'll win the first heat. Montson and Jordan are both out to prove themselves, and they'll overcompensate on the first go. By the second, they'll be tired, and right useless by the third heat. The London Rowing Club will win, but, more importantly, Lord Ashmond will be insufferable after the first heat. Gloating."

"And?"

"And that's when Albie and I should start an argument with him about Leander. We'll crowd him, and Lady Demeroven and Miss Demeroven will have to step out, and then in the heat, with the hubbub, she'll get faint, and as you're trying to drag your father over to break up our argument, he'll just . . . have to catch her."

Gwen gapes at Bobby. That's—that's an excellent plan. Truly. Simple, but crafty. Nuanced in all the right ways.

"When the hell did you grow up?" she demands.

Bobby smirks and nudges her. "We drank a few weeks ago."

"We've drunk for seasons. This—you'll be a right catch next

season, you know?" she says honestly, impressed. Chastened too, since his plan is deceptively simple, and they really should have come up with it themselves.

They should have asked for help a month ago. She's been telling herself she's losing Albie to Meredith—and possibly losing Bobby by extension. But they've been there the whole time, hoping and speculating. Albie would have said yes, if she'd asked. He could probably have even convinced Meredith too. She's just been too busy wallowing in self-pity to notice.

"Let's focus on your parents this season, and you can turn your sights on me next year," Bobby says, taking her arm to pull her back toward their tent, where Albie and Meredith are now standing at the edge. "Oh, look, they're about to start."

Gwen doesn't look at the boats. Instead, she steps back so she can watch the Ashmonds watch their son. Lord and Lady Ashmond stand at the edge of their tent along with their hangers-on, leaving Beth and Lady Demeroven a row behind, and likely unable to see. Gwen notes that neither looks particularly put out about this. Lady Demeroven's fanning herself like it's the end of days, and Beth—

Beth looks straight at Gwen. She offers a slight smile and then turns to her mother. Gwen looks back at the river just as the starting gun goes off. They're well and truly underway of this ridiculous charade, and there's nothing left but to see it through and hope Bobby can deliver.

Montson and Jordan row like there's no tomorrow. As Bobby predicted, Leander easily wins the first match, outpacing the LRC's scull by at least a full length. Her tent is groaning but the Ashmonds are cavorting. She can hear champagne being popped, whoops spilling through the air.

"Yeah, let's see if they can do it again," Bobby says loudly, nudging Albie next to him. "Beginners' luck."

Albie stares at his brother for a moment and Gwen watches them exchange a series of nods and small gestures. She's never paid much attention to their relationship. Bobby's never been much more than a nuisance, but now—now it seems he's sly and clever and persuasive.

"Jordan can't make another round, and I'd be surprised if Montson's not keeling over already," Albie adds, his voice echoing across the water.

She glances over and spots Lord Ashmond frowning at them. "I don't know, they won by a full length," Gwen says, her voice light and easy, but louder than perhaps it should be.

She hears Lady Demeroven agreeing and has to hide a smile. Gwen glances over at them and Beth stares back at her, perplexed.

"Two rowers simply filling in—there's no way Leander makes it another round," Bobby says quickly.

"The LRC's got this locked up. You wait and see," Albie adds.

Lord Ashmond scoffs absurdly loudly and both boys lean around Gwen to make eye contact.

"You don't agree?" Bobby calls over.

"Well, his son's racing. He's bound to be biased," Albie says, smiling affably at Lord Ashmond.

"I am no such thing," Lord Ashmond exclaims.

Bobby steps around Gwen and Albie squeezes her waist as he follows, the two of them beginning a tirade of challenges and statistics that Lord Ashmond meets with glee. She supposes besting her father's nephews will only add to his sanctimonious disdain. Make him feel tall.

She wonders if he's poorly endowed. What else could make a man so rich this pompous?

"What are they up to?" Meredith asks, stepping up to Gwen's side as the argument escalates, just as Bobby predicted it would.

"Have they had much to drink?" Gwen asks, going for innocent.

"No more than you or I, seeing as it's not even noon," Meredith says flatly. "Oh dear."

Bobby has stepped into Lord Ashmond's space, the two of them nearly chest to chest. Of course, Lord Ashmond towers over Bobby. He looks absurdly childish squared off that way and Gwen feels her bubble of excitement deflating into anxiety.

Father may actually have to step in.

She glances around and finds him already moving toward her, his eyes on the escalating altercation. Lady Ashmond's wringing her hands and Gwen notices a few older gentlemen moving toward the cluster, as tall and intimidating as Lord Ashmond, and possibly less concerned with appearances.

She may have just aided and abetted a brawl.

"What are your cousins doing?" Father asks as he reaches Gwen.

"I'm really not sure," she says honestly, watching Albie brace Bobby from behind. Lord Ashmond leans down, spilling vitriol about the boys' father and how Ashmond used to trounce both Viscount Mason and Father in scull racing when they were lads.

As if any of them could do damage in a boat these days.

"Sod it all," Father says, starting forward just as Lady Demeroven drags Beth out from the tent, the two of them stepping back carefully into the sun. One of Lord Ashmond's men knocks over a chair.

"Father, don't make a—" Gwen starts, but he's already striding across the small gap of lawn between the tents.

Gwen follows after, no longer concerned with their plan. Lord Ashmond's just pushed Bobby into Albie, and the boys are building up toward fisticuffs. She has to stop this.

She takes another step forward only for a hand to close over her wrist.

"Don't." Gwen turns, surprised, and Lady Demeroven slides her hand up to take Gwen's arm. "You don't want a black eye, and none of them can take the scandal of accidentally knocking you one," she says lowly.

Beth steps up on her other side. Gwen glances at her, both of them wide-eyed. It takes her a moment before she turns to Lady Demeroven.

"Should you be standing with me?" she asks, too anxious and overwhelmed to find a subtler way to ask.

"Your father is about to defend your cousins from that clod. No one will blame me for watching over you in his stead right now."

She gives Gwen a tight smile, though Gwen can feel the tension in her frame from the vise of her arm.

"Okay," Gwen whispers.

Beth takes her other hand, the tangle of their fingers hidden by their bumping skirts.

"What possessed Bobby?" she asks as they watch Lord Ashmond's friends trying to step between the boys and Lord Ashmond.

Father's visibly restraining Albie, who's yelling obscenities that Lord Ashmond is spitting right back.

"Walk it off, Lord Ashmond," Father shouts as he wrestles

Albie behind himself and steps up, wrapping an arm around Bobby's torso to hold him back. "Your son will be in another race in minutes, we'll return to our tents, let calmer heads prevail."

"So you can keep bribing honorable men into your heathen schemes? I think not," Lord Ashmond shoots back, pressing forward.

Father sidesteps and pushes Bobby out of the way. Gwen gasps as he and Lord Ashmond press chest to chest. With Father, it's an even match.

"Your mangy nephews have no business here," Lord Ashmond spits.

"They've as much right as anyone. It's you who's turned a sporting bet into a fight."

Gwen watches in horror as Albie pulls Bobby back. Lord Ashmond's men—others from the House of Lords—encircle Father and Lord Ashmond.

"He's going to end up on the floor," Lady Demeroven mutters.

Gwen bristles. "Father can handle himself."

"Lord Ashmond," Lady Demeroven clarifies. "Your father has a mean left—"

CRACK. Father throws a punch that spins Lord Ashmond into the chairs, sending him toppling headfirst into the grass. Lady Ashmond shrieks in dismay. Bobby and Albie rush back in to restrain Father as the other Lords gape.

"Go back to your betting," Father spits out as Lady Ashmond attempts to help her husband up.

But he doesn't need the help. In a blink, Lord Ashmond has risen from the chairs and launched himself at Father. The two go down in a flurry of fists and linens, rolling on the grass like two common urchins. Both sides hurry to try to pry them apart. Beth squeezes Gwen's hand so hard it hurts and Lady Demeroven holds her back when Gwen goes to surge forward.

This is her fault. He's in this fight because of her. She has to stop it—

The Lords manage to pull Lord Ashmond off Father, but not before they each get one more punch in. Lord Ashmond clutches at his jaw as the men force him away, his wife caterwauling after them. Bobby and Albie help Father off the ground and everything goes quiet.

She can distantly see another race underway, knows the commoners on the river have been watching, can almost hear their own tent tittering. The Ashmond tent has entirely cleared out. She doesn't know where they've taken Lord Ashmond, but she hopes it's somewhere to be doused in cold water, the lout.

"Father," Gwen exclaims.

Lady Demeroven finally loosens her grip and Gwen rushes forward, dragging Beth with her. Father turns and regards them, squinting. His white suit is stained green, and she can tell he'll have a livid bruise and swollen eye tomorrow, but otherwise he looks remarkably unscathed.

"You always could take a punch," Lady Demeroven says. She comes up behind Gwen, placing a hand on her waist.

Father rolls his eyes, testing his jaw and brushing off Albie's supportive arm. "And you always could pick the rottenest of the bunch," he returns.

Gwen winces, but Lady Demeroven simply pulls a lace kerchief from her skirts, stepping up to dab at a trickle of blood that's making its way down Father's face. Lord Ashmond must have nicked him with a ring.

"What were you thinking?" Lady Demeroven asks. Beth steps close to Gwen, hiding their hands amid their skirts as they glance at each other.

"You'd rather I let that man hit my nephew?" Father asks, making no move to stop her ministrations. "Should you be doing this?"

Lady Demeroven stills for a moment before shrugging. "I doubt this will be the most exciting part of the story. Boys, go get some cold water," she instructs, leaning around Father to look firmly at Bobby and Albie.

The boys jolt into action, slipping off into the tent.

"Are you staying the night here?" Lady Demeroven asks.

"We took the train," Father says, gently taking the handkerchief from her to press it hard against his temple.

Gwen watches as Lady Demeroven hovers close, a hand on his chest for a long moment before she steps back. "You'll want to get a steak from the inn before you head back."

"Yes, I'll certainly look a sight beside Gwen then," he says, chuckling. "Violence is never the answer," he adds, looking at Gwen and Beth.

"Fat lot of good that advice has done you," Gwen says, the words slipping out.

Father merely laughs. "I'm just fine. Though, Miss Demeroven, I suppose you should watch the rest of the race, cheer on your intended, as his parents—"

They all glance into the Ashmond tent, utterly empty.

"Yes, someone should support Lord Montson, I guess," Lady Demeroven agrees. "Girls, why don't you join—Lady Meredith, isn't it?"

"Yes." Beth startles as Meredith appears beside them. "We'd

be happy to have Miss Demeroven with us for a few hours if you'd like to, um, see to things, Lady Demeroven?" Meredith offers.

"Thank you, dear," Lady Demeroven says kindly. "Walk me to the boathouse?" she asks Father.

"Are you sure that's wise?" Father asks.

"I'm simply making sure you aren't going to involve the authorities. He made the first move against your nephew. I'm smoothing things over," Lady Demeroven says archly.

Father just shakes his head. "All right. Gwen, take good care of Miss Demeroven. We'll be back," he says, gesturing for Lady Demeroven to precede him.

Gwen watches as they move through the empty Ashmond tent and out of sight, walking close but unconnected. Holy hell—

"Did that actually work?" Meredith asks.

Gwen gapes at Meredith.

"Did what work?" Beth asks.

"Oh, it took all of two seconds to realize Bobby was up to something. Come on, I could use a drink."

She takes Gwen's free arm and strides back toward the tent, forcing Gwen to tug Beth along behind her.

"Did you plan that?" Beth hisses as they cluster back under the tent.

They huddle by the refreshments, far from Albie and Bobby. The boys are preening under the attention of their schoolmates. Beyond them, the next heat lines up on the river. Gwen couldn't possibly care less about the race.

"No," Gwen tells Beth. Meredith quirks an eyebrow and passes them each a flute of champagne. "Well, not—not like that. Bobby thought he could distract Lord Ashmond and we'd get your mother to faint, like we planned," she tells Beth, deflating at her flat look. "It made sense at the time."

"Who could have known Lord Ashmond would get that drunk this early in the day," Meredith says, shrugging.

"He could have been badly hurt," Beth says softly.

"Father wouldn't injure him too badly," Gwen protests.

"Your father," Beth corrects. "Or Bobby, or Albie. I didn't—why did you involve them in this?" she asks, part shock, part indignation.

"It wasn't intentional," Gwen cuts back.

"It's not as if you were being particularly subtle about it," Meredith adds. "The two of you glancing at each other every minute. It was clear something was afoot."

Gwen winces and Beth sighs. Meredith laughs at them both.

"Do you think our parents knew?" Beth asks.

"Oh, no," Meredith says quickly. "They're shockingly oblivious to everything but the politics right now, and though it wasn't a *good* plan, your mother did look halfway to a fainting spell for a while there before the fight."

"At least I can stop forcing drinks on her," Beth says, shaking her head as she takes a sip of champagne.

"She seemed remarkably together after the fight," Gwen notes, glancing over at the Ashmond tent. No sign of the Ashmonds or their parents.

"Oh, she's good in a crisis," Beth says, waving it off. "I do wish we could see where they went. Hard to know our next steps with them out of sight."

"Hard to know how they're avoiding the Ashmonds. I can't imagine this will make the earl any more inclined to let the two of you see each other," Meredith says, looking between them.

Gwen cocks her head. Beth glances at her and then looks back at Meredith. "What . . . exactly do you think we're trying to do?"

Meredith considers them and then looks back at the cluster of boys. Gwen notes that all of the Lords have disappeared as well. She wonders if the two camps are elsewhere, planning political machinations in light of the Havenfort/Ashmond brawl, as she's sure it will come to be known.

"Based on the little I've heard from Albie, you're trying to match up your parents. I'm entirely unclear on the motivation."

Gwen glances at Beth, who's simply staring at Meredith.

"That's . . . yes. We just think they could be happy together," Gwen offers.

"And provide you some leeway in finding marriages yourselves, I expect, though you've left it a little late, Beth, to get out of this one."

"I know," Beth says softly.

"Do you really want to? I know Lord Ashmond is an unmitigated arse, but Lord Montson seems sweet enough, and he does like you very much."

"I know," Beth repeats. Gwen swallows hard as Beth raises their hands for Meredith to see. "But Lord Montson isn't who I'd like to spend my life with. And my mother will be miserable, much as she keeps insisting it's best for us both."

"Oh," Meredith says softly before glancing around the tent again.

But no one's paying them any mind. All of the men are eagerly watching the races. Beth should probably be cheering for

Montson, but Gwen won't give her up. Won't pull her away. Won't shy away from the look Meredith gives them as she returns her gaze, soft and understanding.

"I see."

"If our parents marry, it will mean we can . . . do away with charades and the marriage market. And they'll be happy," Beth adds desperately. "If we thought they were going to be miserable, we wouldn't try."

"We almost didn't," Gwen says, squeezing Beth's hand. "But they've both been nearly as heartbroken as we have, and if there's a chance for everyone to have . . ." She trails off, can't quite articulate it.

"For everyone to get a happily-ever-after, I understand," Meredith says, her smile growing. "Well. I think we're going to have to meet about my wedding much more often."

"What?" Gwen says, inelegant. She'd rather have an ice pick to the eye.

"Beth and I are just going to have to meet to compare notes. And her mother will have to come. And the Mason house has been having terrible mold issues, haven't you heard? So we'll have to meet at mine. And as your father is providing some of the funding and working with Albie's uncle to shore up the vote, I imagine he'll have to come along. And we'll simply need to picnic, won't we?" Meredith says.

"You really ought to have consulted Mere from the outset," Albie says as he steps up behind them. "She's the most devious of all of us, and that's saying something."

He glances at their hands and Gwen slowly tugs Beth's tangled fingers down between their skirts, smiling at her and then at Albie. She never said it plain, but they've both just known.

He's been her companion for nearly a decade through all of this nonsense. She should have just told them.

"Are you all right?" Beth asks as Albie steps around them to stand beside Meredith, taking her hand the way Beth has Gwen's.

"I'm just fine. Bobby's man of the hour now. And I think your father will be fine. I spotted him sitting on a bench with Lady Demeroven behind the boathouse. She found him a steak for his eye."

"Good," Gwen says, tension leaking out of her.

"So I hear we'll be seeing you in a few days?" Albie asks, winking at Beth.

Beth has the gumption to wink back, her hand squeezing Gwen's. Perhaps all is not lost, even if today was utter chaos.

"I think you just might," Beth says gamely.

Chapter Twenty-Five

Beth

Meredith, Bobby, and Albie are a force to be reckoned with. Beth watches in awe as they expertly maneuver their respective relatives. Meredith pairs off her mother with Albie's aunt. Bobby and Albie drag their uncle away to discuss the order of the groomsmen. And then Meredith swoops back in to pull Beth and Gwen into conversation so artfully that Mother and Lord Havenfort are almost required to at least exchange pleasantries.

The Harringtons aren't personae non gratae to Lord Ashmond, but the Masons surely are. These visits are a risk, but they're chances Mother seems eager to take. Their "accidental" picnic at the botanical gardens with Meredith, Albie, Gwen, and Lord Havenfort last week was a thorough delight, and Mother readily agreed to come take tea today. Beth's hopes are rising fast, as well as her chagrin.

"Does all this make you feel exceedingly unclever?" Gwen whispers as Meredith pours them tea, going on loudly about dress hems.

"Painfully," Beth agrees.

She's spent the last month and a half practically glued to Lord Montson's side, and all this time, if they'd just asked Gwen's cousins, they could have been having teas and listening to everyone laugh. It's almost enough to make her vomit.

Her mother and Lord Havenfort are chatting by the open window today, a shade too close together. Lord Havenfort's eye is still slightly purple, but Mother doesn't seem to mind. She's laughing, actually. It's her genuine laugh too—a sound Beth's barely heard in a month.

"Have you picked out a dress yet?" Meredith asks, bringing Beth's gaze back to her.

"What?" she mumbles.

Meredith chuckles. "A dress. You must have one at least in process."

"My mother's wedding dress," Beth says absently. "They're taking it in around the bust and removing the sleeves." She pauses, glancing at Gwen.

"I bet you look quite beautiful," Gwen says, smiling softly at her.

They've allowed themselves more than one quiet minute of peace this afternoon, sitting close together, hands tangled in their skirts. Beth's mind keeps wandering, visions of the two of them sneaking off into this cavernous townhouse to find somewhere—some dark corner—where they could slide beneath each other's skirts and—

"Beth," Gwen says, laughing a little.

"Oh, yes. Right. It does look nice," Beth agrees. "Nothing like it looked on my mother. Father insisted she wear it for their portrait and she looks amazing. I look like a flat little frump."

"You absolutely do not," Mother says as she and Lord Havenfort appear around their side of the table.

Beth looks up at her mother—her always poised, always

glamorous mother. "I don't look half so beautiful as you did," Beth says.

Mother rolls her eyes. But she looks so relaxed and happy. They have to make this work; Beth would try just for the look on her mother's face.

"You are beautiful in entirely your own way," Mother argues.

"I'm sure you look very lovely," Lord Havenfort adds. "You're having it done by Mistress Grinley, I assume?"

"Of course," Mother says quickly. "Only the very best for Beth."

Beth forces herself to maintain her smile. It's costing them a fortune to use the most expensive modiste in London for the alterations, for a wedding she's rather hoping she won't be attending. They're down to a phantom staff, poor Miss Wilson's working herself bloody, and for what?

Gwen squeezes her hand and she blows out a breath, pretending not to worry. If they pull this off—and their parents do look rather cozy—the Havenforts have more than enough to reimburse Mother for the expense.

"Remind me of the wedding date?" Lord Havenfort prompts.

"Eight days from today," Mother replies, tension returning to her posture as Beth slumps in her seat. "In fact, we probably should go, Beth. The Ashmonds are expecting us for dinner, and we'll need to change."

"Oh, but we've just poured tea," Meredith says quickly. "Could we finish? Lord Havenfort, perhaps you could show Lady Demeroven the gardens? The roses there would make such a lovely bouquet for Beth."

Beth holds her breath as both Mother and Lord Havenfort consider Meredith's suggestion. It's forward, but not glaringly so. And Mother does love flowers. It's one of her greater regrets, that they haven't spent enough time in London to cultivate a garden. The ones at the Demeroven estate up north are splendid. Mother sometimes even works them herself.

"I suppose," Mother says slowly. "For another twenty minutes. If you don't mind, Lord Havenfort."

"Not at all," Gwen's father says, offering his arm. "I'm great with flowers."

"I remember," Mother says, quite without thinking given the way her eyes widen.

But Lord Havenfort just chuckles and leads her from the room. Beth blows out a breath and Gwen slouches in her seat.

"Well?" Meredith says.

"Well what?" Gwen asks as she strokes Beth's palm.

"Go to the window. My goodness, you're both dreadful at this."

Gwen snorts and stands, pulling Beth up and then taking her arm to guide her toward the window. Beth fans herself as if she simply must get some air. Meredith immediately joins in on her mother's conversation. Albie, Bobby, and their uncle are far too immersed in what sounds like racing bets to care what Beth and Gwen get up to.

Gwen tugs Beth up to the large picture window where their parents stood some minutes ago, and together they look down at the lovely back gardens. They're even more resplendent from above. Though in fairness, the last time Beth saw them, she was too busy kissing Gwen's brains out before breaking both of their hearts to care for the florals.

Beth spots their parents, chatting together on a stone bench beneath a leafy green tree. She can't quite see their faces.

"Do you think it's working?" Gwen wonders.

Beth forces herself to smile despite their dwindling timeline. "They're not fighting."

"They weren't fighting before you dumped us either," Gwen counters.

"We didn't—" Beth looks up and finds Gwen smirking down at her. "Shut up. They were . . . more than friendly then, but I don't know that that's enough. Mother will be throwing away a sure status match."

Gwen sighs. "And Father's gun-shy."

Beth watches as Gwen leans against the windowsill. She looks beautiful in the sunlight that angles through the window, whisps of her blond hair surrounding her like a halo.

"We'll just have to push them," Beth says, rallying her resolve.

"Right. Shove them, more like," Gwen agrees.

"You think if we threw them both down the stairs, we could lock them up together to heal?" Beth wonders, smiling as Gwen snorts.

She glances back down at their parents. But Lord Havenfort is alone now.

"Beth, time to leave."

Beth sighs and turns to find her mother in the doorway to the Harringtons' library. Gwen quickly squeezes her arm before stepping around her to go join Meredith. They've done all they can. This is all she and Gwen get. A measly two hours and middling progress, if any, in their efforts.

"Come along, dear," Mother prompts, and Beth nods, forcing herself across the room to curtsy politely to Lady Harrington before following Mother out.

"Did you and Lord Havenfort have a good chat?" she asks. They take their bonnets from the doorman and step into the late afternoon sun for their waiting carriage.

Everything's so precise now. Carriages always waiting, schedule always full. She misses the emptiness of their life in the country. Hell, even the first few weeks of the season were more relaxing, when they attended every event in sight. There wasn't this pressure.

There wasn't this sadness, is more like it. She could handle the bowing and scraping and dresses and tulle if every single moment didn't remind her of what she'd lost. And if Mother ever seemed even a tenth as cheerful when they're with the Ashmonds as she did in the library today.

Mother looks back at her, eyebrow raised, before she lets herself be handed into the coach. Beth follows behind, casting one longing glance at the upstairs window before the footman shuts the coach door.

She watches the Harrington townhouse drift away, the carriage swaying beneath them as they begin the short drive home.

"Well?" Beth prompts.

"Well what?" Mother asks, pulling off her gloves to examine her nails.

"Did you and Lord Havenfort have a good chat in the gardens?" Beth repeats.

"It was fine," Mother says, shrugging and refusing to meet Beth's eyes.

"What did you talk about?"

"This and that."

Beth huffs and adjusts her skirt so she can slouch against the carriage seat. "Expansive."

"I don't know, darling. We just . . . chatted. About you, about the wedding, about Lady Gwen. We're . . . friendly."

"Friendly," Beth repeats. "That's how you'd describe it? You're smiling. You've barely smiled at all in the past month."

Mother blinks and Beth bites at her lip. She's meant to be going about this with more tact. But *friendly*? They are so much more than friendly, and Mother's not an evasive woman. She calls a spade a spade. Why must they obfuscate and tiptoe around this?

"I haven't seen you smile like this in weeks either," Mother counters.

"Is that such a surprise?" Beth wonders. "Aren't you miserable? I'm miserable."

"Yes, you've made that rather plain," Mother says dryly.

Beth frowns over at her, waiting for more. She needs Mother to admit that it's terrible—this loveless, thankless match they've found. Advantageous, yes, but dreadful.

"I will admit it's been trying. And I enjoyed these . . . clandestine opportunities to be around like-minded people. But you know this cannot be frequent. We're dancing on the head of a pin simply seeing Lady Meredith."

"Well, she did set up that cake tasting. We'll have to come for that, since we haven't sent for a cake yet, and we are, as you said, almost a week from the grand wedding," Beth says quickly. Mother rolls her eyes. "Come on, you want to be at the Harrington cake tasting. It's the only fun part of this horrible planning."

"Yes, well, there you're right," Mother allows, smiling. "I do think this ruse can probably carry you and Lady Gwen through once you're married. You'll have to visit Lady Meredith, and she'll have to visit Mr. Mason. You'll find opportunities to see each other."

"What, once yearly in the country and then at these group events during the season, if we're even here?" Beth wonders, indignation rising at her mother's casual tone, like it's purely social.

"That's how friendship works once you're married, darling," Mother says, her face carefully flat.

Beth clenches her jaw. "She's not my friend," she insists, staring Mother down.

But her expression doesn't change—blank and serene, as if Beth's words are sliding down a rainy window, impervious to everything without.

"You'll get to see her. Isn't that what matters?"

Beth seethes. "Yes, seeing the person I hold dearest in the world a few days a year makes everything better. Spending the rest of forever with the Ashmonds now feels thoroughly tolerable."

"You will grow to like them more over time."

Mother looks out the window and Beth balls her fists. She knows that deep down, somewhere Mother refuses to reach, she's just as devastated as Beth is—wants out just as much as she does. She just has to get her to admit to it.

"They're horrible," Beth insists. "Concede that much to me. It may be the match of your dreams, but Lord Ashmond is a brute. An oaf."

Mother turns back to her, biting at her lower lip for a moment. She opens her mouth, but then the carriage hits the curb outside of their townhouse.

"Come along, dear. We must dress for dinner."

"You agree with me," Beth insists, hurrying out after her. She keeps pace with her skirts hiked up, less graceful but just as fast as her mother.

"Let's focus on getting ready. Miss Wilson will settle you first while I do my makeup."

"We both look perfectly fine," Beth protests as Mother unlocks the front door and they stomp inside, blinking in the dim, empty foyer.

"We cannot arrive at the Ashmonds' in what we've worn to tea, and you need at least another two layers on your skirt."

"Why?" Beth asks, standing still even as Mother continues toward the stairs. She feels her composure slipping. "Why must we continue this charade?"

"It is not a charade," Mother dismisses, a hand on the railing.

"*Mother,*" Beth exclaims.

Mother turns slowly, the foyer between them. "If the lace bothers you so much, we'll find another modiste."

"It isn't about the lace."

"I know you would prefer to . . . see your friend more, but we've found a compromise. Why can't you be satisfied with that?"

Rage slips up Beth's throat, constricting her lungs. "Gwen is not—"

"That's all she can be," Mother says.

Beth feels the words like a blow to her stomach. It's not that Mother won't acknowledge it. It's that she can't even imagine a world where Beth and Gwen could be together.

"I know it isn't fair, but we will find ways for you to see each other. And someday it will be more than enough. You'll see. These feelings fade. You learn to live with compromise."

Like it's easy. Like living in a purgatory state of sadness is nothing.

Mother waits for some smart rejoinder, but Beth doesn't have one. Of course Mother's fine with compromise. It's all she's ever known. But Beth—Beth wants so much more than empty, ashen compromise, for both of them. This half life will *never* be enough.

"I can't do this. I'm not you" falls out of her mouth before she can think to stop the words.

"Excuse me?" Mother says.

It feels like something has cracked inside her chest, all her hurt surging forward. "The bowing and scraping and bending ourselves to Lord Ashmond's views on everything. Giving up our politics. Giving up Gwen and Lord Havenfort—" Her breath hitches. "We are giving up everything for them. And the way Lord Ashmond talks to you—the way you *let* him talk to you—it's like—" She breaks off, swallowing her words as Mother narrows her eyes.

"It's like what, Elizabeth?" Mother asks, her voice sharp now.

Beth straightens her back. This wasn't part of the plan, but someone needs to say it. "It's like he's Father, all over again. You agree with everything he says, even when I know you don't. You laugh like he's funny. And you let him talk down to you all the time, like you're unworthy of his consideration and should simply be grateful he looks on you at all."

The silence that follows brims with every unkind thing that's ever been said in this house, every slight, every fight and ugly moment. And all of the ways neither of them ever made a move to stop them, never stood up for themselves, never fought Father. They wouldn't have won, Beth knows that. But they can now.

They don't have to submit to repeating the future like it's inevitable.

"I don't want us to live like this. And I know you don't want to either. You can't possibly want to live like this again. Please, Mother, if you just spoke with Lord Havenfort, let him prove to you that—"

"Enough!" Mother yells. "You do not get to have everything you want in life." Her voice is suddenly low and cold, not even allowing for the barest possibility of another way. "You'll have a manor and a husband and a fortune for generations. That is more than anyone can hope for."

"It's not," Beth insists.

"Beth."

"I can hope for more," Beth says, her voice rough as the tears finally fall, as anger gives way to desperation. "You should hope for more."

They stand staring at each other, Beth begging for her mother to value her own life as much as she values Beth's security. To take a chance on their happiness being worth *something*.

Mother just shakes her head. "I have all I've hoped for. I'm going to lie down. Miss Wilson will help you dress for dinner."

She turns and heads up the stairs, shoulders curled inward, defeated, unwilling to hope or want or listen.

Beth's heart clenches in her chest. "Mother," she calls.

But Mother doesn't respond. Beth stands in the completely empty foyer, her voice echoing through the house, all the hurt drifting through the air around her.

CHAPTER TWENTY-SIX

Gwen

"Good, you're here," Meredith says, pulling Gwen through the door before she even knocks.

"What's going on?" Gwen asks, taking in her tight face and plain dress.

Meredith's not outfitted for anything public facing, much less hosting a surprise early breakfast for mothers and daughters. She looks like she just woke up.

That knot of worry at the top of Gwen's stomach twists even tighter. If Meredith isn't actually hosting tea this morning, then Gwen's not going to see Beth today. It's been days since they've had a moment together, longer still since they've managed to have their parents at the same event. The wedding is almost here, and now she won't even get to strategize with Beth. It's time for a last-ditch, desperate effort. But she can't plan that all by herself. They're far beyond her slapdash plans now.

"Come on," Meredith says, steering Gwen down the servant's hallway and through the kitchen.

"Have you heard anything from Beth? Mrs. Stelm said she gave Miss Wilson my last letter, but Beth hasn't replied yet," Gwen says, trying to talk and simultaneously navigate her hoop through the narrow halls.

The servants pay them no mind as they pass, like Meredith must do this every day. But the silence is grating on Gwen. She's anxious enough without Meredith making a mystery of things.

"Meredith, would you please just—"

"Here. You have twenty minutes," Meredith says cryptically, yanking Gwen to a halt.

She opens a narrow door and shoves Gwen inside before she can so much as speak. Gwen turns, mouth open, but Meredith shuts the door on her. Gwen sighs and revolves, taking in the small single bedroom with one high window at street level. It's dim, and cramped, and there in the middle stands Beth in her house frock, hair still braided from sleep.

Gwen's chest clenches as Beth comes for her, shoving her skirt to the side so she can arch up and wrap her arms around Gwen. She presses into her, face tucked into her neck.

"I just wanted to see you one more time," Beth whispers, pulling back only to rise into a kiss that makes Gwen stumble back into the door, hands gripping at Beth's waist to steady them both.

"This was the only time I'm not scheduled to be at the Ashmonds'," Beth says when they break apart minutes later, lips swollen, hair mussed, and cheeks pink. Her hands cradle Gwen's jaw as they lean back against the door. "Mother's still sleeping. She won't talk to me anymore. I can't convince her, I can't make her understand, and I don't think—" She pauses, surging forward into another kiss.

And Gwen lets her, sliding her hands back to splay over Beth's narrow shoulders, clutching her close. This is it then. Lady Demeroven's made her choice. The wedding is in three days. Their second attempt has failed, thwarted by politics and greed and fear. She has to surrender Beth to her unhappy marriage so she and her mother have somewhere to live, money to provide for them, security.

She loses herself in Beth's kiss, clutching at her back. Gwen has a lifetime to grieve. But right now, they have only these twenty minutes in this little room. Their last twenty minutes. She won't waste a moment of it.

"Here," she whispers as Beth breaks away to press kisses down her neck. She gently steps forward, pushing Beth into the middle of the room until she can spin around. "Get me out of this thing."

Beth hums and together they make the quickest work they can of pulling off her bodice and skirt, throwing off her petticoat and hoop. Then she can turn and tackle Beth onto the little bed. Then they can slide hands up underskirts and down corsets, unlacing until they're a mess of half-worn clothes and skin and kisses, gasping against each other for what feels like a small eternity.

This is how she'll remember Beth, bright cheeked and panting beneath her on a small, narrow bed—hair frayed, skirt about her waist, smiling as she comes down from her peak. She'll secret this picture away into her mind. She'll wait eagerly for the brief moments they can have going forward, stolen like this whenever they visit Meredith. Condemned to a quarter life of happiness, but they'll wring every bit they can from it. They'll savor every moment.

"I love you," Beth whispers, stroking at her cheek. Gwen rests her forehead against Beth's, heaving in air as she comes down.

"I love you too," Gwen murmurs, angling her head to sip a kiss from her lips.

But as her sweat cools and her heartbeat calms, Gwen feels the moment breaking around them. The gravity of what's to come presses down on her and she goes to pull back, to offer platitudes or excuses or—something—something to make it better.

Beth surges up, unwilling to separate, kissing her with a ferocity that steals Gwen's breath away and pounds against her heart. Like if Beth tries hard enough, their kiss could forestall the future. As if it can keep them here, in this little secret, away from the world, and reality and—

There's a sharp rap on the door.

"Beth, your carriage is here."

Beth stills, held against her, eyes squeezed shut. She doesn't move, holding to their love, and Gwen steels everything she has to pull away. To let Beth fall gently back on the pillows. To sit up and look down at her lover for as long as she dares.

Meredith knocks again and Beth shakes her head. Gwen stands and tugs on Beth's hands. Beth hesitates and then her eyes pop open, hard and empty. She lets Gwen help her from the bed, watches as she straightens her bodice.

Gwen steps to the side, reaching out for Beth's frazzled braid, and Beth seems to come back to life. She swipes at her hair until it's captured in a messy knot high on her head.

It's devastatingly beautiful. She is devastatingly beautiful.

They stare at each other, inches apart. It feels like the earth has tilted below them, everything wrong and off-angled.

"I'll see you," Beth starts, clenching her jaw as her eyes begin to shine.

Gwen nods, barely keeping her own tears at bay. "You will. We'll write too," she says, forcing lightness and promise into her words. They ring hollow around the little room.

Beth starts forward, but the door jerks open and they cleave away from each other. Gwen hurries back, out of sight of the hall, even though Meredith stands blocking any servant's view.

"Come on," she says, holding out a hand to Beth.

Beth glances at Gwen and their eyes hold for a moment, too much to be said, and never enough time.

And then she's gone, and Meredith snaps the door shut, leaving Gwen leaning against the empty dresser in the dim sunlight from the street above, thoroughly ravished and utterly broken. They were supposed to have three more days.

When Meredith returns some ten minutes later, Gwen has managed through her sobs to step into her hoop and tie it with trembling fingers. Meredith just bends to pick up Gwen's petticoat, helping her slide it over her ruined hair and fasten it over her hoop.

"We'll make sure you see each other," Meredith promises as they get her overskirt down on top of the petticoat.

"It isn't—" Gwen starts, unsure how to explain how much that's not enough. It will never be enough. She wasn't ready to say goodbye. She thought they had three more days.

She thought she was coming here for tea.

"No, it's not," Meredith agrees, stepping around to her front to button the bodice Gwen threw on in a hurry before leaving her empty townhouse. "But it's something."

Gwen meets her understanding eyes. "Thank you."

Meredith smiles sadly. "You would do the same for Albie, and I hope someday for me, if we needed you to."

"I would," Gwen says quickly, grabbing her hand. "If you ever need anything—"

"Be a good cousin to our children, a friend to me, to Albie, that's all I ask," Meredith says, her round face serene and earnest.

"I promise," Gwen says swiftly.

"Good. Now, let's go have scones, and then Albie will pick us up and we'll promenade with my mother."

Gwen deflates. "I don't know that I—"

Meredith gives her a stern look. "You will not go home to grieve in an empty house. Beth has the luxury of being obnoxiously busy. We need to keep you at least half as occupied."

And though it's not enough, not by any stretch, the tea and scones do help. And listening to Meredith and Albie snicker about the ton keeps her breathing. And as the day wears on she finds that the world hasn't ended. She still has her family, her friends. She'll keep moving even though she's been torn apart. It turns out you really can walk through life with an irreparably broken heart. Her father's managed, after all.

That night, when she returns home, a little tipsy from the bottle of champagne Albie stashed in the carriage—of which Meredith's mother happily partook while delivering Gwen home—she finds Father actually at their dinner table. He looks up, giving her an exhausted smile.

And for one moment, Gwen forgets her heartbreak and horror, and smiles back, settling at his side. Mrs. Gilpe brings their plates—a light summer salad with potato soup, easy and bright.

"You look well," Father decides after they've eaten for a few minutes.

Meredith reapplied her makeup, and she supposes she does

look sun brightened from the day. He hasn't seen her frequently enough recently to really know better.

"You look exhausted," she says, taking in the deep circles beneath his eyes, and the slight hollow to his cheeks. "Have you eaten at all in the last few days?"

"I—" Father begins, and then sighs, rubbing at the back of his neck. "I haven't been home much, have I?"

Gwen shrugs and takes a sip of her soup, earnestly trying to hide just how much he hasn't been home, and how much she's missed him. It's one thing to lose Beth—to feel like she's losing him too . . .

"How are you, really?" Father asks.

Gwen blinks. "I'm fine."

"I doubt that," Father says softly.

Gwen sinks back against her chair, the ache of it charging back up her chest. "I had hoped—" She pauses. Had hoped what, exactly?

"You thought there was still a chance Beth might abandon her match, her security, her safety, and come live with you?" he asks gently.

Gwen looks over, surprised. "I—no, no, I . . . didn't," she argues, her voice brittle.

She knows that won't happen. That it can't. It's why they schemed and tried and pushed. But Beth can't just walk away from the life the Ashmonds can give her. Gwen knows that. She's cried about it enough.

"I hoped so, when I was your age," Father says, and Gwen meets his eyes, surprised. "Thought that at the eleventh hour Cordelia would give up her advantage and come back to me, marry me and live a small but happy life. I believed it might happen right up until the church bells rang. And it broke me."

Gwen watches as he regards her, paternal and protective and experienced. "What did you do?" Gwen asks, feeling her heart breaking all over for him and herself.

"I drank, and I partied, and I got a good girl in trouble, and got you," he says steadily.

Gwen swallows hard. She thought he didn't know she had heard him and Mrs. Gilpe—hoped he'd thought that she'd just been sick. She hasn't had the heart to mention it.

"And I would do it all over again to get you," he says firmly, reaching out to take her hand. "But I can't pretend it was easy or how I wanted to bring you into the world. And your mother, rest her soul—you can do better than me, Gwen. Find a good man, or hell, a good woman who can stay with you. We can go to Paris. I hear from friends it's much more . . . open about these things right now."

Gwen blinks. He—he would take her to Paris, to meet a nice woman—"But what about the title?"

"We can worry about that later," Father says, shrugging like it's no longer important. "If I can push this vote through, I don't really give a damn what happens after."

"And you wouldn't . . . mind? If I never married?"

"I just want you to be happy," he says simply.

Gwen sits for a moment, soaking that in. Words she's wanted to hear for ages—she can stand down, she can let go of the season, she can simply be herself.

But what does it matter if it won't be with Beth?

"What about you?" she asks, seeing one shimmering last chance.

"What about me?"

"If you don't care, after this vote—if it doesn't matter—why can't you be happy too?"

Father snorts. "What do you mean, Gwennie?"

Gwen summons the last dregs of her courage. Beth gave it her all; Gwen has to at least try. "Ask Lady Demeroven for her hand. Take your own happiness. And who knows, you could get an heir—a planned one. And even if you don't—"

"Gwen—"

"She's miserable too. She hates the Ashmonds, and Beth says it's like watching her submit to her father all over again. Can't we—can't you try, just once more? Ask again."

The ease falls from his face, that guarded, aloof expression she so hates settling over him. It's the look he wears at balls. The way he looks with women. Detached and poised and uncaring.

"You may be a glutton for punishment, but I am not," he says stiffly.

"What?"

"The teas with Meredith? Do you think you've been subtle?"

Gwen leans back, surprised and defensive but with no way to argue it. "I—"

"How you and Beth deal with the pain is your business, but I did my time. I let that woman stomp all over my heart, twice. I won't do it a third time."

Gwen blinks and before she can formulate another argument, before she can say anything, he stands and tosses his napkin onto the table.

"You're a good girl, Gwennie. I love you very much. But leave me out of this. I won't have us utterly destroyed by the Demerovens again. We will move forward with our lives, and someday this will be just a painful memory, I promise you that."

He turns and strides out of the room, leaving Gwen alone, for the second time today, heartbroken and winded.

CHAPTER TWENTY-SEVEN

Beth

Beth runs her fingers over her engagement ring, spinning it on her finger, trying to let the hypnotic motion drown out the world around her. She sits across from her mother, watching her poke listlessly at her dry chicken while Lord Ashmond bloviates. They're here for a consolation dinner one day before the wedding, one day after the MCA vote, which passed. And Lord Ashmond is still a livid purple.

Beth hasn't had time to let it sink in—to know she does have an escape if she ever needs one. If she ever wants one, she can argue her case, can escape the Ashmonds, can go find Gwen, can disappear into the slums and live a happy life with her lover.

But then she looks across at her mother, jaw tight and back straight as Lord Ashmond continues to rail. She cannot leave her mother here with these people. They are either in misery together, or they leave together. And while Beth thinks she could live a life of poverty with Gwen, loved and cared for, even without a single luxury or comfort, she cannot doom her mother to a loveless poverty.

And so they're here, listening to her father-in-law-to-be go on and on about the evils of women, while his wife and son nod absently along. Beth still doesn't know if Lord Montson believes a single word his father says, but she knows he never fights him on it.

She knows, too, he's as powerless as she is to defend the act. His whole inheritance depends on acquiescence to his father's every opinion, as does hers by proxy. But still. Still, he could say something on her behalf.

"Any woman who would abandon a husband simply on the cause of . . . what did they say, Harry?"

"Emotional distress," Lord Montson says around a mouthful of potatoes.

"Emotional distress," Lord Ashmond sneers. "Women are in emotional distress at the drop of a hat, literally. Didn't you weep the other day, dearest, when your hat fell in the mud?"

Lady Ashmond nods placidly, her eyes distant and a bit empty. Beth wonders if her mother isn't the only one to have dipped into the laudanum.

"How could a woman differentiate between the average distress and something deeper then, if all it takes is a hat?" Lord Ashmond continues. "Preposterous. How a man behaves with his wife is no business of the courts'."

"Unless he's beating her," Beth feels herself say, clamping her lips shut as the whole table turns to look at her.

She hears Mother sigh quietly, but has more pressing matters now, with Lord Ashmond glaring at her. Lord Montson looks on in surprise.

"I only, well, I only mean that, in some extreme cases, I suppose it is the business of law enforcement if a woman fears for her life. But, ah, that was covered before the MCA in extreme cases, wasn't it? So I didn't . . . I didn't mean . . . anything by it," she peters off, unable to stand tall in the face of the earl's glower.

"I'm sure Beth understands the difference between petty words and assault," Mother chimes in.

"Right," Beth says quickly. "I only worry for those young ladies married to much older men, who might have different . . . customs, that's all," Beth defends meekly.

Lord Ashmond works his jaw, not wanting, it seems, to insult his son's bride-to-be. He really might think it's the right of the husband to beat a wife bloody if he wants. Barbaric.

"Beth knows her place," Mother says.

"That she does," Lord Montson agrees, glancing at his father before sending Beth a strikingly winning smile. "And that she never needs to worry about such things from me."

"Yes, yes," Lord Ashmond says, apparently mollified by his son's promise not to beat Beth senseless.

Which seems like faint praise to her, the very least he can do. But she returns Lord Montson's smile anyway, grateful at least to be out from his father's scrutiny.

"Beth knows her place," Lady Ashmond repeats. "And understands what it means to be in this family. Dirty laundry should never be aired, publicly or privately. Marriage is a sacred bond."

The whole table turns to look at Lady Ashmond. That implies—

"Quite right," Lord Ashmond agrees, patting his wife's hand, a little too hard given the way the silverware rattles. "Disputes should be settled privately, and family business is just that—for the family. Don't you agree, Lady Demeroven?"

Beth watches her mother take in the tableau of the

Ashmonds—his heavy hand on Lady Ashmond's frail one, his bravado, his insistence that all ills and disagreements are settled in-house—by him.

"Lady Demeroven, you don't think young ladies should be going to the courts for matters they could resolve at home," Lord Ashmond prompts when Mother has done nothing but stare.

Beth swallows, unease settling into her stomach. Silence doesn't bode well when it comes to her mother.

"Of course she doesn't," Beth says softly, forcing a smile for the Ashmonds. "You—you know our position on the MCA."

"The right one," Lord Montson says quickly.

Beth presses her nails into her palms.

"Lady Demeroven?" Lord Ashmond prompts. "I know your late husband agreed. Stand-up man, he was."

And that, somehow, seems to be the last straw.

"My husband was a lout who spouted the same abhorrent drivel and used to backhand me for every slight. If I could have taken him to court and gotten half of his estate, I would have, and I would tell Beth to do the same should your son ever, ever," Mother says, turning a hard look on Lord Montson, "raise a hand to her. And I would support her use of the new law immediately."

Beth gapes, as does Lady Ashmond, while Lord Montson just stares, wide-eyed. What—

"Think very carefully about your next words," Lord Ashmond says, his voice deathly even and low.

"Or what?" Mother asks, leaning back in her chair.

Something has broken within her, Beth can see it. Stretched taut and snapped.

"And you?" Lord Ashmond asks, turning his glare on Beth, who fights to stay sitting straight. If her mother can do it, so can she. "Do you feel the same?"

Beth glances at Mother, who doesn't acknowledge her, glaring right back at Lord Ashmond. Beth takes a breath and meets Lord Montson's wide eyes.

"I would give my husband warning, that if he ever struck me again, that would be it. I won't—I won't stand to be beaten," she says slowly. "Arguments don't warrant divorce, but I won't stand to be abused. I have value and deserve to be treated well. I believe your son agrees."

Lord Montson stares at her and then nods quickly. But his face goes flat when his father turns his glower on him. Beth watches as he withstands the scrutiny, and suddenly that quick little nod isn't as comforting. "He'll be kind to Beth when his father isn't around" isn't quite the assurance she wants.

"Harry knows his place," Lord Ashmond decides. "And I suggest you learn yours," he adds, turning back to Mother. "Whatever you thought of your late husband, you will only speak of him kindly in this house. He was a good, strong man, who fought for his ideals. I imagine he's rolling in his grave to hear you even contemplate using the act, or Beth."

Mother clenches her jaw and stays silent.

"And you," he adds, turning back to Beth. "You will be patient, and positive, and obey my son in all ways, and if you do, you should never have need to speak such progressive, hurtful things again. You will do as he says and defer to him in all ways."

Beth stares at her father-in-law-to-be. "I—" She looks to Lord Montson, but he won't meet her eyes. "I—" she starts again, her chest tight.

She won't be beaten. She won't be yelled at. She will not repeat what her mother endured.

"No, she won't," Mother says, and Beth feels her heart plummet. But then Mother stands up. "If those are your conditions, Lord Ashmond, that my daughter submit to anything your son wants, without question, be it verbal or physical, or simply his abhorrent taste in unseasoned food, then we will have a problem."

"Lady Demeroven, you misunderstand," Lady Ashmond says softly, before yelping as her husband's grip on her hand tightens.

"You will sit down this instant, we will have another round of drinks, and we will speak of this no more, or there will be serious consequences," Lord Ashmond says darkly, his voice ice-cold.

Mother and Lord Ashmond glare at each other for what feels like an eternal, awful minute. Their whole future teeters on this moment, and Beth can't dare to believe—

"Then we have a problem," Mother says, her voice even and devoid of emotion. "Beth, gather your things. We'll be leaving now."

Lord Ashmond stands abruptly, rocking the table. "Be very careful, Lady Demeroven."

"Or what, you'll hit me?"

Lady Ashmond squeaks. Lord Montson gapes. And Beth hastily folds her skirts, hope pounding violently against her chest.

"I will end this engagement and your name and your daughter's will be dragged through the mud," Lord Ashmond threatens.

Mother laughs. *Laughs*. "And? Your opposition failed. Parliament is about to be out of session. I don't know what damage you imagine could be done to our reputations, with your own so low as it is. Couldn't drum up the votes. Let yourself get beaten by Lord Havenfort."

Lord Ashmond pushes back his seat and Lord Montson finally, finally stands up. "Father," he cautions.

Beth slips out of her seat and scurries behind her chair.

"Get out," Lord Ashmond booms. "Get out."

"With pleasure," Mother says, nodding to Beth. "Lady Ashmond, if you ever need help," she adds.

Lord Ashmond takes a menacing step around the table toward Mother and Lord Montson bodily blocks him. Beth hurries around the table to grab her mother's hand. Mother squeezes her palm and turns on her heel, marching for the hall.

"Beth," Lord Montson calls as they reach the doorway.

"Good luck, Harry," Beth says, offering Lord Montson a bland smile over her shoulder before Mother walks them out of the room. They stride quickly down the cavernous hallway, their shoes slapping against the marble floor.

They hit the foyer and the startled porter automatically opens the front door for them, allowing them to spill out onto the street. The doors slam closed behind them and they trip down the stairs to stand on the sidewalk, heaving in air in the cool summer evening. There's no carriage waiting—of course there isn't.

"What was that?" Beth asks, turning to Mother, who's flushed and a bit disheveled, but standing taller than she's seen her in months.

"I—I don't know," Mother admits, meeting Beth's eyes. "God, I just—that man—"

"Is abhorrent," Beth agrees.

"Yes," Mother says, reaching out to brush a stray hair from Beth's face. "Yes, you're right. You've been right for a long time, and I thought—I thought I could do this, live this way again, but I can't. You were right, Beth," she repeats.

Beth smiles slowly, shocked and relieved. Laughter bubbles up from her chest. A high giggle escapes and Mother's face blooms into a smile of its own, until they're teetering there in front of the Ashmond house, gripping at each other to stay standing.

Mother gains enough control to turn them and begin the long walk home. Perhaps they can find a coach for hire closer to the park, but the streets are empty. It's Thursday evening, and everyone is at home, or at the club, celebrating or mourning the MCA.

"I am sorry," Mother says a few minutes later as the glee seems to leave them, exhaustion and shock in its wake.

"For what?" Beth wonders.

She's a bit numb now, but she thinks she'll be incandescently happy in a few hours. Even with no plan ahead of them, and the house about to be taken—they're free. They're *free*.

"I know he wasn't your choice, but you at least liked Lord Montson, which wasn't nothing," Mother says.

Beth shakes her head, squeezing Mother's arm. "Don't worry about that."

Mother stops, pulling Beth to a halt. "I do worry though," she says and Beth turns to meet her eyes. "I just blew up your marriage, and now—they'll be coming to take the house in two days, oh, Beth, what did I do?" she says, panic bubbling up all over her face. "What have I—"

"I don't care," Beth says quickly. "I never wanted to marry him. And I didn't want to watch you acquiesce to Lord Ashmond, and now I don't have to. We'll figure it out."

"But," Mother says, her face pale under the lamplight.

"We'll figure it out," Beth promises, happy to take charge now, since Mother saved them both. "We can stay with Meredith, I'm sure, for a few days."

"She's about to get married," Mother protests.

"All the more reason. Her mother will need a friend," Beth says simply. Mother shakes her head. "It will be fine."

"I just ended our one chance at security over a stupid argument," Mother exclaims, her voice bouncing over the cobblestones. "It will not be fine."

But Beth—Beth feels a surge of power, of promise, of hope.

"Not our only chance," she says slowly. "Not at all. Come on."

She takes Mother's hand and begins pulling her down the street, toward the corner that will take them one of two ways.

"Beth, stop," Mother says, but Beth can't stop. They have somewhere to be. "Where are we going?"

"To get you your happy ending," Beth says firmly, laughing as Mother splutters. She turns them down the street, away from their townhouse.

"Stop. Where are you taking us?" Mother demands, pulling them up short beneath a streetlight.

"I told you. Your happy ending. It's still there," Beth insists.

Mother stares at her for a moment, confused, until it clicks, and she blanches. "No, no, Beth, there's no way—"

"You wanted me to have a husband who would be good to

me. Who would have a title and the money to support both of us. Who would treat me well and love me, right?"

Mother frowns down at her.

"Right?"

"Yes," Mother says tightly.

"Someone who was genuine, and had good morals, and fought for good things?"

"Beth—"

"Lord Havenfort is all of those things, but for you. You spent my whole life with a lout—you said so yourself. Now you should spend the rest of yours with a gentleman."

Mother's mouth falls open and Beth laughs, trying to tug her back along. But Mother holds tight to her hand, an anchor there beneath the streetlight.

"Beth, you're not—I can't—he won't take me," Mother says, her voice suddenly rough.

"Of course he will," Beth counters, too filled with hope now to second-guess herself. "He loves you. He's been a wreck since we parted ways, drinking and throwing himself into politics. But he loves you. He has for years."

"I've broken his heart too many times," Mother says. "I can't—why would he take me now?"

"Because you're ready now. And because you're you," Beth insists.

"I'm not—"

"What—beautiful, learned, witty, fun, and a match for absolutely anyone? Lord Havenfort may have cracked him one, but Lord Ashmond looked destroyed tonight and you didn't lift a finger, barely even a brow!"

Mother snorts. Beth can't remember the last time her mother looked at her like this—vulnerable and still so young, and open, and seeking Beth's approval. Her opinion matters now. Has always mattered.

"Come on. He's no scarier than Lord Ashmond, and infinitely more handsome."

Mother laughs a little and lets Beth tug her up the street, moving more slowly, but following all the same. All they need to do is put them in the same room together, free of previous obligations, contracts, and responsibilities. She's sure of it.

Doubting it now would only make her as pale and frightened as her mother, and Beth doesn't have time to wonder and worry. There's a fire in her stomach and a tingle in her limbs as she drags Mother the four avenues until they're standing outside the massive Havenfort home. The last time she was here, Gwen—

No. This is her mother's moment. There will be time for her own reunion after.

"Darling," Mother whispers, wrapping her free hand around Beth's arm and squeezing. She's practically trembling.

"It's right there. You just have to reach out and take it. Twenty-two years, Mother, and it's just minutes away now."

Mother turns and meets her eyes. Beth takes in the wide, wet sheen in her gaze, her shaking hands, her pale cheeks. She smiles reassuringly and squeezes her mother's hand.

"Tonight, just think about what you *want*. Nothing else matters."

"And if he says no?"

Beth takes a deep breath and keeps her smile. "Then you and I will live cozily in a hovel somewhere and we'll be happy there too."

"Beth, I can't let you—"

"You and me. We'd be scandalous ladies about town. And we'd be fabulous," she says firmly. "But that's not your future. You're going to be married to one of the wealthiest men around, and he's going to treat you like a damn queen."

Mother huffs and glances about, like the actual queen could be loitering somewhere nearby, eager to be insulted.

"Mother, you can do this," Beth insists.

"I can?"

"What's scarier? Telling a good man you love him, or spending your future alone?"

"But I wouldn't be alone," Mother says slowly. "I'd have you."

Beth smiles and leans up to kiss her cheek. They left their bonnets at the Ashmonds'. Shame; they were good bonnets.

"You'll have me either way. But you could have a lot more than just me, if we knock."'

"I don't need anything else," Mother says, gripping at her hand. "Truly."

Beth nods. "I know. But let's have more anyway. What do you say?"

Mother pulls her close for a moment before the decision settles over her. Her shoulders roll back, her neck lengthens, her jaw sets and Beth watches it all, fascinated. Her mother, indomitable, confident, and sure, takes the steps two at a time, dragging Beth along, laughing behind her.

And suddenly her doubts are truly gone. Mother gets what she wants when she looks like that. And what she wants—it's what they all want. A happily-ever-after, as soon as someone comes to the door.

Chapter Twenty-Eight

Gwen

"You're not expecting visitors, are you?" Mrs. Stelm asks as she, Gwen, and Mrs. Gilpe traipse from their card game in the kitchen toward the front door.

"It's gone nine, rude to be calling without an invitation," Mrs. Gilpe mutters, though Gwen's rather sure it's just carried-over frustration from the thorough trouncing Mrs. Stelm was giving them.

"Could be something political," Gwen offers.

Father's in his study, though she believes he has plans to be at the club later. Something about rubbing the act's passage into some smug conservative faces.

Another knock rings around the foyer and Mrs. Gilpe sighs gustily, marching to the door and flinging it open—the porter's on his night off—with Gwen and Mrs. Stelm right behind. She's clearly ready to give the visitor a dressing-down, but her words die in her throat.

Beth and Lady Demeroven stare anxiously back at them there on the front stoop.

"Beth?" Gwen whispers.

"Is Lord Havenfort at home?" Lady Demeroven asks, her voice shaking but stance tall and proud.

Mrs. Stelm, Mrs. Gilpe, and Gwen just stare at her, all of them a little slack-jawed.

"I apologize for our . . . forward arrival, but it really is urgent."

"Right. Yes, I'll, ah, I'll go get him, shall I?" Mrs. Stelm says, glancing at Mrs. Gilpe and Gwen before hurrying off down the hall.

"Come in, please," Mrs. Gilpe says, ushering the two women inside.

They're dressed for a fine evening out, in full hoops and silk, hair piled high and makeup perfectly done. Gwen, by comparison, is wearing an old pair of stays and a housedress, Mrs. Gilpe's in an apron, and Mrs. Stelm's lucky she's not in a dressing gown at this point.

"What . . ." Gwen begins as Beth separates from her mother to come stand at her side.

Beth takes her hand, nearly vibrating, and Gwen glances between Lady Demeroven and her daughter. Lady Demeroven's practically shaking as well, but looks far less sanguine than Beth, who's almost . . . radiant beside her. Lady Demeroven looks like she's about to go to the gallows, actually.

"What are you doing here?" Gwen asks, turning back to Beth.

"What we should have done months ago," Beth says simply, squeezing her hand. "Watch," she adds, nudging Gwen to look toward the hall where Father has paused by the staircase, staring at them all, Mrs. Stelm hovering behind him.

Silence hangs over the foyer, interrupted only by the shifting of fabric. Gwen would break the quiet, but she can't seem to open her mouth, not with the violent hope swirling in her stomach.

"Has something happened?" Father finally asks after the shock has worn off.

He hurries toward them. Mrs. Gilpe moves with Mrs. Stelm to respectfully vacate the foyer, though Gwen's sure they'll be leaving the door to the serving hall open and hovering just out of sight.

"Is everything all right?" Father asks again, striding purposefully toward Lady Demeroven, who's just . . . staring at him. "The girls?"

He glances at Beth, who gives him a wave and a smile. Gwen wonders how she can be so blasé when this feels—momentous, precious, precarious.

"Is it the engagement?" he prompts, turning back to Lady Demeroven, now only steps away, and still standing frozen. "Cordelia, you're scaring me," he insists.

Her name seems to unglue her jaw and Gwen watches as she takes a very deep breath. It looks for a moment like she's about to curtsy, but she keeps sinking, until she's knelt in front of Father, on one—

Gwen gasps and Beth elbows her. But it doesn't matter. Father's now the one shaking, staring down at this woman who has broken his heart, and given him joy, and stayed with him in memory all these years.

"I, um," Lady Demeroven starts. Father's whole body jolts, like she's brought him out of some kind of temporary stasis. "I realize this is . . . abrupt, and forward, and possibly futile. But I, ah, I wanted to apologize, for the hurt I've caused. To ask your forgiveness, if you can give it. And to offer—" She pauses, glancing over at Beth, who gives her a thumbs-up.

Gwen can't believe this. It can't be happening. Did she fall asleep and get carried upstairs and is now living some sort of fever dream?

"Well, to offer myself," Lady Demeroven says, scrunching her nose while Beth laughs quietly. "That sounds terrible. I meant—I mean, I am here to ask you to trust me once more, with the promise that I will never break your trust again, or your heart."

"Cordelia—" Father starts, but Lady Demeroven shakes her head.

"Will you marry me?" she asks, looking up at him, her face broken open, young and shy and hopeful.

She looks a little like Beth and it makes Gwen's chest ache. *Say yes*, she wants to scream. Oh, please, *say yes*.

"Is this—is this for the girls?" Father asks, glancing back at them, his eyes softening at what must be the sight of them, clutching at each other hopefully.

"If it was?" Lady Demeroven asks.

Father looks back down at her. "An arrangement for their sake could be made, but do not ask me thus if it isn't for yourself."

Lady Demeroven's face brightens and she looks up at Father with such adoration and open emotion that Gwen almost wants to turn and give them privacy. Almost, but not enough, because she's desperate to see Father say—

"Then yes," Father says softly, reaching down to take Lady Demeroven's hand and pull her up from the floor.

He tugs her close and plants a kiss on her that makes her squeak and then melt into him, the two of them held tight together.

"Oh my God," Gwen hears herself say. Beth shrieks, the

sound bouncing around the room and breaking their parents apart.

Gwen whacks Beth, but she's giggling too much to do more. Giggling, giddy, shocked, and stunned. Their—they did it. Their parents are—

"Happy, girls?" Father asks, turning to regard them with Lady Demeroven still in his arms.

Beth nods and rushes to hug her mother, who only just steps away from Father to receive her, both of them laughing in delight.

Father watches them fondly before stepping aside, arms outstretched. Gwen finds herself hurrying across the floor in much the same way, wrapping Father up tight in a hug that feels like freedom.

"I'm so happy for you," Gwen tells him as she pulls back.

"Me too," Father says, chuckling down at her. He can't stop smiling, his eyes all crinkled. "And happy for you as well."

"Yes," Lady Demeroven says, and Gwen turns, Father's arm sliding around her shoulders as they face their—what, exactly? She watches Lady Demeroven give Beth a soft smile. Beth's grin widens. "We'll need to discuss the particulars, and obviously you girls understand the charade that will have to continue?" Lady Demeroven asks.

"That we're stepsisters, or that we're still looking for husbands?" Beth asks, looking gleeful.

"Both," Lady Demeroven says, glancing at Father, who nods. "Though perhaps we can forget the rest of this season, and possibly the next."

Gwen feels herself relax into Father's side. "So, you don't mind?" she asks Lady Demeroven, feeling shy but bold at once.

"No," Lady Demeroven says softly, squeezing Beth. Beth's shoulders seem to come down, chin high. "If you're both happy, that's all that matters, and I'm just as happy for you. And better—goodness, better you're together than out there. The things Lord Ashmond said tonight," she says, glancing at Beth, whose smile dims.

"I hope his wife is all right," she says.

"What happened?" Father asks.

Lady Demeroven wrinkles her nose. "I think I've ensured this is a spectacular scandal. I suppose I should have opened with that. We'll be . . . we'll be dragging your reputation through quite a lot. God, we have to formally end your engagement," she adds, looking to Beth.

"I do think storming out rather did that for us," Beth counters.

Father chuckles and all three of them turn to look at him. "Don't worry about our collective reputation. We'll be the talk of the ton for a cycle and then they'll forget us. I would be happy—no, honored, to pen a refusal for Beth, if you'd like."

Lady Demeroven's grin is positively evil. "That sounds wonderful."

"Excellent," Father says, squeezing Gwen to his side before stepping away and holding out his hand for his . . . good Lord . . . fiancée. "Shall we? Breakfast in the morning, girls?"

"We're staying?" Beth asks.

Lady Demeroven takes Father's hand. "I hardly think one more scandal can hurt us, do you?"

"Agreed," Father says, grinning at her before looking back at them. "Have a good night, ladies."

And with that, Father sweeps Lady Demeroven off down the hall toward his study, leaving a flabbergasted Gwen and Beth alone in the front hall, staring after them. They listen as the study door opens and shuts, and then it's just silence, the two of them there, clutching at each other in shock.

"What the absolute hell?" Gwen finally exclaims, turning to look Beth over, the relief and happiness and confusion of the last few minutes skittering over her skin.

"Surprise?" Beth says, laughing as Gwen shakes herself, unsure if she wants to whack her or kiss her senseless.

"How?" she asks, searching for better words, but coming up empty.

"Lord Ashmond and Mother got in a heated row, and that was kind of the last straw. We stormed out, and then she was panicking and I thought, well, why not try just one more time and . . . it *worked.*"

"It worked," Gwen repeats, glancing toward the closed study. They actually did it.

She feels Beth's fingers trailing down her arms and turns back, tangling their hands together. They're both wide-eyed and breathless. Gwen swallows, too many words caught in her throat. Beth is so beautiful, and so brilliant, in her foyer, hers to have and—

"I hope it's all right with you that we're here forever. I really don't think I could stand to say goodbye to you a third time."

Gwen tugs her in, instinctive and awkward. She wraps her arms tight around Beth's shoulders and Beth laughs. "No more goodbyes, ever," Gwen says firmly, the thought burning bright through her chest.

Beth giggles into her neck, lips brushing over her pulse. "Yeah?"

"I'm keeping you."

Beth presses closer, squeezing her waist. "Forever and always?"

"Forever and always and eternity and infinity," Gwen promises, a rush of heady, desperate joy descending through her shock that makes her pull back to see Beth's face.

"For centuries, and eons, and epochs?" Beth asks, her eyes sparkling.

"For every season, and year, and decade, and—" She's halfway onto bended knee before she even thinks about it.

"Come here," Beth says, hauling her up into a thoroughly, exultantly, ridiculously perfect kiss. The silk of her gown beneath Gwen's palms, the press of her lips, the pressure of her hips—it's heaven, and they stay there kissing like it's the end of the world for what feels like ages.

Hers. Hers. Hers. *Forever.*

"You have a room."

They break apart, stumbling out of each other's arms. No longer alone, Gwen looks up to find Mrs. Gilpe and Mrs. Stelm standing in the doorway to the serving hall.

"Right," Gwen says, wiping at her mouth as Beth goes crimson.

"Good to see you, Miss Demeroven. Gwen, you have a shift she can use?" Mrs. Stelm adds.

"I do, yes, right. Thank you. Um, good night. We'll—oh, Beth, you'll love playing cards with—right. This is Mrs. Stelm, and Mrs. Gilpe, our housekeepers," she says, bumbling around the words. Beth laughs, and the two women regard her in fond exasperation.

"Very pleased to make your acquaintance," Beth says, dipping in a curtsy that makes both women grin.

"I like her," Mrs. Stelm says brightly.

"I'm assuming you heard . . . all of that?" Gwen asks.

Mrs. Gilpe rolls her eyes. "If your parents agree, we'll prepare your room for two, otherwise she can have the empty one next to you. And Miss Demeroven—"

"Beth, please," Beth says softly.

Mrs. Gilpe nods. "If you have need of anything, our quarters are down this hall, past the kitchens, and to the left."

"Thank you," Beth says, her eyes going a bit wide.

Gwen reasons the reality of how much has changed has just hit her. She can tell in a few minutes she'll be in her own complete state of paralysis. Best they get upstairs before they're too overwhelmed to bother. And she doesn't particularly like the gleeful look on Mrs. Gilpe's and Mrs. Stelm's faces. Beth is fresh meat, another young woman to embarrass and spoil, and tonight, that's entirely Gwen's job.

"Come on," she says, taking Beth's hand to start the trek to her—their—room.

Beth waves at Mrs. Stelm and Mrs. Gilpe and then laughs as Gwen tugs on her arm, practically dragging her up the stairs. Of course, as soon as they round the first landing, Beth's as eager as she is, the two of them sharing one look before bursting into giggles. They all but sprint up the stairs and down her—their—wing until they reach Gwen's room.

Gwen pauses, Beth's hand warm in hers, the two of them flushed and happy and gloriously free.

"Gwen," Beth prompts. She reaches out and opens the door, nudging Gwen through.

Gwen lets herself be handled and watches as Beth flips the lock with confidence and then comes to stand with her in the middle of the room. It's a mess, with clothing everywhere and a few dishes left about. She's been in a funk for weeks and it shows.

But Beth just grins at her, stepping forward until she can slide her hands up Gwen's chest and draw her into another fiery kiss. And then Gwen doesn't care so much about the cleanliness of the room, or where they'll put all of Beth's things, or how they're going to balance their public and private lives, or what exactly they're likely to face after a letter penned by both of their parents goes to the Ashmonds.

"I love you," Beth whispers against her mouth.

Gwen clutches at Beth's waist and pulls back so she can meet her eyes. "I love you too."

Beth smiles and then slowly spins in her arms. "Help me out of this godforsaken thing?"

"With so much pleasure," Gwen says, reaching out with eager fingers to start undoing Beth's dress. She's going to kiss her lover, and undress her, and touch her, in their bedroom, for the first of many, many wonderful nights to come.

EPILOGUE

April 1858

Beth

"We barely fit," Gwen grumbles, shifting carefully around Beth so they can see into the vanity together.

Beth snorts, reaching out to grab the chair for support so she doesn't stumble into the vanity as Gwen's hoop inevitably bumps hers. The circumference in style is rather large now and Gwen's not wrong, with both of them in their room and clothes and detritus scattered about, it's almost claustrophobic.

But Beth doesn't really mind, watching Gwen fondly as she delicately wipes at her lip line. Together, Beth thinks they look quite the young ladies, a little older, a little wiser, and infinitely happier than this time last year.

After all, they woke up tangled naked together this morning and have nothing more than debauchery planned for the opening ball. It's frankly glorious.

"You should wear blue more," Gwen says, arranging her skirt so it fans out like a peacock's tail behind her to press up to Beth's back.

"You're wrinkling it," Beth protests, but she still angles her head to the side so Gwen can press a soft kiss to her neck.

"And you're beautiful," Gwen replies, grinning at her. They meet each other's eyes in the mirror.

"The green is stunning on you," Beth says, enchanted by the way the deep green silk makes her skin glow and her blond hair seem almost luminous. It only accentuates her stark collarbones and regal neck. "We should go back to bed."

Gwen snorts and Beth blushes, biting her lip for letting that thought slip through. "I'd love that, but your mother will be up here in ten minutes if we don't make it down, and then Father after her, and it'll be a thirty-minute lecture about her nerves and I just can't."

Beth laughs and nods, pushing the chair into the vanity so she can spin around without knocking into both the bedpost and vanity in the process. She reaches out as Gwen does, their hands tangling.

"You ready for this?" Beth asks.

Gwen nods, a mischievous look coming over her face. "Albie promised me he'd have a flask, and Bobby has already promised his first three dances to you. It'll be grand."

"I love your cousins," Beth says fondly. "But shouldn't Bobby be jockeying for a more eligible hand?"

"There's no such thing," Gwen says quickly, and Beth laughs. "And probably, but you know how much he hates dealing with the mothers. You'll ease him in, and then we can both be there for Albie. He's been a pouting wretch about the whole thing."

Beth sighs. "Gwen—"

"He wants us to treat him like normal," Gwen insists.

Beth shakes her head. Viscount Mason passed six months ago, leaving Albie a mountain of debt and estate management catastrophes to sort through. Bobby's spoken of almost nothing but the upcoming season every time they've written, even though Beth knows he abhors most of it. And while she understands both of them wanting to just get on with things, grief doesn't go away like that. Even if you did hate your father. She should know.

"Really. He asked me to be a nuisance. Demanded I cheer him up so he's not pining the whole time."

And then there's that. "If I were stuck in the country with morning sickness, would you want to be all the way down here, attending parties?"

Gwen wrinkles her nose. "Stop, I don't want to feel worse for the poor sod."

"Feel bad for Meredith then. I know her mother says it's just a little sickness, but in her last letter she said it's constant."

"She wrote again?"

"It came earlier today while you and your father were fencing. I'd," Beth starts, looking forlornly at her side table. "I can't get over there in this damn thing. I'll show you tonight."

"Tomorrow," Gwen says firmly. "I have no intention of being sober when we get home."

Beth laughs and drops one of Gwen's hands so they can make their way out of the room. "Yes, Mother will love that. And your father too, come to think of it."

"Oh, posh, he's not going to be sober all night."

"If he wants to sleep in their bed tonight he will," Beth tosses back, thinking of her mother's glare.

It's a relief to have it turned on someone else. Though really, they're all equally liable to provoke her these days. She'd be irritated, but she's just so glad Mother has the energy to have her moods at this point, she'll happily take her annoyance.

"There you are."

Mostly glad, at least. Beth withholds a sigh and Gwen squeezes her hand. They come around the last landing to find Mother waiting in the foyer, looking thunderous.

"We're going to have to sit in the receiving line for ages now. What takes you girls so long? Two sets of hands for everything, how hard can it be?"

Beth and Gwen descend the stairs as Dashiell comes down the hall from the study. He immediately steps up behind Mother and begins rubbing her shoulders. She scowls, but they can all see the tension leak from her frame.

"Come now, darling. I'm a second set of hands and hardly any help at all."

Mother laughs, startled, and Beth smiles. They watch as one of his hands abandons her shoulder to wrap around and rest on the prominent bump beneath her skirts. He's so good to her—has been so good to her, steadfast and at her side through the panic of the past few months. But here they all are, happy, healthy, and with a joyful addition to the family firmly on the way.

She's trying very hard not to think about the actual arrival. The story Mrs. Stelm told her about Gwen's birth is still wrapped around her heart. If anything should happen to Mother—

"You're sure you want to go through with this?"

"Do you truly think I can't handle a simple ball?" Mother snips back.

"All right, all right," Dashiell says, leaning in to kiss her cheek.

Beth forces her shoulders to come down. Everything's fine. Mother looks elegant and radiant in her deep purple gown, adjusted for her growing stomach. Her dark curls are shinier than ever and her cheeks are plump with happiness.

Even if she and Gwen had decided they hated each other after all, Beth thinks all the scheming was worth it for the picture their parents make: luminously happy, unexpectedly expecting, and still utterly wild about each other through all of it.

"Our daughters' penchant for messing about rather than getting ready aside," Dashiell says, raising an eyebrow at them. Gwen simply shrugs and he rolls his eyes. "We still need to wait for the viscount, don't we?"

"Yes," Mother agrees, leaning back against Dashiell and sighing in relief. "He's late."

"He's young," Dashiell argues.

"Beth was never late," Mother says.

"Yes, well, that was because of you, not any natural punctuality on my part," Beth says.

"And James isn't a presenting debutante," Dashiell adds. "He can be as late as he likes and still be desirable."

"Fat lot of good that does us though. By that token we'll be dirt beneath everyone's shoes if he's much later," Gwen says.

Beth elbows her but Dashiell just laughs. "Are you trying to attract a wealthy suitor?" he asks.

"No," they say together, giggling as Dashiell and Mother shake their heads.

"Then it doesn't matter. However, if either of you should meet a gentleman you think might support your life together, we of course will support that," Dashiell adds.

Beth nods, meeting her mother's eyes. Mother winks at her and Beth leans into Gwen as much as she can. Gwen's fingers tangle through her own. She takes a deep breath.

"I doubt we'll find someone *that* open-minded, but thank you," Gwen replies for them both.

"You never know," Dashiell says as a knock reverberates through the foyer. "I didn't think I'd end up a father again."

"Yes, some hardship for you," Mother says, groaning as Dashiell gently pushes her back upright to answer the door. "Be nice to your cousin," she adds as Beth and Gwen approach her.

"We're never anything but delightful," Gwen protests and Beth laughs.

"Of course you are," Mother says, letting Gwen take her elbow with her free hand. "But I meant Beth. It's not his fault he inherited our estate."

"I don't want it anyway," Beth insists, even as a small part of her gut twists at the thought. He's only been in residence for about a month, but it does still rankle.

It's not like they would have kept living in the townhouse, or the northern estate, anyway. But the entire ordeal of handing everything over—of forfeiting their entire life and property simply because he came of age—it just has never sat right with her. They haven't seen him since he arrived in London, and he was a gawky, awkward thing last year when they met at Mother's wedding. And now they're meant to help him find a bride. Like either of them has the slightest idea of how to succeed at the marriage market.

Gwen squeezes her hand. She supposes that's not really true. They did succeed, rather spectacularly, all of them. Just . . . not in a way anyone else would respect. Their reputations have survived, but only just. Really, arriving with them is going to drag James down more than anything else.

"Cousin."

Beth and Gwen stop cold as a tall, broad-shouldered young man bows to them on the front steps. When he stands up, Beth can't help but gape. Gone is the acne and ungainly height. James has filled out into his figure. He's still a touch awkward and long limbed, but it's offset by his strong jaw and beautiful sandy-brown hair and blue eyes.

He's handsome. Truly handsome. A man, now.

"You grew up nicely," Gwen says.

Mother sighs as Dashiell turns a bark of laughter into a cough. James regards them a bit shyly and Beth tries to offer him a genuine smile while she digs her nails into Gwen's palm in remonstration. This is hard enough for the poor boy without her treating him like Albie.

"You look very handsome," Beth says as Dashiell guides her mother toward James' opulent carriage. She'll try very hard not to think about the fact that it's their former money that's supplied it. "Are you excited for the opening ball?"

"I guess," James says, his voice a little timid.

"It'll be a grand time," Gwen assures him, gesturing for him to precede them to the carriage. "We'll help you fall in with the right crowd."

Dashiell snorts while helping Mother into the carriage, giving Beth enough cover to lean into Gwen. "Do you have them?" she whispers, ignoring James' curious look.

"Of course," Gwen says, patting her pocket.

Beth tries to hide her grin as Dashiell hands Gwen up into the carriage.

"Don't listen to them," he says to James, before reaching out for Beth. "Neither's had a successful season."

"Mostly by choice!" Gwen calls out.

Beth clambers up into the coach, arranging her skirts around Gwen's as they perch onto one bench. James shuffles inside, squeezing in next to her. Dashiell settles beside Mother and closes the door. He taps the ceiling and they jolt off.

Mother already looks a little green. Really, they should have stayed home. She knows Mother will be fine, but it does seem more trouble than it's worth for her to be on her feet all night.

"Don't let my husband worry you. Beth and Gwen know many lovely young ladies and they'll be happy to introduce you," Mother says tightly, holding onto Dashiell with one hand and bracing herself against the ceiling with the other.

"And I trust you can see them home if we need to leave a bit early," Dashiell adds.

"I'll be fine," Mother says.

"Yes, of course, you look it."

Mother whacks his stomach and he laughs, scooting closer to wrap his arm around her shoulders. She quickly grabs his free hand and squeezes, knuckles white. But she's smiling.

"Have a good time, don't drink too much, and do try not to be too smug," he continues, looking at Gwen.

Gwen holds up her hands while Beth hides a snicker. "When am I ever smug? I'm the politest."

Even Mother opens her eyes to give Gwen a look.

"I'll try," Gwen promises. "Albie will keep me in line."

Dashiell rolls his eyes. "Beth, you'll try, won't you?"

"What, to keep them from drinking or keep Gwen away from Lord Montson?"

"He's not coming. Something about his new wife being ill," James says. They all turn to look at him and he shrinks back against the seat.

"Ah," Dashiell says. "Well, then, we won't have problems."

"Does that mean his mother is here alone?" Gwen wonders.

Mother nods. "Be nice to her if you can. It's been such a year for them."

"Of course," Beth says, before Gwen can get a word in.

Of the two of them, Gwen remains the most heated about the Ashmond affair. Not that Beth really wanted to run into Lord Montson. She didn't quite jilt him at the altar, but it was close. There will be enough talk without a full confrontation.

"I heard the Yokelys have wonderful gardens," James offers after a few minutes filled only with Mother's quiet whimpering as they rattle over the cobblestones.

"They do," Dashiell agrees.

Beth and Gwen exchange a glance before looking pointedly out the windows. They don't secretly have plans for another tryst amongst those hedges. To reclaim that maze from the pain of last year. They wouldn't risk exposure twice; that would be wrong.

Of course, if they can convince Albie to stand sentinel it might not be so bad. And it isn't like they didn't cover for him and Meredith over the winter when the two of them could barely keep their hands off each other, newly wedded and utterly disgusting.

Gwen squeezes her hand, her thumb stroking at Beth's pulse, and Beth smiles, closing her eyes against memories of last year. Instead, she'll think about last night, and bask in the happiness of their strange little family before she has to share them with the world again.

Gwen

"Oh, there she is," Beth whispers, gesturing subtly across the room to a circle of older ladies.

Through the crowds they can just see her, Lady Ashmond, bright faced and boisterous, making a spectacle of herself without a care in the world. She's been divorced three months and has apparently made the absolute most of it. The civil case was a salacious spectacle. She proved adultery, abuse, and neglect all at once, using a lawyer Gwen is almost positive Father arranged for her to meet.

Now she's free, Montson's hiding up north, and Lord Ashmond hasn't shown his face in London at all, and isn't expected this season, outside of a few crucial votes. Father's been gleeful. And while Cordelia has given lip service to the tragedy of it all, Gwen knows she's extremely proud.

Cordelia is amazing, and if she helped Lady Ashmond, how wonderful. The woman's still a dreadful person, but at least she's no longer mistreated. That's something.

"Having a grand old time," Gwen agrees.

"We should join her," Albie mumbles as Bobby appears with a tray of drinks, handing them down the line.

"Thank you," James says, his voice almost too soft to hear over the milling crowd.

They arrived early in the evening, despite Cordelia's concerns, and the dancing hasn't even started yet. Albie promised her the first three too, so she wouldn't have to stand on the sidelines without Beth. Though honestly, getting drunk with Albie sounds like more fun than dancing.

"They're all staring," Beth whispers.

Gwen glances around. They are attracting a fair bit of attention. It's nothing new, the disapproval. The Havenfort girls and their scandalous mother/stepmother, running out on the Ashmonds. Of course, Cordelia looks radiant across the hall, with Father glued to her side. No more cavorting for him. He's thoroughly henpecked and delighted with it.

Gwen really can't get enough of seeing them together, happy and serene. It was a hard winter. She's never seen Father so worried—bringing doctor after doctor in to make sure Cordelia was healthy. To make sure that the baby was safe. Nerves filled their home, but now—

They're here. Everyone is all right. They've two more months before the baby comes and decides the fate of Father's title. And settles the household bets. She wants another girl, sod the title. But Beth's rooting for a boy, for the variety. Mrs. Gilpe, Mrs. Stelm, and Miss Wilson have a whole pool going with the staff, and she's almost positive Cordelia's thrown something in too. Father definitely has.

"Gwen, the cards?"

Gwen absently pulls out the new set of cards she and Beth have been toiling over for the past few weeks. Last year, she couldn't be bothered, but Beth—Beth has brought new blood to her party games, and they're going to make the absolute most of this season.

They needn't think about the birth yet. Cordelia had Beth, after all, and she's perfect. Everything will be fine.

"Oh, give them to me," Beth says, tugging the cards from her hands.

Gwen takes a deep breath, shaking herself from her dour thoughts. It's time for fun.

They've the whole season, and this year's round of Spot-the-Scion will be one for the books.

"Are you finally going to let us play, then?" Bobby asks, leaning over Beth's shoulder.

He's had as much of a growth spurt as James, and has become equally handsome. He's a head taller than her now. His larger nose fits his sharpened features. And while Albie seems to have grown narrower with the increased family responsibility of the last six months, Bobby's become quite bulky, as if he's spent the past half year boxing and riding and turning all of his feelings into activity. The bulk suits him.

"Only if you think you can keep up," Beth says, holding out her wrist so Gwen can pin the scorecard to the back of her dance card.

She passes cards to Albie and Bobby, and then over to James. She did promise Father they'd introduce him to people. This will give him a crash course in the ton.

Though she's not sure he'll truly appreciate Beth's new rating system.

Beth pins Gwen's card just before the band strikes a few warning chords. Bobby steps around them and offers Beth his hand. Gwen keeps hold of Beth's fingers, gripping tight so she can't step away.

"Don't," she whines, feeling besotted and foolish and utterly unembarrassed by both.

Beth laughs. "Albie, show her a good time, would you, so she doesn't pout all evening?" Albie salutes and Beth grins, gently prying her fingers from Gwen's with a playful smile. She takes Bobby's arm. "All right, young man, show me your moves."

"I've been practicing," Bobby insists, letting her drag him gamely to the floor.

"Do you want to take the first set?" Albie asks.

Gwen shakes her head, glancing over at James. "Can't leave this poor sod all on his own. Demeroven," she prompts, waving him closer so he's not standing awkwardly apart, on the other side of the hole left by Beth and Bobby. "Mason went to Oxford as well."

"Right," James says. "Heard a lot of good things about you," James says, offering Albie a truly uncomfortable smile.

"From Lady Gwen?" Albie asks.

"No," James says quickly. Gwen laughs and Albie smiles. "I mean, no, not—not only from Lady Gwen. My cousin sings your praises. I—" He shrugs and rubs at the back of his neck.

Albie laughs. "No harm done. She's a menace," he adds, nudging Gwen. "But Miss Bertram is a delight."

"She is," Gwen confirms brightly to James. Albie huffs, rolling his eyes at her. She'll never argue over Beth's many, many positive attributes. "And Bobby's become an even better dancer."

"He has," Albie agrees grudgingly. "You two might have been at school together," Albie says, glancing at James.

"We were," James says, eyes tracking Bobby and Beth on the floor.

"Oh?" Gwen says, surprised. He acted as if they were just introduced.

"I mean, I saw him," James says quickly, blinking before turning back to her. "We never had classes together. Don't think we ever spoke. What's this then?" he asks, flipping his scorecard.

"Spot-the-Scion," Albie says. "First one to cross off all the names gets—what?"

Gwen grins. "Full betting rights at Ascot. The winner gets to decide how much we bet and on which races, and gets to keep the spoils."

"We?" James asks.

"Lady Gwen's finally deigned to let me and Mr. Mason into her little debutante game. What's the tally column for?" Albie asks, peering at his card.

"Oh, you have to rate the gents," Gwen says, laughing as Albie rolls his eyes.

"Of course."

"And the second column?" James asks.

"If you spot all the sons in a family, you get a bonus. We've got spares galore this year," she adds, glancing over at Beth and Bobby.

Bobby twirls Beth around with a wide grin. The blue gown, her beautiful brown hair, her gorgeous eyes—God, Gwen wishes she could be the one on the floor with her. Watching isn't bad though. It's giving her all kinds of ideas for later tonight.

She glances at James when she feels her cheeks starting to heat, trying to banish thoughts of a far less vertical dance. She meant to just check in on him, but finds him staring at Beth and Bobby, almost transfixed. A strange protectiveness rises in her gut. He can't be looking at Beth that way. They're cousins.

More importantly, Beth is *hers*.

She takes a swig of her champagne and looks back out at the ballroom, jaw clenched. She can't get jealous anytime a man so much as looks at Beth. If she does, she'll be in a state the whole season. Beth's only becoming more beautiful and graceful, and without the weight of a match on her shoulders, she's downright joyfully dancing with Bobby now.

Her beautiful, brave, smart, funny Beth.

No one deserves her. Not even Gwen. But she's got her anyway, and she'll never let her go to some man purely for society's sake. No matter what Father says, she's not interested in finding someone who will tolerate their "lifestyle." She just wants their life together.

James is still staring when Beth and Bobby finish their set and Gwen finds that she's grinding her teeth. God, how is she going to make it through the season?

She's so focused on her stupid jealousy she almost misses it as Bobby guides Beth back to their little group.

"You didn't dance," Beth accuses Albie.

Bobby grins and Beth and Albie trade barbs, going back and forth about Beth's revamped scorecards. They've become fast friends and are endearing banter partners. They can keep a whole table going if they try. But it's not Beth and Albie's repartee that captures Gwen's attention.

No, it's James staring at Bobby that does it. Bobby's still flushed from dancing, pink cheeked, with his broad chest heaving a little. And James—James looks gobsmacked, hot under the collar, and—

Oh.

It wasn't Beth he was staring at.

"Come, gents, let's get the girls another round," Albie says when Beth has bested him handily at some wordplay Gwen wasn't following.

Bobby slings a jovial arm over James' shoulders and gestures for Albie to lead the way. Gwen watches as they set off, James stiff beneath Bobby's arm, Albie none the wiser.

"You should have danced too," Beth says, looping her arm casually through Gwen's. She jiggles her free wrist, her scorecard bouncing. "I've already got the Kingsman brothers back from Oxford."

"Hmm?" Gwen says, her mind zipping.

She has no interest whatsoever in marrying a man who would simply tolerate her "friendship" with Beth. But marrying a man who has a "friendship" of his own? That has promise.

"Are you listening at all?" Beth asks.

"No," Gwen replies, scanning the ballroom without seeing.

If they could pair James and Bobby off—Bobby who *never* seems interested in women, who's never wanted to marry—then Beth could have Bobby and Gwen could have James and they could—

"Gwen?"

"Double wedding," Gwen says, wincing as it comes out sharp and unprompted.

"What?"

Gwen grabs Beth's hand and drags her back toward the washrooms, ignoring her protests. They slip out of the hall but pass the correct corridor, wending into the house far enough that Gwen thinks they'll have some relative privacy.

"What is wrong with you?" Beth demands.

"I think James fancies men," Gwen says on a rushed whisper.

Beth goes still. "Excuse me?"

"I think he likes men, and I think he likes Bobby."

"Oh," Beth says slowly. "That's unfortunate."

"What?" Gwen exclaims.

Beth shakes her head. "Not—God, not that. Just—he'll need to marry and have an heir, that's all. Unfortunate in that sense. Otherwise, well, I mean, men are generally terrible so there's that too," she says, twisting her fingers together. "You really think?"

"I really do," Gwen says. "He looked like I did, looking at you."

Beth smiles at that. "Hmm. Something to keep in mind, I guess. I'm sure there must be clubs he could go to."

"You're thinking small," Gwen says, smiling as Beth turns an unimpressed look on her.

"Excuse you?"

"James likes Bobby. And Bobby's never shown a single interest in a woman."

"So?"

"So . . ." Gwen says, waiting her out. Beth's sharp, she'll figure it out—

"No. No. We almost killed our parents. I am not embarking on another matchmaking scheme. Especially since we can't marry off their parents to make sure they can be together."

"Again, you're thinking small," Gwen says, feeling a little giddy with the idea.

Not that she'd have anything against living with their parents forever. But this would give them true security, no matter what gender the baby is. Real autonomy. Running two adjoining estates? The possibilities are endless.

"All right, what, then?" Beth asks, sounding a little exasperated. It makes Gwen want to shove her up against the wall and make her really exasperated.

"If we get James and Bobby together, then you marry Bobby, I marry James, and . . ."

Beth gapes at her, eyes moving rapidly. She takes a breath, and then shakes her head. Gwen watches as she plays it over in her mind, a quick journey from preposterous to possible if ever she's seen one.

"Where would we live?" she asks slowly.

"Your old estate. Bobby has a property not far down the way."

"Convenient," Beth mutters. "And you'd be all right with . . . James?"

"I wouldn't be with James," Gwen says quickly. "It would be in name only. They'd live in one, we'd live in the other, and make appearances when necessary. The perfect disguise."

Beth purses her lips, twisting her fingers for a moment before she looks up and meets Gwen's eyes. "Our own house?"

"To run exactly as we please," Gwen entices. "Close enough to visit our parents, but not with them. Our own money. Our own lives entirely. With good friends just up the way for the manly things."

"Husbands," Beth says.

"In name only," Gwen repeats.

"Our own house," Beth says, a smile starting to stretch over her face.

"We'll build you that tree house," Gwen promises. "All four of us."

Beth's smile turns into a grin and she leans up and kisses

Gwen impulsively. Gwen loses herself for a moment and then gently pulls back, glancing around. They're alone, but they shouldn't tempt anything outside of the hedgerows.

"So that's a yes?"

"To trying to convince two young men, who we're not actually positive have that inclination, into a farce marriage so we can live up in the country?" Beth confirms.

"Basically. It worked the first time."

Beth bobs her head. "We have the season."

"The whole season," Gwen agrees. "And if we fail, we're at home with the baby."

"Better stakes than last time," Beth says with a small laugh.

"So?"

Beth considers her for a moment. "You want to marry me through James?"

"I'd marry you without anyone," Gwen says quickly. Beth's look softens. "But since that's not an option, yes. I'd like to take empty vows with James and get you in exchange, forever."

"Me too," Beth whispers. "The marrying you part, not James."

"That would be actually wrong," Gwen agrees.

Beth laughs and takes a deep breath. "Okay."

Gwen feels her whole body brighten, possibility and love and excitement buzzing through her.

"Okay?"

Beth holds out her hand and Gwen laughs, taking it with one decisive shake.

"Let's get them together," Gwen says.

Beth grins. "Let's."

ACKNOWLEDGMENTS

Writing is often a solitary process, but if you have the right team backing you up, it doesn't feel quite so lonely. Sorry to all the other writers out there, but my team is THE BEST.

To Stacy, my wonderful agent, for the guidance and encouragement, support, and excitement, thank you. I wouldn't be here without you, and I'm so glad we're on this journey together.

To Sylvan, my fantastic editor, you bring out the very best of me with so much joy and such great fun. Thank you for believing in Beth and Gwen (and their found, beloved family) as much as I do.

To Larry, my champion manager, for taking a chance on me, believing in me, and hiking with me up this steep steep hill, thank you. To many more years to come. And Devra, thank you for everything.

To Wayne, lawyer extraordinaire, thank you for the guidance and support, for reading, and for so many wonderful chats.

To Leni Kauffman, for the most beautiful, absolute wildest dream of a cover, thank you for giving Beth and Gwen the most spectacular come-to-life.

To the other incredible publishing professionals who have laid hands on *Don't Want You Like a Best Friend*, thank you: Erika Tsang, May Chen, Tracy Wilson and Mark Burkeitt, Christine Vahaly, Diahann Sturge, Shelby Peak, Amy Halperin, DJ

DeSmyther, Jes Lyons, Kalie Barnes-Young, Ronnie Kutys, Andy LeCount, Caroline Bodkin.

To my betas, my friends, my compatriots in the writing and creating trenches, Abby, Becca, Ben, Joe, Lindsay—you make me better, you raise me up, you make me laugh, and I love you all to pieces. I couldn't be here without you. And I owe you so many cupcakes.

To the amazing authors and creatives who have supported this story—Evie Dunmore, Amalie Howard, Carlyn Greenwald, Courtney Kae, Darcy Rose Byrnes—thank you so much for reading and making this year so joyful.

To my wonderful friends, who have cheered me on throughout this whole process, endlessly encouraging and loving, you are the absolute best people this world has to offer and I love you so much.

To Dylan and Dani, thank you for the love and support, calming words, and breathless excitement. Thank you for being there every single step of the way. Thank you for believing in me.

Mom, thank you for all those patient years guiding me through essays, teaching me how to make the conclusion into the thesis. I looked out for repetitions. Dad, thank you for the late-night discussions of story, beats, and dramatic arcs, and the endless Sondheim before-school sing-alongs. I wouldn't be the writer, or person, I am without both of you.

And to you, dear reader, I hope this book brings you as much joy as it has brought me, and that you can see a little something of yourself in it somewhere, and imagine.

ABOUT THE AUTHOR

Emma R. Alban is an author and a screenwriter. Raised in the Hudson Valley, she now lives in Los Angeles, enjoying the eternal sunshine, ocean, and mountains. When she isn't writing books or screenplays, she can usually be found stress-baking with the AC on full blast, skiing late into the spring, singing showtunes at the top of her lungs on the freeway, and reading anywhere there's somewhere to lean. *Don't Want You Like a Best Friend* is her first novel.

Read on for an excerpt from

You're the Problem, It's You

Coming in Summer 2024

Bobby

They haven't invented a liquor strong enough to counteract the absolute banality of an opening-night ball. Bobby Mason stares down into his drink, listening to his brother, Albie, and their friend Lord Cunningham recite a list of debutantes at a rapid-fire pace, all the names swirling into a light buzz. Bobby's not sure how Albie has managed to keep track of this many girls, living up north all year. Perhaps this is what Meredith discusses when they're spending long, loving evenings together.

Guilt overtakes him. He shouldn't think ill of his new sister-in-law, stuck in the country and unable to travel because she's expecting and poorly. If he's being honest, Albie's always the one bringing up engagement gossip, not Meredith. Meredith's a delight. This unending conversation is a pain.

"But I wouldn't put any money on the Steton-Johnson merger," Cunningham says, his slightly nasal voice cutting into Bobby's brooding.

"I wouldn't be too sure," Albie says, chuckling as Cunningham rolls his eyes. "Lady Annabeth goes after what she wants. She already had ten scions last I checked."

"Damn, already?" Bobby grumbles as he looks down at his own Spot-the-Scion card. He's only managed to spot seven society sons, four of whom include himself, Albie, Cunningham, and his cousin Gwen's partner Beth's cousin Lord James Demeroven.

Bobby glances at Demeroven and finds him staring down into his own glass, narrow shoulders high. Cunningham's apparently betrothed to a nice girl up in the country, so he has no need to make a match this season—the poor lucky sod. But Demeroven, with his new title, will need to think about settling down. Bobby is sure Beth's terrible uncle is eager for Demeroven to pop out an heir.

Of course, that's not a unique perspective in this room. Bobby looks out at the sea of debutantes, mothers, and eligible scions in the immaculate ballroom. It's all swirls of soft pastels, tails, and glittering jewels.

Oh, and there's Mr. Yokely, Lord Yokely's younger brother. "Eight," Bobby mumbles. He fishes the small pencil Gwen passed him earlier out of his pocket to mark his Spot-the-Scion card. He's doing pretty well for having spent the first hour dancing with Beth—another ten eligible sons spotted and he might have a chance at winning.

"You got another?" Albie asks, leaning up to see his card. Bobby's got inches on his older brother now. It's still strange to be able to look down at Albie's light brown hair.

"Not much else to do," Bobby offers with a shrug. He does so love his cousin and Beth for coming up with *something* to keep them occupied.

He really should be trying harder. Beth said that betting rights and gains at the Ascot races would go to the winner of their society sons tournament this year. He's not sure if that prize is just among the extended family, as they are, or if it includes Beth and Gwen's young lady friends too. If so, he's doomed. He can never remember enough of the various heirs to fill out a whole card, and they've added the spares this year, too. At least the girls get twirled around the room, giving them a better vantage point to scope out the myriad progeny of the ton.

He notices Albie marking something down on his card. "How many do you have?"

"Fifteen," Albie says, brown eyes twinkling.

Bobby groans. "Demeroven, how are you doing?" he asks, wanting to feel at least a little better about his terrible way with faces and names.

Demeroven looks up, his piercing blue eyes darting about to figure out who addressed him. He looks so uncomfortable. "Um, four?"

"Just us, then?" Albie asks, not unkindly.

"Yes," Demeroven says, sheepish.

"Well, that won't do," Cunningham says, his round cheeks dimpling with a slightly evil smirk. "We'll have to get both of you lads dancing, then, won't we?"

"Oh no. No, no," Bobby says, trying to back away. Albie grabs him about the shoulders, laughing at his expense. "I don't dance."

"You danced with Beth," Albie counters.

"Beth is different," he says hastily. "She doesn't step on my toes."

"I'm sure there are any number of lovely young ladies who can manage a simple waltz without injuring you," Albie says, his grip tightening. "What about—"

"Demeroven's the one who should dance," Bobby says desperately, wincing as Demeroven's head snaps up, a lock of sandy-brown hair falling into those harried blue eyes. "He's new. He needs to meet new people."

"I couldn't, really. I'm sure there must be— Oh, Lord Havenfort," Demeroven says, turning with a relieved smile as Bobby and Albie's uncle approaches them. Bobby thinks he hears Demeroven add a muttered, "Thank Christ."

"Gentlemen," Uncle Dashiell greets, smiling down at all of them. Dashiell Frederic Bertram, Earl of Havenfort, is almost a head taller than most of the men in the room and, with his striking blond hair and features, draws every eye his way everywhere he goes.

Honestly, if Bobby's cousin Gwen *wanted* to find a husband, she wouldn't have trouble. She got all of her looks from her father—statuesque, blond, and instantly captivating. Now, if Bobby could only spot her and her partner Beth in the crowd . . .

"Bobby, would you mind terribly if I stole Albert, James, and Lord Cunningham away? There are several members of our party I'd like you all to meet," Uncle Dashiell says.

And how can Bobby do anything but nod and smile, watching as his only protection, such as they were, is shepherded away to more important matters? He supposes it wouldn't occur to any of them to invite him along. He's of no political import, after all. But that doesn't mean he can't be interested.

Bobby sighs and swigs the rest of his drink, staring out at the ball. Albie's running the estate. Albie's taking their late father's seat in parliament. Albie's doing everything important. All that's left for Bobby is the social season. He's meant to be making a good impression for the family name, but he'd rather be absolutely anywhere else.

He turns and strides back to the drink station to slug back another whisky. But the burn of the alcohol against his tongue turns his stomach and he only drinks half the dram before placing it back on the table. The doctor wasn't positive it was the drink that killed their father, but it certainly didn't help.

The thought curdles in Bobby's throat and he turns to search some more for Beth and Gwen. He doesn't want to think about his wretched father tonight. Nor the mess he left for Albie to clean up.

He just wants to hide away with his cousin and Beth. Let himself be buoyed by their happiness. Neither Gwen nor Beth needs to think about finding a husband. Uncle Dashiell and his new aunt Cordelia, Beth's mother, have made it quite clear they'd be happy to have Beth and Gwen under their roof, protected and insulated against the ton forever. Two young women, in love, hiding in plain sight.

If only his father hadn't been such an absolute brute, perhaps Bobby could have arranged something similar. Ignoring the fact that he hasn't yet found a man he'd ever consider settling down with, of course.

But now it's no longer a possibility. His father is dead. And he's one carriage accident away from being the reigning Viscount Mason. He needs another drink, sod what the doctors said about his father.

He turns to make for the drinks table again, but finds his path blocked by a deluge of satin and skirts. Lady . . . Chiswith (he thinks) and her daughter have snuck up on him and now stand between him and the sweet relief of alcohol.

"Your father was such a lovely man, Mr. Mason. I know I speak for my husband as well in extending our deepest condolences," Lady Chiswith says, her narrow face crinkled in sympathy that makes Bobby itch.

His father was so far in the opposite direction of "a lovely man" that it's almost comical. "Thank you," he manages, looking briefly to Lady Chiswith's daughter, who's fanning herself with a blue feather monstrosity.

"Miss Chiswith would be more than happy to take your mind off your tragic loss, if you feel as though you have enough strength for dancing," Lady Chiswith says.

Bobby notices Lady Chiswith's daughter paling in mortification. He can relate. No need to put them both through misery. "I'm afraid I haven't the strength," Bobby says seriously, trying to project Albie's pleasant, polite smile at the woman. He's sure it doesn't come off half so well on his face. "Another time," he adds, looking at the daughter.

Her shoulders relax and he silently pats himself on the back. He bows and quickly retreats, striding across the room as if he has somewhere to be. But even with that dance dodged, he sees hungry maternal eyes tracking him from every cluster of attendees. Like he's a piece of fresh meat. Which he supposes he is, though he's hardly a prize.

The second son of a lightly disgraced gambler with an alcohol problem—surely there's someone better for the many daughters at the ball tonight. But the wandering, watchful eyes say otherwise, and, oh dear, he needs to find the safety of his cousin and Beth, now.

He searches for a flash of blond but can't see Gwen anywhere. Beth's far too short to find from this far away. He about-faces again, considering heading out to the small terrace, before he nearly bumps into Demeroven.

The shorter man hovers just outside the hall to the velvet-lined parlor, where many of the gentlemen and parliamentarians have set up camp for the night, far from the fray. Demeroven should still be inside. Bobby can just see Uncle Dashiell's head in the chamber beyond.

Instead, Demeroven has nearly pressed himself back against the wall, blocking Bobby's more furtive path out to the terrace. And though he's not Beth or Gwen, Demeroven is still better than the roving mothers.

"All a little much?" he asks, focusing on Demeroven's discomfort instead of living in his own.

Demeroven's head snaps up, those wide blue eyes staring up at him like he's just appeared out of thin air. "Oh, um, a tad," he says, his voice stiff.

Bobby nods toward his side and Demeroven moves jerkily so Bobby can slip into the gap between him and the pillar that mostly blocks them from the rest of the room. Together they watch the swirling dancers. It's a little quieter here and Bobby lets himself relax.

He's been wracking his brain, but he doesn't remember meeting Demeroven at Oxford, though they were only a year apart. He thinks he would remember if they'd been introduced. It would be hard to forget Demeroven's striking gaze, patrician nose, and the sharp line of his jaw. Though perhaps he's clenching his teeth?

"Anything good on the agenda, you think?" he asks, gesturing back toward the clustered parliamentarians, hoping to put him at ease.

Demeroven glances at him before staring back at the floor. "Not really."

Bobby waits, but the man doesn't elaborate. "I thought the Medical Act sounded interesting," Bobby tries again. Anything but talk of marriage.

Demeroven just shrugs. "It's all a lot of chatter, really."

Bobby stares at him, surprised. "My brother says the briefing Uncle Dashiell gave him was rather interesting."

"I guess," Demeroven says, looking unconvinced.

Bobby clicks his tongue. If he were about to sit in parliament for the first time, he wouldn't be dismissing all the upcoming bills as prattle, but . . . he's sure there's a weight of responsibility that might make it all seem onerous.

He'd rather sit through a hundred boring sessions in the Lords than dance, but fine.

"You know, the Matrimonial Causes Act last year has had a dramatic effect already. Did you see Lady Ashmond earlier? She seems to be much happier as a divorcée."

"Good for her," Demeroven says.

Bobby blows out a breath. This is Beth's cousin. He has to extend him some grace.

"Well, I hope you find an act that piques your interest," Bobby says, forcing lightness into his voice. "I'd hate to think you'd be bored to tears all season."

Demeroven toys with his cuff links, eyes fixed toward the ground. "Every time anyone brings up a point that's remotely interesting, somehow the conversation turns to the events for the season and the racing bets. Endless talk of racing bets. How men who make our laws can be so enthralled with mindless, vulgar gambling, I'll never know," he says in a rush.

The man is certainly making it difficult. "Surely there must be something of interest. I hear the games of whist at the club get rather competitive," Bobby says.

"I don't gamble," Demeroven reiterates.

"You don't have to gamble to play whist," Bobby replies, trying not to take it personally. "Uncle Dashiell says you were good at maths. You must like cards."

Demeroven shrugs again, shoulders slightly hunched. "I'm decent at whist, but I won't abide playing for money, not with them, anyway."

Bobby watches the way his glance shifts back to the parlor, disdain on his otherwise handsome face. That won't do. "You'll have to get better at pretending."

"I beg your pardon?"

"There's no way you'll survive at the clubs with that attitude. Find something, low-stakes games, darts—anything—to make you seem approachable, or you'll be marked for the season." Demeroven's shoulders stiffen and Bobby winces as he tightens his jaw again. "I only meant . . . Well, you'll need to find a way to survive at the clubs is all. Connections are important. I could suggest a few clubs that are less . . . lordly, if you like."

He starts to say more, but the flat look Demeroven turns his way sours the words in his throat. He was only trying to *help*, for God's sake, no need to look at him as if he's dirt on the man's shoe.

Still struggling for any way to keep the conversation going, Bobby turns at a touch to his elbow. He wilts in relief to find Beth at his side, smiling up at him while Gwen offers her hand to Demeroven.

Demeroven nods stiffly at them. "Lady Gwen, Miss Bertram."

Bobby nearly pushes the man into his cousin's arms, watching Demeroven sedately escort Gwen onto the floor. They make a striking couple once they get moving, his lithe build and her tall, stately frame, twirling gracefully. It seems unfair that Demeroven should be both that attractive and a good dancer, especially when Gwen's always complaining that Bobby's dancing skills pale in comparison to Albie's. He *has* gotten better over the last year; she just refuses to acknowledge it.

"You two getting along?" Beth asks, sidling into Demeroven's empty space.

Bobby looks down at her, rolling his eyes at her eagerness. Always wanting them all to get along, to be happy—dreadfully loving of her. But he can't resist her big brown doe eyes. And with her rich brown hair falling in ringlets from her braided bun, she's almost angelic.

"He's . . . fine," Bobby lies, looking back at the dance floor. Can't miss Gwen, her blond hair styled in much the same way, a head taller than most of the girls, and inches taller than Demeroven, for that matter.

"Do you think you could invite him to visit the clubs with you?" Beth asks.

Bobby turns back to her, eyes narrowed. "Why?"

"Well, he doesn't know anyone. And I remember how lonely I was in the first few weeks of the season. It would be nice for you to introduce him to a few people, help him make friends."

Bobby bites his tongue against the honest retort—that most of his friends have up and gotten married, the poor lads. Cunningham is still about, and Prince, somewhere, though he thinks he's heard that Prince has gotten engaged too.

"I'm not sure he'd like the clubs I attend," Bobby says instead. It's enormously true, but feels safer than baring his own lonely soul.

It's not that Beth wouldn't understand, but she has Gwen. A constant friend, a live-in companion—the love of her blasted life. And he's just . . . second fiddle to his brother, who barely has any time for him anymore.

"I'm sure he'd find them interesting," Beth counters. "Please? I'd hate to see him fall in with the wrong crowd."

Bobby sighs. Albie would tell him to do it—help ensure that Demeroven votes with the liberals, sympathetic to Uncle Dashiell's positions. Help erase the stain of the previous Viscount Demeroven—Beth's late, horrible father. A new voice for a new generation.

And if even Beth—who has every reason to resent Demeroven for coming of age, inheriting her late father's estate, and nearly leaving her and her mother destitute last season—can find it in her heart to help him, how can Bobby refuse?

He spins the new gold signet ring Meredith got him, engraved with his initials, around on his finger and watches Gwen and Demeroven continue dancing into another set. He supposes showing Demeroven the town wouldn't be the worst way to spend a season. He's handsome and learned, even if he seems to be a dour, reticent chap. Bobby has always liked a challenge.

"What do I get if I do this for you?" he asks, looking back at Beth.

"The pride of a job well done and a possibly enduring friendship isn't enough?" Bobby narrows his eyes and she laughs. "How about my undying gratitude?"

Bobby huffs, pretending at greater exasperation just to see

her eyebrows crease. He so loves riling her up. Almost as fun as getting Gwen angry.

"Fine."

"Oh, thank you!" Beth says brightly, wrapping her arm through his. "God, doesn't she look beautiful?"

He watches her watch Gwen, her eyes wide, a small smile on her face. Doting, in love, besotted.

Gwen's not the most graceful of the dancers, but there's something in the confident way she carries herself—and maybe a little in the way Demeroven is an actually adequate partner. "She does," he agrees. "And so do you."

"Oh, don't bother—Gwen has been laying it on all night."

"Yes, what a hardship, to be beloved," he says.

She laughs and squeezes his arm. "Shall we find you someone to sing your praises too?"

Bobby fights a shudder. "No, no, turning Lord Demeroven into the toast of the ton is more than enough of a project this season, I think."

Beth hums, giving her attention back to the dancers.

It's not making laws, or making a difference, but shaping Lord Demeroven into a moderately respectable lord is *something,* at least.

James

He closes the heavy front door to the townhouse and rests his forehead against the cool wood. If he never attends another ball in his life, he could die a happy man. Between the politics, the dancing, and the endless stream of mothers and daughters he disappointed with his utter lack of social flair, he's exhausted.

Dancing with Lady Gwen and his cousin Miss Bertram wasn't terrible, but spending the night surrounded by their chatter, with Lady Gwen's cousins Lord Mason and the younger Mason chiming in, was almost dizzying.

He's not sure if it's the hour, the faint buzz of alcohol in his system, or the lighting, but he thinks his mother may have purchased yet another bust. The statues and paintings all seem to meld together in the narrow, tall space of the foyer. It's oppressive.

But it isn't as if he tried to stop her. At least it gives her something to focus on, now that she's here and separated from her friends back home. His stepfather couldn't wait to get to the city, but he knows his mother took much solace in the community she'd made in Epworth.

She may have purchased herself an entire set of evening ball gowns for the season, but she didn't even make it out of bed today. Her lady's maid, Miss Marina, said it was a headache, but he thinks it's likely just melancholy. They don't deal well with change, he and his mother.

His stepfather, on the other hand—

"'S that you, Demeroven?"

James winces, considering making a break for it up the stairs rather than facing the smoke-filled haze that is his stepfather's study. What should be his study.

But if he doesn't face the man now, he'll be banging down his door tomorrow, bright and early, demanding a full report. So James shuffles across the narrow hall and into the study, coughing at the smoke. The man could at least crack a window.

The space is filled with heavy, half empty bookshelves. His stepfather brought down his own dark, dour chairs to face the enormous desk left behind by the late Viscount Demeroven. The room has a strange, out-of-time feeling, half full, half considered, half his stepfather's and half a dead man's. There's nothing of James in here at all.

His stepfather looks up from yet another financial ledger. Ever since they arrived, he's been nose-deep in the late viscount's London accounting, not that he truly knows the first thing about managing an estate. Though neither does James, really.

His stepfather's beady eyes peer through the haze, his round, ruddy face set in a scowl. "You're home early," he grunts.

James bites back the automatic retort that he is a man of age now and needn't answer to his stepfather any longer. He's in control of the title now. He's the new Viscount Demeroven. His stepfather's—the gentleman Mr. Griggs'—reign as regent to the estate is over. James is about to sit in parliament, for God's sake. This is, in fact, his house now.

But the words never manage to pass his lips. Instead, he shrugs, like an insolent little boy.

His stepfather frowns and takes a swig of the late viscount's brandy. "Did you meet Lord Henchey?"

James shakes his head. "No. Lord Havenfort introduced me to a fair few, but they were all his lot."

His stepfather groans. "You let that man walk all over you, didn't you? I told your mother you didn't have the backbone for it."

James tries to straighten said weak backbone, curling his fingers into fists as his stepfather slips into one of his tried-and-true rants. James is meek. James is fragile. James is bad with people. James isn't cut out for this life, and if they'd just spoken to the late viscount, they could have ensured that Stepfather maintained official control of the finances once James came of age. But no, Stepfather is saddled with this lump of a boy instead of the man he needs.

"I'll do better," James cuts in, his ears ringing with phantom previous lectures. "Tomorrow. I'll make sure to meet Henchey. Brighton wasn't there, for the record."

"Of course he wasn't. Wouldn't waste his time with something so frivolous."

James yawns theatrically. "Right, well, I'm knackered. I'll see you tomorrow for dinner."

He ducks out of the room before his stepfather can get another word in and pads back across the foyer and down the corridor to the kitchen. He can't face his bed just yet, not with his stepfather's tirade still ringing in his ears.

Instead, he collapses at the long oak staff table in the red-tiled kitchen and lets his head fall into his hands. He just needs a few minutes for the echo of his stepfather's words, the latent sound of the orchestra, the chatter of his cousin, her stepsister, and the Mason boys talking too fast and too furious to fade away.

But as he stares at the backs of his eyelids, Bobby Mason's face fills his mind. His broad jaw, his thoughtful hazel eyes, his frown at finding James as lacking as everyone else always does—

Their chef Reginald smacks a plate of scones down in front of James and he jumps.

"Jesus," James says.

Reginald pours him a glass of milk, plops it down beside the plate, and strides around the table to sit heavily across from him. His blue eyes sparkle with interest and James wants to hide his face again.

Reginald has been teasing secrets out of James since he was small and Reginald was just a kitchen hand, plying him with cookies and shielding him from his stepfather whenever possible. Often his only refuge, and friend, Reginald knows every one of James' tells, which is bloody annoying sometimes, even as the smell of the scones does release the tension in his shoulders.

"So?"

James groans and stuffs half a scone into his mouth to stall.

"Come on, tell me. Is he everything you thought he'd be?" Reginald asks.

James feels himself flush. "Shut up," he mumbles.

Reginald grins, rubbing his hands together. His dimples make his smile almost irresistible, but James does not want to discuss this. Not when the night felt like such an unmitigated failure.

"All right. How was the dancing?"

James stuffs another scone in his mouth and Reginald laughs.

"Really? Anyone of interest?"

James shrugs. Lady Gwen wasn't a terrible partner, though she hardly seemed focused on him. Lady Gwen and his cousin, Miss Bertram, are thick as thieves and seem to be able to communicate with nary a glance between them, always laughing and filling out their Spot-the-Scion cards.

"It was fine," he says after he gets the scone down. Usually they're his favorite, but he's parched from all the dancing and alcohol.

He takes a long drink of milk, closing his eyes to hide from Reginald's raised eyebrow.

"Fine," Reginald repeats, waiting him out until he can't drink any more. "You must have met *someone*."

"Lord Havenfort introduced me to the lords," James mumbles, taking another scone simply to crumble it to bits on the plate.

"And?"

"And they were rather boring," he admits, finally looking up to meet Reginald's eyes. "A lot of whose wife was where and which daughter was available."

"Any of those daughters the ones your mother keeps harping on about?"

James sighs. "Plenty."

"And how many did you dance with?"

"Two?" he guesses. He really wasn't paying much attention to anyone but his cousin and Lady Gwen. "The rest were friends of my cousin's, and they're all already taken."

Reginald reaches out for his own scone with a frown. "Your mother won't be happy."

"I went, didn't I?"

Reginald gives him a disapproving look. James crushes a bit of scone between his fingers, agitated.

"There'll be other balls," he says.

Reginald bobs his head. "Of course, of course." He takes a bite of his scone and chews thoughtfully. It almost lulls James into a false sense of security. "And Mr. Mason?"

James groans again and drops his head. "Stop it."

"You've got to give me something," Reginald insists. "All those summers when you were home from Oxford, waxing poetic, and you never even talked to him. Surely, *surely*, you spoke tonight."

James squeezes his eyes shut, bracing himself, before looking up to meet Reginald's rampant curiosity. "He's fine."

"Fine?" Reginald huffs. "That's all I get? My years of loyalty, my sympathy biscuits, my words of wooing wisdom—"

James shushes him, his shoulders going up as he glances back toward the foyer. But all is quiet, which means, for better or worse, no one is coming to save him.

"Tell me you at least plucked up the courage to talk to the man now that you're tangentially connected."

James blows out a breath and looks back at Reginald. "We talked."

Reginald glowers at him. "Out with it, Viscount."

The title makes him wince and straighten his shoulders all at once. He's a viscount now. He can face his cook's teasing. He danced, he rubbed shoulders, he . . . made possibly the world's least charming impression on blasted Bobby Mason—

"Well?" Reginald prompts.

"He's nosy," James decides, returning to picking at his scone so he won't have to look Reginald in the eye. "And Lady Gwen says he's a poor dancer. My cousin likes him, but it seems he's truly just a pretty face."

He trails a finger through the remains of his scone in the ensuing silence, hoping perhaps Reginald will take that as enough truth for the night and leave him be. Instead, when the silence has lasted long enough that it's uncomfortable, James raises his eyes to find Reginald waiting, entirely unconvinced.

"That's it? The great Bobby Mason, wonder of Oxford, protagonist of half your stories, is just a stuffed shirt? Surely not."

James shrugs. "Don't know what else to tell you," he says, playing at nonchalance. "He's gotten pretty muscular since school." Reginald's mouth twitches and James hurries to add, "And all he wanted to talk about was the Medical Act."

"That's not enough substance for you?"

"And the clubs," James says quickly. "He kept telling me I'd need to learn to gamble."

Reginald furrows his brow and James works to keep his face blank. He probably didn't need to lay it on quite so thick about the gambling, especially given what Lord Havenfort told him about how the late Viscount Mason wasted away the Mason fortune before his untimely death. But he doesn't want to talk about the clubs, doesn't want to think about having to hobnob with more of these men in small, crowded spaces. Doesn't want to consider them judging him and finding him as lacking as his stepfather does.

And since he doesn't like to frequent the usual clubs, he hardly thinks he'll get along with Bobby Mason, who seems to be all about them. Better that he never discovers how little Bobby Mason could care for him.

Not that he's been dreaming of meeting the man since school, only to find himself tongue-tied and anxious to the point of rudeness in the face of his beauty up close. No. He just simply doesn't care what Bobby Mason thinks. He doesn't care what anyone thinks. It's easier that way.

"Well, if Bobby Mason isn't the catch we thought, were there any other pretty faces to consider?"

James glances back toward the hallway to the foyer again and waits, listening. But they're still safely alone.

"Not really," he says, turning back to Reginald. "Wasn't a lot of time to look or talk to anyone outside of Lord Havenfort's lords, and they're . . ."

"Not who you're looking to meet," Reginald agrees. "Well, Thomas' standing invitation is still there. He would love to have you at the club, introduce you to some nice gentlemen."

James feels his shoulders coming back up. "Right."

Reginald's eyes soften. "It'll be just like back home, only fancier. You'll see."

"I guess," James says, thinking of the small back room at the Inside Inn near Epworth. The comfortable chairs, the worn wooden table, the back door that led out to the woods. Safe, guarded, secluded.

He can't imagine how Reginald's brother, Thomas Parker, could possibly create a space that secret or comfortable in London. His club is supposed to be the safest refuge for men of a certain persuasion in the city. But James doesn't know how that can be true when it feels like there are eyes everywhere.

"Give it some thought, that's all," Reginald says. He pushes back his chair and gets up. "It's not like you're going to meet a nice man elsewhere."

James nods and looks back down at his plate, the crumbs of his scone too closely resembling the shambles of his life.

"What would you like pressed for tomorrow? I'll tell Gabriel on my way to bed."

James lets out a low moan. He'd almost forgotten. "I don't care." He puts his head back into his hands.

"Come now, it's your very first day. We need to make a good impression."

James is tempted to tell him to sod off, but he knows Reginald is right. Even if just to keep his stepfather off his back, he needs to make some effort. "Nothing my mother bought me. Classic, elegant, simple."

"Aye-aye," Reginald says merrily, drawing James' gaze up to find him posed, hands on his hips. "We'll make you the best-dressed young lord in parliament. On my honor."

"Sod your honor," James says gruffly, laughing despite himself as Reginald lets loose a low, rumbly chuckle. The man's too charming for his own good.

"Get some sleep, yeah? Gabriel will have everything ready come morning."

James forces a smile and watches Reginald head out the servants' door and down toward his room. Tonight was exhausting, and tomorrow promises to be even worse. Him, a sitting lord? Him, making laws? Him, the blockhead who couldn't even be charming to the man he's fancied since university—how is he ever supposed to impress the House of Lords?